THE ENFORCER ENIGMA

BY G. L. CARRIGER

The San Andreas Shifters Series
Marine Biology: San Andreas Shifters Prequel (FREE via gailcarriger.com)
The Sumage Solution
The Omega Objection
The Enforcer Enigma
The Dratsie Dilemma

The Tinkered Stars Series
The 5th Gender
Crudrat (as Gail Carriger)

STEAMPUNK AS GAIL CARRIGER

The Finishing School Series
(four young adult novels, beginning with *Etiquette & Espionage)*
Spies, girl power, and flying food

The Delightfully Deadly Stories
Polite lady spies

The Parasol Protectorate Series
(five novels, beginning with *Soulless)*
Adventure, love, and silly hats

The Supernatural Society Stories
LGBTQ+ proper subversive activities

The Custard Protocol Series
(four novels, beginning with *Prudence)*
World travel, cat shifters, and stolen tea

The Claw & Courtship Stories
Werewolves in cravats and the ladies who romance them

The Enforcer Enigma Copyright © 2020 by GAIL CARRIGER LLC
Cover assembled by Starla Huchton of *Designed By Starla*
Cover © 2020 by GAIL CARRIGER LLC

Version 1.0
ISBN 978-1-944751-17-3

THE ENFORCER ENIGMA

SAN ANDREAS SHIFTERS

G. L. CARRIGER

ACKNOWLEDGMENTS

Lexi Blanc and some of her lyrics began with the creative genius of author Alex White. I must apologize for turning their fictional alter ego into a raving bitch. I tried to save her, but the needs of the plot outweighed the duties of friendship in this matter. I am ashamed.

I owe a writer's debt to Hugh's husband, who knew not one, not two, but *three* words for that "sharp manmade rubble stuff that is used as retainer along shorelines in Sausalito" (riprap, shot rock, and rock armor). Also my darling other Smokeys, who had to listen to me sing country as part of our readings, not once but twice (MK summarily serenaded me with *fangs, fangs, fangs* every time we met in the hallway – thank goodness her voice is better than mine). I love making my fans giggle, but making my friends giggle? There's no greater pleasure.

Thanks to a certain sensitivity reader (you know who you are) who agreed to read for me, even though this was "totally not his thing." To Starla who got this cover finished well before I'd written the book, because I found the perfect model and I wanted the three covers to "look pretty together." And thanks to Sue and Flo for their excellent editing. Without my team, everything would take a lot longer and be a lot less tidy.

Finally, thanks to Olivia Wylie and the Parasol Protectorate Fan Group for the dratsie tip. I had no idea otter shifters were a thing, and my world is now better for having Trick in it. I hope you love Trick too, 'cause he's up next – poor Deputy Kettil.

CHAPTER ONE
TAKE ME HOME, WEREWOLF PACK

Colin knew they were going to cause problems the moment they walked in the door. It was so obvious, in fact, it transported him to some Old West movie full of clichés.

Two men swagger into the tavern. They approach the bar and start harassing the little lady in charge. No one realizes there is a lone gunman in the corner. Cue twangy yet suspenseful music.

Except, of course, it wasn't at all like that. The tavern was instead a quirky well-lit cafe in a busy tourist town. The kind frequented by locals who knew what they liked and ordered it quickly, and tourists who got confused by the awesome power of daily specials and were a pain to everyone except the bottom line. The cafe was called Bean There, Froth That, because the owner was an idiot. Everyone else called it the Bean. It was early evening – one of those chilly fall nights that descended suddenly in the Bay Area. No warning, no wind, just penguin-ass-nipping cold because, unlike the East Coast, the West has never learned to do autumn properly.

The two men who swaggered into the cafe bumped Colin's table. Which was on point for Old West baddies. They both wore double-breasted pinstriped suits. No hats. Colin was disap-pointed – baddies should wear hats. Also, neither shirt nor tie appeared under said suit. Just suit jackets over hairy chests.

They bumped him on purpose. Yes, Colin did like the small table near the door, but it was well out of normal foot traffic, so they'd jostled him on purpose. The newcomers smelled like briny prey – browned butter and kelp – yet they were big enough to be threatening. Colin hadn't met any face-to-face, but he still knew selkie blubber when he smelled it. So these were not really men at all, but shifters.

They didn't act like regulars but they sure weren't tourists. Which meant they were infiltrating pack territory – his pack's territory. Colin really didn't want to get involved, but selkie tended to have mob connections. Besides, his textbook on *The Reality of Sense Perception* wasn't addressing the shifter sensory experience. He hated human-centric philosophy. So he marked his spot, set it down, and watched.

One of the selkie (Colin decided to call him Blubber Bozo One) leaned over the counter in a film-perfect loom.

"Yo, fag," was his charming opening statement.

"What can I get you, sir?" The barista, Trick, dove into his role of *little lady in a Western shoot-'em-up*. Trick's attire was relatively understated for the part. He was wearing a long-fringed scarf and one dangling feather earring, which was good, but otherwise jeans and a t-shirt. Colin liked Trick because it was really hard not to like him. Colin was annoyed by this, as he tried not to like *anyone*. The fact that Trick had made it through his defenses was really… well, tricky of him.

"Get me? You can get me the goods. Now!" Blubber Bozo One loomed even more loomy-like.

Trick was barely over five feet, always cheerful, with never a bad word to say against anyone. Through the relentless application of a crooked smile, sweet greeting, and always remembering Colin's order (decaf latte with whipped cream on top) he'd endeared himself, despite Colin's best efforts.

Colin knew Trick was some kind of shifter, because he smelled of wet riverbanks and fresh hay, but he didn't know what kind. Trick's scent was closest to that of a kelpie, but Trick was far too small to be a water horse. He wasn't a merman either – no salty pong. Plus Colin's pack had contact with the local kelpie (there could be only one) and the local merfolk pod, and Trick certainly wasn't either. He was, in fact, a bit of a mystery.

"I'm sorry, what?" Trick batted his lashes at the bozos. Colin suspected this was a defensive mechanism.

Colin wasn't supposed to get involved. *Wolves do turf, not surf*, his dad often said. But Colin hated his dad almost as much as he hated the word *fag*.

"Listen here, you slimy little shit, you're *Inis*, aren't you? Inis is holding our goods and owes us. Took forever to track your ass down."

"Inis? You're after my family?" Trick's dark eyes went even rounder than normal. "I don't speak to them. Or, more properly, they don't speak to me. Whatever. We don't speak!"

"I don't care if you're in with 'em or not. They vanished with our goods and you didn't vanish good enough."

Trick backed away from the counter, hands up in front of his chest. "Dude, I've not seen them in, like, *forever*. Even if I did, I don't have any money, let alone *goods*. Whatever those may be. I work as a barista. Come on!"

Colin ached for the little guy, he looked so scared.

"You're still *Inis*." Blubber Bozo Two was even more intellectual than One.

Colin wondered if he had any kind of weaponry in his bag. *Does a half-eaten peppered salami count?*

Trick tossed his one earring back as if it were a lock of hair. "You want me to change my name? I'll go down to DURPS tomorrow and fix that right quick. I never liked it anyway."

"Don't be cute. Just be paying us back with goods or cash. We ain't picky, slimy little fag."

There's that word again. Sure, Trick looked super gay but Colin admired that. Even envied him a little. If Trick had the guts to wear makeup and earrings, Colin should have the guts to act like the werewolf he was and defend the poor thing. *Wolf the fuck up, you wuss.* Colin shut his laptop, then tucked it (and the disappointing *Reality of Sense Perception*) away in his messenger bag.

It was a Tuesday night, after dinner, and in a suburban town, so it was only locals at the cafe. At the opposite side of the front section sat the straight couple who came for date night and made moony eyes at each other over Mexican hot chocolate. Against the side wall sat dour old Floyd who liked to knit, and blessedly never tried to make small talk. (Colin supposed he could nick the man's knitting needles and stab the selkie with them, only that'd get blood on the guy's knitting, which was probably rude.) In the back was the lesbian couple who'd recently added a third and came in to play board games.

They were all regulars who probably loved Trick, but they were also all human, and this was shifter business.

So Colin stood and picked up his empty coffee cup – it'd work to bash a head in a pinch.

Colin was one of the world's least threatening werewolves. Even as a wolf he wasn't big or vicious. As a human he was the opposite of butch – a lackluster mild-mannered nerd who disappeared into the background so well he'd once considered a job in espionage. One of his older brother's super-hot college buddies described Colin as a *washed-out twinky stick figure*. To be fair, the buddy hadn't known Colin overheard him say it. And while cruel, it *was* accurate. Or maybe Colin had simply turned into that person from then on. He envied Trick, partly because he himself hadn't the guts to be a true twink – flashing skin and taking names. He wore baggy clothes, his face was inclined to petulance, and his temperament towards silence. At twenty-two, he was insipid in coloring and timid in personality, not the type to go up against blubber bozos.

Still, someone had to help Trick.

So he sent a 911 text to his Alpha and jumped into the fray like a piece of wilted lettuce – AKA he slouched into line behind the selkies. Speaking of which, the word *selkies* sounded wrong. He wondered if *selkie* was like the word *sheep*, both plural and singular.

Blubber Bozo One turned to glare at him. "Who the hell are you?"

Fucking A, sea folk had horrible noses. Couldn't the man

smell a shifter when he was standing next to him in a coffee shop?

Trick looked at Colin, eyes swimming in hope. "Can I get you another latte, Col?"

"You doing okay, Trick? These guys aren't bothering you?" Colin could see the confusion in Trick's eyes. That Colin, of all people in that café, would attempt a rescue. Quiet, grumpy, fragile-looking Colin. The shy student who barely said anything, just studied by himself in a drafty corner.

"Uh, no man, I'm cool, I promise." Trick didn't mean a word of it.

Colin turned his attention back to the bozos. They were big, outweighing him by a hundred pounds each, at least. But he bet they were slow. Plus he'd have some advantage if he shifted into wolf.

He pulled his gray hoodie off and tossed it back to his table. He liked that hoodie and didn't want it to get torn when he went to wolf. Of course, it slithered to the floor. Now it was all cafe-sticky. *Sigh.*

"I really hate shifting form, but if you guys won't leave off harassing the staff, I guess it's gotta be done."

"This ain't your business, whatever four-footed fuzz-butt you are."

Colin huffed. "Hell it *ain't*. This is pack territory. You can't come in from offshore and just start harassing my favorite barista. I don't care what arrangement you have with his asshole family. You got a legal complaint, you take it to DURPS. You got something locally vested, you bring it to my Alpha."

"Pack? Alpha? You're a werewolf? You sure don't look like one."

Blubber Bozo Two added the profoundly eloquent but apt "Fucking werewolves."

Colin thought of his mild-mannered marine biologist Alpha, who was the strongest wolf he'd ever met. "Looks can be deceiving." They weren't in his case, but the selkies didn't need to know that.

Trick was staring at him with wide eyes. "You're seriously a wolf shifter, Colin? I'd no idea. Cool beans."

Colin grinned. "I'm a pathetic one, Trick, but I'm still made for fighting on land. Selkies sure aren't."

"Which is why we carry these on turf, to even the odds." Blubber Bozo Two pulled out some kind of gun.

Colin didn't like guns, so he had no idea what kind it was. It was a big, metal, loud surrogate for a tiny dick – like all guns. He pulled his gaze away and back to the selkies. He'd read that victims of gun crime got fixated on the weapon too easily.

"Well, aren't you smart selkies? You shoot me and bring the whole pack down on your head, not to mention our local allies. Brilliant move."

Blubber Bozo One only crossed his arms, pretending to relax. "Bullshit. You're a loner. There are no packs in the Bay Area."

Colin rolled his eyes so hard the world tilted on its axis. It was a phrase people kept parroting at him like it was a mantra. *There are no snakes in Ireland. There are no werewolves in San Francisco.* "You mean, there *weren't* any werewolves in the Bay Area. Now there are. Your information is out of date. My pack moved in over the summer. Now you're stuck with us."

"No," said Blubber Bozo One, pulling out his own gun and pointing it at Trick, "we aren't."

"Well, this escalated quickly." Colin pretended extreme boredom and examined his fingernails. "Just so you know, our pack allies include a kelpie, several powerful kitsune, and one sublimely bitchy Magistar. Not to brag or anything."

"Now I *know* you're lying out your ass. Ain't been a Magistar in these parts in my lifetime."

"You really need to keep up with the local news. Max *hates* being dismissed as purely hypothetical," replied Colin.

Trick, suddenly oblivious to the danger, was now staring at Colin with his mouth slightly open. "You don't mean *Max*? Morning blue-eyes Max? Hotness with the snark and Asian god prince come down to preach the gospel of running in tight leggings for the good of all mankind? *That* Max? I *love* Max.

Terrible taste in coffee, but I try not to hold that against people."

Colin nodded. "He's Beta-mate in my pack."

"He is? Cool. That the big hunk who comes in with him sometimes?"

"Bryan. Yeah, that's our Beta. Also Max's familiar." Colin let himself be proud of that. Bryan and Max were something to be proud of. Special. Unique.

"Nice. I didn't know I was surrounded by wolves."

"Pack house is just up the hill." Colin gestured with his mug towards the back of the cafe, away from the ocean.

The bozos did not like being ignored. "Good little faggots, now that you've got that cleared up. You still owe us, Inis."

Trick glanced at them as if he'd momentarily forgotten they were there. "How much?"

"Huh?"

"How much was my idiot family in it, before they ran?"

"Two hundred grand."

Trick cast his hands up to the heavens. "Two hundred! What the fuck? Well, I don't have that kind of money. I can't even make rent. You can threaten all you like, nothing will come of it." Trick gave one of his patented half-smiles. "Beat me up, you might get blood outta *me,* but you can't get blood from a stone."

"Impasse," added Colin. "Because I'll sure try to get blubber out of a selkie. You two smell delicious."

"You think you can move faster than a bullet, asshole?" Blubber Bozo Two asked, cocking his head as if in admiration.

"He can't, but I can sure try," said a deep rumbling voice from the entrance to the cafe.

Colin glanced back even though he really didn't need to. He knew the voice.

Judd had managed to open the door without the bell sounding, because he did things like that. He could move unbelievably quietly for such a big dude.

Judd was everything Colin was not in terms of threatening and werewolf. He was massive, rippling with muscles, full of scowls and teeth and power. He smelled wonderful, because he was pack and enforcer, which meant the scent of safety and protection, but also because he was *Judd*. And Judd had smelled like the pinnacle of yummy from the moment they met. Judd was also the hottest thing in Colin's universe.

Trick seemed to agree. "Ohmygod, whothat?"

"That mine," Colin hissed back, hoping Judd was too far away to hear such an unsubstantiated claim. It was only an impossible wish, a fantasy, but Trick was so cute and bold and charming that Colin couldn't let him even think of pursuing Judd.

"Share?" suggested Trick, hopefully.

"No."

Kevin pushed into the cafe after Judd. This time the bell jingled. Kevin was the other pack enforcer. He was as tall as Judd and almost as muscled but somehow less threatening. Probably because he was always smiling and cheerful. He was also a true redhead – disgustingly jock and inexcusably hot about it.

"How about that one?" asked Trick.

"That's related. Don't even."

The selkies were focused on the two enforcers, as they should be, much greater threat. Which allowed Colin and Trick to pretend to relax with banter.

"Well, wasn't your family blessed genetically." Trick leered at Kevin.

"Stop, please, that's my brother you're drooling over."

"So. That's *your* problem."

"He's tragically straight."

Trick pouted. "Well, fiddlesticks. So they're basically the cavalry?"

"More like the musculature."

Trick nodded, tossing his earring and grinning happily. "Oh, I see, enforcers. Goodie!"

Colin may not know what kind of shifter Trick was, but now that Trick knew he was in the presence of werewolves, he could guess at pack dynamics. Sometimes it sucked being the face of shifters in the modern world, everyone always knew werewolf business.

Still, at least Colin wouldn't have to test his wilted-salad fighting skills. "Yeah. Enforcers."

Judd had always intended to check on Colin. He usually walked past the cafe a few times when the kid was studying there. Why he couldn't just study at home, in the pack house, where it was safe was beyond Judd's comprehension. But if Colin wanted an overpriced drink in the company of humans, Judd would keep an eye on him and his stupidity.

Then Alpha texted him: *911 from Colin. You always know where he is. Go fetch.* Judd had never moved so fast in his very long life.

True, he'd move fast for any of his pack. He was an enforcer, that's what he did, but Colin was his favorite. Such a sweet, smart innocent little thing. Colin was, so far as wolf-Judd was concerned, the best chance at mate he'd ever met. Maybe he even thought of him as his mate sometimes – carefully, cautiously, deep down where the word might never pass his lips or become a longing in his eyes. It was a fragile hope that came with the safety of pack, and from wanting to belong for so long. Not that Judd would act on *mate*. Colin was too young for that. Far too young for Judd. Still, the kid needed looking after. Yet Colin never asked for help, ever. So a 911 from Colin meant something bad.

Sure as shit, the cafe was in crisis when Judd arrived. It smelled of burnt beans, stress hormones, and something fatty and damp. The humans were sitting frozen in shock while Colin faced up against two huge dudes with guns. Judd felt his canines begin to drop at the sight.

The cute coffee-slinger behind the counter vibrated in distress. Judd had never been inside the cafe. Why would he? But he'd noticed the barista through the window. Pretty, sparkly little thing, appealing and tasty no doubt. But not Colin.

Judd paused to scoop up Colin's fallen hoodie. It smelled like him, warm spices and red meat. Like a Christmas roast from back when Judd lived in Scotland. Familiar and tasty. His canines receded. Judd carried it over. Handed it to its owner. Unspoken reassurance: *I'm here now, you won't need to shift.*

He stepped forward, interposed himself between Colin and the... He sniffed. "Selkie. Bit outside of your territory, aren't you?"

He gentled Colin around and behind him. "Whatcha gonna do, kid, beat 'em up with a mug?"

Colin snorted. "Overprotective lug. I only wanted a refill. They started it."

"Course they did." Judd had no doubt of that. Colin wasn't a troublemaker. In fact, he went out of his way never to start anything. Not to garner anyone's notice. He must be awfully riled to have stepped in. Or he really liked the barista. Because the barista *was* the type to start trouble. Judd had no doubt *that* bouncy sparkle was involved.

Judd leaned around the salty buttery smell of the selkie to get a whiff off the pretty dark-eyed shifter at the espresso machine. He was all wet mud and cut grass. A scent Judd hadn't smelled in decades.

"Well, hello there, little dratsie. Colin didn't tell us about you. Aren't you just the cutest?"

Judd sensed Colin tense behind him. Hoped it was jealousy. Got mad at himself for that because he was too bloody old for Colin. Or jealousy for that matter.

"Max too," replied the dratsie, grinning at him. Playful cheek was to be expected from his kind.

"Huh?" Judd didn't follow.

"Your Beta-mate Max. He's also one of my regulars. He could have told you I was serving here."

"Max doesn't notice anything with his nose. Humans are almost as bad as selkies." Judd wasn't above a jab at the two assholes who'd threatened his favorite pack mate.

"And Colin does notice things?" asked the dratsie, eyes big and interested.

"'Course he does. Look at him, all sensitive and quiet. Sees everything, this one does."

Colin snorted. "Yeah yeah, *smells,* more like. Except whatever he is. I mean, I knew Trick was a shifter, just not which kind. Figured he didn't seem like a threat, no point in causing a fuss."

"And yet here we are, fussing. Because dratsie always cause a fuss. Trick, is it? That's apt." Judd frowned. How could Colin not have taken greater care of himself, let alone their territory? An unknown shifter working right here? In their town? In their cafe?

The dratsie bristled at Judd's words.

Judd placated. "Now, now. I know you don't mean to. Chaos is your nature."

Trick cast his eyes up to heaven. "It *is* our nature. The problem is when others take us seriously. They really shouldn't."

Kevin, who'd been mostly glaring at the two selkie and covering Judd's back, said to his brother, "And you didn't think the pack should know we had one of these dart-zee critters in our town? Hanging out with you in the evenings, making you drinks? Feeding you!"

Clearly both enforcers felt the same way. This pleased Judd. Also, now that Kevin had said it, he didn't have to.

Colin barely tolerated his brother's protectiveness on his best days. "No, I didn't. There's plenty of shifters around."

"Yet Alec knows every single one living or working in Sausalito." Oh, Kevin was mad.

Colin wasn't touching him but Judd swore he could feel him tense up. "Thanks bundles, Kev. I didn't know I was supposed to suck up to the Alpha every moment of every day. About what? Look boss, there's an adorable barista, smells a bit fishy, down at the cafe. You might wanna check my nose on this one."

"That's *exactly* what you should've done!" Kevin snapped back.

"Trick doesn't deserve me telling on him! He's got a right to his own privacy and his own existence without our interference." Colin would not back down from his brother.

"Aw, Col, you think I'm adorable?" the dratsie preened.

Judd hid his amusement. The pretty man reacted so typically, even in the middle of a crisis. He'd missed dratsies.

The selkie remained silent throughout. Presumably trying to determine their odds of survival. Three werewolves, two of them enforcers, was a whole different operation from one skinny ginger upstart loner. Even with guns to even the odds. Plus, they had to know more pack would arrive soon. Enforcers came first, but the rest of their pack was never far behind. The selkie had threatened a vulnerable pack mate – the smallest and youngest. It simply wasn't done. The Alpha was coming. No one wanted that.

Judd risked a glance back at Colin. "Shitgibbon, you're a pain in the ass. It ain't brown-nosing if we could have put this dratsie under our protection. Then we'd know to keep the selkie off his back." He didn't want to be harsh, but Colin's safety was at stake.

"Why would you want to do that?" wondered Trick, genuinely curious.

Colin seemed to agree. "Yeah, don't we have enough problems?"

Judd looked between the two of them. "Because he's your friend, Gingersnap."

"He is?" Colin looked surprised, then resigned.

"I am?" Trick looked surprised, then delighted. "I mean, I've been *trying* like hell to get there, but you never know with him."

"Fair point." Judd nodded. "But he stepped in to protect you with a coffee mug so I'd say, friends is a pretty good moniker." He always liked dratsies. That this one was trying to break through Colin's shell was awesome. Poor Col needed more friends his own age. Trick struck Judd as a relatively young dratsie. Although, like with kitsune, it was difficult to tell for certain.

One of the selkie was sick of being ignored. "We going to shoot something, Wade?"

"I take it your Alpha is on his way?" The other selkie asked, resignation in his voice. He pocketed his gun.

"Yep," said Kevin, cheerfully.

"Forgive me. How rude." Colin leaned around Judd to indicate the two selkie with a graceful hand. A hand Judd spent a lot of time wanting all over him.

Elegant fingers pointed. "This is Blubber Bozo One and Blubber Bozo Two. Bozos, these are the San Andreas Pack enforcers, Judd and Kevin."

"Charmed, I'm sure," said Kev.

Judd thought Colin was so cute with his snark – when he let it out.

Blubber Bozo One took a deep breath. He looked Judd firmly in the eye. How fun, a challenge. Judd pulled himself up and puffed his chest out. He was aware of how threatening he was as a man – big and Black with resting grumpy-face. Add to that the knowledge that he was a werewolf enforcer and most shifters just ran away from him. These two selkie were remarkably resilient. Perhaps Judd was going to get to punch something after all. That'd be nice.

"There are more in your pack?" asked the bozo.

"When have you known two enforcers and a youngling to be the only members of a wolf pack?" Judd was annoyed by the ignorance underpinning the question.

The selkie looked terrified. Good. Finally. "How many of you?"

Kevin grunted. "Enough."

Judd grinned. "If you're real lucky, Isaac and Tank will show up."

"And if you're real unlucky, Max and Bryan will," added Kev, amusement clear in his tone.

Blubber Bozo Two put his gun away.

"Fine," said Blubber Bozo One. "We get your point. You're a big pack. I suppose strawberry wonder-boy here wasn't lying about your allies either?"

"He tell you about the kitsune?"

"Yeah, and a kelpie."

"And a Magistar! Max!" piped up Trick, proud of his new insight into one of his regular customers.

"All true," confirmed Judd, pleased with Colin for bragging about their achievements. The San Andreas Pack had grown significantly in the short time since they moved to Sausalito. Not just with a coveted Omega, but with honest friendships, and neighborhood solidarity. Judd had been in many packs over the years. But this was by far the most inclusive. He loved it.

Speaking of which, he added one more extended member of their pack. "We got us a couple bad ass chefs as well."

The selkies looked confused. "How is that threatening?"

"Pepper's balls are bigger than yours, and Lovejoy is a beast with a spatula. You ever worked in a real kitchen?" Judd asked.

"No."

"I rest my case."

The two selkies backed away, but they weren't done. They were mob muscle after all. They'd watched too many Italian flicks and cared too much about image.

Blubber Bozo One said, "The moment he's on his own, he's ours. You can't watch Inis's back all the time."

Judd and Kev exchanged looks.

Kevin nodded. "Yeah, we can."

Judd knew Alec would agree and Max would insist. "He can come stay with us. Plenty of room. That'd be okay, right little dratsie?"

Trick looked quite cheerful. "Am I being press-ganged into joining a cult, or gang-banged into joining a pack? Option two, please."

Cheeky little thing, wasn't he? "No bangs. No cults. Calm down."

Trick pouted. "I take offense. I'm never calm. I'll stay where I am, thank you very much."

Kevin crossed his arms and glowered. "Because the place you're staying now is safe?"

Trick fiddled with his earring, looking embarrassed. "Well, I've been sleeping in my car, moving it to different parts of the headlands, you know? Rent these days is a crapshoot."

This time Judd definitely felt Colin stiffen behind him. The kid's breath huffed out in shock. But before either of them could protest, another voice joined the conversation.

A loud roaring kinda voice. "You've been doing *what*? Sleeping *where*?!"

Judd relaxed then. Because while it wasn't his Alpha, it was the next best thing. The cops had arrived. Probably as a result of one of the shocked cafe humans dialing 911 after seeing guns.

Judd swiveled to look at the door. He took it as an opportunity to place a hand on Colin's side. Offering reassurance. Colin shuddered but didn't move away. In fact, he leaned into Judd's touch, slightly. Colin hadn't flinched away. Judd took that as a win. Werewolves were normally tactile creatures. Colin wasn't, but not for lack of need. He simply held himself back. Thrilled by this chink in Colin's amor, Judd was careful not to take advantage. Staying as still as he dared.

Turns out it wasn't the cops, but only one cop, Deputy Kettil. Who had probably given his partner the slip... again. Still, even Deputy Kettil alone was guaranteed to put fear into a whole blob of selkie. At almost seven feet tall and weighing more than Judd cared to guess, the bear shifter put fear into basically everyone. Except, apparently, Trick, who snapped back, "And what business is it of yours where I sleep, Deputy?"

Before whatever that was about could ramp up, Colin also started to yell at the dratsie. Colin. Sweet, mild-mannered, little Colin. Apparently, he was equally upset by Trick's sleeping in his car. "Patrick Inis, why didn't you *tell* me?"

Judd didn't know Colin could get that loud.

"I didn't know we were friends, Col. Not *that* kind of friends. I didn't know you weren't sleeping rough yourself. Poor student, alone all the time. You sure dress like you're homeless."

"That's cause I've terrible taste, not lack of resources. You're an idiot." Colin's tone softened to kindness.

"But adorable, remember?"

"Yes, yes, adorable." Colin huffed in exasperated fondness.

Judd was getting uncomfortable. Were they flirting? Did Colin know how to flirt? Did Colin *like* the dratsie? Was it a good idea, under those circumstances, for Trick to come stay with them at the pack house?

Fortunately for Judd's peace of mind, Kevin interrupted the

love fest. "So the dratsie, whatever that is, is with us? And he ain't your problem, selkie bozos. Whatever you want from him, he's got a pack at his back now, so you'd best get your needs met elsewhere."

The selkies stalked out at that. Kettil glared at them but clearly didn't want the hassle of making any arrests just yet.

"Please tell me we're done here?" The bear shifter glowered at the cowering humans in the cafe. "Since *someone* saw fit to call this in, I got a mountain of paperwork to do now. Which one of you is Julie?"

One of the board game lesbians raised her hand, looking slightly sheepish.

"You called. Lemme take your statement before you go. The rest of you can shove off."

Trick said, snippy, "Stop scaring my customers, Deputy!"

"Don't start, nibbler. It's past closing time, in case you forgot. I'll come by, get your statement in the morning."

"At your regular time, for your regular drink, I imagine." The dratsie matched attitude with attitude.

"Of course. Because after I leave here and you close up, you're going to go home with them, and sleep surrounded by wolves, safe. Otherwise, I'll know about it and be *none too pleased*, you hear?"

"Surrounded by wolves, you say?" Trick wiggled his eyebrows at Judd, Colin, and Kev.

Judd chuckled.

Deputy Kettil threw his spade-sized hands into the air. "*Alone* but surrounded. You know what I mean."

Judd knew the pack's Omega, Isaac, had been counseling the deputy for ages about his failing love life. Now Judd wondered if Isaac knew Kettil took so much interest in adorable dratsie baristas? If maybe the berserker's problems stemmed from insisting he only dated women. Bear shifters, so stubborn.

"Only because I want to. Not because you're ordering me around!" snapped back Trick.

Kettil pointed two fingers at Judd. "You gonna make his safety a priority, enforcer?"

"*None too pleased*," griped Trick. "Who *says* that?"

Judd briefly closed his eyes, seeking strength. "You two are bloody exhausting."

The deputy only moved his fingers to include Colin. "Like you don't have your own shit to figure out."

Since the deputy was one of Isaac's regulars, he'd started coming to pack barbecues the moment he moved to Sausalito. Clearly, he thought he knew things about Judd. Which was annoying. But in the interest of keeping the peace, Judd only bothered to glare at the bear in return. "Yeah yeah."

Kettil nodded, calming down at last. "You three yappy-yaps okay to see me later tonight? I'll come by your den to get your statements?"

Colin whined in annoyance. "I have an exam tomorrow."

"Then you shouldn't go around antagonizing selkie," barked back the deputy. "I expect to find you studying when I arrive."

"Yes, officer," grumbled Colin.

Judd was secretly pleased that Kettil had ordered Colin back home. That way Judd didn't have to. "Kev and I will be there too. Only we didn't see much of it."

"I still want your statements."

Trick came out from behind the protective shield of his counter. Bounced up to the group of wolves and stuck his hand out.

Kevin shook it, then Judd.

"Patrick Inis, real nice to meet you both. Thanks for inviting me to stay."

"Judd Day and Kevin Mangnall. San Andreas Pack enforcers. Nice to meet you, Patrick," replied Judd.

"Call me Trick." The dratsie twinkled up at Judd. Big round black eyes and inquisitive, pointed chin. Trick might have recently been terrified for his life, but you'd never know it. He was practically vibrating with excitement, either at formally meeting them, or having a place to stay for the night. Poor thing, no one should have to sleep in the rough.

"So, Judd, *dratsie* is what you're calling me? You somehow Scottish?"

Judd chuckled. "Confused, are ya? Don't I look Scottish?"

Trick grinned back, willing to play along. "No accent."

Judd barked out a laugh. What a cutie pie. "I spent some time there, long ago. Another lifetime, really. But you're not either? Scottish I mean."

"Irish. You know, by blood and fur and all that rot."

Judd didn't know the Irish word for *dratsie*. "So that makes you what exactly?"

"Dobhar-chú."

"That's a mouthful."

"What's it mean?" asked Kevin. He had no tact because he never needed it, not looking the way he did.

"What kind of shifter does that make you?" asked Colin at the same time. Who did have tact, but apparently decided he didn't need it with Trick.

Judd grinned. Gestured for Trick to take it away. He'd never out a shifter that didn't want it. But he knew any dratsie worth his salt liked to brag.

Trick gave a little flourish and a kind of curtsy. "Otter shifter, at your service."

CHAPTER TWO
WE'VE GOT AN OTTER BY THE TAIL

It turned out to be harder than they thought to settle Trick inside the pack house.

Colin would never have guessed it, but the playful young man (well, *otter shifter,* because *of course* he was) could be stubborn. He agreed to move his car into their driveway, but refused all offers of a room inside the big house.

He wouldn't budge on that point, but he took them up on a meal and a shower, which Colin figured was a win. He understood pride combined with an inability to trust.

Most of the pack was home and getting ready to eat dinner when they arrived with Trick in tow. Half of them kept night hours so this was technically breakfast for them, having just woken up. A few (like the Alpha and his mate) worked day jobs, so this was their dinnertime. It was custom for as many of the pack as could make it, to collect for an evening meal around eight or so.

Colin would have been horrified to join a big group of hulking shifters after a day spent working in a cafe dealing with humans and bozos. But Patrick Inis took it all in stride.

Colin retreated to the living room, where he could stay out of the hubbub and pretend to study, while still keeping an eye on things. He wasn't sure why, but he really wanted Trick to like it at the house. Like him, like his pack, and enjoy himself with them. Trick was just so cool. Colin wasn't good at making people feel welcome, so he did the next best thing and provided quiet reassurance from afar. Or he hoped that was what he was doing. Mostly he felt awkward about the whole situation. But that was nothing new for Colin.

Kevin took Trick on a tour of the house and grounds, introducing him to everyone as they came home or woke up. Judd joined Colin in the den, making him feel both comforted and on edge. He sat across from Colin, not too close, and read the local paper which he'd stolen from the cafe.

Isaac and Tank came downstairs, sleepy and affectionate, both wearing what amounted to a uniform in the clubbing world – tight black t-shirt with confusing logo and black pants (in Tank's case, BDUs). Tank worked as a bouncer at the same club Isaac bartended. Their boss had accommodated a co-schedule rather than lose either one because the mated pair preferred to stick together.

Colin shuddered at the idea. He yearned for a mate or husband. He'd settle for *partner*. He didn't care the title, so long as there was someone who put him first in the world. However, that didn't mean he wanted to spend all his time with that person. It was Alec and Marvin's arrangement that Colin admired. The two spent a great deal of time apart and then glowed incandescently when they were together. Or maybe that was just Marvin's love of sequins? Either way, they had separate jobs and separate lives most of the time, and were always delighted to see each other again.

To no one's surprise, Marvin and Trick instantly got along after introductions. What did surprise the pack, though, was Max's easy acceptance of the barista in their midst.

"Good," was all the Magistar said upon hearing that Patrick was staying with them indefinitely. "Someone who can make a decent cup of coffee at last."

"Says the man with repulsive taste in coffee," shot back Trick without flinching.

The most powerful man in that room only flipped Trick off in good humor.

"You two know each other?" asked Marvin, curious. "Max, did you make a *friend* and not tell us?"

Max eyed the cheese platter Lovejoy had put out to stave off hunger pangs. "Sure thing, sparkles. This one keeps my morning drip line of overly sweet caffeine in full supply." He smacked his lips.

Trick nodded. "I invented a sticky bun-flavored latte just for him."

"It's heaven!" crowed Max. "And it's mine. *All mine!*" He glared around – as if anyone else would want such a thing.

Colin curled his lip, then noticed most of the rest of the pack was equally repulsed.

"You go on with your bad self, snuggle-bun," said Bryan fervently.

Max bit into a piece of cheese violently.

The front door opened and closed. The last and most important member of the pack was finally home. The rest of them immediately focused on him. Not that they all ostentatiously turned their heads or anything like that. It was more like flowers following the sun. A tilting reorientation, so to speak. Although not *that* kind of orientation.

Colin had a complicated relationship with his Alpha. Alec was powerful, which in Alpha terms meant he was capable of great control over himself and others. He could take away Colin's free will, if he wanted to, with one well-executed VOICE command. He was mild mannered yet freakishly charismatic. He was a brilliant intellectual, a marine biologist, for goodness' sake, who performed bumbling nerd with consummate skill, yet could kill most anyone with graceful efficiency. Colin had never seen a faster wolf shift or a more precise third form. Alec was like an espresso Alpha, concentrated, intense, necessary, and *you better wake up right the fuck now.* Also probably best when immersed in frothing milk, which Marvin could speak to, no doubt, and might explain Alec's love of the hot tub. The fact that he was physically smaller than most Alphas, and most of his own pack, was irrelevant to his power over them.

Being in Alec's presence made Colin buzz with need. He

wanted so many things from his Alpha – comfort, approval, safety, blessing. As if Alec were a god, or a father, or a cult leader. All those desires utterly terrified Colin. So mostly he bottled them up. He tried not to need his Alpha. He tried to be cool and calm and unruffled around Alec. But he could never stop the jolt of joy that always came when Alec first walked into the room.

The Alpha hung up his lab coat and glanced around, his eyes meeting and checking on each of his pack members. He noticed Trick, of course, as a stranger in his house puttering in his kitchen with Lovejoy and Marvin. But he assessed the man as unthreatening, and then made certain all his wolves were good.

This was done via wordless glances with Bryan, his Beta, and Isaac, his Omega – a nonverbal communication of security.

To Bryan: *Are we all safe?*

To Isaac: *Are we all happy?*

Whatever response he received from both masters of impassivity, it relaxed the Alpha's shoulders and put a smile on his face.

Marvin left the kitchen at a trot and flew into his arms. "Boyfriend!"

"Hello, my sweet sea-bean."

A few more murmured words of sappy adoration were exchanged, and then the merman was back in the kitchen, flushed and chipper. Colin worked hard to keep the yearning out of his eyes and scent. The way Alec focused all his Alpha intensity on his mate, and yet was so gentle with him. Colin wanted that.

Instead of his normal evening routine, which dictated a quick moment alone in his office, Alec stuffed his bag in a cubby by the door and came into the den.

To Colin's surprise, the Alpha's attention was on him. "You all right, Colin?"

Colin frowned. *Why wouldn't I be? Oh!* "The 911 text?"

"Yes." Alec moved around the couch and crouched in front of him. He removed Colin's textbook. Took both of Colin's hands in his.

The Alpha's touch was unbelievably reassuring. His hands were fine and strong, not too big but confident and sinewy. Colin hadn't realized he still carried the weight of the selkie confrontation. He'd been holding onto it, muscles tense, until Alec touched him. *Alpha, here.*

Colin looked over at Judd, sitting behind Alec on the other side of the coffee table.

The enforcer was watching them, his big arms flexing and relaxing. Colin was seized by the ridiculous idea that what he should have been doing, from the moment he got home, was snuggling in Judd's lap. That Judd also needed reassurance. That they ought to be reassuring each other, and because they couldn't, Alec had to handle them both.

Colin looked back into his Alpha's kind hazel eyes. "I'm fine. Judd and Kev arrived at the cafe and then Deputy Kettil. Have you met Trick? We brought him home with us. He needs a safe place to stay. I hope it's okay with you. Judd said you wouldn't mind. And he's such a sweetie, and he's in danger, and he's, well, kinda my friend."

Trick appeared, not quite bouncing, subdued even, hovering at the edge of the sunken den. "Like a stray kitten off the street. Hi, Alpha. Thanks for taking me in. I'll try not to be a bother. I know you don't need the hassle. I pinky-swear promise not to overstay my welcome."

Alec squeezed Colin's hands gently, still looking into Colin's eyes. *You're one of mine, nothing happened, and you're safe now*. The feeling washed over him, a necessary terrifying important thing.

Colin had to force himself not to cry. He had no idea why. He thought it might be relief.

Finally, Alec let him go, stood up, and approached their newcomer. He raised one hand to Trick's face, cupped the side, gentle, intent on the dratsie now. Focused attention under which even Trick stilled.

"Oh, wow," said the otter shifter.

"You'll stay forever if you need to, okay?"

"Oh, I couldn't impose. I couldn't…" Trick flushed, uncomfortable and yet painfully hopeful.

"We have nothing but space," said Max, who'd followed Alec to the den with a glass of grape juice. He folded his lanky frame into one of the really comfy chairs. "So long as you don't mind the construction."

Alec smiled, still focused on Trick. "We're remodeling the old girl, making improvements, making it better as a pack house. You'll stay." His tone was firm.

"Okay. If I could just park my car up the driveway? Sleeping there is fine. I don't want to put you out."

Alec clearly didn't like that idea at all but he also knew when not to push. He wasn't a dominating Alpha, just a persuasive one. "We'll talk about it over dinner."

He dropped his hand from Trick's face.

Trick scuttled back to the kitchen. "Marvin, I mean, whoa. Dude! Intense boyfriend is *intense*."

Marvin smiled big from where he was chopping clams. "Imagine being the focus of all of *that* in bed?" He waggled his almost non-existent eyebrows for lascivious emphasis.

Trick dropped the spoon he'd picked up in shocked delight. "I can't even! You lucky bastard."

Marvin shimmied his hips. "I know, right?"

Lovejoy, captain of his kitchen domain, grumbled at them both. "Less talk, more chowder." Lovejoy wasn't singing much these days or dancing about the house. Colin worried about him.

Colin turned back in time to see Alec and Judd clasp hands briefly. Judd was looking up at their Alpha from where he sat, almost worshipful.

"He's fine," was all Alec said.

"Thank fuck," Judd replied.

Colin looked away. This was a private moment between an Alpha and his enforcer. It was not for him, a lowly unranked pack member, and the weakest of the lot, to witness.

He returned to his book. Then he remembered.

"Hang Ten Viking and his assistant Phil are coming by later, take Trick's statement and talk to us about the incident at the cafe, and stuff."

"Who?"

"Colin's moniker for Deputies Kettil and Zarlenga," Judd explained, voice full of humor, which made Colin oddly proud. "Since Kettil's half Scandinavian and surfs in his off hours and Zarlenga, well, why do you call him *Phil*? Isn't his first name Luca or something?"

Colin didn't glance up from his book. "Yeah, but he *looks* like a *Phil*."

Alec laughed. "He does. Right, I'll get ready to charm 'em."

"Just keep Isaac with you," suggested Colin, because Deputy Kettil adored Isaac.

"Fair point."

"Omega super power, makes our Alpha seem charming?" suggested Judd.

"Are you saying I'm not charming on my own, enforcer mine?"

"Never that, Alpha."

Judd found dinner entertaining. The combined force of his pack crumbled when hurled against one stubborn dratsie. No matter what they said or did, Trick refused to sleep inside the house.

A direct attack never worked on an otter shifter. Slippery bastards. Judd could have told them that from the start. It took a half hour of expressive looks and coded phrases, but eventually the pack determined how to cope with Trick.

They would make sure Trick's beat-up 1982 Rumble Bunny was parked inside the garage. Judd and Kev would move all the motorcycles out. That would at least put a roof over the dratsie's head. Plus the garage shared that same roof with Max and Bryan. Max owned the property, but he refused to live in the big house. Instead, he preferred the small apartment above the garage. Bryan slept where his mate slept, of course.

So that kept the dratsie safe, for now. Judd mentally organized a guard detail. Who could do extra patrol while Trick slept? Who could provide escort to and from the cafe each workday? He'd have to look over everyone's schedules. He was both worried and pleased to have a new pack member to care for. Whether Trick liked it or not, he'd been adopted. Judd was enforcer enough to take pride in every new opportunity for protection, and every sign of an expanding pack.

The pack silently agreed that they'd work on Trick. Persuade him into their den and a proper bedroom over time. Judd figured that the best approach would be to get the dratsie inside for showers and dinners regularly. Then they could keep him gossiping as late as possible. Then he'd fall asleep on one of the couches in the den. They were hard to resist, those couches. The poor little otter worked long shifts at the cafe. Judd nodded to himself. He'd mention the scheme to Alec later.

Judd adored their sunken living room. Partly because he'd helped to remodel it. Partly because it was his ideal den. Their shared living area was open plan, which was actually a really old-fashioned idea. Like a longhouse from Viking times. Or the great hall in a certain castle of Judd's early werewolf days. It had a dining table that expanded to seat twenty, a fancy kitchen (at Lovejoy's insistence), and the awesome sunken den area.

The den was two steps down into a massive sitting area, around a huge fireplace. It was full of comfortable scratch-resistant leather couches and armchairs, cowhide rugs, stainless steel tables, and outrageous throw pillows. Marvin was into sequins – teal and turquoise. Recently, he'd added a few sea-colored fuzzy blankets and chunky knit floor pillows. Their friendship group continued to expand and it was getting cold enough to move barbecues inside after dark. Kitsune and cat shifters liked to lounge about on floors.

Judd also liked the den because Colin curled up there to do his homework regularly – when he wasn't at a cafe. Colin always occupied the smallest couches, his books spread around him. Judd liked to join him there. Not on the same couch. That was pushing things. But close enough to be aware of him, and soothed by his proximity and scent.

Colin was such a skittish little thing. After many conversations with Kevin about his brother, Judd still hadn't managed to coax away his shyness or entirely understand it. Of course, it's possible Colin wasn't attracted to a hulking, dangerous-looking dude like Judd. But Judd hoped that it wasn't that. Or, if it was, that Colin could get over his fear enough to realize they were perfect for each other. It was just taking a lot of time. And Judd had already waited a hundred years for this man.

"He might not be into you, dude," Kevin pointed out. "Not swing your way, so to speak."

"Everyone swings my way," Judd had responded, puffing out his chest. Arrogance was expected of an enforcer.

Kev had laughed. He had his own fair share of arrogance, and a propensity to misuse it. "You know what I mean. I mean he might be scared. What with me for a brother. And our dad for a father."

Judd nodded. They'd talked about it before. Kevin adored Colin. He worried about him *all the time*. He hadn't realized, when he left for college, that he'd abandoned his younger brother to something bad. Since Colin never talked about it, neither of them knew exactly what happened during those four years. Judd suspected that, at the very least, Colin had been profoundly neglected. All respect to Kev, because when he realized what was happening he got Colin out. But something remained damaged in Colin because of those four years.

Kev said once that he worried his brother was broken beyond repair. The rest of the pack thought he might be, too.

Judd didn't. Or perhaps it was more, that he hoped if Colin was broken, it was like a break in one of those Japanese cups. The kind that could be repaired with gold and made into something imperfectly precious and whole again.

So Judd sat close to Colin when he could. He rarely touched him. He took pleasure in the fact that since Isaac had entered their lives, Colin spent more time in the den. He would sit by himself, while the others puttered about the house. But he was there. When he wasn't in the den, he went to the cafe or school. He let himself be around other people. Had even made a friend.

When they'd first moved in, he'd spent most of his time in his room alone.

Small shifts become big hopes, Judd supposed. He looked over at Colin now, sitting next to Trick at dinner, looking relaxed and happy.

Eventually, the discussion moved on from Patrick's predicament to other matters. Trick wanted to know what everyone did for work. How did the pack function? Where had they moved from?

They chatted happily, talking over one another. Except Colin and Tank, of course. Neither of them ever said much. Tank was content in silence. Colin just rarely volunteered information.

Dinner was also an opportunity for the pack to reconnect. It was customary for them to all check in with Alec at mealtimes. The Alpha and his mate had the most stable jobs. That was for the best, but it meant they were away from the pack for eight hours at least every workday.

Alec worked for a private biotech company, well funded and within his specialty. Marvin worked for the Coast Guard in marine recovery and rescue. As a merman, he was perfect for the job and it played to his strengths. Although he sure wasn't military-minded. Bryan picked up sporadic shifts as a medic with Marin EMS. He didn't want anything more permanent. He needed flexibility because of his familiar duties. Tank and Isaac had just settled into their new schedule at Saucebox. Lovejoy had recently given up his bakery job. He and Pepper were trying to make a go of it in the food truck business. Pepper was a brawler but an amazing chef. Lovejoy was so easygoing, that their partnership seemed to be working well so far. His kitsune lover, Mana, was off on some grand tour with her drag show. Colin figured that's why Lovejoy was so subdued these days. But customer foibles occasionally whipped him up into a verbal frenzy.

"Can you believe he ordered the carpaccio roll, but wanted me to *cook the beef*? Humans!"

Lovejoy and Pepper weren't expecting the food truck to turn a significant profit until next year. Although they were taking on catering jobs over the holidays. The pack was trying to decide if they should invest in a small car for commuting into the city or invest more in promoting the food truck.

Trick offered up the loan of his *Rumble Bunny*, but the others balked at that. For one thing, it was still the dratsie's home. Judd decided he'd sneak some work in on the engine while Trick was at the cafe. Make certain it was running okay. Max said they could use his *Cheetah* if they liked, but everyone laughed at that idea. First of all, Max himself barely fit inside it.

Second, as Kevin put it, "One good earthquake and the whole thing will fall apart."

"Be nice," replied Max. "The rust is the only thing still holding it together."

Alec redirected them back to finances. "So, for now, we help with the food truck and save on the car. Look into wet weather gear for the motorbikes." He looked at Colin. "Does that leave us enough to hire a contractor for the house?"

Judd tried not to sigh. This was the boring part of pack life.

Colin, however, perked up whenever finance paperwork and spreadsheets were under discussion. Judd figured it was a character flaw he could learn to overlook.

"If we roll the profits from Heavy Lifting into that instead of back into the business."

Since Kevin and Judd's corporate front for the pack had unexpectedly turned into a profitable business venture, none of them had time to actually work on the remodel anymore. They did, it appeared, have the means to hire a construction crew. It was just a matter of finding the right team. This was their pack house, after all. A bunch of hard-hatted humans in their territory harping on about sportswear, shaving, and snickerdoodles – or whatever it was humans talked about – was bound to mess with their carefully cultivated werewolf aura.

They decided they'd ask around at the next full moon barbecue. See if their local friends knew anyone interested in working on the furry side of the street.

Alec turned his attention onto Judd. "Any new contracts, then?"

Judd felt a thrill of pleasure. He was about to reap Alpha approval. He'd just confirmed a great new contract. Neither enforcer was computer savvy, but Colin had set Heavy Lifting Security up with a simple website and all queries came through email or by referral. Judd could check email. So he vetted queries right after he woke up each day, because Kevin couldn't be bothered.

"Yeah, I bid us out for local bodyguards to a visiting shifter celebrity. Xavier recommended us for the gig. She wanted extra private security, specifically werewolves. Word is she asked after Kevin by name. So I guess we got ourselves a reputation."

"How'd you know that's the reputation she's after?" leered Kev, who was a bit of a slut. In the best possible way, of course. Also, in a very dramatic way. He had a habit of falling madly and inappropriately in love with any woman smart enough to put him in his place. Occasionally, he even attempted to juggle several such women at once, without any juggling ability what-soever. Not the sharpest pickle in the jar, that one.

"I don't know which way she wants you, but I asked for double our normal fee because it's so last minute. Starts tomorrow, in fact. She didn't even bother to negotiate."

"Should've asked for triple," said Lovejoy.

"Truth." Judd nodded at him. "But you know I'm not great at this kind of thing. I only do the contracts because Kevin is worse at them. Still, this fee alone should pay to start the upstairs remodel. We really need another bathroom. Anyway, she's in town for this huge concert. Mount Tam, Saturday night."

Colin cleared his throat.

Judd stopped talking and turned to look at him.

Everyone else hushed and listened too. Colin rarely said anything at pack meetings. He probably felt he wasn't allowed to, since he didn't contribute to pack funds. As the youngest and smartest, he was encouraged to stay in college. The pack eagerly supported his education. But Colin saw himself as a freeloader. Sometimes, Kevin prodded his brother into admitting to good grades at dinner. Judd was absurdly proud of how brilliant Colin was, especially with computers. Judd was too old to be anything but a Luddite. He admired a man who spoke the language of the beeps and clicks.

"Judd, I do hope it's not the singer I think it is," Colin said, even as he blushed because everyone was staring at him.

Judd figured Colin knew that Lexi Blanc was in town because of *Instalamb* or something. "I hear ya, Gingersnap. Country music, pah. But her money is good. It's only the one concert. The rest is local TV and shit. Shouldn't be too bad."

Colin sat back, pushed his food away. "I'm gonna be sick."

Judd got it – an entire concert of country music was no joke. But even Judd didn't think it warranted *that* extreme a reaction.

Kev looked up, shoveling chowder into his face. "What's up, bro? She a total diva?"

"Judd didn't tell you the *name* of the celebrity who's gracing our amphitheater with her presence this weekend?"

"What do I care? Job's a job."

"It's Lexi Blanc. Isn't it, Judd?" Colin's voice was shaky and flat and wistful and angry all at the same time.

Judd could only nod, confused.

"Ohmygod!" squealed Lovejoy. "I love her! *Fangs, fangs, fangs! Fangs in the morning dew! Fangs in the—*"

"Please don't sing, Lovejoy. Not country. Not at the dinner table," Judd remonstrated.

"Yeah, Lovejoy, have you lost all sense of decorum? You've even come to dinner without your gloves!" mocked Max.

"I know, right? Where did I put my straw bonnet?" Lovejoy played along.

Trick giggled at their antics.

Judd couldn't look away from Colin's pinched face. Why was he so upset? It was a good contract. Lexi Blanc, country music legend, the first werewolf singer to make the charts – sexy, sultry Alpha goddess of every good ol' boy's heart. Everyone loved her. Except, apparently, the Mangnall brothers. Because, out of the corner of his eye, Judd saw Kevin also go white as a sheet.

"Oh fuck me, no. Judd, tell me you didn't already sign it!" Keven, his fellow enforcer, actually yelled at him across the table. They always sat so one was facing the big windows and the other the front door.

Judd tore his gaze away from Colin to glare at Kev. This was a perfectly normal contract, why was he freaking out? "Uh, *yeah*. The money's insane. The contract was a digital rush job. I signed it a few hours ago."

"You're running the op on your own, then. Or we'll pull Tank and Bryan from their crap jobs for a bit. Better yet, get Isaac to help."

"Hey now," rumbled Tank, mildly.

"I could ask for time off. I'm only running spotter for a human ambulance team over next few days." Bryan offered, ever the peacekeeper.

Isaac only sat watching. He was waiting to see if he needed to intervene and mediate. Judd and Kevin often teased each other, so it was hard to know if Kevin's anger was genuine.

Judd, however, did know. This was out of character for his partner. He stared at Kevin, trying to read his body language. The other enforcer was vibrating with rage and what... Fear?

"Well, I'm out, no matter what!" Kevin's jaw was set, the shape so much like Colin's. Their lips were different, though. Colin's were fuller, especially on the bottom. Judd always wanted to tug on that lower lip with his teeth. It was an inconvenient urge but apparently irrepressible.

Judd shook his head at Kevin, staying firm. "No can do. They asked for you specifically, remember? You're named in the contract. I *told* you. You've got the reputation to beat with celebrities these days, apparently. All that flirting."

"Well, shit a brick," said Colin, surprising everyone. He almost never swore. The rest of them were confirmed potty mouths. Colin was proper and educated and stuff.

Trick was watching the whole exchange with wide eyes.

Kevin stopped eating. Everyone else did as well, in sympathetic shock.

Kevin *never* stopped eating.

Kevin rubbed a hand over his face. "It's not my reputation she's after. It's my relation."

Judd frowned. "How so?" He looked at Colin. "How'd you know she was coming to town?" His stomach churned. Had he made a horrible mistake? He tried to make a joke of it. "Are you her number one fan, Gingersnap?"

"Nope. I'm her number two son." Colin still had that funny look on his face.

"What?!"

"Lexi Blanc is our mother," Kevin explained, voice flat.

"I guess Kev doesn't tell you everything, Judd." Colin pushed back from the table and ran from the room.

"Oh shit," said Judd, meaning it. He turned to their Alpha. "Did you know about this?" He pushed his chair back to go after Colin. To comfort and apologize. His Gingersnap was hurting. Judd had to make it right somehow. He'd no specifics of the brothers' history with their mother. But it clearly wasn't good.

"No," snapped Kevin, "I'll go."

Alec stood then. Alpha. Dominance. "Neither of you go. Isaac?"

"On it." Isaac jumped up and trotted up the stairs with alacrity.

"Well, isn't this terribly dramatic and exciting," said Max.

Alec turned back to his enforcers.

Judd felt guilty even though there was no way he could've known. He glared at Kevin across the table. Both of them were now standing. "You could've *said* something!"

"How was I to know my fucking mother would try to hire us? I haven't spoken to her in over a decade!"

"Both of you, sit."

It was a mark of how agitated they both were that they ignored their Alpha.

"She's famous, you wanker!" Judd swore. "You didn't think this pack needed to know that your mother's, oh, I don't know, *the fucking queen of country music*?"

"She doesn't *mean* anything!" yelled Kev back.

"Clearly she does!" Judd gestured to the two empty spots at the table. The absence of Colin. His baby was hurt! Worse, Judd was the cause. Idiot Kevin.

"BOTH OF YOU WILL SIT."

Power rolled off their Alpha. Real power. The kind that forced compliance.

They sat.

Trick said, into the resulting silence, probably to Marvin. "Is it always this exciting? It's like that new soap opera – what's it called? Oh yeah – *The Nights of Our Afterlives.*"

Marvin said, "Always, darling. And we haven't even gotten started yet. Wait until you meet our kitsune friends. They're nothing but drama. It's fantastic. Lovejoy, pass the seaweed salad please? Trick, darling, would you like some?"

"Don't mind if I do."

Judd was still held in stasis by his Alpha's command. Everything in him screamed to follow Isaac. Chase after Colin. Fix this somehow.

He felt the VOICE leave him.

Alec let out a huge sigh. "Anyone else want seaweed? No? Good. Slimy bits of salty grass if you ask me. Right. Kevin, start talking. Tell us all about your mother."

CHAPTER THREE
MAMMAS DON'T LET YOUR BABIES GROW UP TO BE WEREWOLVES

Colin really didn't mean to be a drama queen, he honestly hated causing a fuss. Especially on Trick's first dinner with the pack. But really, he couldn't be expected to behave calmly when mothers were sprung on him over clam chowder.

He sat, slumped on his bed. Of course he was looking at the one photo he had of her from before... Before she was famous, when she was still his mother. He didn't keep the photo out, or keep it with him. It was usually hidden in a corner of his wardrobe. And yeah, he had a wardrobe because the pack house was too old to have closets, one of the many reasons for the remodel.

The photo showed all four of them. It was from too long ago for Colin to remember where they were. His mother stood on one side, looking much like him – same lips and chin, same coloring, although somehow less fragile. Those features looked great on a woman; on a boy they were insipid. He was only about four, almost white-blond and covered in freckles, sitting on his dad's shoulders. His dad looked pleasant, still serious with no smile, but content in a way Colin couldn't really believe was real. His dad was big like Kevin, ginger too, his hair that same darker, better red. Kevin was standing between their parents, one hand in each of theirs – mid-swing, in motion, and blurry. Colin was looking away, content on his perch and unaware of the camera. Kevin was looking up at their dad, cheeky, searching for approval. Their dad was looking at their mother, not turned to her, but aware of her and not the camera. Their mother, all big smiles and big hair, was looking directly at the lens – poised, charming, gorgeous, and already leaving them.

A knock came at Colin's bedroom door.

He sighed, stood to open it, wondering who they'd sent. He hoped it was Judd, as he owed him an explanation. Poor big lug. Judd hadn't known what he'd committed them to. Kevin should have told him about their mother months ago. Judd didn't like drama, always said he was *too old for that shit* whenever Marvin threw a hissy fit.

Colin really hoped it wasn't the Alpha at his door. Alec wouldn't understand any of it. He knew this because he'd met Alec's mother several times. Alec and Bryan's mom was the type to have eschewed the bite and stayed human. She avidly collected deviled egg platters with flower patterns, bleached her hair with peroxide, and decorated her nails with fake gems. But she never had a bad word to say to her boys. Colin and Kevin's mother, on the other hand, was the type to first, name her boys *Colin* and *Kevin,* and second, abandon them to pursue a career as a country music singer under the ridiculous stage name, Lexi Blanc.

But it wasn't Judd or Alec at his door, it was Isaac. Of course it was Isaac. Isaac fixed things and Colin was broken.

Isaac, who made Colin feel safe and open and needy in a way that didn't worry him the way it did with Alec. Probably because Isaac exuded some kind of soporific wolf pheromone. Their Omega didn't smell like anything. Or, to be more precise, he smelled like pack and comfort, and Tank, who was also pack and comfort. As an Omega, Isaac's whole function was to grease the social working of the pack machine. Isaac was also some kind of gossip savant at getting shifters to talk.

Colin didn't want to talk. He wanted to wallow and suppress his feelings until he could walk back out there and face up to the fact that Judd was about to spend more time with Colin's mother than Colin had in living memory. Not to mention his brother. His big, strong, straight, perfect enforcer brother. Who never seemed to care much about anything.

But this was Isaac, so Colin gestured for the Omega to come in. The man's face was warm and sympathetic. He took a seat at Colin's small desk, turned the chair to face the bed, waited for Colin to join him.

Colin wondered if Isaac might understand his feelings more than the others did. Isaac, who grew up in a cult run by an abusive narcissistic enforcer father. Colin figured they had parallel parenting, his being a narcissistic mother and an enforcer dad. He shied away from the *abused* moniker. He wasn't sure if he qualified. He didn't want to diminish Isaac's experience with his own, which wasn't that bad by comparison. So instead, Colin just never talked about his childhood. He never even looked it up on the internet to see if there was a definition. Did forgetting your second son existed count as abuse or just neglect? And what exactly distinguished the two?

"What was that about, Col?" asked Isaac, gently.

"I don't really want to talk about it."

"Okay. So your mom is famous?"

Colin passed over the photo. Proof because she still looked like herself there, younger and human, but there was no mistaking famous werewolf singer Lexi Blanc.

"Now that I know, I can see that you look a bit like her."

Colin gave a humorless laugh. "I look *a lot* like her. One of the few gifts she gave me and it's a crapshoot."

"You're beautiful, Colin."

"Cute, Isaac, nice try. I'm an emaciated orange clown doll."

Isaac actually winced, then looked angry. "Stop that. You aren't. Your mom was voted the most beautiful woman in the world a couple of years ago. How can you not see that translates to you too?"

"I'm a dude. It doesn't work that way."

Isaac shook his head. "So you got baggage with your mother."

"We talking parents now? You wanna tell me about yours?"

Isaac twitched. "Okay, touché. But you're old enough to

know the damage done, regardless of who did it originally, eventually is your responsibility and not your excuse. Especially not an excuse for poor behavior towards others when we have guests. You're not a pup anymore."

Colin nodded, feeling even more ashamed. He took the photo back. "Yeah, I know. And I'm sorry."

"Apologize to the Alpha and Judd and Trick, not to me."

"I will."

"Please talk to me about it?" Isaac's voice was soft.

Colin found himself wondering if it wouldn't help to tell the Omega something of his childhood. It had been such a long time ago. *I'm a mess,* he thought, *just like her.*

"What happened with your mother?"

"Yeah, what happened?" Judd was there, standing in the open doorway, occupying most of it. He leaned against the jamb, huge arms crossed over his chest, backlit from the hall so it was difficult to make out his expression.

"I'm sorry I snapped at you."

The big enforcer shrugged. "It'd help if I knew why."

Colin sipped a tiny breath and nodded. It was a fair request. He owed him.

"I don't know much about my mother. If that's what you're after," Colin started, hesitant and defensive.

Apparently, he really did think that all Judd wanted was more information on his bodyguard client.

Shitgibbon. Judd intended to break that contract. He just wanted Colin to be okay. He wanted to bust across that room and scoop him up. He wanted to lick off the smell of tears.

"She took the bite right after I started kindergarten. As soon as she knew she'd survived, she took off. I don't remember much about her. I was so young when she left. I only really know the void she left behind."

Isaac touched Colin's wrist.

Judd wanted to be doing that. Wanted to caress away the

tension in Colin's hands. They were clenched so tight. They were too beautiful to abuse like that.

"What did that void look like?" Isaac asked carefully.

Colin gave a humorless chuckle. "Dad used to clip articles out of magazines for her to read when she got back. Every week he'd set them out in a fan shape on our coffee table and no one was allowed to touch them. This shrine of hope that she'd return, when everyone knew she never would. It was pathetic but weirdly beautiful."

"And you, how was he with you?"

"Oh, he wasn't."

"Wasn't?"

"I don't think he said ten words to me at any one time after she left. He talked to Kevin about pack or sports or hunting. But then when Kev left for college, things were just silent. He didn't want to see me, so I made sure he didn't, easier on both of us. I wasn't what he wanted. I was small, and weird, and nerdy, and, you know..." He unclasped his hands and flopped one wrist. "Super fucking gay. What dad wants to notice that?"

Judd winced. Colin's abandoned father had perpetuated his abandonment. He'd coped with homophobia through neglect. Judd ached for child Colin, who'd endured loneliness like it was some earned punishment. Judd, at least, had chosen loner status. "He wasn't physically abusive, was he?"

Isaac looked at Judd with a frown. As if Judd shouldn't ask such a thing straight out.

Judd flinched. Maybe he shouldn't? He was probably being indelicate. But he needed to know. After all, Colin's father was still alive. Judd could still get across the country and challenge the man. Kill him. Be back in forty-eight hours.

Colin shook his head, looked at Isaac. "Is it wrong that sometimes I wished he was? That he would notice me enough to hit me? Fuck, don't tell Max, please." Max who *had* been hit, probably a lot. "I mean, it wasn't great in high school, everyone pushes around the weird gay kid and it's not like I could play hooky. School was the only thing I was good at. I *let* Dad ignore me. If I were a different kind of child, I would've acted out, gotten into trouble, brought home endless boyfriends, anything to get his attention. But I didn't."

"Instead you took neglect as your due and faded away." Isaac patted Colin's wrist – a brotherly kind of comfort. Judd admired his ability to be undemanding, as Colin hadn't flinched.

Judd glowered. He was angry at the pain in Colin's tone. "And Kevin didn't notice *any* of it?" Judd wanted a scapegoat. He threw Kev to the proverbial wolves, even though he considered the other enforcer his friend.

"I was always pretty quiet and Kev was the opposite. He's so bright and noticeable and very…"

"Straight?" suggested Judd.

"Straight. But also an enforcer." Colin flapped his hand at Judd as if to say, *Well, you know what that means.* "Something to be proud of, more like our father. More like a real werewolf. Besides, by the time it got really bad, Kevin was out of the house."

"Bad?"

Colin winced. "Puberty wasn't kind to me and I was late to it. Kevin left right when I went into high school. It was… rough for a while there. I was… am… this skinny rag of a person, all elbows and freckles. Covered in zits, with big lips and bad hair. Perfect bully bait. I got this scholarship to a private high school. So even if the youngsters from our old pack had been inclined to protect me, which I highly doubt, they weren't around. I hadn't taken the bite yet. Didn't think I'd survive it and never intended to try. Thought I'd graduate, get some scholarship to a West Coast college, and run. Forget that shifters even exist. Just be human."

"Why did you take the bite, then?" Isaac asked with real interest. He'd never had a choice – Omegas were born werewolves.

"It was the only time Dad wanted me to do anything." Colin shot a quick glance at Judd, looking up through pale lashes. Judd guessed he didn't want to elaborate.

Even so, Judd moved into the room, listening hard.

Isaac's calm Omega presence worked its magic.

Colin stared at the floor with vacant eyes and continued. "I think he hoped I'd die in the attempt." Another quick glance up at Judd. Checking for disapproval.

Judd worked hard to keep his face neutral.

Colin added, "I think we both hoped I'd die."

Judd felt something in him fracture at that kind of despair – breaking around a lump of sympathy. He'd lived his whole long life in many ways and places. He'd experienced horrible things – poverty, war, bad packs, cruel Alphas, long stretches of endless loneliness. But he'd never really known despair. Not that kind.

"I won't take the job with her. We'll cancel the contract." Judd hoped the quiver in his voice wasn't apparent.

Colin shook his head, hard. "We'll get sued. Not to mention, we'll be in Xavier's bad books. You know how Xavier gets. His reputation is riding on Heavy Lifting. We really can't afford to be on the outs with him. He's Tank and Isaac's boss and he's got a ton of power these days with the local shifters. He's a good ally. You can't just back out because I'm a dramatic little idiot. And don't let Kevin tell you he can't handle it, either. He's always been way better about her leaving."

Judd questioned that. Kevin was older. Kevin would have remembered their mother more. Kevin was used to being worshiped. He would resent and hate being abandoned, but hide it well.

Colin looked up from the floor, finally. He sucked in a breath. "It's not like I really blame her, given how Dad was. You know she was only sixteen when Kevin was born? Twenty for me. I think the marriage was pack arranged too. I doubt she ever loved Dad. Who wouldn't want to escape that? Get away from his cold power."

"Will Kev be okay with the contract if you are?" asked Isaac, even though it was clear Colin wasn't okay with any of this. But if Col wanted to put a brave face on everything, Isaac seemed disposed to let him.

Judd sighed. He would have pushed the matter. But Isaac was an Omega. He supposed Omegas knew best.

Colin shrugged. "I don't know."

"You gotta learn to talk about this shit with your brother," Judd said, unable to help himself. Kevin had probably kept Lexi's identity from the pack because he didn't know how his younger brother would feel. And now Colin didn't know how his older brother felt. They should fucking communicate.

Colin gave a sad lopsided smile. "Family code. Don't talk about shit that hurts. You're old, you should know that one."

Judd snorted. "I'm so old I know better, kid."

There was a moment of quiet. Everyone stilled. Judd wanted Isaac to leave so he could sit on Colin's bed, gather him into his arms. Not so much for Colin's comfort as for his own. But he was afraid Colin would flinch away. That would break Judd's heart even more. Plus, what right did he have to offer comfort?

Eventually Isaac spoke, absentmindedly and softly, as if he were reminding himself of something. "You know, they're supposed to take care of us. Parents are supposed to look after us, and love us, and talk and hug and all that sappy stupid stuff. You know that, right?"

"Yeah." Colin stared back down at the floor. He looked fragile, sunken in on himself.

Isaac's voice firmed. "No, I mean, do you *know* it – all the way down to your bones? The ones that break and reform. Really *know it*. I don't think we heal, without that knowledge. You get to blame him. And her. You get to hate them even. I give you permission, if you need it."

Colin didn't say anything. He was probably afraid of breaking down. Judd suppressed his own need to cry.

Isaac nodded. Point made. His Omega timing clearly telling him not to push. Judd envied him that.

Isaac stood gracefully and left the room. He nudged Judd further into it as he left. A weird kind of permission. He shut the door and Judd was alone with Colin. Together.

Yet Judd was at a loss. What should he do? He usually knew what to do. Maybe not what to say, but action. He was good at action. Now, he was at a loss. He hadn't a life experience to share. He didn't know how to reach Colin and provide comfort. Even if he did, Judd wasn't the right person to do so. Judd represented everything that repelled Colin – big, fierce, older, enforcer. Just like good old Dad. He didn't want to loom. He didn't want to scare Colin. God, *anything* not to scare him.

The silence stretched out between them, unraveling all Judd's dumb longing.

Finally Colin's voice trembled out, small and barely audible. "Forgive me for snapping earlier? You didn't know."

"Done." Judd figured that if he didn't know what to do, the best thing was to ask. Colin might be young, but he seemed to know his own mind. "How can I help make this easier for you?"

He meant them having to work for Colin's mother. He meant dredging up lost family and old wounds. He wanted to be given a task, something that would make everything better.

"What do you need?" Judd asked. Tense. Ready to leave. Ready to be rejected. Ready to not fight, when fighting was all he was good for.

"Would you? Maybe…" Colin hesitated.

"Anything," Judd said, probably injudiciously. But Colin so rarely asked for anything. Judd was sure whatever he wanted, Alec would accommodate.

"Maybe a hug?" Voice so tentative, as if Colin shocked himself with the request.

Judd had never felt more surprised in his life. He'd also never moved so quickly across a bedroom. And that was saying something.

Colin had no idea what possessed him to ask for such a thing. *A hug! Really? As if I'm the kid Judd always calls me.*

He'd spent his whole life training his needy body not to desire touch. He'd thought for so long that he wasn't going to be a werewolf, that he'd better learn daylight distancing. Everyone knew humans were less interested in touch than wolves, so he'd cultivated the skill of denial. He'd thought that to be strong and independent meant no contact, or as little as possible. That's certainly how his father behaved.

It had become a kind of reactive physical tic. Every time Colin craved contact, he withdrew further into himself. Eventually, he shied away from even the most casual of touches. He knew it worried the rest of his pack, and he hated to worry them, but by the time he and Kevin had joined, it was already an established habit. In a weird way, he was proud of it. As if it meant he didn't really need any of them.

Maybe some part of him thought it would be a step in the right direction, turning to Judd for physical reassurance. Perhaps this was a way to prove that Colin could be fixed, wasn't irreparably broken.

But mostly he let himself ask for a hug because of the look on Judd's face. Colin had never been looked at with such naked longing before. As if the enforcer would do *anything* to make Colin feel better. As if he hurt *for* Colin, felt all the things that Colin never let himself feel. Because that would be wallowing, and strong men endured without complaint. Maybe Colin could give a little back in gratitude for such empathy. Maybe a hug would make *Judd* feel better.

The moment the words left his lips, Judd approached. The enforcer could move fast – he was a supernatural creature, after all. Barely a blink and he was sitting on Colin's bed, close but not touching. Colin tried to stop himself but he still flinched.

Instantly, Judd stilled, as if Colin were some frightened woodland creature in a children's cartoon.

Colin resettled himself and leaned a little towards Judd.

The big man let out his breath slowly. Colin could actually see Judd consciously relaxing the muscles in his shoulders and arms, unclenching everything to appear as approachable as possible. Judd's eyes, dark brown and worried, stayed focused on Colin's. So intense was the look, Colin lowered his lashes, because otherwise he wouldn't find the courage to make the first move. And it would have to come from him, a verbal request wasn't enough. Judd would do nothing without Colin's physical welcome. They were creatures of body language, not conversation.

Colin imagined climbing into Judd's lap. He would straddle

him – plaster his whole chest against the man, absorb his warmth, inhale him through his pores. But that was too much – too gay, too girly, too desperate, too many things Colin found repulsive about himself. His father's voice singing a litany of failings.

So Colin scooted close and leaned into Judd from the side.

Judd turned, angled towards him, and opened his arms, waiting.

Colin firmed his resolve and collapsed against the enforcer. His favorite man. His favorite person. His favorite werewolf.

The hug was awkward and off-center, but the best one Colin had ever experienced.

His brother hugged him sometimes, and his Alpha once in a blue moon, and Marvin in a flighty, absentminded, one-armed way. But this was different.

Judd was big enough that Colin could barely fit his arms all the way around the man's massive chest. Waist maybe, but that was too low and too close to the man's perfect ass, so Colin kept his arms raised. He could have wrapped his legs around Judd, of course, but he wasn't going to let his brain go there again.

Judd's wonderful scent surrounded him, something rich with meaty musk, almost edible, but also safe. He smelled the way a warm comfy leather sofa felt to sink into. Or the way that first bite of a perfectly prepared steak bursts over the tongue.

Colin burrowed into Judd's neck, breathing deeply. He nuzzled his cold nose just above Judd's collarbone, where the skin was thin and impossibly soft. He pressed his eyes and forehead into Judd's throat, using the warmth there to stop himself from crying.

Judd stayed still, probably a bit scared, afraid Colin might bolt, no doubt. It was a valid fear – Colin *really* wanted to bolt. Desperately needed to. But he fought the inclination, let himself like this insignificant thing that he wanted more than anything.

Cautiously, impossibly slowly, the enforcer returned the hug. He wrapped huge arms around Colin, tightening them hardly at all, not wanting to cage him or imply Colin was trapped in any way. He didn't stroke or pet, didn't try to take any additional touches, just crossed his arms over Colin's back. He could do that easily; Colin was stupid skinny. Judd's big hands curled over Colin's lower ribs, molding the shape, not gripping at all.

"This okay?" rumbled out Judd's deep voice under Colin's chin. For the first time, Colin caught the hint of an accent that had been muted by decades in the New World. Something European in origin, that formed the word *okay* unnaturally, but with great precision.

"Yeah. This is great." Colin was surprised to find it was great. He wasn't lying at all.

He still wanted to bolt, but that was because he liked it too much. He decided to be kind to himself, because Isaac had said it was fine to do that. Because, he realized, surprised by his own insight, that the pack was always unfailingly kind to him. Especially Alec. If the Alpha could extend Colin some measure of grace, perhaps he could extend that same grace to himself? Perhaps it didn't mean he was weak, it just meant he was loved.

It felt right to be there, held by someone stronger. Leaning on someone else. It also felt scary.

Colin started gathering his courage, reminded himself not to relax so much that it implied trust. Taking a deep shaky breath, pulling the last of Judd's scent into his memory, Colin pushed himself away.

Instantly, Judd lowered his arms. "That was great, kid. Thank you."

"For a hug?"

"What, you thought I didn't need them too?"

Colin had thought that. Judd always seemed a bit impervious to the needs of man or wolf. "But you're so strong."

"Hugs don't make me less so. Needing touch isn't a failing. It's natural."

"For werewolves."

"For anyone, Gingersnap. Shifter or human. Even Max likes a hug on occasion and he's more prickly than a hedgehog surfing a pincushion."

Colin let himself consider that maybe hugging his pack

mates wasn't that big a deal. He'd have to examine the idea more closely, later. "Why do you always call me that?"

"Gingersnap? It's my favorite cookie. Although, to be fair, I prefer the soft chewy version. And you are ginger. Don't you like it?" Judd looked... What? Nervous? Hesitant? Prepared to be crushed?

Colin actually liked *Gingersnap*. It made him feel spicy and interesting. Plus no one else had ever had a special name for him, only Judd ever bothered. "It's fine. Why do you always call me *kid*?"

"'Cause you are to me. I'm decades older than you. Over a century, even."

"Surely you aren't *that* old. Besides, werewolves get that way. Big age differences. You're a lot older than the rest of this pack, too."

"Yeah. But you're the youngest here." Judd sounded a bit too defensive.

Curious.

"So you use the word *kid* because you're trying to remind me, or yourself, of how young I am?" Colin felt he was being rather daring. The implication that there was some reason Judd needed to establish distance. Which was preposterous. Colin didn't really believe Judd was interested in him as a lover, but it was fun to tease him with the idea. *Kid* seemed to imply a chink in Judd's armor.

Judd gave a dry rumbling chuckle. "Probably both. You know I find you wildly attractive, right?"

Colin laughed. It had to be a joke. "You are sweet. Trying to make me feel better."

Judd tensed, defensive. "I know your father made you invisible... Well, I know that *now*. And I know that you had a rough time in school, and that your mom left you, and all that shit. Sure, you were an awkward teenager, but you do realize you grew out of it? You do possess a mirror." He waved a hand at the one above Colin's dresser.

Colin was offended. There was no need for Judd to lie to his face. He *had* been feeling better. But the idea that he was anything more than an ugly, wimpy failure was absurd.

He inched away from Judd. *Ah, physical distance, my old friend.*

Judd looked at the ceiling and sighed.

Colin retreated to the head of the bed to hug his knees to his chest, because he really wanted to hug Judd again and his knees would have to stand substitute. Even though he was upset with the enforcer, Colin wanted to reward Judd for trying to make him feel better, for liking him enough to lie. For implying that Colin was even slightly worthy of Judd's casual affection, let alone his romantic attention.

"Oh" Judd's voice was infinitely sad. "You *don't* realize." He leaned across the coverlet, easy for him to do, the bed was only a twin. He raised a hand to Colin's face, waited to see if he would flinch. Instead, Colin closed his eyes in anticipation (and to stop himself from jerking back).

Judd cupped Colin's cheek. His hand was so big it covered most of the side of Colin's head. It was warm, rougher than the skin of Judd's neck, but still smelled like him. Colin wanted it there, always.

He tried not to whimper.

"You are beautifully intelligent, infinitely precious, and profoundly lovely," Judd said. "And if you'd let me, I'd tell you that every day until you believed it."

Colin didn't know how to respond to that. Were he a braver creature, he might ask Judd to prove it. Because words were cheap and not to be believed. But he wasn't sure what form that proof would take, and he was terrified by how Judd might demonstrate sentiment. Judd who was all action, all the time. He wanted Judd in his bed for more than just comfort, he wanted him forever. He suppressed the tiny hesitant hope of a mate. Colin couldn't trust this went beyond proving a point, so his fear won.

Still he allowed the caress, even reveled in it. He thought that was probably some kind of progress.

A knock came at the bedroom door.

Colin's eyes popped open.

The door burst wide. Crashed against the dresser. Only one pack member wouldn't wait to be told to enter Colin's room, and treated doors with such reckless disregard for their safety.

Kevin.

Judd's hand lowered from Colin's face, but not before Kevin saw it.

Colin glared at his brother. Annoyed, yet grateful for the interruption.

"Kettil's here to take our statements," Kev said, and then, "Whoa. What's this? Finally making a move, are we?"

"Shut up, Kevin," said Judd and Colin at exactly the same time and in exactly the same tone of voice.

CHAPTER FOUR

NOTHING IS MORE IMPORTANT THAN A GOOD EDUCATION

"We need to talk," Kevin said to Judd, after they'd given their statements. He smelled distressed, sour.

Judd didn't want to leave Colin facing Deputy Kettil's looming authority alone, but he seemed to be handling it okay. It probably helped that Alec and Isaac insisted on staying with him. They stood, stoic sentinels of the couch kingdom, glowering at the cops in their domain. For his part, Colin spoke in a measured, thoughtful way. Eloquent, even. Colin wasn't afraid to talk in public. At least, Judd didn't think he was. It was more that Colin only spoke when specifically encouraged to do so. He needed to know his input was welcome. Even though Deputy Kettil was in a terrible mood, he seemed to understand Colin's personality. He made it clear that he was on their side. He was grumpy about the situation, not the victims of that situation.

Kettil was intent on establishing Trick's sleeping arrangements first. He seemed to hold the pack personally responsible for the fact that they hadn't convinced the dratsie to stay in their guest room. The deputy was somewhat mollified when told they'd gotten Trick and his car into their garage. Max and Bryan were directly above where the dratsie now slept. Kettil was no less grumpy, but the knowledge did calm him down.

"We're working on it," was all Alec would say, his tone strongly suggesting that the bear shifter drop it.

The enormous berserker's uniform creaked as he sank back into the plush armchair. He glowered. His partner stood behind him with a notebook, stone-faced and impassive.

"Trick takes careful handling." Isaac tried to mollify the beast – acting in his capacity as Omega counselor and friend. "He's got a lot of pride for such a cheerful little guy."

"You're telling me," grumbled Kettil.

Before Isaac could ask why the bear shifter cared so much, Kettil whipped out his own notebook and began quizzing Kevin and Judd about their end of the selkie confrontation.

The interview hadn't taken long. There wasn't much ground to cover. Judd wondered about Kettil's uniform. Did the sheriff's department have them custom made? What was the point? If the berserker shifted, he'd bust out of the thing. It was kinda funny to imagine. Wouldn't it be more practical to have shifters who served on the force in robes? Uniform robes? Judd would have to share that idea with Marvin. Marvin worked for the Coast Guard. He'd love a military-issue robe. Especially if he could get epaulettes on it, and brass buttons. But did robes confer sufficient authority? That was the question.

Soon enough Deputy Kettil, not in a robe, dismissed the enforcers.

"Patrol," suggested Alec as they stood to leave the den.

They would have done it anyway. As pack enforcers, Judd and Kevin patrolled the grounds constantly. Especially when weaker members were in residence. Colin was there. And Marvin. And Max. They ought not to think of Max as weaker. But the enforcers did. He was mortal and physically vulnerable, for all his immense power. And Marvin might be able to make most shifters bleed out their ears, but he was such a cute sparkly little thing, it was hard for them not to think of him as weak. And Colin? Well, Colin regularly called himself *weak* in tones of disgust. Like the enforcers weren't honored to look out for him. It made Judd sad to think about.

Perhaps *weak* wasn't the right way to put it. But Judd found it difficult not to constantly categorize pack mates into those who needed his protection in battle and those who did not. Kevin was the same way. It's what made them enforcers. Now they had Trick to care for, too.

Alec had probably ordered them to patrol, to prove to the two cops that they were taking Trick's safety seriously. Politics. Bah.

Judd and Kevin went to the cloakroom near the front door, where they might strip with subtlety. Not that Judd didn't want to strip in front of cops. Show them how strong he was. How capable. Show off the sharpness of his teeth and claws. But it wasn't done to drop trou and change shape in front of official visitors.

In the privacy of the cloakroom, Kevin stopped Judd from shifting with the dreaded phrase, "We need to talk."

Judd preempted his friend. "I know, I know. I'm way too old for your little brother. What you saw upstairs was comfort, not a pass. Colin is messed up in the head about who he is and what he's worth. Which is *everything*, before you get huffy. Not to mention how beautiful, and smart, and lovely he is."

"Beautiful, huh?" Kevin had a funny expression on his face. Hard to interpret. Usually the other enforcer was an open book.

Judd scented the air for clues. Scared of how this might go. Also upset with Kevin. That Colin has no ego at all, believed himself garbage, was partly Kevin's fault.

"Why the hell didn't you get him out sooner, Kev?" Judd challenged.

"Oh, so my little brother's fucked-up feels are my fault? How is that fair?"

"How long did you leave him alone with your father constantly cutting him down?"

Kevin's face was all bravado mixed with agony. "I never saw dad *do* anything. He never hit him. Never even yelled at him. I thought they'd be fine."

Judd shouldn't be mad at his friend. He knew that enforcers only noticed action. Enforcers weren't subtle. They didn't do nuance. He knew this because he was exactly like that himself.

Kevin pushed on. His face was red and his fists balled at his side. "It was just, you know, this *nothingness* between them. And man, I needed to get out. And once I was free of all that, I stayed away, because I'm a fucking coward where my parents are concerned. They put it all on me, you know? Kevin will follow in his father's paw prints. Kevin is the golden boy. Kevin will be the perfect enforcer, just like good old Dad. I thought maybe if I were gone, the fucker would stop looking at me to relive his glory days. I actually thought he'd notice that he had another son. I'd no idea he'd just keep ignoring Col forever."

"You never called? You never asked? You never came home to check up on him?"

Kevin was sullen. "I came back on holidays. They seemed okay. Dad's an enforcer, for fuck's sake. He should know his job. If nothing else, Colin was pack and his responsibility!"

Judd wondered that Kevin could be so blind. "Your brother was withering from neglect. Still is, like your dad gave him some kind of disease. He had it done to him for so long. He thinks that's all he's good for."

"I know, all right? I know." Kevin lashed out.

Judd probably should have expected that.

Kevin stepped forward. Bumped chest-to-chest with Judd. Both of them big and posturing and hurting for something they couldn't just beat up and fix.

"*Now* you know." Judd was still angry. It was mostly at his own inefficiencies which he saw reflected in Kevin. Judd was upset that he hadn't found the Boston pack sooner. Hadn't spotted Colin and scooped him away. Judd had been lost in a loner's melancholy. Unobservant, even when he first noticed the kid. Everyone who should have loved Colin and looked after him had failed.

Kev prodded Judd's sternum hard with two rough fingers. "You fucking forget, Judd, I was just a kid myself. And yeah, part of me thought he'd run away. Hoped he'd run. Whole Boston Pack thought he'd run. What's a brilliant boy like that want to stay with werewolves for? He's smarter than all of us put together. I thought he'd reject the bite and get away from all of it. I *told* him that. Every time I was home, I told him he could stay with me at school, couch surf as long as he needed, to do his applications and stuff. Everyone knew he could earn a full ride to any university he wanted. He's off the fucking charts on those dumb standardized tests humans like so much. He might have gone to university at sixteen if he wanted to."

Judd puffed out his cheeks. He gave a curt nod, tried not to be resentful. Here he was putting all his expectations of good behavior on Kevin, just like Kev's father had. Expecting the golden boy to solve his family's problems.

Judd had no life experience that compared to theirs. When he was made wolf, colleges didn't really exist, certainly not any for his skin color or accent. He'd learned to write so he could code messages for a spy ring run out of the London docks. Most of his friends back then were illiterate.

Still, still. "None of that excuses the fact that you left him there to rot."

Kevin sagged – all his posturing lost to misery. "You think I don't know that? You think I don't curse myself every time he flinches away from one of us? From me! I'm his goddamn brother and hugging him is like holding a broken glass figurine. So sharp I don't know if it'll cut me or him or both of us."

Kevin started stripping out of his clothes, fierce sharp movements. It was time to patrol. He didn't want to talk about it anymore.

Judd hadn't realized how much guilt Kevin carried. But then again, Kevin *should* feel guilty, shouldn't he? Except that also became a burden for Colin to carry – his brother's wounded gaze.

Judd would have to forgive Kevin, because they worked together. And so that Kevin could forgive himself. Judd owed Kevin for all the months of easy friendship. For the way they seamlessly fought side by side. For the way Kevin let him take point. Never challenged him, although he'd been Alec's enforcer first. The big redhead was happy to be the Alpha's left hand to Judd's right. Judd owed him the truth, at least.

"Look, I know you're trying to be all protective big brother. But that's too little too late now, we both know that." He was not above getting in one last dig. "But all I did was hug him. Short and awkward. Then I touched his face, as you walked in. But you know wolves, touch is how we console. And he did ask for it. I wasn't making a pass."

Kevin glared at him, skeptical.

"No really, he asked for a hug. I'm as shocked as you are. And, yeah, you're right to be mad at me. I did want more. Do want more. But I'd never push or take advantage. I know I'm far too old for your bother. Too much enforcer. Just, you know, *too much.*"

"True. You are." Kevin was suddenly all pleasant agreement. That funny look was back on his face from before, when he'd caught them touching. The one that made Judd nervous because he couldn't read it. "But I also know you're super experienced in the ways of gay sex. I don't want him taken advantage of by someone else either. If he really is finally waking up, maybe interested in being touched or even fucked, sooner you indoctrinate him than some random human."

"Holy shit, this is your *brother* we're talking about. Slow down." Judd did not like the idea of Colin suddenly going off and getting freaky with a bunch of humans, rebelling at last. He'd seen that happen before, when guys first came out of the closet. For some it worked. For others it was a new form of self-punishment – an attempt to prove their own worth through sucking as much cock as possible. Validation through others' desire.

Kevin waved his own crassness off. He was totally naked now, head tilted in thought. "If he really did ask you for a hug, that's a good sign, right? It must be a good sign."

Judd frowned. "Unless you think it's a sign he's about to dive in without any experience at all."

"Diving into a bathtub full of lube, we hope."

Judd winced.

Kevin ignored this. "Look, he's been so closed off for so long I never felt I had to worry about him, even when he started college. Only now he's got you all up in his business."

"I know, like I said, I'm—"

Kevin didn't let Judd finish. "Yeah, yeah, *too old.* But I also know you, man." He waved to encompass them both. Standing there, naked. About to change into wolves and patrol together. The gesture also encompassed moving across country, fighting off enemy packs, protecting their friends, sharing the same house, hanging out over beer and roast beast in the backyard. They were coworkers. They were pack mates. They were friends. They were the pack's enforcers, the right hand and the left, the strength of the group made manifest in flesh. They relied on each other. They trusted each other. Was that enough to translate to family? Judd didn't know.

Kevin surprised him. "I believe that you've got his best interests at heart. On the other hand, I really don't know about those college boys he hangs out with, or those human creeps down at the coffee shop, or a fucking barghest sniffing his ass, or something shitty like that. Sexually, the little fucker is really repressed. I think you should help him out with that."

"What!"

Kevin nodded. "You have my permission to seduce him. I think you should teach him what's good and all that. You know, gay butt sex stuff, two cocks in smooth places. Seems to work well for the rest of this pack."

Of all the ways this conversation could have gone. Judd stopped folding his clothes and stared at the man. "You're a bloody lunatic, you know that?"

"I'd take him aside and give him *the talk* if he was straight, but he's not. I trust you. I bet you're great in the sack."

"Oh, you think so, do you?"

"Well, *yeah*." No shame from the straight man on this. Kevin had learned fast to flirt and take shit like any old queer after they moved to San Francisco. The redhead puffed up his chest, grinning huge and easy. This time the posturing was in fun, not anger. "Besides, you're like the gay version of me. So of course I think you're the best choice as Professor Sex God."

"Kevin, your mind is a warped place. I'm *nothing* like you."

Kevin shrugged. "Enforcers, rah! We do physical really well, in all things. That includes sex. So, yeah, go to it. Not that you need my permission, but you got it."

"I don't know what to say."

"Thank you?" suggested Kevin.

Colin didn't mean to eavesdrop, but he'd been showing the deputies out and the two enforcers were still changing, hadn't yet gone on patrol, when his brother started yelling.

Kevin was kinda loud and boisterous, so normally Colin would have ignored this. But then he smelled the acid pulse of fighting pheromones.

Colin had a really good nose, he just didn't tell anyone that. He'd tried not to rely on it too much. It seemed too animalistic for him, the reluctant werewolf. Still, this scent worried him. Judd and Kevin tussled and bantered with each other often, but they'd never fought each other in anger. Colin thought he should enter the cloakroom – maybe the presence of a weaker pack member would mitigate the situation, especially if he called out in distress.

He paused, hand to the door. They were talking, not fighting anymore. From the tone, whatever had caused the spike in rage had passed. He would've moved on, except he realized they were talking about him. Which meant they'd been fighting about him too.

To his mortification, he heard his brother tell Judd that he had permission to seduce Colin. After that, Kevin said that he bet Judd was great in the sack. To Judd's face! Which Colin believed with all his heart, but he was now blushing furiously.

Colin breathed deeply and let himself roll out from under the shame of it. His brother clearly thought that Colin was so sexually inept that he needed to be pimped out to a friend. That hurt. But also, to be fair, it was kind of true. And if this was a way Colin got to have Judd? Well... he was both ashamed and excited by the idea. He was also pleased by Judd's apparent acceptance of the proposition. At least, he hadn't dismissed the idea out of hand.

Colin didn't linger; the two enforcers were about to patrol.

He didn't want to be caught eavesdropping. He hurried back to
the den. Alec and Isaac had gone off about their evening activities, leaving him to his studies in peace. No doubt this was intentional. Both the Alpha and the Omega knew when a pack mate
needed time to process. Colin had a lot of processing to do. Even
more now.

He picked up his epistemology book and tried to concentrate,
which resulted in him reading the same paragraph six times.
Finally, he put the book away and picked up one of Marvin's
sequined throw pillows. They were fun to play with because if
you stroked them one way they were teal and the other more
silver. He could paint patterns into the sparkles.

Colin had always known he was gay but he'd also never
wanted to sleep with a man. Not until Judd. He wasn't familiar
with that part of himself at all – the part that felt desire or lust.
Maybe this was because it had never been allowed to form in the
first place. Sexually, he was stunted. Other ways too, but clearly
this defect was obvious to his brother. And now Judd.

Colin wondered sometimes if being so invisible to his family
and his old pack had made bits of his identity go invisible to
himself. Not gone, just faded away into colorlessness. At a time
when he should've been dating, kissing, figuring out who he was
and what he liked, his sexuality had been offensive to the one
person who was supposed to love him unconditionally. His
father. So he'd learned early on not to let who he was show, let
alone what he *wanted*. Although that hadn't stopped him from
wanting. Not in the beginning. Not in those first flush teenage
years of awakening. It was already hell being part of his father's
pack. Try being gay and surrounded by big muscled biker werewolves all the time, often naked. In self-defense, he suspected
that his own mind had basically shut his sexuality down.

Colin sighed. Introspection was exhausting. Still he was
ready to admit something. He loved the idea of fucking Judd.
Not just hugging his chest and sniffing his neck. And even if he
wasn't worthy of the enforcer as a long-term romantic partner
(and he *wasn't*), if Judd really was willing to sleep with him as a

favor to Kev, Colin had to admit he wanted that. Wanted him. Badly enough to take a pity fuck.

Would it be taking advantage of Judd's good nature if he accepted sex under the guise of education? Maybe. But Colin did like learning, and he did want sex. It's just that he'd been so long without it he didn't really know how to start. Plus once Judd came into Colin's life, he hadn't really wanted anyone else. All the boys in his classes and at the clubs had seemed just that, boys. Not right. Not Judd. He did want to learn to be good at sex, and as a lifelong student he knew that he could excel if given the right training. He'd read the books. He'd watched the porn. He just didn't have any practical experience. It was like a science class without the lab component. Colin was also smart enough to know he'd let his own retiring human nature take things too far – his wolf side was starving for touch. If he let it go on much longer, he'd spiral into an irreversible depression. The fact that his brother had needed to set him up was, of course, humiliating. But in one way or another, Colin had been humiliated by Kev and Kevin's friends his entire life. At least in this, he knew what was really going on. He knew Judd's interest was as a favor to his friend. He knew Judd was doing it out of sympathy and for the good of the pack. He knew going in that it wouldn't last.

Presumably, Judd had to be at least a little attracted to him, or he'd refuse because he wouldn't be able to perform. At least this way Colin could learn what it would be like to really be the focus of the big man's lust. He was also self-aware enough to realize he liked the idea because it was safe. Right now he was too scared to try for a real relationship with anyone his own age, let alone someone as glorious and wonderful as Judd. This way, Colin could have a little piece of the man risk free. Because it would only be until Colin had learned the basics and then it would end. That was appealing.

Colin decided to be bold and approach Judd with an offer. Wouldn't it be fun to play the enforcer at his own game? Pretend all innocent, that he had this idea – would Judd teach him sexitimes? He would bat his (nonexistent) eyelashes and pretend he'd never overheard them concocting their scheme.

The very next night, when Judd came back from his first patrol, Colin would go to him and make him an offer. He practiced what he'd say. *I've been thinking about hiring a professional, and then it occurred to me, when you hugged me and smelled so good, that perhaps you might be interested, Judd sweetie pie.* Okay, maybe not sweetie pie.

Yes, this was a good scheme. This would work. And it would maybe turn his brother's manipulating on its ass. If Colin pretended it was all his idea, it gave him the power, and the ability to impose boundaries.

Bolstered and pleased with himself, Colin was also nervous about the task. He could have done it that very night, but he wasn't *that* brave. He needed at least twenty-four hours to come up with a proper plan… and an alternative to *sweetie pie*… and an outfit. He should wear something sexy, but he didn't own anything sexy. He scuttled upstairs and hid in his room, upending his closet, just in case.

Everything was blessedly quiet on the property. The stone and sea, the fog and dirt familiar now and comforting. It had been a wild evening. It was nice to have a calm night. The enforcers did find a doe and her fawns attempting backyard infiltration. It wasn't time yet for full moon hunt, so Judd and Kevin merely chased them off. They then peed the fence line to warn them *here be wolves*!

It was a good pee.

Judd left Kevin to finish running a wider sweep plus additional urination obligations as needed.

He returned to the pack house first, shifted, but was still wide awake. So he decided to review the new contract. See if there was any way to get out of it. He couldn't believe he'd accidentally committed them to looking after Colin and Kevin's *mother*.

Unfortunately, it was ironclad. Like it or not, they had one day's grace before Lexi Blanc descended upon them.

He was crushed not to find Colin in his usual study spot. He must have gone to bed early, cut up over Judd's blunder. Accident or not, Lexi Blanc in their lives was Judd's fault. Judd wanted to approach him about Kevin's suggestion. Of course he wanted to. Right now. Too eager.

He was a lecherous old wolf.

As a distraction and precaution, Judd focused on learning everything that he could about Alpha Bitch Blanc. He wasn't great on the internet. He wasn't incompetent either. He started a file on her, printing out any articles of interest.

Of course, the questions he really had could not be answered by the internet. Why had she demanded Kevin be part of her team? Did she just want to see him again? Check in? Or was she trying to rebuild a lost relationship? Why only Kevin? Did she know Colin was also with them? Colin wasn't mentioned on the Heavy Lifting website at all, even though he'd built it and acted as tech support. But he was a registered pack member. How much was Lexi Blanc like Colin's father? Did she only care for Kevin because he was the big, strong enforcer, the perfect werewolf, the golden child?

The rest of the pack often joked that Judd was intent on printing out the whole of the World Wide Web, in case it went away while he slept. It was more that Judd didn't trust himself to be able to find anything a second time.

Once he had a good stack of things to read, he went back out to the den, settled in for a long night. Kevin would take first shift. In a few hours, Judd would do the rounds again while Kevin napped. Then they'd swap. They tended to keep nocturnal hours. Most of Heavy Lifting's gigs were at night. Even regular humans did the kinds of things requiring bodyguards at night. So when they were home, they ran patrol on a schedule. With Trick and possible invading selkies, they'd be doubly watchful until the others awoke. Then one of them would take over. Judd checked the schedule. Tank was on morning detail, since

Saucebox was closed Tuesday nights and he'd have had a chance to sleep.

As if summoned, Tank came downstairs right then. Trouble sleeping, probably, as he too kept night hours. Or perhaps he just wanted a snack. In his usual quiet fashion, he noticed Judd and wandered over. Sat opposite. Didn't say anything.

"Am I an idiot, Tank, to even try with Colin? Am I too big, or too crass, or too much like his father? Do I risk him running from us? Am I pushing him out of the pack?"

Tank arched a brow. "Colin, huh?"

"Sometimes, I feel like he just needs to know he belongs."

"He knows."

Judd frowned at the huge man. Tank was so big he wondered, sometimes, if he carried bear shifter genes.

"He does?"

"He's not like me, Judd. I needed that. He's different." Tank was, when you got him talking, sometimes quite wise.

Judd encouraged him gently, "So why is he so scared all the time?"

Tank sighed. "Colin knows he belongs with us. He just doesn't think he deserves it."

Judd nodded.

Tank picked up one of Judd's printouts. "What am I looking for?"

Judd explained about Lexi Blanc.

Tank nodded.

They read about the celebrity, and country music, in companionable silence. Much better than actually experiencing celebrity or country music, Judd supposed.

CHAPTER FIVE

KISS A WEREWOLF GOOD MORNIN'

Colin made a concerted effort not to see Judd until the following night.

Wednesday was his biggest class day anyway. Alec gave him a ride to school on his way into the lab, since their schedules matched up. The Kentfield campus was out of Alec's way, but the Alpha insisted.

Alec needed to check up on Colin and Colin needed him to want to. He tried to become comfortable with that need while focusing on the familiar roadways, houses, and businesses they drove past. He didn't look directly at his Alpha, but he let himself enjoy knowing he was there. Next to him.

"You doing all right, Col?" Alec asked, steering carefully through the morning traffic.

For a horrible moment Colin thought Alec had heard about the seduction game. Then he realized that the Alpha was actually asking about Lexi Blanc.

"You mean my mother coming to town?"

"Yeah. You scared us a bit last night." Nothing but warmth and mild interest in his Alpha's voice. Alec was trying not to pry. He was failing, but it was nice to know he cared.

"I'll be okay. It's just a bit freaky to have her go from absent void to body-checking my reality."

"I can see how that might be awkward." Alec didn't push,

just waited patiently to see if Colin had anything else he needed to say.

Silence.

The Alpha cleared his throat. "So. Aside from her coming, are things okay with you?"

"Yes, Alpha." *Aside from trying to lose my virginity to a much more experienced older man, who I'm totally into, and is way too good for me.*

"School is going all right this semester?"

"Yes, Alpha." *Aside from the one teacher who picks on me, either because I'm a shifter or gay, and the stupid epistemology class that ignores all us supernatural creatures as if we were second-class citizens.*

"How's that epistemology class?"

Sometimes Colin swore the Alpha could hear his thoughts. "Not great. I mean, I get needing to study how knowledge works, but it doesn't even begin to address the shifter experience."

"Oh, and why should it? Do shifters fundamentally think differently from humans?" Alec was great at playing devil's advocate. Colin should have known he'd immediately latch on to a philosophical argument.

"Well, we have different senses, better in some cases, worse in others. Wouldn't that affect our processing of the world around us, and by extension our knowledge base both collectively and as individuals? Isn't shifter knowledge, by definition, different from human knowledge?"

"I suppose the counter-argument would be, except that the reality we all perceive and interpret around is essentially the *same* reality, either way."

Colin nodded, glanced at his Alpha furtively. "They call that the essential Truth of Reality. And yet we are flawed beings and we must, by definition, filter that reality through our own senses. Therefore, shifters have a reality that is fundamentally different from human reality, because we *experience* the same world differently."

"Agreed, but by extension, every individual person would

also perceive reality differently from every other person, shifter or not." Alec had a small smile on his face, enjoying himself. Colin's chest swelled with pride. He might not be the strongest or the bravest in Alec's pack, but he was the one who could match their Alpha for brains – that had to count for something.

Debating obscure points of academia was one of the reasons Colin loved Alec so much. Their Alpha was so smart and so interested in things. They could drive for thirty minutes discussing the reality of sensation and scientific truth and not even realize any time had passed. Challenged, Colin had to stay on top of the discourse and couldn't think about his mother or Judd even once. Which was probably why Alec did it.

Of course, Colin thought about either his mother or Judd most of the rest of the day. He even, during a break between classes, went to a little thrift store and looked longingly at a t-shirt with a unicorn on the front and the slogan *too fast for rainbows*. He knew it would fit, but it would be very tight and was short enough to show a strip of stomach above the waistband of his jeans. His stomach was flat, but still, that seemed horribly daring.

So he left without it.

Who cared, right? A unicorn t-shirt couldn't possibly be all that seductive. Could it? But then, what was *sexy* on someone who looked like Colin? He snorted to himself. A puffy jacket and parachute pants, most likely. Ski mask over his face. What was he thinking, that he even considered being in Judd's bed? Except he'd heard that conversation and Judd said he was willing. And there was that time at the barbecue when Judd flirted with him. More than one time, in fact, at more than one barbecue. His head spun.

He decided he'd not let himself talk himself out of wanting Judd. Unicorn t-shirt or no unicorn t-shirt.

Judd woke in the late afternoon at his usual time. He dressed and went instantly to the cafe. Lovejoy was on Trick detail but he needed to be relieved, as he had a catering gig.

The walk downtown was full of dumb humans. Judd caught a toddler on a tricycle just before he darted into traffic. The mother was breathless and grateful. Judd sneered at her. A fierce big dog charged him, off its lead. Judd growled at it until it sat back on its haunches, confused. The young owners came panting up, apologizing for Milton having *gotten out*. Judd sneered at them. Honestly, how did humans survive?

The Bean was quiet and stayed that way while Judd sat at Colin's table at the front. Trick was always good for a laugh, though. The little dratsie came and sat with Judd during slow times. There weren't many but Judd enjoyed the company when he got it, even if Trick insisted on teasing him mercilessly.

"So what are your intentions towards my new best friend in the whole wide world, Colin Mangnall? I need to know, you hear? Are there leather slings involved? Tubs of lard perhaps? Rubber gloves?" A playful slap to Judd's arm. "You look like a man with a latex fetish."

"What, pray tell, gave me away?"

And so forth. Trick was great fun. He was also going to drive the wolf pack completely batty. Judd rather looked forward to it.

Eventually, Tank arrived to take the last shift. He wasn't working his bouncer gig until late, so he could stay until closing, make sure Trick got home safely. Judd wondered, amused, if Trick would start in on Tank with fetish wear shock tactics. Tank might surprise even a dratsie with his answers – should he say anything at all.

After a low-key pack dinner, especially when compared to the previous evening, Judd shifted into wolf form and went on patrol.

Colin was the only one downstairs when he returned. Judd didn't approach him. Gingersnap seemed awfully comfortable in the den surrounded by his books. Instead, Judd went to the office to use the pack computer and look up more on Lexi Blanc. This time he had security questions in mind: Why did she need extra protection for this leg of her tour? Was she having stalker issues? Or was it something even more sinister?

There was *a lot* to read – tons of gossip, several fan forums, hundreds of interviews, and way too many videos. Lexi Blanc had her own WooTube channel. She was a very big deal on Instalamb with over a million followers. *Many* of her fans acted more like stalkers.

Judd started jotting down user names. Those who took too much interest in the singer and her location. Those who claimed a personal relationship. Those who seemed overly interested in her staff and daily routine. He'd get a solid list going, then start trying to find out real names and whether they lived in the Bay Area.

Lexi Blanc looked *a lot* like Colin. Way more like Colin than Kevin. Judd wondered if that had impacted Colin's father's mistreatment of him. That he had this half-formed ghostly reminder of his lost wife lurking about his house. Did Colin and his mother sound alike, too? Smell alike? Certainly, Colin was way more masculine – Lexi Blanc put true meaning into the words *curvy* and *voluptuous*. Even Judd, who'd never favored women in his bed, appreciated her figure. He thought Colin also had her hair but that she dyed hers a darker red for the stage. Still, Colin was much better looking. His beauty less bold, more refined and ethereal. He had her cheekbones on a thinner face, her big eyes under fiercer brows. His lashes without makeup were so pale they were difficult to see, just shimmers of rose gold.

Judd examined a paparazzi shot. A candid photo of Blanc and her team leaving a building after some kind of magazine photo shoot.

"Who is *that*, always with her?" Judd asked himself out loud.

Colin answered him. "That's her stylist, Risa Ostrov. Human."

Judd turned. His Gingersnap was lurking in the doorway. Judd cursed his comfort with Colin's smell. He hadn't been alerted to his presence. Judd was slightly embarrassed to be caught prying, even though he needed to do the research for his job. He was also thrilled. He couldn't remember a time when Colin had actually sought him out. Voluntarily entered a room with only Judd in it.

"How do you know that, Gingersnap?" He wanted to scoot back and pat his knee. Colin could sit on his lap. They could cuddle and look at the computer screen together. But they weren't there yet.

Still, it was progress when Colin pulled a chair away from one of the other desks and sat next to him. Close was good. Close was more than they'd had before.

Colin's cheeks were flushed. "I know everything possible to know that is public facing about Lexi Blanc. And before you ask, no, I haven't ever hacked private files to find out more. I work hard not to care *that* much about her. But I do follow her online. She is my mother, after all. I can't help myself. It's like picking at a scab."

"Scab or open wound?" Judd asked, softening his voice.

"Scab. Honestly. It was easier for me than Kev. I really don't remember much about her. The fact that she left me is kind of an intellectual *huh* more than anything else. How did it impact my psyche exactly? I don't know. But it's not painful. Kevin actually knew her, and so far as I can tell, she really liked him. But she still left. That had to have hurt him a lot." He shrugged. "I might hate her for abandoning me in theory, but only so much that dumb internet reporting is sufficient substitute. Kevin needs to pretend that she died. He ignores her, while I've always checked in. I've got a vanity alert on her name. I even lurk in her fan group on Tailtale sometimes."

"You'd flag up as one of her possible stalkers, then."

Colin shook his head. "Unlikely. I'm good at hiding my tracks. Better than most, as I've never written her an email, a comment, or a letter in my life. With stalkers, you look at the ones who are moved to engage, right?"

Judd shrugged. "I'm not a cop, so I don't know for certain. I may talk to Deputy Kettil about this. But I think you're right."

Judd passed Colin the list of user names he'd gathered, plus any location data and notes he'd made on each. "These are some of my red flags off forums and the like. I'll delve into those that act particularly proprietary and entitled plus live in the Bay Area."

"You know you could keep this list on the computer, right? They even have such miraculous things as digital spreadsheets these days. I know, I know! Crazy talk." Colin's pretty face was alight with the pleasure of teasing, almost unguarded.

Judd caught his breath and tried to act normal, keep up the witty repartee. "Pen and paper came first in my life."

"Fingers came first too, yet you eat with a fork for the sake of practicality and politeness."

Judd shrugged, loving that Colin felt comfortable enough to poke fun. "Most of the time. You saying a spreadsheet is *polite*?"

"Certainly better than your craptastic handwriting."

"I was taught by lady spies. What do you expect?"

"Were you really? Cool. Well, it is practically code."

"Exactly why I avoid computers, too easy to crack."

"Barbarian Luddite," said Colin, voice warm. Then he started really looking over the list. He indicated a few he too had encountered and found suspicious or had additional information on. "I think that one is on the East Coast. That one is deployed. That one is actually a stooge. She's on mother's publicity team or something. Could even be that stylist you notice always with her, Risa. Or possibly her manager or what have you."

"How do you know that?"

"Just from the way the user talks about mother's schedule. Also the way they ask questions of the group. They try too hard to keep interest going, rile up the fans. The user seems intent on making certain the algorithm stays engaged."

Judd nodded and made notes next to each name.

They continued that way for a while, Judd happy to have Colin there, next to him, sharing his space. His own, small ginger-flavored miracle.

"You trying to distract yourself from homework?" he asked at last.

Colin nodded. "Yeah, a bit. This epistemology stuff is super dull. You wanna use my laptop for your research and keep me company in the den? More comfortable and we can spread out a bit."

Judd jumped at the chance. Colin was basically inviting him into his territory. This was an even bigger deal than joining Judd in the office. Sure, it was a bit less private, but it was also a space that Colin felt secure in. Judd wanted him safe.

So Colin loaned Judd his laptop and they shared one of the big couches. Judd sat normally, facing the coffee table. Colin curled sideways and, greatly daring, allowed his feet close to Judd's leg. Eventually, almost as if he didn't realize he was doing it, Colin had wormed his sock-covered toes under Judd's thigh. For warmth, of course.

Judd pretended not to notice. But the joy that simple touch brought him was ridiculous. Absurd how much he hungered for and savored the tiniest scraps of this beautiful man's affection.

Finally, Judd closed the laptop. He picked up his notes to examine them closer, identify any patterns. He had about two dozen suspects. For half of those, he had real names. Three lived locally. He thought that was pretty good for a night's work from a barbarian Luddite. He picked up the contract. He'd printed it out, because *of course* he had. The job started tomorrow night. He would take point because Kevin was going to hang him out to dry on this one as much as possible. Which was fair.

The pack house was quiet. Even though werewolves were instinctively nocturnal, by midnight everyone who was going to be out working *was* out working, and everyone else was asleep.

Judd felt nested in Colin's cozy little world. Lights twinkled across the bay through the big windows. Otherwise, the den was surrounded by the tops of trees. They were alone with the smell of earth and ocean and pack. They sat, lit only by two low lamps as the coals in the fireplace faded to red.

Colin's toes wiggled under Judd's thigh. It tickled. Judd put down the contract and looked up at him. That had been intentional, designed to attract attention.

Colin's big green eyes were regarding him, heavy lidded. Sexual, but also nervous and full of questions.

"So I was thinking," he began, voice fractured and vulnerable, "and maybe this is a really stupid idea. And you should totally say no if it's something you're not into. If *I'm* something you're not into. But... I do really love the way you smell. And I did like that hug up in my room a lot. So I'm wondering if you might be interested in me. Like, you know, interested in showing me, uh, stuff."

Judd was shocked. Colin could have knocked him over with a feather, or a foot wiggle, for that matter. He was also thrilled, and honored, and skin-pricked with joy and terror at the responsibility.

Colin petered out. For once, he lacked precision in his speech. He held perfectly still. His chest barely moved with his breaths. His desperate eyes were fixed on Judd as if Judd were about to kick a puppy. Or hand Colin a puppy. One of the two.

"You want me to do performative hugging on a regular basis?" Judd tried to relieve the tension. Clearly Colin had been working up to this for hours.

"No. I mean, yes. I mean, kinda?" Colin let out a sigh. "I want you to teach me."

"What exactly? You're way better educated than I am. There's not a subject in the world that I know better than you." Judd wanted everything clear. Because he wanted everything.

"Oh, nothing academic. Although I bet you know more about modern history post-Saturation than most historians."

"Firsthand accounts are unreliable. You know that."

Colin pressed his hands together, uncomfortable. "We're getting off topic and this is challenging enough as it is without you bringing history into it. Look, please. I want you to show me how to... you know... do *sex*."

"What?" Judd felt his brain kind of stretch and snap back with the shock of such a brazen request. How brave was Colin? And how much had he underestimated his Gingersnap?

"Like have it, firsthand experience-wise."

Judd took a deep breath, treading carefully, cautious. Proud as he was of Colin's bravery, Judd's whole heart was in this. Colin's timid offer was close to tormenting him with possibilities. He had to be certain. "Flattered as I am, if you can't talk about sex, then you shouldn't be having any."

Colin narrowed his eyes, straightened his shoulders, and firmed his pert little chin. "I would like you to take me upstairs, regularly, and for a while, until you think I'm at least qualified to pass a 101 level class on the subject of getting freaky. We could use either your room or mine, but probably yours, because I suspect you're better equipped. Although I do have some toys and lube. I'm not a compete ignoramus. And in that room, whichever it is, I want you to screw my brains out, in all the ways and in all manners possible. Because I suspect you'd be really good at it, and I could learn all the things you like, and I like, and how to please a lover. Then I wouldn't be so scared to date. And I would try to make it as good for you as possible, so it wouldn't be a hardship."

Judd sat there, gobsmacked and ridiculously proud – mulling over every word, trying to decide what to *do*.

The feet under his leg started wiggling again, this time in discomfort.

Judd almost jumped forward to tackle Colin. Press him down into the couch. This beautiful boy who was offering Judd everything all at once, when Judd had thought it was a dumb, impossible wish. Colin offered it as if Judd would be doing *him* a favor. As if this wasn't Judd's dream. As if sexing Colin up was some terrible obligation when it would be Judd's greatest privilege and joy.

Judd tried to make a joke of it. "Until you're tired of me?"

Colin shook his head, all sweet earnestness. "Oh, I don't think that's possible. Only until you're tired of me, or you think I've learned all of it."

"*All* of it, really?"

Colin clearly thought Judd was still pressing him to talk about sex openly. His full lips tensed and then he said, voice steady and confident. "Yes, *all of it*. Hand jobs, blow jobs, ass play, rimming, fucking, toys, and maybe some Dom sub games like rope or a blindfold. I don't think I'm into pain, but I want to try everything, and I trust you, so will you?"

Judd had never thought he'd hear the word *trust* come out of Colin's mouth. He said the only thing he could, because this small act of requesting had taken all of Colin's courage. "Of course I will. And you can stop it, anytime for any reason."

Judd knew he was agreeing to something transient. But if he said *no* merely because of the limited time frame, it would hurt Colin terribly. Plus, what would stop Colin from asking someone else? Finding another teacher. No one else would take as good care of him. No one else would induct him properly into the wide joyous world of pleasure. Certainly no one else would be as kind. Judd would give Colin everything he asked for and anything he needed. At cost to himself. Because Judd wanted every small scrap of Colin that he could get. Even if it was only to be used as a seed for self-actualization. Surely, he could be happy having Colin until someone more age-appropriate came along.

So Judd reached down and tugged gently up on the back of Colin's knees. Pulled, so Colin had to bend them, scoot his butt forward, closer. Judd bracketed Colin's face with his hands. Speared his fingers into silky red hair.

Finally, he kissed those pretty lips. The bottom one, slightly fuller than the top. Both of them lush. Edible.

Colin tasted the way Judd hoped he would. Warm and spice-filled with flavors all his own. Rich like chocolate, hot like cinnamon, earthy like cardamom. Specialty Gingersnap.

Colin's mouth was unsure. His lips trembled under Judd's at first. Then they were transformed by eagerness. When Judd pressed for entry, Colin opened to him. When he swept his tongue in gently, Colin responded in kind – tongue tentative. Judd coaxed him to be bold. Pulled slightly back, nibbled that ridiculous lower lip. Colin did the same, teeth slightly too sharp, perfect.

Judd needed to breathe but he couldn't resist one more fierce press before he drew back. Colin was panting. Happy.

So was Judd. "You're a fast learner, Gingersnap."

Colin's face flushed crimson. It was from pleasure this time.

"I'm an excellent student, I'll have you know. So you'll really do it?"

Judd set his heart aside. It was going to get crushed. He didn't care one iota. "Yeah, I really will."

Colin couldn't believe it. He'd netted himself a shark. Or was that a wolf in sharkskin? Regardless, the biggest of big fishes wanted him. Biggest badass for certain. Oldest of the pack. Kevin was probably as physically powerful, but in sheer magnetism Kevin was all show, Judd was real strength. Yet there Judd sat, looking wide-eyed with awe… at Colin.

As if Colin had done something amazing. In just making a request. In just taking his cues from one simple kiss.

Okay, it hadn't been *that* simple. Judd kissed him like it was the punctuation mark at the end of a sentence – a purposeful pause in time and breath. Contemplative and thorough. It had been a really *good* kiss. At least Colin thought it was – hard to know for certain, as he had limited experience in the matter.

He looked down at Judd's lap. If the bulge there was any indication, Colin hadn't done too bad reciprocating.

Judd cleared his throat, voice even deeper than usual. "Look, Gingersnap, I gotta be certain. I don't want you feeling any kind of pressure. Are you sure it's me you want? I can be a bit much."

Colin wondered if that had happened to Judd in the past. He could see how this man – big, aggressive, possessive, loud – could be overkill in a lover. Judd occupied space in a way that many would find threatening. Colin, on the other hand, really liked it. When they were in a room together, people never noticed Colin because Judd drew most of the attention, like some gravitational anomaly. He certainly drew Colin's attention.

Colin liked it because that pull meant Judd could be depended upon. It was as if he were there to take on the weight of the needs of others. Needs that Colin felt as stressors, because he couldn't fulfill them. But Judd was not weak like that. Judd could shoulder the burden of pack expectations.

"You're not a bully, Judd." Colin needed him to know he wasn't being pushed into anything.

"No, maybe once a long time ago. But I'm too old for that now, takes too much effort and my ego is fine. I don't gotta prove anything, anymore. But that doesn't mean I'm not a lot to handle."

Colin struggled to articulate his feelings. "You are a little *intimidating*?" He suggested it as the right word, hopeful that Judd wouldn't take offense.

"I'm a large Black man, Gingersnap. One way or another, most of my many lives, others have felt threatened by me."

Colin felt inadequate to the task of explaining in the face of such a life. "I'm not saying things right."

Judd's eyes were wounded. "I'm too big, too much, aren't I? For you, I mean. Reminds you of bullies, and assholes, and family shit."

"No that's not... I mean, you..." Colin felt the heated tingle of shameful misunderstanding. He was getting this wrong, somehow. He was messing up.

Judd pushed on. "That's why Alec is such a good Alpha for you. He's not physically very imposing."

Colin felt compelled to get this right. "It's one of the reasons." He licked his lips. "But I was trying to say that for me, it's more the wolf side of things. Enforcers are all..." He trailed off, helpless. He wanted to say *intimidating* again, but Judd hadn't responded well to that word.

"Big and angry," Judd substituted, examining Colin's face.

Colin felt exposed. This wasn't working. He pulled away to sit up properly, turn from Judd – alone at the end of the couch. He picked up and fiddled with one of Marvin's sequined pillows, looking at it so he didn't have to cope with the injured intensity in Judd's eyes.

Colin needed to somehow show the enforcer that he didn't feel diminished by him or his rank. He struggled to be honest without causing more harm. "Also contentious and challenging. It's part of what you do for the pack – keep it moving, keep it from stagnating, keep the Alpha from becoming a tyrant.

Enforcers are a different kind of wolf, different kind of personality, from the rest of us. You're more independent. Guardian and
protector, yes, but also able to distance yourself from the pack,
to think about us from the outside – the way a cop does with
civilians." As a kid, Colin had researched enforcers. After both
his father and his brother, he wanted to know everything. If he
survived the bite, was it was something he would suddenly
become? No, as it turned out. Not even slightly.

Judd nodded. "Yes, but that means that we enforcers can turn
sour. Spoil like meat left out in the sun. Go mad on the loneliness of having to choose to *stay* all the time. Or get caught up in
our own heads, warped by the solitary grandeur of the rank."

Colin frowned. "Like what happened with Isaac's dad?"

"Exactly. And maybe a bit of what happened with yours,
after your mother left. More than any other werewolves,
enforcers are anchored by close friendships – family, mates,
spouses. Not to mention the presence of another enforcer. Why
do you think your brother is the way he is? Always dating. So
desperate to be loved."

Kevin was rather infamous in the pack for constantly
seducing inappropriate women, often more than one at a time.
Drama fluff-monger, Marvin called him.

"I don't—" Colin stopped himself. He was about to deny his
response to that innate enforcer nature, but that would be disin-
genuous. "That *does* scare me sometimes, about you."

Colin knew Judd would assume he meant Judd's intensity,
but it was really about his inclination towards loner status. Judd
had joined their pack as a loner. He'd been one for a long time
prior. Sure, he'd had packs before, up in Canada. Back in Europe
too, probably. But he'd *left* them. And he never talked about
those packs, or why he left, which meant, to Colin, that Judd
could pick up and leave them too. Leave Colin. Anytime he
wanted.

It wasn't Judd's presence that scared Colin, it was the possibility of losing it. Even if theirs was only a temporary sexual
fling with an inevitable ending already place. Colin feared the
total loss of Judd in his life, as a friend, as a protector. The very

presence Judd feared was too much for most people, but Colin craved it. He loved being around Judd in their house, lover or not.

He risked a glance over. How to put *that* into words in a way that wouldn't make Colin look pathetic? "Not necessarily your size, just that you're an enforcer."

Judd tilted his head in query. "That's because of your father, you think?"

"Probably. But the horrible thing" − Colin's voice hitched a little, and he dug around in some dusty part of himself to unearth his gravest sin and lay it before Judd − "is that enforcer nature also comforts me."

"Because of your brother?"

Colin nodded, slowly. Was that it? Even after Kevin left, he'd been a beacon of hope in Colin's life. His strong older brother, who'd liked him. Who'd once looked after him. Colin hadn't run away to join his brother, but he'd always known he *could*. Mostly, that had been enough. And now, with his new pack?

"But it's not…" Colin waved his hands about to finish the sentence − they were more articulate than his tongue. Then he remembered that he didn't do *that* because his hands were *too gay*. He forced them into stillness, giving way to words. "I've never been the type to run to anyone for comfort."

"Because it wasn't ever offered?"

"Yes. Maybe because of that. Maybe I was born like this." Colin was thinking that there was something about him that meant he was unlovable. But that was way too pathetic to say aloud. It was whining. They were embarking on something physical − this was no time to confess emotional hang-ups to a prospective teacher meets fuck-buddy.

Or whatever he and Judd were about to become.

CHAPTER SIX

IN THE DEN AGAIN

Judd now knew it was possible to ache with pain for someone else. He wondered how he could make sex not just bearable but joyful for this fragile being across from him. It would be safest to temper enforcer aggression with passivity. The last thing he wanted was to scare Colin in any way. Unfortunately, *passive* didn't come easy to him.

Judd lay back on the couch. He stared up at the ceiling. He let one arm flop to the floor and the other wedge between his body and the couch back. Belly exposed – playful and vulnerable.

He kept the need out of his voice. "So come here. Lie on top of me. I won't hold you too tight. I won't confine any part of you. I'll just lie under you."

"Like a mattress?" Colin's voice was shaky, but he moved to Judd. Cautious as a kitten in a new place. Eager as a kitten, too.

"Like reassurance. I'm here because I want to be near you. You can do what you will with me and with that sentiment. You cannot hurt me, Gingersnap. I mean to prove that I will not hurt you. And I will not ignore you either."

"So I'll know what that feels like too?"

"Exactly."

"It's a good approach. How'd you get so wise?"

"I've been around a long time, remember?"

Slowly, Colin lowered himself to lie on top of Judd. He gifted Judd with all of his weight. It wasn't a lot, but also it was, because his Gingersnap was pressed against him from neck to calves. They were both still hard from that kiss. Colin was tense and not just sexually. He was nervous but he was trying.

"It's not too much for you?" Colin asked. Ridiculous question.

"See how I suffer?" Judd arched his hips so Colin could feel his interest. Colin needed to know that Judd wasn't indifferent. That he wasn't just playing along for the sake of friendship. He was passive, but he was also engaged.

"Oh yes," Colin gave a tentative body wiggle.

Judd realized that this kid might actually be the death of him. He'd gotten himself into a situation where everything would depend on his control. He had to be patient and wise and gentle. Yet Judd was an enforcer. He'd never been anything more than an enforcer. He'd wanted more – the patience of a Beta, the control of an Alpha. But he was over a hundred years old, and he was still only an enforcer. Wolves don't learn new rank. It was genetically coded in, like the color of their fur. Yet now Judd was setting himself up to lean on strengths he didn't have. Colin was going to test him to the limit.

Colin wiggled again.

Judd felt a nicely sized dick press against his own. Which was, of course, one of Judd's biggest weaknesses. He loved a twink with a big cock, the juxtaposition of fragility and weaponized pleasure. Also, Judd really loved getting fucked. He wasn't ready to confess that yet. It destroyed his image. He was an enforcer with a reputation to maintain. But now he was looking forward to that part of Colin's education even more.

No doubt Colin assumed that Judd would top. Colin had a messed-up perception of gay dynamics. Judd liked that too, just not as much. He intended to show Colin carefully and thoroughly how good penetration felt. But he was also going to show Colin how to fuck him. And Judd already knew that would be his favorite part. He certainly hoped Colin was game. The eager cock pressed against his seemed damn near perfect in that regard. Already testing Judd's patience and control. The patience and control he didn't come by naturally.

Judd forced himself to relax into the big comfy couch. He remembered that his role was as educator. "Here's what I think, Gingersnap."

Another wiggle. "Yeah?"

"I think I'd like your hands all over me."

"You would?"

"Oh yeah. I dream about those hands of yours."

"You do?"

"Seriously, yes. I dream about lots of parts of you. But your hands, kid, they occupy too much of my thoughts."

"You don't need to keep calling me that."

"Kid?"

"Yeah, I mean are you still trying to remind yourself I'm too young for you?"

Well, yes, of course Judd was. It was worse now. Now Judd had to remind himself not to take advantage. Not to fall in love. So much more was at risk.

"I'll try, Gingersnap, but it might take me a while."

Colin nodded, bumping his chin. "That's fair. So now, I can touch you?"

"Please."

"All over?"

"Anywhere you like. You should know the goods before we start sticking them into each other. If we're gonna go all in, don't you wanna know what you're getting as your part of the deal? We wouldn't want you disappointed."

"Judd, sweetie, that is so completely not possible." His voice was amused.

"Don't lose that."

"What?"

"The *sweetie*."

Colin gasped. "Really? Even in public, in front of the rest of the pack? I could call you that? You don't mind them knowing?"

"Of course not." Of course Judd wanted to be publicly owned by Colin! Who wouldn't want that? "I expect Alec and

Isaac will rake me over the coals for taking advantage of you, but I'm not afraid to be seen as yours. Temporary or not. Can't keep a secret as smelly as sex in a pack. And you're mine while we do this, okay? No one else for either of us."

Colin bumped him with another nod. "No one else, promise. As if I could look at anyone else while sharing your bed. Ridiculous man. Remember, you take up all the oxygen in the room."

"I'm sorry."

"I know, but I like it. We established that. Back to touching?"

"I've no idea what you're waiting for. Talk talk talk. Who knew you were so chatty?" Judd allowed frustration to enter his teasing.

Colin, amazingly, laughed.

Judd felt like he was king of some very small ginger castle. He lay still.

Colin went to work torturing him.

Torture it certainly was. Those pristine graceful hands fluttering over him – long tapered fingers tentative at first. Colin started with what he could reach while still lying on top of Judd. A stroke down Judd's dangling arm with one hand. Fingers started by wrapping around Judd's bicep. Colin was unable to get them all the way around. Judd was secretly proud of that. Colin then stroked down over the crease in Judd's arm. Around the coarseness of his elbow. He licked his lips, eyes sparking with orange.

Frowning, frustrated, limited by his position, Colin leaned up and scooted back. He straddled Judd's upper thighs. Judd forced himself not to move. He wanted everything all at once, so fiercely and so much.

"Would you take your shirt off?" Colin asked.

Judd swallowed, nodded. Tried to think only about the importance of the kid asking for what he wanted, voicing a desire. When really Judd was so proud to be asked. Delighted by the opportunity to show off. To this boy. His Gingersnap.

Judd's answer was to sit up, strip out of his t-shirt, easy and quick.

Colin stared down. A pink tongue-tip poked out between his

full lips. His eyes went almost completely orange. Judd was flattered. He preened under the arousal he'd caused.

"Oh, wow. I mean. I've seen you bare before, but never for me to touch."

"All for you," rumbled Judd. Wondering if his own eyes had gone yellow.

Judd knew what he looked like. He knew it was pretty darn spectacular. His body was most of what he had to offer a potential lover, since his brain wasn't anything to write home about. Certainly not for someone as brilliant as Colin.

But his body was great. Of course it wasn't to Judd's own personal taste. Brawny brute was not what Judd yearned for in a lover. Judd was built for fighting. He'd put muscle on easy and kept it on after becoming a werewolf.

He'd been very fit and very strong when he took the bite. Back then, it was thought a man had to be as physically powerful as possible to survive metamorphosis. They didn't know about the triple helix or recessive genes or shifter sequencing. Judd had trained for years, ran the highlands for hours, helped local farmers with their harvest, lugged boulders for stonemasons. He wasn't sure if that helped him to look the way he did now, or if it was mostly genetics. Either way, he was enforcer enough to be smug about his body.

He was aging, very slowly, but it was there. After Saturation he'd had to shave – once a year or so and these days he occasionally caught some silver. Still, he stayed as fit as the supernatural lifestyle permitted. So he didn't look that different from when he'd been bitten, decades ago.

Colin seemed to appreciate it. Those beautiful hands, stroking over Judd's body, felt reverent. They worshiped the coarseness of the tightly curled hair on Judd's chest. The fine fingers brushing over his nipples were full of wonder.

"I'm not all that sensitive," Judd admitted. This was meant to be an education after all. Colin should know this kind of thing. "But I do like a little pain on 'em. The jolt of it – teeth and the like."

"Yeah?" Colin scraped Judd's left nipple with his thumbnail.

Judd shuddered. This almost-mate of his was a quick learner. Of course he was.

Judd reminded himself again to teach. "Not all men are like that. Some of us don't really feel anything. Pain is just painful. Some of us have really sensitive nipples. Can get off on them being licked."

"Which one am I?" wondered Colin. He'd said he'd done some self-experimentation, but clearly not with nipples.

Judd grinned up at him. "Why don't we find out?"

Colin swallowed. "You want my shirt off?"

"If you feel comfortable with that."

"I don't look like you. All muscled and stuff."

"Part of the appeal, I promise." Judd stopped himself from saying that he'd already seen Colin naked. Only once a month or so, but Judd always peeked. He couldn't help himself. Colin didn't like spending time in wolf form. He only did it out of necessity on full moon. He always tried to strip and shift fast, hunched to hide his human body. No flexing or strutting about like some werewolves Judd could name... including himself.

"I'll like it, I promise," he insisted.

"You like twinky guys?"

Judd accepted that the twink moniker was normal in gay culture these days. But the way Colin said it made him sound ashamed.

"Very much." Judd purred and arched a little under Colin, reminding him of his ever-hardening arousal.

"Would you prefer it if I were more..." Colin stopped touching Judd and fluttered his hands, mouth twisted in bitterness, "...*femme* or something?"

Judd didn't like the self-hatred he saw.

Colin often did that with his hands. He'd start talking with them, graceful and beautiful, then muffle them. Force them to his sides. Stifle himself.

Judd was in a trap. If he said yes, Colin would take that as a criticism that he wasn't femme enough. If Judd said no, Colin might take *that* as a criticism, that he was too femme. Or did

Colin want permission? Was he seeking approval for a secret need?

Colin's hands returned to petting over Judd's chest. The boy's cock was still hard, but his gaze was intense, yearning for something more than just sex… validation.

Judd took a deep breath, watching as those hands rose and fell, pale and stark against the dark of his own skin. "I'm gonna be blunt, Gingersnap. I don't want you misconstruing anything about this. About us. I'd like you no matter how you looked or talked or acted. But I can't deny I'm attracted to the part of you that's a contrast to me. *Twink* if you insist. It's probably my protective enforcer nature. I enjoy how you fit against me, under my chin. I adore the idea of picking you up and tossing you onto my bed. That's sexy to me."

"But, how would you think… would you still like me okay if I dressed like Trick? Or Marvin? Would you still wanna sleep with me then?"

Judd stopped himself from grumbling *of course*. He'd love it if Colin was a bit more femme. His Gingersnap would look hot all gussied up with lip gloss and wearing something silky. But this really wasn't about what Judd liked, it was about Colin's desires and identity. "You want to wear makeup, Gingersnap, then you wear makeup. You want color on your nails, do that. You want silk or lace next to your skin, they got whole websites of men's lingerie now. I think it's all sexy. Especially on you. You want skirts instead of pants, you do that."

Judd allowed frustration into his voice. They lived in a time and place where such things were possible. Judd remembered all too well when they were not. Why couldn't Colin take advantage of the freedom of *here* and *now* if he wanted to?

Judd sighed, of course he knew why. Colin was vested in being unnoticed. Colin had diminished every part of himself to remain invisible, even the part that was gay. Especially that part. Could be Colin had always wanted to dress pretty, just never let himself. Not that Colin's old pack would have allowed it. They would have beat the shit out of him for *being a fag* for *looking like a girl*. Judd needed to be kind about Colin's fear, because to dress that way was to stand out. And Colin hated to stand out, yet he clearly yearned to be pretty.

Judd tried another tactic. "You'd look great if you dressed sexy. But you don't have to just because you're slender and beautiful. It's not like there's some required uniform for your body type. Hoodies and baggy jeans are fine. Comfortable. Who am I to advise? I never give what I wear a second thought."

Colin's face shuttered. He stared at his hands where they rested on Judd's chest, unmoving and curled slightly, like they'd died there. Those elegant hands that felt like a benediction on Judd's body.

"I'm not like them, you know."

"Like who, Gingersnap?"

"Like Marvin or Trick or Max or Isaac. I'm not bold. I don't live in my skin the way they do. Either skin or fur. I'm not fabulous or sparkling or amazing or special. I'm just gay."

Judd's heart clenched. Was this part of Colin's pain? An inadequacy based on comparison to other gay men?

"You be whatever you want to be, Gingersnap. You wear whatever you want to wear. There's no set standard on what *gay* looks like, despite what Hollywood has done to us. Christ, they can't even get werewolves right."

"But you can say that, because look at you. You're totally butch." Colin traced Judd's pec with his fingers, as if indicating the power there. "You've got it covered. I can't be that either. I mean, look at me!" Frustration and self-loathing leaked into Colin's voice.

Judd lifted his dangling hand to scrub at his face. He knew what he looked like, what he was. There'd been crap all his long life for things he couldn't control about his appearance – big, Black, powerful. But he *had* passed as straight whenever he needed to. He understood that counted for a lot in this world, even now. He was aggressively masculine. Partly because he was an enforcer, but also as a result of his childhood. Rough upbringings make posturing part of a man's personality, even before becoming werewolf. But Judd also hadn't passed in so many other ways. He'd been called out by his skin, his accent,

his wide-armed way of walking. Colin had been called out by
the fine beauty of his hands, the fullness of his lips, and a
yearning to put glitter on his eyelids.

"I like the way you look just fine, Gingersnap. But appearance doesn't dictate who you are inside. Look at Mana."

"She's fabulous too."

"You don't have to make a splash – you just have to know
how to swim."

"Well I don't. I don't know anything. Most of the time I can
barely stay afloat." Colin wasn't talking about sex anymore.

Judd pushed up onto his elbows, stared into the lost face
above him. "No one can teach you how to be gay, baby. Not
even me. I mean, I can help you with the sexual side of things,
but gayness is more than that. It's like, no one can teach you how
to be happy. You have to figure that shit out for yourself. But I'll
tell you something private, because I think it'll make you feel
better. I look like this. I'm aggressive. I'm crass and rough. I fit
enforcer well, always have – gay or not. And I'm not like Tank
or Bryan – there is no submission in me. I might have been
Alpha had I had the gene, and the right species of bite. We'll
never know, now."

Judd moved so he was leaning back against the arm of the
couch, sitting upright even more. But he grabbed Colin's wrists
when his Gingersnap would have backed away. He tugged,
gently, mindful of his strength. He pulled Colin forward. He
kissed those delicate hands, one after the other. A demonstration
of dominance, and touch, but also service. Colin needed to take
this seriously. "But I like taking dick as much as giving it, and
no one would ever guess that from looking at me."

Colin's eyes went big and round, his mouth an "o" of
surprise. "Really? You *like* that?" Against Judd's stomach
Colin's hips twitched. His cock flexed. A bright splash of
crimson spread across his cheekbones.

Judd was delighted. His almost-mate liked the idea of
fucking him, did he? Good.

Colin's eyes went quickly up and down Judd's body, assess-
ing, needy, bright yellow. Then he swallowed, focused on Judd's

face. His expression was still lost but his body had relaxed after Judd's confession. Judd had told Colin a truth that others considered a weakness. It balanced out Colin's insecurities.

"You're so much yourself, Judd. So comfortable. I figure it comes with age."

Judd nodded. It probably did. He'd hidden bits of himself for a long time. He didn't do that anymore. "Yet you thought you knew what I liked in bed because of what I look like. Because of what I show you as part of this pack. You thought you knew what kind of gay I am because you know what kind of wolf I am."

Colin nodded. "But I don't, do I? There's more than just... that."

"Taking dick? Yeah, there's more. Because big parts of who I am aren't in the way I act or look or what I do in bed. Just like they aren't in the way you fade into the background, or don't like talking to new people, or find comfort in puttering about the kitchen when there's a group in the house – because you think of them as invading your space so you invade Lovejoy's. Or the way you have to wash every single potluck container at a barbecue."

Colin's brows arched. He was surprised Judd had noticed. Of course Judd noticed! He noticed everything about his Gingersnap, his beautiful pack mate... his mate.

Judd pressed on. "I'm pretty sure you don't want to be thrown over the back of this couch and reamed just because you're slender and prettier than anything I ever saw, and flutter your fingers when you're excited. What we want and need, what I'm like in bed, what you are, that is not visible on the outside. That's not there to be shifted from one form to the other on the surface. That's bone deep. Or boner deep, if you prefer."

Colin relaxed a bit, smiled small and shy. "I'd like to find out."

"Wanna dick me out, do ya, kid?" Judd let himself be a bit crass. Trying to get that gorgeous blush back on Colin's expressive face.

"But I don't know what I'm doing."

"No one knows what they're doing the first time. And I was always gonna have more experience than you."

Colin took a sip of air. Fluttered his hands around. Then wrapped them over Judd's big ones. Tentatively, Colin smoothed thumbs against Judd's wrists. His voice was hesitant. "You have been thinking about me... Me? That way? Like, inside you?"

Judd sighed. "I think about you a lot, Gingersnap. More than is healthy, I suspect." He didn't tell him the truth because that was creepy. He didn't explain that back then, not too long ago by his standards, before Colin was made werewolf, Judd had barely had time for the Boston Red Paws. They were just another biker pack, near his territory. Fun to hook up with for a ride or a hunt on occasion, nothing more. Until that one night, when there'd been this newly minted ginger wolf pup. Unsteady and surprised to be alive. All red hair and big eyes, knobby knees and full lips, too pretty to be real.

Judd just stopped.

Just stopped.

Stopped wanting to move on.

Stopped wanting to be alone.

Stopped wanting *anything* but Colin.

Judd badly wanted to be worthy of something so newly minted precious and copper shiny perfect. He'd made inquiries about the Boston pack, about enforcer positions. He heard rumblings of a new Alpha, of a queer pack. He let himself hope as he hadn't hoped for a long time, for acceptance and belonging.

He wasn't going to tell Colin any of that. Because Colin only needed him long enough to learn how *to sex,* as he put it. Yet Judd had changed his entire world so he might belong with him for eternity. He'd settle for pack mate, so long as he got forever.

So instead Judd told Colin a different truth. "You spend a lot of time trying not to be seen. I always saw you, from that first night. Been looking at you, full on, for a while now."

"Me?" Colin squeaked.

Judd shook his head to stop from sighing. "You spend so much energy trying not to be noticed, you stopped noticing things yourself. Except threats, of course. You're safe now. None of us here are out to get you, or belittle you. We all just want to love you, one way or another. I'd like to love on you all ways, learn some stuff about what's under your defenses. What you smell like when you come. How soft you are behind your knees." He turned his hand up, encouraged Colin to stroke over his palm.

Colin was focused on touching Judd, but also listening hard. Not yet ready to say anything.

Judd pushed on. "I want you, Gingersnap. In my bed, all up in my space, and in my business. No bones about it, okay? Regardless of how this thing plays out between us, you will never be bothering me. You will *never* be in my way, or unwelcome. You got it? I would love to help you learn what you like. What kind of gay you want to be. And if we stop fucking, that won't end. I won't leave you behind, like they did."

Colin's face was wracked with fear and hope. But he was taking Judd's words seriously. Maybe even believing them a tiny bit.

Judd pressed. "You got me?"

"Yeah. Yes. Yes, Judd, I got you."

"Good. Now, we're gonna stop this fooling around for tonight. Don't get me wrong, I want my hands on your cock, and yours on mine, like nothing else right now. But you need to seriously think on things. Talk to Isaac if you can. He's good on this kind of shit. But I'm ready for the next lesson whenever you are. I'll wait as long as you need me to if you need time. But for tonight, I want you to pause and think about it. Okay?" Gently, lingering over his mate's exquisite body the entire time, Judd separated them. Lifted Colin, put him to the side, wanting badly to stay touching, but obsessed with the importance of choice. Especially with Colin so young.

Colin's full pretty mouth was pressed straight and firm, eyes narrowed. "Okay. I got it. I'm sure. But maybe you need time to think, too." Colin was annoyed at being pushed away when his decision was already made. Plus he was sexually frustrated. Judd was pleased to see both those reactions, and that Colin wasn't trying to hide them. Had a backbone, and it was important to know that he would use it on Judd.

Judd stood, cock aching. He scooped up his discarded t-shirt. He didn't put it back on, just carried it in a ball and strode away. At the bottom of the stairs, he checked back, to make sure Colin was ogling his ass.

Colin was definitely ogling.

Good.

Fortunately for Colin, since he didn't get much sleep, his first class wasn't until two the next afternoon. As usual, at that hour, the pack house was empty, everyone either asleep or at work.

He drank some cold coffee out of the pot – caffeine wasn't necessary for werewolves, but he liked the taste. He didn't bother with breakfast, remembering he still had half a salami in his backpack and that would do. He geared up for a motorcycle ride, grabbed his bag, and was off to campus.

He had a lot to think about, but strangely it wasn't Judd and sex that occupied his brain while he rode. It was his mother. (Which was more than enough to kill any of those first thoughts had they tried to develop.) He wondered if she wanted to see him, if she would even bother to reach out. He wasn't sure if he desired her interest or was terrified by the prospect. Bit of both, most likely. He also didn't know what he would do if she reached out. He admitted to being curious. By unspoken agreement, he and Kevin never talked about either of their parents. But this meant he knew very little about his mother.

His afternoon class was applied mathematics, which was one of his favorites, but even that didn't totally distract him. Weirdly his brain seemed to have latched on to the fact that today his mother was *in* the Bay Area, and was going to give a concert *that* weekend. *His real live mother* was going to meet with Judd and Kevin that very evening to discuss security. His mother, whom he barely remembered. It was all very strange and surreal.

Nevertheless, when he was out of class and strapping his

helmet back on, contemplating the best way to extract his motor-cycle from the herd of scooters and bicycles that now surrounded it, the very last thing he expected was to actually see said mother in the flesh.

A stretch limo pulled up next to him. An honest-to-goodness *stretch limo*, not even the new sport utility kind that were better suited to the hills and curves of Highway One.

Colin glared at the ridiculousness of it, feeling self-righteous about his own choice of vehicle (not that he had much of a choice – werewolves and motorcycles were kind of a trope these days).

The limo put its hazards on and stopped, right there in the street next to campus. *Entitled prick,* thought Colin.

The back seat window rolled down, as if they were in some mobster film, and a face Colin knew from the media, if not his own memory, looked out at him.

"Well hi there, sugah," she said, in a drawl as fake as her hair color.

"Hello, Mother."

CHAPTER SEVEN
CAFE RIDERS IN THE SKY

Lexi Blanc, in the flesh, right there in front of Colin. Well, in a stretch limo but still, right *there*. Colin stared at his mother, some alien creature here to abduct him, or experiment on him, or something. He half expected a probe to unfold from her bouffant hairdo.

She was unbelievably beautiful. He knew that from her online images but up close, in person, was worse. She was Alpha – most female werewolves were – and she had taken pains to focus all that Alpha charisma through her appearance, like a magnification lens made of face powder.

Besides, Alpha power only really worked well in person. A photograph of Alec couldn't convey to the world how safe he smelled, how bossy-kind he was. How Colin always knew that Alec had the pack's best interests at heart. And how Alec was only disappointed when Colin failed himself or hurt the pack.

A photograph of Lexi Blanc, even a video of her, couldn't show Alpha-ness. Meeting her face-to-face, Colin felt it in his bones – that he was a lesser wolf, a rank-less weakling, hers to play with and manipulate. She knew she was his superior. She knew she could order him to do anything and he'd probably do it. And he knew it. Without his pack to buffer him, to protect him from another Alpha, Colin felt belly up, exposed, shaky, and terribly alone.

He wanted to bolt. He didn't know if she had VOICE, but if she did, he was within range. Running would do him little good. But he didn't want to move any closer, either. He didn't want to smell her. Didn't want to be comforted, if her scent reminded him of a childhood he'd never had. Didn't want to feel his hackles raise if she smelled like a stranger or an enemy.

She didn't do or say anything further, just stared at him. Her lips were so much like his, and her chin and eyes, her hair artfully streaked and darker red. But still red. There was no denying that face – he saw a version of it every morning in the mirror.

Colin stood, frozen, staring back – motorcycle helmet still half on his head.

Maybe a few seconds passed, maybe a minute. A part of Colin registered that she'd catch attention soon – in *that* car with *that* face, someone was bound to recognize her. So he wasn't at all surprised when she rolled the tinted window back up. In fact, he expected it. Expected her to just drive on. Leaving him wondering why she'd bothered to come looking for him, or if it was all a coincidence.

But the limo stayed where it was. The door she'd just been looking out of popped open.

More than anything, Colin wanted to ask her *why*. Not why was she here, or why had she come, but why had she left in the first place? Not for himself, but for Kevin. Kevin, whose pain was bright in his childish memory. Colin didn't really remember his mother, but he remembered his older brother's misery more than he remembered his own. His big, bright, charming older brother who'd sobbed in his bed across the room until Colin started climbing in next to him, hugging him close. Kevin who'd wailed that child's word *why?* into Colin's neck as if he were the younger sibling.

Colin knew down to his shifting bones that his brother still wanted an answer to that question. Why abandon Kevin, who'd tried so hard to be perfect for her? Kevin, who she'd praised for his achievements in sports, for his physical beauty, for his bold personality. Kevin, who she'd looked at with such pride, her golden boy, yet who she still left behind.

Their dad was clearly an asshole. No surprises there. Colin was a disappointment, weak and inferior. He'd been deemed insufficient from the moment he was born. He knew exactly why she'd left *him*. But he needed an answer for his brother. Kevin would never ask her himself.

Colin took his time locking his helmet back onto his bike. He walked over slowly to that open limo door – not out of reluctance, but to keep any eagerness from his step.

Inside the limo was a surprise.

His mother, of course, and her ubiquitous stylist Risa Ostrov, but also two familiar faces. Familiar not from Colin's paparazzi research or any show Lexi Blanc had ever performed, but from Colin's own recent history.

"Well ,well, well," said Colin, because if he was to be in a gangster film, he would play the damn part. "What have we here? Agents Faste and Lenis, back in San Andreas territory already? I'd say it's nice to see you again but given the company you're keeping, this can hardly be a good thing."

It was a dig at his mother, but she seemed unaware of the slight. Or uncaring.

She was sitting in front of him in a flowered wrap dress with strappy sandals, long legs crossed at the ankle, and perfect makeup. Her eyes on Colin's face were not the avid ones of a long-separated mother, stupid of Colin to even think that. They were mildly annoyed, as if he were some government questionnaire she had to fill out, and she was wondering if she could make her assistant do it for her.

He took a cautious sniff, relieved to find that Lexi Blanc smelled like a stranger. A strange Alpha werewolf in his territory mixed with face powder and hair product – human ones that were scented with chemicals and greed. Colin could smell Agent Lenis too, another Alpha, but cleanly wolf, earthy meaty power, a scent his instincts had catalogued before. Agent Lenis's scent was that of *tentative ally* – not *safe* but not *enemy* either. Agent Faste smelled of berserker – honey fur and boreal forests. Risa, the human, smelled as all humans did, slightly like prey but also of perfume and skin cream, shampoo and deodorant, all the scents that most humans who worked closely with werewolves were asked to avoid. Curious that his mother didn't restrict the products used by her human companion. Had Colin been a more aggressive wolf, he would have pointedly coughed.

He narrowed his eyes at Lexi Blanc. "Mother dearest, I had no idea you were working for the SBI."

His mother pushed a single coil of artfully arranged hair back over her white shoulder with one fine-boned hand. Colin realized, with a start, that her hands were just like his too, gracefully tapered and elegant.

"Don't be silly, darling, they work for *me,* of course."

Agent Lenis snorted loudly at that.

Agent Faste, as always, was a lump of inscrutable, unflappable refrigerator-sized disinterest. Or apparent disinterest. No doubt the berserker observed everything.

"She's lending us a hand." Agent Lenis, as another, older, Alpha, wasn't going to let his mother get away with claiming superiority.

Colin was secretly delighted by this. "What does the SBI want with a country music singer?" he asked.

"Never you mind that, sugah, I wanted to talk to you."

"Funny, mother, that's never motivated you before."

Colin looked hard at the two SBI agents. What was going on here? Had they used his mother to get him away from his pack? Shifter protocol dictated they go through Alec to officially interview him. Was this a work-around to get him alone? Why him? What could the SBI possibly want from him?

"Why me, specifically?" He ignored his mother and glared at Agent Faste, who'd always seemed a nice enough dude for a bear shifter. Plus he was super hot, best thing in that car to look at.

"Because you're my darling sweet little boy," replied Lexi Blanc.

That actually made Colin's stomach roll. So he continued to

ignore her and talk to the SBI team. "What are you after? What's going on?"

"Apparently you had a little dust-up with some members of the Pinniped Syndicate."

Colin was deeply confused. "I did?"

"The selkie are in town, snookums," said his mother, smiling sickly sweet.

Colin narrowed his eyes at her. "Seriously, just stop." He turned back to the agents. "That thing at the cafe the other night? That was some assholes who thought a friend of mine owed them money. He didn't. End of story."

"Patrick Inis, yes. We've been watching him for a while." Agent Lenis curled her lip.

"Oh, that must be exciting for you. Poor thing slaves away at that cafe more hours than he should, then sleeps in his car. I'm sure he's a veritable fountain of criminal activity."

Agent Lenis rolled her eyes. "Yeah, yeah, whatever you say, kid."

"Hey now," replied Colin. No one but Judd was allowed to even think about calling him *kid*, Alpha werewolf or not.

"And yet, the Pinnipeds made contact with him, so he must be some kind of dirty." Agent Faste's tone was mild.

Colin bristled and went for the limo door. That was more than enough of *that*. "You lure me in here using my estranged mother and then accuse my friend of being scum with no evidence? What exactly is going on, agents?"

"My pup has some fire to him, even if he is an unranked skinny little wimp," said his mother with something like pride.

Colin decided that he hated her. Not that he'd been far away to start with, but still.

It hardly mattered because she immediately lost interest. "Risa, is my nose shiny? It feels shiny."

Risa passed Lexi a small mirror. Lexi held it to examine her face and hair. Like she was in a 1950s commercial.

"You have Patrick Inis with you now, at your pack house?" Agent Lenis was not about to let things ride.

Colin nodded. He wasn't revealing anything. The SBI could

source Trick's location soon enough if they looked at Kettil's report. "Yeah, and we set a guard while he's working at the cafe, plus the local deputies said they'd drop by to check on the regular."

"You think the selkie will try again?"

"They seemed very eager."

"What did they say to him? You were there."

Again something they could read in Kettil's report, although Colin supposed the sheriff's department wasn't noted for its speedy filing of paperwork, or its general eagerness to cooperate with the feds.

Was this what they were after? Contacting Colin for information on the local selkie mob? "They wanted a lot of money off him. Or they thought he was hiding a lot of their money from them. Or goods or something. Which is crap, because poor Trick has been scraping to make ends meet the whole time I've known him. Clearly he's not sitting on thousands of dollars! I wish he'd told me how bad it was for him. I would have asked him to stay sooner."

The two SBI agents exchanged meaningful looks.

"Are you the reason she hired Heavy Lifting for her events while she's here?" Colin asked them, referring to his mother as if she weren't still sitting in front of him.

Lexi Blanc did not like to be ignored, so she answered. "Certainly not! I have some kind of creepy stalker following me around, stealing my stuff. I wanted extra security, and any firm employing my son must be a good one. Kevin is an excellent enforcer. I'm sure he'll make a remarkably good bodyguard."

"You know nothing at all about him," snapped back Colin.

She shrugged, like that hardly mattered. "He's my pup, of course I know him."

Colin saw some measure of discomfort on the two agents' faces at that. So they hadn't known about bodyguard werewolves incoming. Mother was playing them, too. Colin narrowed his eyes at the feds. "You did know that she hired Heavy Lifting to provide extra security while she's in town? Our pack is going to be all up in her, and apparently your, business." He turned back to ask the question that had bought him into the car in the first place. "Why are you messing with him, mother?"

"Who, dear?"

"Kevin. You leave him the fuck alone. Just like you always have."

"Sweetie, how adorable, are you trying to be protective? Don't bother, it's not in your nature. Are you two actually close brothers? That's nice. I did good, then."

Abruptly, Colin had had more than enough. He didn't need to ask her why she'd left Kevin behind, she didn't care for anyone but herself. She had wanted a career and they'd been in the way. Kevin being the perfect son didn't change that fact.

Colin turned back to the SBI. "Are we done here?"

"Tell us more about your friend, Trick," insisted Agent Lenis, iron in her voice. Not quite a command, but close.

Colin wanted to show his neck. The act of resisting made him grimace. So he ended up baring his teeth at the Alpha. Not a wise move.

She rumbled out a warning at him and her eyes flashed yellow.

Colin swallowed and tried to find a backbone somewhere. "You wanna question me, you come at it through my Alpha like a proper shifter should, or you run it up official channels and arrest me, like a proper fed should. This skulking limo action isn't right, and you know it." They could probably make him talk. Every shifter in that car was a higher rank and a heavier hitter than he was. Not that he had anything more to say. Not that he was hiding anything.

Colin was counting on at least Agent Faste being decent. This was a crappy way to go about things, and they all knew it. Perhaps the berserker could be made to care?

He turned his big eyes on the bear shifter, knowing he must look desperate.

"We just want to know what would make a pack of were-wolves take in an otter shifter," pressed Agent Lenis.

"Compassion. You should look up the word. Bet none of you have ever heard of it."

"Look at my little one, pretending he has big teeth. It's so cute." Lexi reached over as if she were going to pinch Colin's cheek. He wanted to bite her hand. Instead he flinched away. He was really good at that.

"No touching!" he barked at her.

She pouted. "But I'm your mummy."

"What kind of sick game are you all playing?" Colin suddenly, fiercely, wished for his pack around him. Alec's quiet strength, Isaac's calm certainty, and Judd's supportive fierceness. Yes, Judd. How would the enforcer act in this kind of situation? Stupid question. Judd would never have gotten into the limo in the first place. Judd always went all rigid when surrounded by outsider Alphas, almost military in his responses. Taciturn. Guarded.

Colin swallowed. "I'm calling Alec."

The agents exchanged another series of expressive glances. "Fine. But we'll need to talk to that otter friend of yours."

Colin made a rather rash statement then, but he could think of no other way to protect Trick. "He's pack now. You better do it to protocol."

"I didn't see anything filed with DURPS to that effect. In fact, your little river friend there isn't even registered as a local shifter. He's an illegal, and we can take him in for questioning with no warrant if we want."

Colin didn't think that was true. "Off of our pack lands, out from under our guardianship, seriously? I don't think so. Otherwise, you'd have done it already. Instead, you came after me. Via my mother. Sideways and sneaky."

Silence met that. There was some reason they wanted to leave Trick free-roaming and didn't want to be seen visiting the pack. Colin wasn't an idiot, he could figure it out.

"You're using him as bait, aren't you? When he didn't do anything! What happened to protect and serve?"

"That's not our motto, that's the cops'."

"So what's yours? Successfully bother innocents?"

"Trust me, red, if there's Inis around, Inis are involved. He did *something*. Inis don't leave the family business and they are never innocent," said Agent Faste, sounding almost sad.

It was the sympathy in the berserker's voice that made Colin question his gut. Was Trick actually involved? Had the otter shifter lied to them? But then that act of questioning his own instincts made Colin even more angry. He wasn't going to mistrust a friend simply because some feds were hounding him (even if it was just a coffee shop flirt-friend like Trick). After all, these feds were using his mother to get at him. Colin always believed in judging people by the company they kept. The agents were not doing well in that regard.

So he said, "We're done here." He knew his Panda Rights. He took off his backpack, began to strip out of his leather riding jacket.

He started to recite. "Colin Mangnall, San Andreas Pack. I formally request the representation of my Alpha and that he be alerted that I'm in custody for protocol violations. I have the right to remain shifted. Anything I do as a wolf cannot be influenced by an Alpha not my own. If my Alpha cannot come for me, an Alpha will be provided on my behalf. I request Ms Trickle, kelpie. She can be found locally at the DURPS headquarters at the Marin Civic Center in San Rafael. I will now shift." It was getting darker, but the sun had not yet set. It would be difficult and painful for Colin to shift prior to sunset, but it was his best recourse at this juncture. Agent Lenis could VOICE-command him to stay human, but after declaring his rights in front of witnesses, that would be highly illegal.

"Kid's gotten stronger since last we were in town," said Agent Faste, confusion in his tone.

Agent Lenis sighed big and deep. "Fucking San Andreas Pack got themselves an Omega."

Agent Faste laughed. "'Course they did. I forgot about that. They got a Magistar and a familiar, too. That's a complete set." His bright gaze moved between the two female Alphas. "Bet your lot fucking hate it. San Andreas is now the most powerful pack in the country, full of gay dudes and mages and mermen and all kinds of shenanigans." Agent Faste returned his attention to Colin. "Keep your shirt on, Mangnall. You're free to go. We aren't detaining you."

Colin tugged down his t-shirt, pulled his hoodie back on, and put his leather jacket on top. Picking up his backpack, he glared at Agent Faste; the berserker stayed calm and impassive under his pointed disgust.

"You should pick your friends with greater care, old bear."

"You can pick your friends and you can pick your breakfast, but you can't smother your friends in hollandaise sauce." Agent Faste was a bit of a weirdo, probably why Agent Lenis did most of the talking.

Colin thought about Judd smothered in hollandaise sauce and said, "Yeah you can, you just need the right kind of friends."

With which he got out of the limo and slammed the door hard behind him. It was petty, but it made him feel good. And they let him go.

They let him go!

Colin's first instinct was to call Judd. Or his brother. Or both. He did neither. He bent over, put his hands to his knees and hyperventilated for a bit. He managed to not throw up, which was a victory, since his stomach was all kinds of freaked out and he still hadn't eaten anything that day. His mother, so many Alphas, all them intensely *wanting* something from him, forcing him, and he hadn't yielded. He had resisted. At least, he thought he hadn't yielded. And he'd left with his own intel, too. He now knew that others beyond the selkie were after Trick. That the government thought Trick was dirty, thought Trick was trouble. That Lexi Blanc was working with the SBI. Were they protecting her? Was she some kind of spy for them or something?

Colin did some yoga breathing, got himself back together, stood up straight. Then he did the right thing, he called his Alpha.

And his Alpha called a pack meeting.

It wasn't even dark when Kevin busted into Judd's room and woke him up from a really hot dream.

"What?" he growled. "We aren't meeting with the client for another two hours."

"Pack meeting." Kevin's eyes went wicked. "You look flushed. Nice dream?"

"Your little brother featured in a starring role. There was a neon mesh jock strap involved. You sure you wanna hear about it?"

"Yech, no. Dude. I mean, *dude*! That's *not* cool. I gave you my blessing, but I *so* don't want any specifics."

"Which is what I tell you every time you screw a woman. Now you know what it feels like. Plus, maybe if you didn't divulge every tiny detail of every sexual encounter, they'd feel a little less like bragging rights and more like people you actually cared about."

"Now you're giving me advice on my love life? What, you got everything suddenly sorted with Colin, so now you're all Captain Magicdouchnugget Superdick?"

Judd groaned. "It is way too early for you to be all up in my biscuit. Pack meeting? Isn't Alec still at work?"

"He's headed back. And you gotta get up and dressed because we're meeting at the *Bean*."

"Pack meeting in public? At a cafe? What the hell?"

"I know, right? But apparently it involves Trick and he's working. So we take the pack to him."

"Weird."

"And you'll never guess who called the meet."

"Alec, of course."

"No. I mean, yeah Alec summoned us, but the reason for needing a meeting came from Colin." Kevin went off to rouse the others.

"Wait. What?" Judd was out of bed and dressed in record time, even for a shifter. Even for Judd, who wore jeans, t-shirt, boots, and nothing else most days. He didn't hold with underpants or socks – too many layers between him and wolf.

Down in the kitchen, Judd waited impatiently. He was gonna

leave for the cafe alone. They could damn well meet him there. Then Kevin, Lovejoy, Tank, and Isaac ambled in. He shepherded them all out the door without allowing for any conversation. He practically ran them down the hill. They arrived at the Bean in less than ten minutes.

Alec had claimed a family emergency and left work early. His lab was usually good about that kind of thing. Marvin was at sea, looking for a lost shipment of bullion-level prosciutto. Preserved meat was a serious business in a town with high shifter numbers. Bryan and Max were already at the cafe. They'd been on Trick detail all afternoon. They'd set themselves up on the wireless. Max doing whatever it was that he did that revolved around being the only Magistar in California. Bryan was probably reading Burp reviews. He'd been charged with finding them a general contractor. Normally Max and Bryan spent their time together practicing in the yard. Away from the house and pack, they played with quintessence, learned enchantments, and stank the trees up with the smell of coolant and ozone.

When Judd arrived, the two of them were happily ensconced at Colin's table near the door. It was weird for them to be huddled behind computers at a cafe. Out of character. Although Judd supposed even Max, magical being though he was, had email to answer. There was always email.

Alec came in next, looking impossibly geeky in his lab coat. His hair was sticking up. He'd been running his fingers through it. He did that when he was worried.

The focus of the pack swung in his direction. Palpable yearning. Even the humans sensed Alpha power.

"We should take over the back." Alec pointed to the family zone at the rear of the cafe. It was full of books and board games.

Fortunately, the cafe was mostly empty. The lunch rush was long over and the post-work evening crowd had not yet arrived. Americans didn't have the concept of afternoon tea, a fact that, even all these years later, Judd still found a grave character flaw.

Those few humans in the place were giving them wary looks.

They deserved it – a gang of big burly dudes, a bit too loud, a bit too pushy. The weirdness of a geek in a lab coat coming in and ordering them all around just made them seem extra creepy to humans.

The writer in the corner gave them a horrified look. She packed up her things, scampered out. The couple in the window started finishing their muffins with a will.

"Everyone order something so we look like we belong," instructed Alec. "Except you, Lovejoy. You'll pinch hit as barista, please. We need Trick at our meeting."

"Beautiful boys!" Trick sang out, "What can I froth for you?" He was clearly delighted to have his place of work invaded by werewolves.

Dutifully they all stood in line and ordered. At cafes that catered exclusively to humans, none of the drinks were that exciting to werewolves, let alone other shifters. But Bean There, Froth That had two stickers in its window – the rainbow and the moon. Which meant this was a queer-friendly place that tried to accommodate shifters. Those stickers were probably Trick's doing. In addition to the requisite pastries, the Bean carried eggs baked in baskets of bacon, fish pies, and sardine banh mi sand-wiches. For drinks, Trick did interesting things with frothy milk, bone broth, fish sauce, and clam juice. The Bean was considered very hip as a result.

Judd got himself a steamed milk broth with sour cream and cinnamon sprinkled on top. He thought it was similar to what Colin got, so he wanted to try it. Then he went to wait impa-tiently at the back.

Alec gave Judd a long look. Then sighed. "Tank, you guard the door, please." Normally, that was Judd's or Kevin's job. But if Colin was in trouble, Kevin would want to be part of the discussion. Judd was grateful that his Alpha understood that Judd *had* to be there too.

Trick whipped up their drinks in record time. He even had Colin's ready for him. Judd was tolerably certain that no one had told him Colin was coming.

Although, this *was* about the time Colin usually stopped by the cafe on his way home from school.

Judd sipped his drink – meh – and worried.

Turns out he was right to worry.

Colin's beat-up old motorcycle coughed to a stop outside. He drove it up onto the sidewalk. Deputy Kettil would have a fit if he saw it, but the kid was clearly in a hurry. Colin was usually law-abiding, even on a motorcycle, which Judd didn't understand. Wasn't that the *point* of a motorcycle – that they could get away with shit and no one would catch them? Except a motorcycle cop, of course.

Judd chose a seat on the couch at the very back. He had a good view of the front door. He jostled Kevin for it. His fellow enforcer let out a long-suffering sigh, and took the chair opposite instead, facing the employee entrance at the back. Both doors were now under enforcer surveillance.

Judd examined Colin closely as he came in. His face looked troubled, but he didn't appear overwrought or injured in any way. He gave a nod to Tank at the front and moved quickly to the counter. A few words exchanged with Trick, and Colin scooped up his drink and rushed to the back.

"Should I ask Trick to put up the *closed* sign? He needs to hear this too."

"You sure we shouldn't hear it first?" Alec's tone was delicate.

"No, Alpha. That's kinda the point, actually. It's not private pack business."

Alec nodded. "Lovejoy, you're up."

Lovejoy chugged the last of his drink – iced milk mixed with clam juice – and went behind the counter.

"What are you doing?" came Trick's offended squeal. "No, you can't just take over for me! This is my responsibility! It's my *job*. Do you even *know* how to run an espresso machine?"

Whatever Lovejoy replied was lost behind the steaming gurgle of said machine kicking up. Lovejoy did something that mollified the dratsie. Trick came sashaying back to them, carrying his own drink.

"If I get fired for this, I don't know what I'll do, you guys. I mean I'm grateful for you taking me in and all, but *darlings,* you can't just come to my place of business and take over, all looming studly hotness and lotharios frothing my milk…" he trailed off.

Alec pointed at Colin. "Start talking."

CHAPTER EIGHT
MAY THE FROTH BE WITH YOU

Colin took a deep breath. A precise carefulness was in his voice when he spoke. Judd knew that this meant he'd practiced what to say into his helmet on the ride over. Judd breathed with him, for reassurance.

"Okay, so when I left class today my mother was waiting for me curbside."

"What!" barked Kevin.

"Yeah, in this massive dumb limo. Anyway, you'll never guess who she had with her. Agent Faste and Agent Lenis. Well, and her stylist. But anyway, the SBI are here in town and they're all up in our business."

"Fantastic. Are they after her for something?" Kevin sounded more resigned than surprised.

Colin grimaced. "I don't think so. I believe they're protecting her or using her for something connected to their current case. They had lots of questions for me. So I figured they were maybe using her to get to me. It wasn't like she actually wanted to see me or anything."

That was said for the benefit of his brother. As if Colin were reassuring Kevin that Kevin was still the favorite child. Or at least that Lexi Blanc would have ignored both of them, had she not been ordered to reach out to Colin.

"Anyway, the SBI is in town because they're investigating

something Trick-tangential. Sorry, Trick. And I'm pretty sure it's *the goods* those selkies were after. Because, Trick, they really only wanted to ask me about you and what happened Tuesday night."

"Me?" Trick placed his hand to his chest in a parody of a Southern belle. "Little ol' *me*? But why? I don't *have* anything. My family hasn't given me anything. I swear. You can search my car if you like, boys. They can search it if they want to. I mean, seriously, dudes, the SBI is after me? I swear, I haven't *done* anything illegal. I'm just a barista!" The little otter was working himself up into a freakout.

Isaac stood and moved over to him. The Omega placed a hand on his upper back and began rubbing in circles.

"We don't think you're involved, Trick." Alec's voice was soothing, Alpha power behind it. Which meant Alec really *didn't* think Trick was playing them false.

Colin said, "But I do think it's likely your family is involved. The SBI is a pain, but they aren't *that* incompetent. I mean, if both the government and the mob are after you, what were your people into, Trick? You left them a while ago, right? And you didn't register with DURPS here because you were scared they could track you if you went on the record. Right? So your family must be into something *not* great."

"Tut tut tut, Trick," said Max, who used to work for DURPS. He still had a lot of friends there. "You're an unregistered shifter?"

Trick started wringing his hands. "My family really sucks, Max. They'd come after me. Like *seriously* come after me. Or at least make contact and want me to *do* things for them. And I don't wanna do those kinda *things* anymore."

"What do they do, Trick? What did they make you do in the past?" Alec's tone was firmer, more power to it.

The dratsie crumbled under the weight of Alpha displeasure. He started blubbering and trying to talk at the same time. This resulted in incomprehensible babble.

Isaac rubbed his back harder, crooning. Bryan went over to him, as well. He offered Trick a napkin and told him it would all be all right. That they didn't blame him for anything his family might have done.

Even though it wasn't directed at him, Judd could feel the Beta's calming influence.

Judd almost wanted to comfort the dratsie, too. Except, somehow, Trick's family had put Colin into an uncomfortable and possibly dangerous position. Judd would not have that.

He suddenly realized that Colin had been questioned and bullied by his *mother*. The same mother he hadn't seen since he was a baby. He must be wrecked and emotionally wrung out. Not to mention Agent Lenis was the worst kind of bossy Alpha. Poor Gingersnap.

Judd looked over to find Colin wasn't watching Trick. He was staring at Judd, his face full of sad longing.

Judd took a risk. Smiled tentatively and patted his leg.

In a flash, Colin was across the room, curled into his lap.

Everyone but Trick froze and stared at them.

Colin had, on occasion, sat next to Judd at a barbecue. But he'd never sat in his lap. He never initiated any kind of physical contact with any of the pack.

Judd was impossibly proud to be the first. *Look at me,* he wanted to crow, shoving it in all their faces, *he trusts me.* Which was kind of what his actions said right now anyway – openly cuddling Colin in the middle of a cafe. Big strong enforcer, made soft-bellied and sweet. *Look at me, look what I got! Look at this precious, beautiful being who chose me. Isn't it glorious? Aren't I lucky?*

"Fucking damn it! Who had this week in the pool?" That was Kevin, of course.

"Marvin, I think," said Lovejoy, from where he leaned over the espresso machine.

"No," said Max, idly licking the foam off the top of his tiramisu latte. "Wasn't Marvin."

A throat was cleared at the front of the cafe.

Tank gave them all a cheery wave.

The others grumbled. They threw twenty-dollar bills onto the coffee table. Kevin gathered them up and delivered them to Tank with ill grace. "You can collect from Marvin yourself, damn it. How'd you know?"

Tank shrugged, grinning big, and stuffed the wad of cash into his pocket.

Alec, who clearly hadn't been in on the wager, nevertheless let it play out with only a single raised eyebrow of mild annoyance. "If you're quite done, gentlemen?"

Judd shrugged and snuggled Colin against him. Careful not to squeeze too hard. Happy to have his rich scent mingle with that of the cafe. He should pretend to be annoyed. But how could he, when he had what he wanted in his arms? If his Gingersnap was going to let him close in public, Judd intended to take full advantage.

"Holy shit," whispered Colin in Judd's ear, face hot against his cheek. "They had a bet going?"

"'Course they did."

"'*Course* they did? Were you in on it?" His voice rising, Colin was prepared to take offense.

"Don't be silly. We aren't allowed to bet on ourselves. That's insider trading."

The rest of the pack tried manfully not to smile or stare, but they did not hide the fact that they were listening avidly to the conversation. Judd took this as unilateral support and reveled in it.

"But you knew it was going on?" Colin waved one elegant hand about.

"Well, I figured it might be. Didn't you?"

"Oh my god, no!"

"Kid, I've been circling you from the moment I joined San Andreas. This pack isn't stupid. Frankly, I'm glad Tank won. Seems he had the most faith in me."

Colin looked up and around at the silent men carefully not looking at them. "Everyone else thought it'd take us longer to get together?"

"I thought it'd be at least another year." Max sounded almost gleeful, even though he'd lost. He was the only one staring at them openly. Max had no subtlety.

Fortunately, this ridiculousness was the perfect thing to calm Trick. He stopped crying, watching the back and forth with bright dark eyes.

"I kind of love you guys," he said.

Judd whispered into Colin's ear, tolerably certain the dratsie (at least) couldn't overhear, "I suppose we shouldn't tell him there's a new bet going on him?"

Colin nuzzled Judd's neck and whispered back, "And Kettil?"

"Of course."

"I want in."

Judd chuckled. "Of course you do, Gingersnap. Talk to your brother about it."

"I will. And I wanna talk to you about him."

"Something happen with your mom you've not told us?"

"Yeah, and I don't know if I should say something to Kev about it. I want your advice."

"I'm here for you. But later, okay?"

"If you're all quite done?" Alec sounded extremely prissy. Looked it too, all buttoned up in his white lab coat.

They quieted.

Alec turned back to Trick. "Your family, Trick. Please give it to us straight. We need to know so we can keep you safe."

Trick took a deep breath. "That's the problem, they're crooked as the night is long. Fences mainly and some money laundering. Mostly we – they – move stolen goods, get things across state lines, or out of the country. River otters, you know?"

He spoke quickly, nervous but eager to accommodate. Barely pausing for breath, he pushed on. "People don't really remember the waterways in this day and age. The selkie dominate all offshore action, but they also deal in interstate byways. Dratsie accommodate that. It's not like there's a territory conflict – we like fresh water, they like salt. Makes for a decent working relationship, actually. I mean, if you're a criminal. I was raised to the game. But, to be honest, I kinda sucked at it. I'm not good at hiding things. I mean look at me, I'm out and fabulous. There isn't a subtle bone in this fantastically tight bod." He gestured at himself. He was wearing a red mesh top that fell off one shoulder, ridiculously huge fake eyelashes, and an extremely tight pair of plaid pants. Judd thought he did, in fact, look fantastic.

Trick continued. "I really didn't enjoy skulking and hiding. Somehow I was born with a code of ethics. Mamma said she shouldn't have put me into a human school. I found theater and took to it like it was religion. Got sexed up with human males, learned how *not* to steal for a living. Then I swam away as soon as I could. I was underage when I left. I've been running from them ever since."

"You didn't want to be tried as an adult, did you?" suggested Max. Max wasn't a particularly ethical person. He tended to think in terms of practical choices.

"That too."

"Makes sense that the selkie would come after you. If your family had been hired to get something of theirs overland to California so that they could take it offshore." Isaac's tone was soft and soothing, reasonable.

Colin said, "The blubber bozos said they were after almost a quarter of a million dollars."

Trick nodded, miserable. "Yeah, but I really don't have it, guys. And knowing my family, they could be moving it in any number of ways. I've no idea at all what form it would take. Art, artifact, jewelry maybe. Portable property of some kind, something easy to liquidate at this end. Probably waterproof."

Colin's quick mind was already connecting the dots. "That would explain the feds too. If dratsie and selkie are moving stolen goods, that's squarely in SBI jurisdiction."

Judd wanted to squeeze him for his brilliance, but refrained out of dignity.

Trick groaned and rubbed his face. "Deputy Kettil is going to hate me."

"Your family is not your fault, sweetheart," said Judd, trying to express support. It was easier to believe in the dratsie when he had Colin, warm and lovely, in his arms.

"Speaking of which, what the hell was mother doing involved with all this?" Kevin looked hard at his brother.

Colin straightened, but didn't stop leaning against Judd. "Now, *that* I don't know. It was really weird, guys. She summoned me over and the agents were just there with her in the car, and they asked me questions and she mostly sat looking supercilious and pretending to be nice to me."

"Supercilious? Big word much," teased Judd.

Colin got prim. "It's the right word. I'll use a big one if I want to." He paused and grinned. "Why do you think I'm with you?"

Judd smiled back. "Nice one, Gingersnap."

Colin frowned. "Oh, and the SBI didn't know mother had hired Heavy Lifting."

"So she isn't happy to be working with them, if she didn't tell them about us." Kevin looked almost hopeful.

"I don't know!" Frustration colored Colin's voice. "She's awful. Like, what is her problem? Seriously, Kev. Yuck."

"Yeah. Bet you're glad you don't remember her now, aren't ya?"

Alec cleared his throat. "So, I have the SBI in town kidnapping members of my pack and interrogating them without permission. And we have a visiting celebrity Alpha werewolf with a security problem, and someone trying to move thousands of dollars of stolen goods through my town via dratsie fences to the selkie mob?"

"That about sums it up," said Judd, grinning at him.

"Just your average day by the Bay, then?" Max actually sounded excited and interested for a change.

"This is gonna be fun, right?" piped up Lovejoy from behind the counter. He had no customers. Either Tank at the door was scaring them off, or things really were that slow in the late afternoon at Bean There, Froth That.

"Fun for everyone but Kevin and Colin," said Isaac.

"And Trick," added Colin.

"Yeah, dudes, Sorry about your mom being, you know, sucky and all," added Lovejoy.

"Family's a bitch," sympathized Max.

"Literally in this case." Kevin was enough himself to crack a bad joke.

"This is *so* going to be fun." Max took a long drink, blue eyes fierce with evil ideas.

"What's the plan of attack, Alpha?" Judd looked at Alec. "We got us a meeting with the lady herself in about an hour. Not sure if the SBI will be there, or if they're gonna make a run at Trick."

Alec nodded. "Max, are you and Bryan okay to stay with Trick? You're the only things the SBI really fears, plus you can certainly handle a few selkie if they come after him again. That works with your schedule, right Bryan? Your shift's not until nine, I think."

Bryan shook his head. "I'm off tonight."

"We were just going to blow up some seaweed or something in the backyard. Coffee's better here." Max smiled in a way that suggested it wasn't a joke. "Coffee's always a better idea."

"And, hopefully, less explosive," added Bryan. "Still, I think I'd better hit the head and shift, just in case."

Alec nodded. "Good plan."

Bryan was only really effective as Max's familiar when he was a wolf. Max could do some serious damage without Bryan's assist, but he was way more accurate and powerful with a were-wolf mate at his side.

Max pouted. "Aw, there goes all my scintillating conversation."

Everyone chuckled. Bryan gave the love of his life the finger. The only one of them less chatty than Bryan was Tank.

Poor Trick took it seriously, though, because he wasn't familiar with pack dynamics. "It's okay, Max, I'll talk to you when I'm not serving. Plus some of the regulars will be in after five. I know you're not friendly with the evening crew, but a few of them are real nice. You can make new friends. It'll be fun." He clapped his hands.

Max looked horrified. "Please don't bother. Seriously, Trick, *please* don't."

Colin went restless in Judd's lap.

"Yeah, Gingersnap? You got something to add?" Colin needed to be encouraged to contribute.

"Trick, do you know your Panda Rights?"

The otter shifter nodded.

Judd figured if Trick came from a crime family, P-Rights had been drilled into him since birth. The Inis family probably had some crooked lawyer on retainer.

Colin tensed, nervous but determined. Judd gave him silent support. "Good. 'Cause I told them Alec was your Alpha, so if the feds or the cops hound you, feel free to claim his protection and shift, okay?"

"Oh Colin, you didn't! What a nice lie! That's so sweet of you." Trick looked like he was about to launch himself over the coffee table to land in Judd's lap too and hug Colin.

Alec snorted. "Not exactly a lie, Trick. I told you you're ours now. I protect what's ours. I don't know how otters handle groups, but you're part of the San Andreas Pack as long as you need it. I'd be honored if you used me as your Alpha for the sake of protocol. We'll get you registered and make it all legal once this mess blows over." He showed his age by dipping his head and adding, "If you still want me for Alpha, of course."

Trick looked genuinely confused. As if he really couldn't understand anyone wanting to keep him around, or maybe he just didn't know what to do when an Alpha was nice to him.

Alec continued. "Kevin and Judd, you're already slated for the meeting with Blanc."

Judd nodded.

"Unfortunately," said Kevin.

"I think you should take Colin and Isaac with you."

"What!" barked Judd. He didn't want Colin exposed to that woman again.

Kevin seemed to feel similarly. "Surely Tank or, better, you and Isaac would be more appropriate?"

In his arms, Colin sagged.

Judd glared at Kevin. Now Colin thought his brother didn't want him around and didn't have faith in him as a pack mate.

And after Colin had been so brave today. Judd risked a tentative rub at the small of Colin's back.

Alec held up a hand. "This isn't a war, enforcer, think strategically."

There was a kind of white noise in Colin's ears. He sat up and leaned forward in Judd's lap. He focused on putting down his drink, because he was suddenly afraid that he'd spill it. His fingers felt numb.

Kevin didn't trust him.

Judd, reactive, put both hands to Colin's hips to keep him there, in his lap. For his own comfort or Colin's? Colin couldn't be certain. But either way it was… nice.

"I'm not leaving," he reassured the enforcer.

But I don't want to see her again, he wanted to cry to his Alpha. *I just got away from her. And now I have to go, not only because my Alpha asks it of me, but because I must prove I can, to my dumb brother.*

"Alpha, that's not fair." Judd's voice was a grumble of defense, enforcer challenge.

Alec shook his head. "That's why I'm sending Isaac as well. Tank's too submissive to be useful when there's no actual fighting involved. No offense, Tank."

The biggest wolf of their pack looked up from his station at the front. He was far enough away by human standards to make his reaction seem odd, but werewolves had supernatural hearing. "None taken," he rumbled back. They heard him just as easily.

"And why not you?" Judd was not backing down.

Alec shook his head. "If the SBI is still with her, that's way too many Alphas in one place. Even without Agent Lenis, if it's just me and Lexi Blanc, we won't share territory well. I can tell you that for certain. It would be better if I never met her face-to-face."

Colin had a revelation at that. Even though he'd never talked to Alec about what it had been like for him as a child, Kevin probably had. Before Kevin left for college, his eyes used to look at Colin with nothing but sibling affection mixed with elder brother annoyance. Afterwards, there was always guilt in Kevin's gaze. So, of course, Kevin would have talked to Alec about it. About what he feared. About how damaged Colin had become.

And Alec was Alpha. The Mangnall brothers were *his* pack. So if Alec had to confront their mother, knowing what she'd done to them? If Alec had to witness one moment of her behavior towards them? There'd be teeth and blood and mess. Because Alec was civilized and sweet, a young geeky biologist, but he was still Alpha. They were *his*, and she'd hurt them, and he couldn't breathe the same air as her under those circumstances.

But this was still a political situation, especially with the SBI around, Trick's safety on the line, and Heavy Lifting's reputation in play. So Alec, who fought smart all the way up until he couldn't anymore, refused to put himself in a position of having to muffle his instincts to protect – unless it was utterly necessary.

Colin realized he was staring at his Alpha, mouth open. "You *can't* go, can you?" Alec would try to kill his mother. Lexi Blanc would open her mouth and he'd just *hate* her too much.

Alec's smile was brief and pained. "Not yet. We need to know more, we need to know everything. But if necessary, I'll take her out of play. Right now, it's not necessary. I'm not necessary."

"I am," said Isaac.

Colin wanted to cry out that he himself wasn't necessary either. That he'd already done his part! Except that in figuring out why Alec couldn't go, he understood why he had to.

"With Isaac there, having both Kevin and me will help."

Isaac nodded. "You'll throw her off balance. She obviously wanted to keep you two separate. Otherwise, why approach you individually, and hire Kevin separately? We need all her sins thrown at her at once. I want to see how she is around you as brothers. Plus you're stronger together. You always have been. That's when it all went wrong, no?"

Kevin nodded. "When I left for college."

A small part of Colin suspected that Alec was sending him back, so that he, Colin, learned he *could* be strong in the face of his mother. "Okay, but Kevin I need to talk to you first. It's not pack business. I don't wanna do this in front of everybody."

Alec's hazel eyes were soft. "Whatever you need, Col, we're here for it, or not here, as the case may be."

"What about me?" wondered Trick.

"You stay working, like you have been doing. Tank, Max, and Bryan will keep you safe. Couldn't ask for better protection, I promise."

Colin said, "I'm sorry, Trick, it can't be easy for you. The SBI basically admitted they were using you as bait."

"So long as they don't have anything they can charge me with." Trick shrugged. "I really didn't *do* anything, I know that. I do feel better with Max here. I had no idea you were so deadly, Max-i-pooh."

Max-i-pooh? mouthed Kevin.

Judd huffed in amusement.

Colin tried not to grin.

Max didn't take offense. Instead, he waggled his eyebrows suggestively. "It's always the ones you least suspect."

Trick nodded enthusiastically. "I know, right? I mean, look at Colin there, so fierce. He totally came to my rescue."

"Oh, stop." Colin could feel himself blushing. He was the opposite of fierce. But he supposed that, to Trick in that moment with the selkie looming over him, Colin might have come off as a bit of a savior. It felt good, in retrospect. Like for the first time in his life he'd been a *real* werewolf. A contributing member of the pack. Of course, he'd also basically gotten them into this whole mess.

"You guys are kinda fabulous, you know that, right?" Trick glowed at them.

Alec hid a smile and then looked pointedly at his enforcers. "Well, what are you waiting for? You have a celebrity to guard. Wouldn't want to be late. And Judd, I'm tolerably certain you should be wearing socks when you meet the reigning queen of country music."

"Aw, Alpha. Do I have to?"

Alec rolled his eyes and waved them off.

With very little fuss, they made their way back to the pack house after that.

Colin wasn't quite sure what to do. He was about to go on a proper operation with Heavy Lifting, like he was important. He'd run com and tech for them in the past, but only remotely. He'd never gone to a client meeting. Even though this was only his mother, it seemed significant.

Kevin came to fetch him from his room. His brother was dressed in dark wash jeans and a clean black t-shirt – formal wear for Kevin Mangnall.

"What are you wearing, Col?"

"What I always wear, Pinky. Hoodie and jeans."

Kevin said something odd then, as if he had insight into Colin's true desires. As if he were his real brother, who shared confidences, who'd never left him behind. "I always thought you'd dress prettier when you grew up. Softer. I don't know. Up to you, of course."

"I don't own anything pretty," confessed Colin, which was intentional. For all he'd eyed the unicorn shirt and petted that cashmere sweater yesterday, he'd never let himself actually buy that kind of thing.

"You should go shopping with Marvin some time."

Colin frowned up at him. "Kev, you aren't trying to push me into some preconceived notion of *flaming*, are you?"

"No, I'm trying to push you into something I think will make you happy."

"Okay then." Colin dipped his head, face heating.

"Col?"

"Yeah, Kev?"

"I'm sorry I left you behind."

"It's okay." Colin felt a rush of something in his ears, clawing non-sound. He wasn't sure he wanted this. Not right now.

But Kevin had that set look on his face, the one that came before a game when they were kids, or before a hunt when they were wolves. "No, it isn't. I didn't really know what he was like. Or I did know, but I didn't realize how bad it would be for you without me. I realize that *not knowing* is hardly fair as an excuse, and not really worth anything. But there it is. I didn't know."

Colin needed to nip this in the bud. This wasn't their relationship. Guilt he was accustomed to deflecting, but he would *not* be an object of his brother's pity. "It's okay, Kev, really. You were perfectly right to go to college. That's normal."

"It wasn't right at the time, though. I'm your older brother. I was supposed to look after you. It can't be fixed now, but, well, there is it."

"No, it can't be fixed." Being firm hurt a little, but Colin couldn't bear the weight of his brother's emotions. He'd too many of his own to deal with. He tried to be a little more kind. "Please don't worry, Kev, I'll figure myself out."

"With Judd."

"I don't know that sex with a really hot guy is the solution to all my problems, but I aim to give it a try."

"Okay then. But I'll always worry. I'm your brother."

Colin wished Kev had worried a bit more in the past and a bit less now. But he had his own concerns and questions. "You don't mind? You know, me and Judd?"

"Why should I mind? Because Judd is my friend? Our enforcer pairing?"

"I don't want to be taking him away from you."

"He was never mine to begin with. Besides, I think he'll be good for you."

Colin decided he wouldn't bother to change clothes. If he was going in to meet a client as part of Heavy Lifting, he was acting the role of tech support. Being in a hoodie and jeans was practically required. No one expected much from the geek of a security team.

Kevin finally asked the real question, "What was it you needed to tell me?"

Colin faced his brother, ready to have it out.

Kevin was trying to be brave, trying not to hope for much from their mother, but Colin could smell the wishes on him.

Colin gave him what he could. "She knew you were fine, that you were a good werewolf, a good enforcer. She was proud of you, in her way."

"But she didn't *ask* about me, did she?"

"I'm sure she knew she'd be seeing you later."

Kevin dipped his head, swallowed, forced a smile. "Was that what you wanted to warn me about?"

"She doesn't really care about either of us, I don't think, Kev. I'm sorry."

Kevin nodded, hands clenching into fists at his side. "She cares, but as if we're lost pieces of art she once created. Like we were songs she wrote and gave to some other singer to perform. She cares because she thinks of us, when she thinks of us at all, as leftover parts of herself."

Colin would have replied that maybe she felt that way about Kevin, but she didn't think of Colin as anything but a mistake. But if it helped his brother in any way to believe that, Colin wasn't going to stop him.

"So long as you don't expect anything from her."

"I know better," Kevin said, and maybe he could even convince himself.

"Are you sure about that?" She'd had her claws deep into Kevin, before she left. She'd been shiny and special and wonderful, Alpha and mother. Certainly Kevin, who admired strength and women and glory, would have found her difficult to resist.

"I'm sure."

Colin met his brother's eyes, green like their mother's. Like his. "Okay then, let's do this thing."

CHAPTER NINE
COLD-HEARTED WOLF

Normally they would have met with Lexi Blanc and her team at the venue to do a walk-through. But the amphitheater was a beastly drive. It was atop a mountain in the middle of nature. Plus Heavy Lifting knew the layout well enough already. They'd run a couple of ops there in the past. So instead, they met with Blanc at her rented house in Mill Valley. Of course, she'd rented an *entire* house for the weekend. She couldn't possibly stay in a luxury hotel suite like an ordinary celebrity.

There was no bodyguard waiting for them, which was a mite disturbing. Judd assumed they'd been hired to augment her existing team, not to replace it. The place smelled like humans, plus the slight pong of *wrong* Alpha, plus mossy garden and damp redwood.

Blanc's stylist, Risa Ostrov, met them at the door. She ushered them inside, not even bothering to introduce herself. She was a short female of indeterminate age. Judd wasn't great on human ages until their hair started going gray or falling out. Risa's skin was artificially tan and artificially tight, sort of stretched back from a beaky nose, towards blonde hair cut in a sharp bob. She was like a human corn chip, the kind with the powdered cheese flavoring. She wore a very long dress, probably designer, the exact color of nacho cheese, which added to Judd's chip theory.

The house was an insane 1970s Nor Cal bachelor pad, built down the mountainside, full of fancy stairs and sunburst inlay. There was a sunken marble tub in the middle of the living room floor. Most everything else was glass – sculptures, vases, furniture.

Judd didn't really want to go inside the place. It was made for humans or cat shifters, something with a great deal more grace than werewolves. Risa led them through and over to some open sliding glass doors.

Lexi Blanc was relaxing with her team on a glass-enclosed patio that nested in the treetops. She looked even more like Colin in person than she had online. The major difference, aside from gender, was that Blanc tried too hard and Colin didn't try at all.

She was drinking a beverage but Judd couldn't smell what it was because the stench of human chemical fragrance dominated – perfume, body wash, and hairspray. It was hard to even smell that Blanc was werewolf at all, let alone Alpha. Judd wondered if that was a conscious choice, or just the life of a celebrity who catered to humans. It was disgusting.

She wore a vibrant blue blouse, matched cowboy boots, and a pair of incredibly tight white jeans. These had rips all the way down, as if she'd clawed at them in her wolf form. She didn't stand to greet them. In fact, she ignored them completely.

Judd took point. Kevin was in his sullen state, the one he sank into after bad breakups or losing at Fantasy Fangball. Colin lurked at the back, still in the living room. He looked like he was trying to sink into the floor. Judd could only hope he avoided the marble tub. Isaac was a reassuring presence at Judd's side, observing everything. Technically, the Omega outranked Judd and should lead the conversation, but Isaac rarely worked bodyguard duty with them, so Judd got to negotiate. If Blanc proved very difficult, the Omega would interject. Isaac was a bartender by training – he could coax people into opening up but didn't, as a rule, favor a direct approach.

Judd, on the other hand, defaulted to aggressive yet professional. It's what he was good at. "Good evening, Ms Blanc. I'm

Mr Day, this is Mr Mangnall, Mr Mercer, and Mr Mangnall. We're from Heavy Lifting. You hired us for extra security this weekend. Can we talk with your existing team?"

A breezy laugh met Judd's question.

"Did I say something funny, ma'am?"

"Don't be silly, Mr Day. *You* are my team. I dismissed my previous bodyguards days ago."

"You... *dismissed* them? Why is that, ma'am?"

She gave a contrived shrug. The silk of her top fell away to expose one creamy shoulder. "Things kept getting stolen and they couldn't seem to find out who was doing it. I figured it must be one of them."

"What kind of *things*?"

"Just little stuff, mostly. Like my favorite rhinestone sunglasses and the belt part of a costume. *Things* like that. Really only valuable to me and some creepy fan or whatever."

"So you think you might have a stalker?"

"No, idiot. I just *said*, I think it was one of my previous bodyguards. It hasn't happened again since I dismissed them. Honestly, I had hoped Xavier would send someone a bit smarter. Even Kevin must be smarter than you. And let's be fair, no one would ever call him the sharpest pickle in the jar. Why are you in charge?" She turned in her chair and looked Judd full on for the first time.

Colin's glorious eyes were staring at him out of a woman's face.

"Oh, well, you are a fine specimen." Her expression was eager, possessive, and Alpha. Judd wondered if she'd hired Heavy Lifting to see if she could steal the San Andreas enforcers to her pack. To guard her back and follow her lead. Bonus that one of them was her own son.

She licked her lips. "I suppose your Alpha's not good enough to understand muscles don't mean leadership ability. Still, you're certainly stunning."

Judd was insulted enough not to reply. Some fake-Southern white lady Alpha was sticking claws into him like it was her right? Like he was her personal appetizer? Hang the bloody contract. Alec would support him if he took her head off, right?

Isaac moved, fast. The Omega's hand was on Judd's arm. His gaze was firm on Judd's face. His back was to the Alpha.

"She's baiting you." He didn't try to lower his voice. "Don't let her."

Judd nodded. The roaring in his ears faded under Omega influence. But why? What tactical reason did Blanc have for winding him up? Was she trying to fissure them? Drive a wedge between Judd and her sons? Did she not realize whose side they fell on? Did she actually think she could still command Kevin's loyalty in any way?

Kevin was red-faced, sputtering. He was also dealing with seeing his mother for the first time in years.

Surprising everyone, Colin moved fast through the doorway onto the patio. "You're truly awful, Mother. I'm so glad you left before I had any idea what you were. You're nothing but a…" words seemed to fail him, probably because he didn't swear often so wasn't particularly good at it. "…*coprolite*!"

Everyone blinked at him. No one else knew what a *coprolite* was. Colin seemed pleased with it, though. So it must be pretty bad.

"Now, now." Blanc tossed a lock of hair back over her bare shoulder. "I thought we already had our little talk, baby-cakes. I am sadly not interested in anything you have to say. Now, is that my lovely Kevin? My, but didn't you grow up big and strong, and so much like your daddy. I sure hope you have a better temperament. That man could grump his way into next Sunday." She gave a musical chuckle.

Kevin looked at Judd. "We out?"

Judd nodded. "Oh, we are so out. Colin?"

Colin was the only one still looking at his mother. "Can I hurt her? I mean, I've never wanted to actually hurt someone before. Could I try? I'd give it my all, mauling her nose off or something. She doesn't need a nose, does she?"

Judd shook himself. He couldn't let Colin do anything. It

was sweet of the kid but Colin would only get injured. Lexi Blanc was a lot stronger than her son.

Blanc seemed to realize she was pushing things. "Ah ah ah, boys. Sugah, show them that contract. Heavy Lifting promised me two enforcer werewolves as bodyguards plus additional support, for all afternoon and evening tomorrow, plus the concert on Saturday. Did they not?"

Her, presumed, manager nodded. She was a rail-thin blonde with big hair, who fit in seamlessly with Blanc's other human pets. Judd suspected Blanc had selected her for vast talents in the arena of silent agreement.

Blanc continued. "I doubt you'll be able to find replacements who meet those specifications at short notice. You are, after all, the only pack in the Bay Area. Plus I have that nice Xavier's bond on your reliability. You wouldn't want to disappoint me *and* him, now, would you, boys? I'm quite sure that I have more money and more lawyers than you do."

Judd thought Max could probably take her one way or another in that regard, but they really did rely on Xavier's good will.

"Fine. But keep the personal comments to a minimum, lady," he said.

"Oooo, so fierce. Such impressive growling and rippling biceps. Risa, I want them all in nice tight t-shirts. Keep with my color theme. If they're to be in my entourage, they must match." She gestured at Isaac, Judd, and Kevin. "Well, those three need shirts − obviously they'll be doing the real work." She seemed not to realize that Isaac was an Omega. *The* Omega. Which was good.

She tilted her head, coy. "Why *did* you bring my *other* son?"

Colin wilted.

Judd didn't actually think it was possible to hate her more than he already did. "We're a full-service team, ma'am. That includes tech. Colin will be manning our ear-buds and when the time comes, he'll monitor the concert security feed. We brought him today because we thought we'd be talking tactics with your *actual* bodyguards. Not making small talk over drinkipoos."

He wrinkled his nose at the large bottle of bubbly on the coffee table. Disgusting stuff.

"Oh, how precious. He's your pocket geek." Another tinkling laugh.

"I think we need Max. He's the only one bitchy enough to go up against her." Isaac sounded almost in awe of Blanc's evil.

"Forget Max, let me eat her," replied Judd. He couldn't imagine Colin and Kevin growing up with this female. Much as he hated how alone Colin had been, and how neglected, at least he hadn't had to bathe regularly in this kind of poison.

Colin seemed to think the same thing. "With a nice Chianti? Man, I'm so glad you left us behind, *Mother*." He spat the last word at her. Reminding her he existed. That he was connected to her, whether she liked it or not.

Judd brought them back around to business. "Is there anything actually relevant that we should know? So that we can better protect you tomorrow and at the concert?"

"Isn't it *your* business to know that?" Blanc fluttered her fake eyelashes.

Judd tried a different tactic. "Will the SBI be there?"

"At the concert? I don't think so, but I'm not their keeper. Honestly, I don't know why they wanted me to help them talk to baby-cakes in the first place. He's so useless."

Colin gave a dry chuckle. "Dude, I have no idea why I ever gave you a second thought."

Blanc turned those achingly familiar green eyes on Colin. "Neither do I, sugah. I assure you, I never did give you a *first* thought."

Judd shook his head. "Wow. Okay. We'll enact standard protections, then. I assume you have an itinerary for us, at least?"

The angular manager passed him one.

"Also, I'd like a list of the items that were stolen." Judd pointed at Risa. "Can you draw that up for me?"

The woman gave him a tight-lipped nod.

Judd continued. "We already know the security and layout of the amphitheater. We've worked gigs there before. Anything unusual about your show – scenery, production elements, props? You do any aerial work, Ms Blanc? Anything dangerous or requiring outside experts? Fireworks? Any external contractors we'll need to vet?"

"It's all in the itinerary," replied the manager, taking a large gulp of her champagne.

Judd couldn't believe this. What a waste of time. "Fine, then. Anything else before we leave? Anything we need to know about tomorrow's activities, interviews, transportation?"

The manager only rolled her eyes.

Blanc turned her back on them. "I've seen enough. You'll do for while I'm here. You're dismissed. Risa, be a love and show them out."

Before Judd could say that they could find their own way out, the stylist stood. She hurried over to them.

"Don't mind her," Risa said as she held the front door open for them to leave. "She's always extra snappish before an event. She doesn't mean it."

"Oh, I think she does," replied Judd.

The door closed behind them and they bum-rushed the truck.

Normally, Judd would have at least swept the grounds. Even with the contract not starting until tomorrow, he would have felt honor-bound to protect a client who had no security of her own. But this time, he just followed everyone else into the king cab.

He drove away faster than was strictly safe.

"Oh my god. Guys, I'm so sorry." Colin from the back seat. "She's disgusting!"

Judd could practically feel Colin trembling with affront. "Sadly, I've experienced far worse in my lifetime. I suspect Isaac has too."

He could see Isaac shrug out of the corner of his eye. The Omega sat behind Kevin on the passenger side. "Most of my life was spent in a cult. So not quite the same. But even I can tell that that woman is truly vile."

"Was she that bad when we were kids?" Colin asked Kevin.

Kevin was slumped in the passenger seat. "This was *such* a bad idea." He buried his head in his hands.

Isaac sighed. "Perhaps you should be grateful to know how awful she is. She left, so you never had to deal with her again. It's an odd kind of closure, but it's *closure*, right?"

"Finally using that advanced psychology degree, are ya?" Kevin snapped back.

Isaac flinched. "I'm only trying to help, dude."

Kevin was instantly contrite. "Sorry. Argh! I'm really sorry, Omega. It's just... look... I really don't wanna be related to *that*."

Colin murmured from behind Judd. "At least you don't look exactly like her. Imagine how I feel."

"This is a mess!" Kevin clearly wanted to shift and run. Instead he was stuck in a moving vehicle.

Judd tried to deflect. "Isaac, assessment?"

Without Alec there to rein them in, Judd wasn't sure how to control the situation. His instinct was to lash out, to hit or to maim. Even now, when he was surrounded by pack, he wanted to hurt something. Someone. Lexi Blanc. So he leaned on the Omega.

Isaac's voice was confident. "Narcissist. Profound lack of empathy. But probably not an actual psychopath. Technically speaking, an Alpha like that should be put down. However, she's a loner. If she had a pack, they might stabilize her. Or she might turn demagogue. It all could be a side effect of celebrity status – being in the public eye all the time. However, being surrounded by human sycophants is probably a good thing. They have become her pack, and they obey her every whim. I bet she's horribly nice when the cameras are on. My official advice would be to limit her direct interpersonal exposure to most shifters. Humans are regrettably accustomed to her kind of personality. Her DURPS file probably has a note to that effect. The SBI could be in town monitoring her because she's unstable. Although that wouldn't explain their interest in Colin or Trick."

Judd agreed. He also thought it unlikely that Blanc herself was involved in criminal activities. She might even have made up the theft story for additional attention. "Right. Let's just get through this weekend and satisfy our contract. Once Heavy

Lifting isn't in play, Xavier can't get mad if anything happens to her."

"I think we should introduce her to Max," said Colin, snide.

"She thinks *she's* the queen of mean." Kevin perked up.

"Or Mana. Can you imagine?" The smile was in Isaac's voice.

There was a short, awed silence while they all pictured their tiny formidable drag queen kitsune friend going up against Lexi Blanc.

"Lives would be lost," whispered Colin.

"Whole continents," Isaac intoned, somber.

The mood lifted.

Whatever Blanc had intended by being so awful, the four of them remained steadfast. They'd bonded even more under the duress of her presence. Like having survived a battle. After so many packs, so easily fractured, this one was the gift Judd had always hoped for and never thought he'd get. Rather like Colin.

"Colin?"

"Yeah, Judd?" Colin leaned forward so Judd could feel his breath on the back of his neck. Judd shivered like a giddy teenager.

"What's a *coprolite*?"

Then the most wonderful thing happened. Colin started to laugh.

"Judd?" Colin pulled Judd aside and let the others get a head start through the yard to the pack house.

"Yeah, kid, you doing all right?"

"My mother's personality should come with one of those warning labels – side effects may include headaches, rashes, and murderous tendencies."

Colin was deflecting, of course, and he knew Judd could tell.

The enforcer smiled but also pressed. "And?"

"It was fine. She mostly ignored me. I know you find it

strange, and it's probably unhealthy, but I *like* being ignored. I find it reassuring."

"Man, I hope you never realize how much I noticed you, then."

Colin felt his cheeks warm. He dipped his head. "That's a nice thing to say. So I was wondering…" He faded off, losing words and courage.

"Out with it, Gingersnap."

"Would you maybe consider… Could we start the… lessons tonight?" His stomach boiled with fear but also with *want*.

"I still got patrol and you still got homework. And Alec is gonna want to talk to us. Make sure we're all doing all right. Especially you and Kevin. But then, yeah, I want you in my bed."

"You do?"

"Just to sleep, sweetheart."

"Oh." Had he changed his mind? Colin couldn't stop the disappointment in his voice. The boiling turned to all fear. A blurred throbbing took over his ears, like an alarm set to his heartbeat – rejection, rejection, rejection.

Judd turned him, tipped his chin up with two fingers. "Listen to me, Gingersnap. I want to rip that dumb sweatshirt off you. Show you everything all at once in the worst way. But it's too soon. I need you to be sure that you're ready for this. I need to know that you want it to be me. I think one way to do that is for you to sleep touching me. Get accustomed to close contact. Get me used to your scent, and my scent all over you. Also get you used to seeing a man like me as safe and yours to do with as you will. Okay? It is absolutely not that I don't want you. It's that I want this to be good for you. Right now we are both too stressed. Not to mention suffering the repercussions of country music bitch exposure."

Colin nodded, still disappointed but he supposed that made sense. "I understand. Should I wear pajamas?"

"There's no need to go that far." Judd sounded seriously offended. "The very idea that a werewolf would wear clothing when sleeping. Preposterous!"

Colin gave him a nudge. "Look at you with the big words."

"Brat."

"I prefer Gingersnap."

"Yeah, me too. You should study in my bed. I like the idea of finding you there when I get back from patrol."

Colin's pulse calmed. He warmed with pleasure at that simple statement. No one had ever wanted him around and in their space before. He adored the image of himself curled up with his books in Judd's room, Judd's scent all around him.

"You like that idea too?" There was a hesitancy to Judd's tone that made Colin eager to reassure him.

"I love it."

Wolf Judd returned to his room after a long run. Colin was curled up there. Colin in his private territory. He almost barked in joy. Possessive pleasure shivered over him – *his* mate in *his* room. The smell of them, together. Heaven. Although sweat and cum would make it better. The wolf side of Judd didn't care about waiting or finer feeling, he just wanted.

It had been a hard patrol. Kevin needed to run. Leave behind his mother and her cruel disregard. He'd faced up to sins. His sins. Hers. Ones that he'd not noticed before. Ones he could not control. They hurt him and yet he couldn't physically repair them. So Kevin ran to escape. Judd knew. Judd had done the same many times before – stretched muscles because his heart had stretched too far.

Judd had no parents. He wasn't one himself. The notion of motherhood was somewhat alien. Still, he knew that identity was caged by upbringing. Kevin faced a disconnect forged by time. Had Kevin romanticized his mother until this night? Or was he simply embarrassed by her behavior?

Either way, Kevin ran. Judd kept pace. A watchful eye upon him. Sometimes protectors safeguarded each other. Judd split his attention between Kevin's frantic form and possible enemy infiltration. Kevin was pack mate. Kevin was friend, but Judd was ever the enforcer. Worse, Judd was the only enforcer still functioning. Kevin was injured. Not visibly, but any wolf worth his nose could smell the distress.

They caught the SBI at the border of the headlands. A car carefully *not* in pack territory. The two agents had the windows up. Kevin snarled, fierce and angry. Fortunately, he had enough sense left to stay out of sight in the coyote bush. Judd approached the car, hackles up, ears perked, tail engaged, and teeth covered. Judd was grateful he couldn't smell them. In his heightened state of wariness, scenting Alpha Lenis might have caused him to challenge her. She was not the kind of Alpha to tolerate defiance. As it was, Judd sniffed at their black car. Then he ostentatiously peed on one of the tires.

As he trotted away, he heard Lenis swearing at him and Faste laughing heartily.

He coaxed Kevin back to running. They left the SBI to their own devices. Judd was pleased. The pack knew where they were. And it was bound to be uncomfortable, sitting in a car on stakeout for hours, the scent of another shifter's mark upon them. Judd liked that they suffered.

Kevin eventually returned to the pack house.

He shifted to report on the SBI sighting to Alec. He also spoke briefly about the meeting with Lexi Blanc. Judd stayed a wolf. He wanted to keep things short, save the bulk of the human-talk for tomorrow. Judd longed to leave, to see Colin in his room. But also worried for Kevin.

Alec understood Judd's dilemma. Of course he did. "Go on upstairs, Judd. Thanks for taking point today. Kevin, come here."

He opened his arms so the big redhead could rush into them, bury his face in his Alpha's neck, and breathe him in. Alec, smaller and slighter, didn't buckle under the man's substantial weight or unfettered emotions.

Judd could only guard his friend. Alec could support him. They were lucky – *Judd* was lucky – to have such an Alpha.

Judd felt it all right to leave Kevin then, and bounded upstairs. Beyond eager.

There Colin was. Looking up from some textbook. Smiling

huge at seeing Judd still a big black wolf. He looked small but perfect in Judd's big bed.

"I love your shifted eyes." Colin patted the comforter.

Judd jumped up next to him. Responded to the praise by looking up out of bright yellow eyes. He thought they were creepy. Fierce. But his mate liked them. His mate could look as long as he wished.

Colin tugged gently on Judd's ears, stroked his furry cheeks. "I'll tell you a secret. I like them because I think they're almost the same color as my hair. Yellow with a bit of orange. Like we match just a little." His hands dug into the thick ruff at Judd's neck. "You're such a big wolf, so much more impressive than me."

Judd shifted then. His bones reformed into human limbs. His fur retreated to become the tight short curls on his chest, and head, and groin. Paws grew into big hands, claws shrank into short nails. His eyes went from dark yellow to dark brown.

When Colin would have stopped touching him, Judd said, "I like the petting, please keep going." And he felt like he'd won a prize when Colin continued.

Judd closed his eyes and lay across the bottom of the bed, as if he were still a wolf. His head was near Colin's crossed legs. Judd was naked so he curled in such a way as to show as little aggression as possible.

"You're not afraid of my wolf's size?" Judd asked.

"No. Not in either form. Both wolf Judd and man Judd are impressive, but I never once thought you'd hurt me. Of course, I never thought you'd see me as anything more than pack duty, either."

Judd closed his eyes "First lesson, Gingersnap. Anything we do together is because we *both* want it. We *both* think we'll enjoy it. Please never think that I'm with you out of obligation. If I saw you in a club I'd pick you up. I could show you my favorite porn. You'd see you're exactly my type. Okay? I held off until now because you're too young and I'm too jaded." And because he wanted to keep Colin forever. Judd reminded himself to keep things light. Anything too deep and his mate would run scared.

Colin cupped Judd's cheek, then slid his hand down as if he were memorizing the contours of Judd's face with those graceful fingertips.

"I love your hands. I love them on me." Judd admitted, keeping his eyes closed.

Those hands fluttered as if unsure of the compliment. "I don't like… They're very feminine."

"They're graceful and perfect and yours. Say *thank you*. Take a compliment."

"Okay. Thank you."

Silence descended.

Colin continued to stroke Judd. He ran one fingertip over Judd's eyebrows. He smoothed one hand around the side of Judd's head. Judd kept his hair short. Not that it grew much, not on a werewolf. Colin seemed to like that. Those fine fingers appreciating the shape of Judd's skull. It was very symmetrical. Judd preened and dozed.

He idly wondered if Colin was back to reading his assignment, or if he watched Judd while he petted him. Judd was afraid to open his eyes, in case that caused his mate to stop. In case Colin saw the real wanting of his heart under the desire in his body. So Judd lay still, hardly dared breathe, let himself drift on touch.

Judd had been made wolf during a time and in a place when touch was sacrosanct. It was touch that kept him trying with each new pack. That glorious feeling of fur and fur, skin and skin. Not sexual, just togetherness. He'd ended up leaving because of personality or power struggles, racism or homophobia. But he was always driven to seek another pack before too long, because of touch. How Colin had gone so long without it, flinching from contact, was a mystery to Judd.

So just this, Colin's hands on his face, was more centering than a thousand runs, or a million deep conversations.

"I love being petted," he said to Colin. *Especially by those amazing hands*, he added in his own head. Clearly his mate didn't do well with compliments. But praise for an action he'd undertaken seemed to work okay. Judd would have to remember that when they were fucking.

"You love being doted upon, like a big ol' cat." Colin's voice was pleased. He ran the backs of two fingers down the side of Judd's neck.

Judd did wonder sometimes what it would be like to be some other shifter. Not a werewolf but a supernatural creature more connected to his heritage, like one of the big cats. What would he have smelled like? Looked like? Many of the African shifters were lions or leopards.

Judd guessed his parents had been slaves in England. Least-ways, he assumed that's how they got there. They were dead before he was old enough to know to miss them. He'd been gutter-raised and rough-hewn but *free*. He'd turned street smarts into spying for the werewolves when he was still a child. Some high-up political type had recruited Phineas. And Phineas knew all the ways that *young* and *poor* and *Black* went unnoticed in the London slums. Turned out, the things that made Judd hungry and desperate also made him useful. Judd hadn't minded work that fed *and* entertained. Hadn't minded Phineas's mentoring, either. In fact, he'd enjoyed it. So when Phineas decided to join a pack in the north, Judd followed. There he learned about touch and safety and friendship. So when a loud brash Scottish Alpha with a propensity for small dogs and slim cigars offered him the bite, Judd took it. Turned out his werecat genetics stood him in good stead to become a werewolf. It happened like that, back before they knew anything about the triple helix and the activa-tion chromosomes.

Judd let himself rumble in contentment under his mate's touch. A kind of nostalgic purr for what could never be. "It's likely I was meant for leopards, if my shifter genes came from my dad's line. Lion if they came from my mom. Could even have been both. Better chances of bite survival if I got it both sides. And obviously, I survived."

"You weren't tested before you chanced metamorphosis?"

Judd chuffed in surprise. "How old do you think I am?"

Colin stopped stroking him.

Judd opened his eyes.

His Gingersnap wasn't reading. He'd put his books off to one side. He was, in fact, staring at Judd and blushing furiously.

Judd rescued him. "No concept of genetics when I was bitten, Gingersnap. Not that I knew of, anyway. Back then they believed surviving a supernatural bite had to do with souls and creativity."

Colin's pretty eyes went wide. "But that means you're—"

"Yeah, Pre-Saturation."

Colin's luscious mouth parted in wonder. "How old were you when the world burned?"

"Over fifty. About a decade as a shifter, some of that with my first pack in Scotland. They didn't suit when all was saved and settled. After Saturation we were twitchy in our skins, scared of new power and new limits. Living with *quintessence* all around us, all of a sudden like that – made some of us sick and some of us crazy. The rest of us just had to muddle through. Also, that was before packs knew about enforcers."

"Knew what?" Colin hadn't resumed petting.

Judd sighed and sat up. "Gammas, they called us. I know, these days the term is thrown around for all sorts of ranks and all kinds of shifters. Back then, gamma is what they called a were-wolf enforcer. And they thought there could be only one gamma per pack."

"But that's ridiculous! Everyone knows…"

"Enforcers are the strong arms of the pack, yeah. Right arm, left arm, we come in pairs. Seems stupid, now, but before Saturation no one knew. So when it became clear I was gamma and there was already one in the pack, plus the world being on fire, I was booted. I didn't trust myself for a while after that. Instinct said they needed both of us. Tradition said they didn't. Took me a long time to believe in my wolf again. Then it took a long time to get over being suspicious of tradition."

"You mean you're not, anymore?" Colin's tone was ironic.

Judd tilted his head. Fair shot. He *was* trying, yet he still devalued things done for the sake of having always done them.

"You ever wish it were different? That you'd been a werecat instead of a werewolf?" Colin asked.

Judd struggled to explain the philosophy that a very long life had given him. "I like where I ended up. Here. Now. It's a good place with good people and a great pack. Because of where I've been, I *know* how lucky I am. I'd not feel as contented now if I hadn't followed that path. How I lived, where I started, my own history. It got me here. So I'm good." *Better for you,* he almost added. Better for sitting close to one shiny copper man who needed love and care almost as much as Judd needed to give it.

But Judd's age had given him that too – recognition. Knowing that they would suit, even young and old. His wolf side considered Colin entirely his *mate.* And Judd was so old, his human side was more melded to his wolf than most. The opposite of dementia. Very few shifters were so much at peace with both sides of themselves that they let the wolf breathe behind the human. Although, in enforcers, the wolf always lurked closer to the surface.

But Judd's age had also given him the patience not to push. Colin needed to lose some of his new-penny shine. Not that he needed to be diminished, just grow into understanding.

"And then you were a loner?"

"On and off. Hard to fit in. A man like me in this new world."

"A man like you? Werewolf? Enforcer?"

God, the kid was so young. "Black, Gingersnap. Black. Not to mention gay. Did a lot of guide work up in Canada, hunting and tracking. It's quiet up there. Or it was. Ran with a couple of decent packs, but those that were okay with my skin color weren't okay with my liking dick. Also, it took a long time for everyone to figure out that one gamma should be two enforcers. That my instincts were right. So I made myself packs of humans, sometimes other shifters. It helped to weather the loneliness, but it's not the same. I've been waiting for this pack, seems like all my life. Almost got tired of waiting, a time or two."

"I'm lucky, huh?" Colin's voice was all wonder. "I get to

have this sense of belonging right away. This is only my second pack."

Good that his mate could realize that. "Sure are. And I know you had it rough in your last one. I'm not diminishing that. But it's fine to let go of that experience. Enjoy what we're building here."

Colin nodded but didn't look convinced.

Judd smiled. "I get it. That is, after all, the hardest thing in the world."

"What is?"

"Feeling safe."

"I feel safe right now, with you."

Gingersnap was going to be the death of him. Judd wanted to pounce at such words. Work him over with sex and love and confidence. Show him how right he was to gift Judd with his trust. But that was the enforcer burning in him, the wolf. That was action and physicality and getting lost in passion. Judd needed to guard against that part of his nature or he'd scare Colin away.

"Second lesson, Gingersnap. I know it's not your thing, but I *always* want you touching me – petting, leaning, grabbing, riding, humping. Any or all of that. Your hands on me are about the best part of any day. I only just started getting them and already I want more. All the time. Anytime you like."

Colin dipped his head, smiled. Put his hands back on Judd. This time he reached forward to stroke Judd's bicep. Judd was leaning on his elbows to look up at Colin.

"I want those hands around my cock. I want those long graceful fingers of yours opening me up."

"Oh. Fuck. The things you say." Colin was lobster red.

"Would you like that, baby? Your strong lily-white hands on my hips gripping and digging in as you fuck me?"

"Judd." Colin's voice was a low, shaken hiss. "You're so much more than I should get to have."

Judd decided not to unpack that. Decided instead to roll over, expose his belly – offer seductive vulnerability. Show Colin that he was turned on, eager.

Colin gave a little gasp. "I thought you said…"

"Not tonight, yeah? But see, it doesn't mean I don't *want* to. Doesn't mean I won't talk dirty. Doesn't mean we can't talk, share what we like. What you want to try."

"With you? I want to try everything."

Judd let his head drop back. Looked at his mate upside-down.

Colin licked his lips, his eyes avid on Judd's groin. Made Judd wonder if Colin had eyed his ass while he'd been curled the other direction. His Gingersnap seemed to like his ass a whole lot. He hoped that was a sign Colin really did want to fuck him.

"I'd say you could explore further. But your hands all over me right now would be too much."

Colin was clearly turned on but also overwhelmed and terrified. He let out a long, shaky breath. "That's nice to know. But you said you wanted to wait and I'm gonna respect your boundaries. Even though you're a tease. I'm not sure how I'm gonna get to sleep." He moved to his knees and pushed up, gesturing down so Judd could see the large bulge that pressed against his loose sweatpants.

Judd chuckled. "What a pair we are."

"Tomorrow, the real lessons start?"

"You've had some already."

"You know what I mean. Tomorrow, you promise?"

"I promise. Now let's brush our teeth and climb under the covers. Even if we can't sleep, it'll be nice to cuddle. You can pet me some more."

"Oh I *can*, can I? Seems you get more out of it than I do."

"You love it."

Colin climbed out of bed, made his way out into the hall towards the bathroom. "I really do."

CHAPTER TEN

I'M SO LONESOME I COULD HOWL

Colin awoke to the warm joy of being held. He awoke to touch down the length of his body, something he'd never had before. He didn't flinch away but he did come awake with his heart stress-beating, terrified by need. The smell of want and *other* overwhelmed him. His own lust and desperate desire transformed instantly into a terrifying red flashing behind his eyelids. *Need, fear, need, fear* like a heartbeat, like the throbbing in his cock.

He thought he might hyperventilate.

And he really had to pee.

Grateful for the excuse, he threw himself out of Judd's bed and dashed to the bathroom down the hall. After washing his hands, he leaned hard on the sink, stared at his scared white face in the mirror. Tried to hate himself only a little for what he knew he'd do next – leave Judd to wake up alone.

Walking back, he paused at the door of his own bedroom. He let himself look longingly down the hallway towards Judd's room. For some reason, in that moment, a part of him wanted desperately to change into a wolf. Him! The shifter who rarely shifted. He supposed choices were simpler in that shape.

Marvin emerged from the master suite at the far end of the hallway, fully dressed. Or as fully dressed as Marvin got. He wore a wide-necked pink shirt, raspberry yoga pants, and fuzzy socks.

That decided Colin. He couldn't possibly walk to Judd's room with Marvin watching him do it. Marvin, who was gorgeous and confident. With a nod to acknowledge the Alphamate, Colin opened the door to his own room.

"Where do you think you're going?" hissed the merman, jogging down the hallway to him.

For a skinny dude, he was awfully heavy on his feet. Colin supposed that had to do with the fact that his other form was all fins and big shiny tail.

"To my room," Colin explained, obviously.

"You can't leave his bed before he wakes up. That's just rude!"

"You knew I was in there?"

Marvin gave his naked form an arch look. "Sweetie, everyone knows. Nobody cares. Now go back. Don't be an idiot."

"But I'm not…"

"Whatever you're going to say is stupid. Don't be stupid."

Merfolk were funny about love. They were predominately female and their pods were matriarchal and matrilineal. Their shifter gene passed from mother to daughter. Mermaids chose land shifters or humans to breed with and rarely mated for any length of time. Mermen, when they happened at all, were often gay and always sterile. Marvin once implied that most mermen were seen as decorative accessories or pets by their pod, useful mainly as spies, sent out to infiltrate land-bound creatures. Before Super Saturation, mermen attended human schools, and led human lives. Even in the modern age, mermen usually chose land – forming relationships, friendly or romantic, outside of their species. Marvin was on speaking terms with his former pod, which currently made its home in the San Francisco Bay, but that was about it. He'd always known he would leave his family. And he'd always known he would do it for love.

Alec said that Marvin had swept him up like a tidal wave. Insisting that they be together. It had been as close to love at first sight as mates could get, except for the fact that they'd known each other in high school. Marvin had courted his Alpha wolf with cans of sardines and aggressive flirtation. He still looked at Alec as if the Alpha hung the moon – an expression that had serious meaning for werewolves. Alec, of course, utterly adored him.

"You don't understand," Colin protested. *How can bold, charming Marvin understand anything?*

Marvin's pale brows pulled into a fierce frown. "I don't need to understand, I *know*. I *know* that man adores you and he's waited for you a very long time. I *know* that you slept in his bed last night and now you're abandoning him. I *know* he'll doubt himself and your interest. And I *know* everyone will believe that you care more about what others think of you than his feelings. I *know* that your mind right now is muddled, but your actions are all that matter."

"Oh," said Colin.

"Exactly," replied Marvin, crossing his arms over his slim chest – bangles on his wrist, boiling accusation in his changeable blue eyes. "You listen to your Alpha-mate. I may not know packs but I'm really good at affection. It won't hurt anyone, including you, if you go right back in there and climb into that big warm bed with that hot-as-fuck man. And I also *know* that you really, really want to do that, anyway."

Colin really, really did.

Marvin hugged him then. Colin started to flinch and then remembered he liked Marvin, and maybe he liked hugs from his pack too. Just when he was getting used to it, Marvin pulled away, grabbed him by the shoulders, turned him, and frog-marched him back down the hallway. Colin let him. He could have resisted. He may be the weakest of werewolves but he was stronger than a mere merman!

Marvin pushed him into Judd's room and closed the door behind him with a firm click.

Judd's room.

Colin didn't really belong. He felt the panic rise again. He reminded himself that it was only temporary. He reminded himself how nice it had been to pet Judd last night. How the enforcer had relaxed under him. How he'd looked, like a carved basalt statue of an ancient god, smooth and perfect. Judd had liked it. Liked Colin. Liked what Colin did to him.

Colin made his way over and stood for a long moment, staring down at Judd.

The enforcer had mostly kicked off the covers, which were now tangled around his feet. Colin hadn't been cold without them, because Judd had slept all night wrapped around him. Of course Judd was a cuddler. He'd admitted to it openly, almost proud of his need for skin-to-skin contact. Enforcers were physical creatures, quick to anger and quick to passion, often preferring to communicate with body language. Sometimes people said enforcers had more wolf in them. Of course, Judd would want to sleep using Colin as his own personal pack mate bolster pillow – guard, protect, possess. My pillow. My Colin.

Colin reached out a hand – startled by his own need to touch. Startled by the white of it against Judd's skin. A dead fish of a *thing* – spoiling Judd's beauty.

He jerked away.

Judd had said things about Colin's hands. He'd said he dreamed of them. Colin hadn't really believed him, thought maybe the man was just trying to make him feel confident and secure.

But then Judd kept saying it. Last night, he'd said he liked Colin's hands *on* him – petting him as man or wolf. Then he'd suggested precious dirty things. Things Colin very much wanted to do. Yet all of Judd's fantasies had featured Colin's hands. Which was kind of amazing, since Colin had spent most of his life hating them. Weird thing to hate about himself, but there it was.

Colin stood at the edge of the bed of a man he wanted more than anything and stared at his own hands – feeling stunted and foolish. Long tapered fingers, thin and pale, strong because he was a werewolf but not seeming strong. They were skeletal, too big for his frame but also delicate, as if they were meant for someone else, an artist or a piano player.

When he was a kid, he'd talked with his hands. Fluttered them about – a visual refrain to accompany his words – bright with childish excitement. He'd found his hands better at expressing his feelings than his voice. Until he noticed the cringing disgust in his father's eyes. Then he quieted his hands, his voice, and any indication of excitement. Not sure at the time which it was. He'd learned, later, that it was the hands.

Too effeminate. Too gay.

At meals with his dad and his brother, he would sit on them to stop them moving. There was a time when he mostly didn't eat because of it, until the rest of him became as skinny and as skeletal as his fingers. Kevin, horrified, started taking him for burgers after school. Spending his hard-earned cash from a shitty construction job, to make sure his baby brother didn't have an eating disorder.

Colin explained that he just didn't like the food at home. Really, he just didn't like his hands. His brother worried so much that Colin learned to keep them still enough to lift forks and speak words without grace or flourish. When he spoke at all. So the look in his father's eyes went from disgust to indifference. And stayed that way for a very long time.

So now when Judd said he loved Colin's hands, Colin didn't know what to do with that information.

He sipped a breath and put two fingertips carefully on the perfect curve of Judd's hip. Resting there, his hands weren't fish-like, not really, more fossil or bone, the antlers of a stag, bleached white by time and seasons. Ancient like Judd. He'd no idea Judd was that old. Not just Pre-Saturation but born decades earlier. He must be almost a hundred and fifty.

He certainly didn't look it.

Judd's skin was impossibly smooth, worn by time into comfort, like a beloved cotton t-shirt. Colin stroked over Judd's ribs up to his neck, back down, sternum and chest. He raised his own hand to his face, smelled Judd on his skin.

Lucky hand.

He sat on the edge of the bed, scooted closer, used both hands to pet. Because Judd had said it was okay. And he was so big and warm and easily treasured. Like Colin's favorite over-sized hoodie. A comparison Judd probably wouldn't appreciate, except for the way they both made Colin want to revel in them.

Judd awoke sharp and quick, like most hunters. He relaxed instantly once he realized it was Colin touching him. His dark eyes filled with heat, yellow spiking in from the edges. He licked his lips, parted slightly and tempting.

Colin trailed one hand over those lips, felt Judd smile. A pink tongue poked out, then retreated. Judd opened his mouth more. Colin chanced a finger, allowed it to be caught between sharp white teeth.

They paused like prey and predator in a tableau.

Judd let him go. "Good morning, Gingersnap."

Colin could feel himself blush, but he didn't stop petting because Judd had said that he wanted Colin to touch him all the time, anytime. Judd had *said* that was what he liked about packs – touch, and presumably it was what he liked about having a lover. Colin wanted to be a good lover for this man, the best. And he really did enjoy touching him. He was surprised by all of this because he'd assumed reaching out to another would seem needy. He hated drawing attention to himself. Worse, to come off as desperate. But having been told that Judd needed it, needed him, made it all okay. Because now Colin wasn't asking, he was giving.

"It's tomorrow." Colin's voice shook a little. He wished he could be sassy like Marvin or forward and flirty like Trick. Instead he was all shyness and longing.

"It sure is."

"You promised." *Ugh, how is it possible for anyone to be so un-coy?*

"I sure did."

"Lesson three?" suggested Colin, hopefully.

"You keeping count?"

"I sure am." Colin imitated Judd's tone, trying for lightness. Finding some success, apparently, because Judd emitted a low rumble of amusement.

"Good. So, how do you feel about morning hand jobs?" the big man suggested.

"Very much in favor. But not sure if I'm any good."

"You know how to get yourself off, right? Come here. Lie close to me."

Colin flopped over to his side, scooted away from the edge of the bed. Judd didn't scoop him close, allowing space between them. Colin felt rejected for a moment, until it became clear Judd wanted room to look at Colin's body while he touched him.

Then it was Judd's turn.

Quietly murmuring, he explained what he was doing and why. Because this was in the interest of a good education, after all. He asked permission as he went. "Can I tweak your nipples?" He explained his actions. "Some men are sensitive here. You?" He asked for advice. "Show me how you touch yourself, Gingersnap."

Colin acquiesced, blushing and hugely embarrassed, but so turned on.

Judd put a hand around his own cock, demonstrating what kind of grip he liked. How he twisted over the head.

"May I try?" Colin asked, too caught up in arousal to allow fear to stop him.

Judd, clearly pleased, lay back. His cock was larger and thicker than Colin's own, but not by much. Colin thought it was lovely, perfectly proportionate to his body, so thick and dark when hard. Colin's own equipment was a little outsized to his form. It flushed a rosy red color that entirely clashed with his orange pubic hair. But Judd seemed to find it enjoyable enough, if his attention was anything to go by.

Then Judd's hands were on Colin and Colin lost focus for a while.

Judd's fingers were large and rough, but not too rough – sure and confident. He whispered more questions into Colin's ear, holding him closer now. "Like this, or this? Slower or faster?" A quiz where all Colin had to do was pick an option. No wrong answers. "Keep going, or would you like a change of grip?"

Until Colin lost any hope of intelligent speech and was reduced to whines and moans and *pleases* and *mores* – just *more*.

He came in a red haze of pleasure so intense it was almost pain. It reminded him of the terror he'd woken up with – overwhelming, pulsing. But this was *need, joy, need, joy* instead.

Judd finished him thoroughly, squeezing out every drop. Even though he was too sensitive now, Colin wanted Judd to stay touching him so badly, he bit his lip on the whimper of pain. The crescendo of his heartbeat in his ear was all *stay, stay, stay* and *mate, mate, mate*. It overwhelmed Colin with fear and confusion, because he didn't know if that was what he wanted from Judd or if that was what he was giving him. Or both.

Judd noticed something was amiss and kissed him long and deep, an epilogue to orgasm. Then Judd raised his own hand, covered in Colin's cum, breathed it in, licked it clean. It made Colin shudder, spent cock trying valiantly to rise again.

Colin wanted to give Judd *everything* back. He wanted to smell Judd's cum on his own hands, see Judd fall apart in joy and need, taste him.

"Tell me what to do. What do you like?"

Judd made an approving sound and lay back, putting both of his sticky hands behind his head.

Then he talked Colin through it all. A deep confident voice – occasionally fractured, occasionally cracking with desire – instructing him on exactly how to touch. Colin did as he was told until he realized it was all happening in reverse now.

Judd was writhing under him – hips arching up, muscles glistening and strained. Judd had lost his words, and was making desperate keening noises. His canines were showing. His eyes were completely yellow with need. And it was Colin's *hands*, sure and dauntless, that were causing it all.

His dumb, stupid, ugly, *gay gay gay* hands were on Judd's amazing body – stroking that glorious cock, cupping heavy tightly drawn balls, caressing Judd's ass when he arched up, petting down his thighs when he pressed back. Colin was making *Judd* happy with his hands.

He was doing this.

He was.

Judd broke beneath him, spread open, spurting long white streaks against his dark skin. Without a thought, Colin bent and lapped it up, tasting the brine of a land-bound species, the liquor of the bitter earth. Tasting Judd.

Remembering his own sensitivity after coming, Colin stopped, cradled Judd's cock. Colin was ridiculously pleased with it for having given up itself to his ministrations – having rewarded Colin for newly learned skills with the best kind of praise.

Judd was supine and melted below him, eyes heavy-lidded, bright, and wary – but so pleased.

Colin's gaze drifted down, saw the glistening wet that his own tongue had left behind on Judd's stomach. He stared at his white hands cupping Judd's spent cock. Hands that had just given so much pleasure. And he realized that maybe they were, in fact, just a little bit beautiful.

CHAPTER ELEVEN
LIVE LIKE YOU WERE UNDEAD

Before their meeting with Blanc, Judd reviewed the itinerary with care. Then he organized the team to check in on Trick. He wanted to make sure the dratsie knew the SBI had been spotted near pack lands. He also wanted to gauge Trick's reaction to that information.

In the café, Judd kept Colin close, not ready to let his mate out of touching distance. It was too soon. He had a wolf's need to mingle their scents.

Colin didn't seem to mind.

They made quite a stir, trooping into Bean There, Froth That early in the afternoon. Judd bumped fists with Tank, who was sitting at Colin's table keeping an eye on the door.

Judd explained to Trick that Tank would remain on guard until he needed to leave for his bouncer duties. At which point, Bryan would relieve him. Trick was pathetically grateful to have a rotating werewolf in residence.

"Oh, darlings! You are all such peaches. Uh, pile of peaches? Peach trees? So much muscled peachy strong heroic goodness for little old me. Thank you." He came out from behind the counter to chat.

"Tank is here for you no matter who shows up, SBI or selkie," Judd reassured Trick.

"Though I'm no good against Alphas." Tank's rumble was

embarrassed. "The SBI can take me. Sorry, Trick." It obviously cost him to admit that.

Isaac bent and wrapped long arms around his mountain of a lover from behind. Held him hard and firm, dug his nails slightly into Tank's arms. It was their way. Pain and dominance grounded Tank. Judd understood, even if it wasn't his thing.

In reaction, Judd touched Colin. Back of wrist, to back of wrist. He was absurdly delighted when, instead of flinching, his Gingersnap looked up at him with a small smile.

Trick didn't seem disappointed in Tank. "But if the blubber bozos return, you're golden?"

Tank smiled. Nodded.

"It's just the feds you can't really handle?"

Judd didn't like how scared the dratsie was of the SBI. Agents Faste and Lenis were a pain, sure, but they weren't *bad*. That Trick feared them made Judd suspicious. Was the dratsie guilty? Was he in on it? Were the selkie onto something?

Then again, if Trick was from a crime family, he'd be raised to fear the authorities. Was this a manifestation of childhood trauma?

Judd went with the safest option. "Agent Faste is a bear shifter. So is Deputy Kettil, for that matter. Even if there weren't Alphas involved, no single wolf can take down a bear. Not even one of Tank's size. So just stay out of trouble, okay, little dratsie?"

Trick firmed up his small frame, flicked long lashes at Judd. Not fake today, but certainly augmented somehow. He'd done his eyes all big and dark, his lips faintly pink and glittering. Judd thought Colin would look hot with makeup like that.

"I won't betray you, enforcer. I promise." It wasn't quite what Judd was after, but dratsie were tricky beasties.

Kevin added, "If you really haven't done anything, the SBI should be fine. That said, unregistered, you don't have legal standing in this area. They don't need justifiable cause to take you in for questioning."

Trick nodded, looking very scared now.

Judd exchanged a look with Tank.

Tank nodded.

Judd said, "Tank will try to get you back to the pack house, preferably *inside* it rather than fight the SBI. Max is your only guarantee of protection. So if they even enter the café, he shifts. You ride him and you run. Got it?"

"But who will take care of the coffee? My customers!" Trick twirled about, arms expansive.

Judd caught him before he could trip over a bag full of yarn on the ground near an elderly human male with a perpetual frown. Judd remembered the human from that first night with the selkie.

The man picked up his bag and hung it over the back of his chair. Gave Trick a tut of disapproval.

"Sorry, Floyd." Trick righted himself and calmed down.

"You'll have to call someone to cover once you get to the den." Judd couldn't give a toss about Bean There, Froth That.

Kevin agreed. "Presumably, there's a boss or an owner of some kind? Guess they'll have to work for a change." Kevin's tone suggested his disgust that Trick seemed to run the café singlehandedly.

Elderly human knitter spoke then, as if he'd been part of the conversation all along. "He's an asshole, though."

Trick looked at him, big-eyed and confused. "Then why do you come here, Floyd?"

"You make a mean cappuccino, pretty boy. Best barista this side of the Bay."

Trick put a hand to his chest. "La sir, you're too kind!"

"The muffins are really good too. Firm yet fluffy."

"Well, there you go, I am the firm-yet-fluffy muffin-man!" Trick wriggled his eyebrows. Grinned at the grumpy human.

Floyd resumed his needle-clicking without further comment. Presumably, he also resumed his eavesdropping. Judd decided not to care. The human seemed disinclined to interfere.

Trick returned to Judd. "I could get fired for leaving the café untended."

"Which is worse – fired, dead, or imprisoned?"

Trick rolled his eyes. "Well, when you put it like *that*."

Isaac added, "We can find you another job, Trick."

"But I really *like* it here."

Judd waved a hand. "Enough. We have a country music star to shepherd around. You'll do as you're told, dratsie."

"Yes, sir!" To Colin, Trick hissed. "Is he always this forceful?"

"Enforcer."

"All the time? Everywhere?"

Colin gave Judd a hesitant glance.

Judd pretended good-humored exasperation with the conversation. Secretly, he was delighted that Trick thought Colin was his. The rest of the pack no doubt smelled them mingled, but the otter shifter would have to guess from body language. Clearly he'd concluded that Colin and Judd were a pair. That made Judd's heart swell with pride.

"I would say *persuasive*," admitted Colin.

Trick fanned himself. "Hooooootttt."

"Dratsie," grumbled Judd, hiding his amusement. He really hoped this one wasn't going to betray them. It would be really fun to keep Trick around. Plus, Colin so rarely relaxed around anyone the way he did around Trick. He'd just admitted to a relationship, in public. Judd couldn't help but be delighted with both his Gingersnap and the pack's dratsie.

Still Trick *was* an otter. Judd had to make certain his instructions were clear. "Tank, you grab him, and you run. Even if he objects. Got it?"

"Ooh, like a recalcitrant princess!" Trick squealed. "You don't mind?" He looked at Isaac.

Isaac grinned. "You get on with your bad self and your favorite fantasies. Tank knows who he belongs to."

Trick seemed a bit startled by that statement. "Really? Wow, okay, cool. Sooo... yeah?" Clearly the idea that enormous Tank belonged in all ways to their pack Omega was a revelation. "Huh. So many rainbows to sparkle under, aren't there?"

Tank only nodded. He, at least, remained serious and focused on the task at hand.

So Judd gave Tank additional encouragement. "You'll be

fine. If anything goes south, you text Alec. Then you call Deputy Kettil. In that order."

"Yes, enforcer."

"Right. We've put it off long enough. Time to face the music."

"Literally," grumbled Kevin.

"You boys don't want drinks before you go?" Trick twinkled at them.

Such a good little barista.

Accordingly, drinks in hand and spirits lighter for having had a bit of otter cheer in their lives, they left the Bean, piled into their truck, and drove off to face their doom.

They arrived at the rented Mill Valley house exactly at the time requested. Lexi Blanc wasn't ready and Judd wasn't surprised. She was the type who enjoyed keeping others waiting.

While Kevin scoped the grounds, Judd supervised Colin prepping the ear-buds. Risa joined them, to make certain that the flower buds chosen looked okay in any paparazzi shots where bodyguards might appear. In accordance with their itinerary and location, Colin had chosen California poppies for the buds. Risa indicated that this was acceptable with a slight sneer.

Judd was disgruntled that he would have to walk about with a poppy draped over his ear. Plus it popped against his dark skin like nobody's business. Not very manly – big gruff werewolf with poppy bling on the side of his head. But Colin had taken initiative on the matter, so Judd refused to complain.

Once Colin pronounced the buds *well draped*, they were permitted inside Blanc's inner sanctum.

Lexi Blanc was in the master suite finalizing her *look*. Whatever that meant. Her makeup was caked on in a way that reminded Judd of the late sixties – cat eyes and bubble pink lips. Her hair was huge and fluffy. Judd supposed it befitted a country music star. He didn't know much about women's dos, but he would bet that there was a lot of fake hair added in to make it that big.

Blanc was sitting in a throne-like chair wearing an elaborate satin and lace robe. There was a makeup artist dabbing at her face and a hairdresser fussing away. Risa, after instructing them to stay out of the way, went to continue organizing outfits for the day. The room looked like a gold-sequined dragon had exploded. It was decorated with ruby red velvet furnishings and there was gold fringe, gold glitter, and gold chain everywhere. Not to mention gold sequins and tassels.

There was a truly spectacular jacket draped over an ottoman, studded and spangled with gold beads and flowers and all manner of metallic extras. A pair of gold snakeskin leggings lay next to it, and then another jacket, gold patent leather, and some kind of corset.

"Surely she's not wearing that on the local news?" Isaac pointed to the pile.

"Wouldn't put it past her," replied Colin.

Blanc ignored them but Risa snapped out, "Of course not! But we *are* sticking with a gold theme for this entire tour. Even podunk small town news stations get gold. The leggings and the blazer, to be precise. She will look *fantastic*."

Judd objected to San Francisco being called a *podunk small town* on principal.

Blanc waved a hand. "I will look perfect. Don't you worry, boys. I have this delicious rose-gold Kennal fringed number for that other event after, something to do with local politics. Risa, what was it?"

"Supermarket opening in Corte Madera, Lexi."

"Right, *that*. And then I'll do the belly chain and the crop-top two-piece, because I simply must put in an appearance at the most happening club in town, Saucy Socks or whatever. You'll stick with me the entire time, boys. But don't *say* anything and stay out of the way. Especially you." She flicked a finger at Colin. "You hardly look the part. Couldn't you at least have worn clothing that fit? Risa, take them away and do something pretty with them."

Dutifully the stylist left off fussing with Blanc's costumes, and gestured for Judd, Isaac, and Colin to follow her.

Judd texted Kevin to get inside *now*. He wasn't going to go through fashion humiliation without his fellow enforcer.

Kevin joined them back in the living room. From there Risa led them down a hallway into a study, or possibly the set of a porn flick – difficult to tell the difference.

"I'm assuming you have badges for us?" Judd glared at the freestanding clothing rack sitting innocently front and center.

"And uniforms."

"I'm sorry?"

"Oh, you four will also have to fit with Lexi's *theme*. I have plenty of shirts on hand from the last team. They were human, so they might be a bit tight on you two." She tilted her chin at Judd and Kevin. "Nothing wrong with that."

"Heavy Lifting has its own uniform."

"Yes, so I see. Black t-shirt and jeans, how original. I assure you, that's not going to work for us."

She began flipping though the hangers, eventually pulling out three sets of black pants and tossing them at Judd, Kevin, and Isaac. They were all of a similar size, although Isaac was leaner. The pants were black, shimmery, and overly tight in the ass.

"Seriously?" said Kevin, looking at his butt in a mirror.

Judd frowned. There was something stiff down the side seams – Velcro? "Oh hell no, these are stripper pants!"

"You think I'd risk quality material like *that* on shifting? They tear away so you can change shape without destroying them. I designed them myself, and they're fantastic. Don't knock it until you try it. Or rip it, I should say."

Isaac was looking at his pair with interest. "Surprise! I'm *naked*!"

"Shock that bad guy, shock him good." Kevin grinned.

Judd rolled his eyes at them. "You two are idiots. But didn't you say the previous guards were human, Ms Ostrov?"

Risa arched an eyebrow. "Did I say these were theirs? That's just the shirts. These came from some backup dancers at one point. And yes, they ripped them off."

"See? Stripper pants. I suppose it's somewhat practical." Judd dropped trou and pulled the Velcro pants on. Kevin and Isaac followed his lead, stripping down and donning the pants without shame. Risa, who had clearly seen it all before, didn't even blink.

Colin, on the other hand, went very red and stood looking down at his own feet.

"What else you got for us? Body glitter?" Kevin was actually trying to flirt with the woman.

"Oh, now that you say it…" Risa was decidedly *not* flirting back.

"No," said Judd, firmly.

Colin added, "That'd be too shiny. Bodyguards shouldn't draw too much attention."

Risa looked at him with a new respect in her eyes. "Good point, peanut. You *are* the smart one, aren't you?" She went back to the rack and pulled down three black shirts.

"Can't we wear our own?" asked Judd, failing to see a significant difference.

"No. These are *monogrammed* polo shirts. Put them on."

They were also a great deal silkier and tighter than anything even Lovejoy would choose to wear. Judd looked down. You could clearly see his nipples through the material. And, to a certain extent, his package under the stripper pants. Just wonderful.

Colin's eyes were very big and he was staring at Judd. He licked his lips a few times before he said, hoarsely. "You look nice."

Judd suddenly didn't feel bad about *anything*. "Yeah?"

"Oh, yeah."

Kevin said, "Yech, just stop it, okay? This is not the time." He looked at Risa. "What are you gonna put my brother in, then?"

Risa contemplated Colin. She tapped her lip with one long glittery gold nail. "You'll be more covert? Less acting the part of muscle?"

Colin nodded. "And at the concert I'll be up in the light box or backstage with AV, whichever has the best feed."

"But we still want you to be clearly one of *ours*, I think."

"Oh, I don't think mother wants to be associated with *me* at all."

Risa didn't respond to that. She started flipping through the rack again. Stopped at a pair of tight black leather pants.

"I shift too, you know," Colin protested.

"You do? Well, then." She found him another pair of the silky stripper pants, only these were made out of an even thinner material, practically see-through, and cut like business slacks. They had a gold pinstripe running through them.

Colin disappeared behind a Japanese screen and reemerged wearing them and nothing else.

Judd tried to swallow his own tongue. Choked. Started coughing.

Isaac slapped him on the back, laughing.

Colin just blinked at him, confused.

Isaac said, "You look really good, Col."

"Don't tease."

"No, really, those are *hot*."

Judd realized that it was quite possible Colin wouldn't believe anyone but him. So he stalked across the room, very aware of the thinness of his own pants and the way they slid over his cock. He wondered if maybe, for once in his life, he should have worn underwear.

He pulled Colin up against him. He slid his hands down to grope his mate's ass, which was a truly spectacular thing with those gold lines running down and over. Judd traced the pattern with his fingers.

"Oh," said Colin, "you really like them?"

"You're spectacular."

Kevin rolled his eyes so hard he looked like he was having a seizure.

Colin's face was hot against Judd's neck. "Okay, then."

Risa interrupted them. "Stop that or you'll get all turned on and mess up the lines. Here, snack size, try this for the top." She shoved a black Western-style shirt with gold embroidery between Judd and Colin, like a wedge.

Reluctantly, Judd let Colin go. He turned away, adjusted himself. He didn't care that the others saw.

Kevin made a retching noise. Isaac smiled like a loon. Risa was busy with Colin.

"Yes," she pronounced firmly.

"It's not too tight?" Colin plucked at the skirt. It hugged his lean torso, draping soft and water-like over his slim waist and narrow hips.

"Of course not, it fits perfectly. And it will also do for the club later if we unsnap it a bit. For now, tuck it in."

"Should I be wearing gold, with my hair?" Colin protested, but tucked the shirt in obediently.

"I'm a genius and I never make mistakes." Risa stepped back, finger to chin, examining him. "When Jojo finishes with Lexi's face, I think a little something on yours."

"Makeup?" Colin sounded half horrified, half delighted. "But I'm not important."

Risa pursed her lips. "Humor me. Now, I'd best get back. We're out of here in a half hour. Be ready."

The rest of the day and evening was a whirlwind of rushing from one obligation to the next. Colin couldn't fathom how Judd and Kevin did the whole bodyguarding thing all the time. There was so much crazy coming at them, and they always had to be watching and defending. He supposed it wasn't that much different from being pack enforcer. Colin was really bad at it. He got caught up in the celebrity of it all, and kept getting distracted from actually keeping an eye out for attackers. He got occasion-ally hypnotized by Judd's ass in that fantastic outfit, or caught up in his mother's crazy shenanigans. Or perhaps it was that his wolf side saw Lexi as the biggest threat, a strange Alpha in their midst. Also, he kept catching sight of his own reflection and getting star-tled by how awesome he looked with a bit of makeup. Not too much, because he wasn't courageous enough for that. But his eyes did look totally amazing framed by liner, and mascara, and a hint of shimmer. He'd paid very close attention when Jojo was putting it on, in case he wanted to try it at home. Unlikely, but just in case.

The stupid stretch limo took them everywhere. Because it was Lexi, Risa, Jojo, the manager, the outfits, and four body-guards, every movement from point A to point B was a production in and of itself. Yet Judd and Kevin seemed to be ever looking outward, utterly unimpressed, their attention solely focused on possible threat. Colin realized, for the first time, that his brother and Judd were actually really good at their jobs. The ear-buds became dedicated to a military-like commentary on positions, threat assessments, and safety. Colin, who had monitored their coms before, had never been on the ground with them at the same time, and found it all rather exciting.

He was part of his mother's entourage, for lack of a better term. Her life was all glamorous photo ops, selfies, meeting fans, and doing interviews. She wore one outfit to the TV station, then changed into a completely different one for the supermarket opening, and finally something else for the club. She had to be photographed, fully posed with the right background, each time. Even though all the outfits were gold.

She was, in public at least, charming, vibrant, and witty. Colin could practically see people fall in love with her. She was also very beautiful, with that full curvy figure and waterfall of red hair – a bombshell. On top of all that, she was an Alpha werewolf – powerfully charismatic.

Colin felt self-conscious in his own ludicrous getup but it hardly mattered, as no one gave him a second glance when she was around. He did catch Judd checking him out once or twice. But only briefly, as the enforcer would instantly continue scoping the crowd. For all his mother drew his attention, Colin never stopped being aware of exactly where Judd stood.

Colin took charge of their com unit base. Risa gave him a leather man-bag to carry it. She pursed her lips when he slung it crossbody-style over his head but there was no way he was risking losing the expensive kit.

Judd, Kevin, and Isaac each wore a poppy-shaped ear-bud

draped over one ear. Perhaps the cheerful flower detracted slightly from their bad-ass demeanors, but there was no doubting they were Lexi's bodyguards. Most people they encountered gave them a wide berth. Colin, on the other hand, stuck with Risa, Jojo, and the manager – Lexi's pack of human sycophants – and pretended to be one of them, rather than security. He wondered what people thought his role was. Defensive running snacks? Offensive twittering. Wide receiver of the sacred snood softener? What other celebrity entourage positions were there?

Judd and Kevin had a series of hand signals and body language codes when they were close to each other, so they barely needed to talk on the coms anyway. Just a head tilt from Judd, and Kevin jumped to guard his flank. But Isaac had to be told what to do, as he rarely worked for Heavy Lifting, and hadn't the protective instincts of an enforcer. He was clearly paying close attention to the conversations going on around him too. It was mostly superficial but Isaac did conversation well, and occasionally he'd talk softly with Jojo, Risa, or Lexi's manager. That had to have affected his alertness, so Judd and Kevin were doing all of the bodyguard work.

There were throngs of fans with banners at the supermarket opening, but there were local cops on hand for that event too. They seemed to have things under control. The fans were mostly human, which made sense, as this was a daytime event. Colin felt this was a good thing, since it was shifters who likely posed the greatest threat to Lexi. Not that there weren't daytime shifters, or those happy to be out and about under the star of evil brightness, it's just that the biggest and the baddest tended to be nocturnal.

Judd did have to muscle one screaming fan out of the way as they entered the TV studio. And Kevin had to clothesline another as they left. It took both enforcers to gently dissuade a large sobbing cowboy from prostrating himself at Lexi's feet on the sidewalk on the way back to the limo. But otherwise most of their day was uneventful.

It was Saucebox that night which proved to be the real problem.

Saucebox on a Friday evening was hopping. It was even more crazy than usual (not that Colin hung out at the club often, if at all). Colin figured that Xavier had circulated a rumor that Lexi Blanc would be putting in an appearance at Saucebox. There was very little Xavier wouldn't do for publicity.

It was no surprise that, when Lexi arrived, the crowded club surged and boiled with excitement. Saucebox attracted shifters. Shifters out for a good time and easily excited. Shifters who loved a celebrity Alpha.

Tank, who was manning the door, let them in reluctantly, told them to be careful for fuck's sake. Isaac gave him a quick neck nibble and reassuring squeeze, but their biggest pack member did not look mollified. Colin wished he had another poppy to give Tank – it would help if they could keep contact with the wolf at the door. And it would keep Tank from worrying too much. He made a mental note to pack extra ear-buds for future operations.

The moment the crowd began to buzz at seeing a star in their midst, Isaac moved to stand in front of Lexi, shielding her. Colin figured this was more to do with Saucebox being Isaac's home turf – his job – than any protective instinct.

Lexi seemed to find this annoying. "Stop that. They only want to see me. Take photos. Adore me." She smiled big for the flashing cell phones.

Judd muscled up close on her left side and barked at her, "It's not as secure as Xavier assured us it would be."

"It's a club. It's fine. This is normal for me. I know you're probably not used to such enthusiasm with your regular clients."

Colin decided not to relay stats on the number of celebrities shot in clubs.

Isaac didn't budge from his shielding position in front of Lexi. This seriously annoyed Lexi – he was now going to be in front of her in all the pictures.

"Move!" She shoved him with a hand on his lower back. Still smiling for the cameras. He didn't budge.

"What the hell?" Lexi was clearly confused at Isaac's ability to resist her Alpha-ness. Colin wondered if she really didn't know (or believe) that the San Andreas Pack had an Omega. Alec had loaned her a fucking gift, and she was pretending Isaac was nothing more than an annoying bug under her shoe. In that moment, Colin genuinely hated her.

"Whozat?" Colin heard a kitsune near Isaac ask. Since Isaac was normally the bartender on Friday nights, these were his regulars. But for once, Isaac wasn't going to give them his attention. He wasn't going to explain, or shift his focus onto them.

"Singer of some kind. Werewolf," someone else explained.

"You know that *fang fa fang fang fang* song?"

"No, it's just *fangs fangs fangs*."

"What's that about *gang bangs*?" This was clearly *not* a country music crowd.

"No *fangs*, just *fangs*. Under moonlight or something."

"Oh! Lexi Blanc? I *love* her. She's so cool."

"I wonder if she smells as good as she looks."

"Bet she tastes better."

"Watch out with that talk. That girl is an Alpha werewolf, you know?"

"Really? I didn't know. She can order me to do anything she wants, I would go belly up for that."

Colin felt slightly sick. Objectification of women and all that but also, yech, that's his mother they were drooling over.

Still the interest, excitement, and lust in the crowd was spiking. It was such a terrible idea to bring someone like Lexi to a place like Saucebox, where shifters hung out, got drunk, and confessed their sins to Isaac in order to feel better. There was no Isaac acting Omega counselor to them that evening, so they were already on edge. Adding Lexi to the mix was like throwing Marvin into a lifeguard convention.

The ear-bud cracked to life in Colin's ear:

Judd: "Isaac, where's Xavier?"

Kevin: "Short little fucker is impossible to see in this mess."

Isaac: "Let's just get her up to VIP first. Worry about X later. Safest."

Judd: "Kevin, watch your three. There's a drooling posse of barghest coming at you."

Kevin: "Where?"

Judd: "Close in! Colin, where you at?"

Colin: "Just behind her. Don't worry about me, I'll shift if necessary."

Kevin: "Col, grab her hips and steer her right. Push if you have to. Isaac, clear us a path."

Judd: "Isaac, you got this?"

Isaac: "No problem. They're used to me being in a hurry and cutting through crowds here. Bartender, remember?"

Judd: "Colin, keep your eyes focused on where you're going. Don't look *at* anyone. Don't challenge, just keep her moving."

Colin: "Ugh. I'm touching my mother. The things I do for this pack."

Kevin: "Sorry bro, that sucks."

Judd: "Kevin, they aren't backing down. To the rear. Stand firm!"

Colin, hands on his mother's hips, pressed her forward, steered her to follow Isaac until they reached the stairs up to the roped-off VIP area. Xavier had a bouncer stationed there. The big man saw Isaac heading straight for him. He had the rope down and was standing off to one side in a jiffy.

Colin let go of Lexi and shoved his mother up the stairs after Isaac.

"Get off me, puppy!" was her only response.

Colin gestured for Risa, Jojo, and the manager to follow. They all gave him dirty looks, but they weren't hearing what he was hearing in his ear-bud. Also, they hadn't looked behind them to see the roiling mass of excitement and agitation that bubbled through the club in their wake.

Colin looked at the bouncer. "Rope it."

"What about you?"

"I'm staying here." *Because I'm a complete idiot.* He glanced longingly up at the safety of the VIP zone. Then he turned resolutely to stand shoulder to shoulder with the bouncer. Okay, more shoulder to arm. The man was big, but didn't smell like shifter, which was a bummer. Colin would have preferred a berserker on his side.

"No offense, boy, but you don't look like this is your regular gig," said the human.

"I know," admitted Colin, "but *they* do."

He gestured at Kevin and Judd, who had swung around just in front of them and were acting first line of defense, keeping anyone from approaching.

There were too many scents, plus flashing lights and loud music. Colin couldn't really follow what happened next. But suddenly someone went flying. It was possible that Kevin had picked him up and thrown him.

It seemed clear that some kind of brawl was imminent.

Colin started unbuttoning his nice stretchy shirt — it would impede movement if he had to shift. He wasn't wild about the idea, but if he must fight, he certainly wasn't doing it in skin.

The bouncer next to him said, "I don't think it's that kinda party, baby boy."

Colin didn't reply. Silly man, a quarter of the people in there were shifters. Didn't he know the look by now? Then again, politeness dictated shifters rarely stripped down in a crowded club.

Speaking of which, there came a very loud ripping sound. Loud enough for Colin to hear it above the yells and growls of the crowd. Velcro, tearing.

CHAPTER TWELVE

Who knew Velcro could sound so ominous?

"Woohooo, take it all off!" cried someone.

Silky black pants came hurtling in Colin's direction. He plucked them out of the air and tossed them behind him onto the stairs. A monogrammed t-shirt followed. Judd's boots, fortunately, did not.

Colin knew it was Judd because Kevin, in human form with a nosebleed and a big grin, was suddenly standing next to him, and a stunning black wolf with brilliant yellow eyes was at his feet.

The wolf bared his teeth, long and wicked sharp. Then he threw his head back and howled.

Technically a wolf's howl is for summoning – a call to hunt, a cry of loneliness, a beckoning to shore up the pack. Occasionally, it was a warning to other wolves. Not exactly something one does at a dance club.

But werewolves also knew that with humans, their howl was a weapon. Like the Velcro, the black wolf's howl cut through all the other noises in Saucebox. Ominous. To prey animals, wolf howls meant that a predator was on the move. It was a sound that might not have an effect on the shifters in the room, but it sure freaked the bejesus out of all the humans. Add the howl to this particular wolf's appearance, big and threatening, and even the bear shifters took notice. Judd was large enough to be an Alpha and he was solid black, a creature of myth and shadows. Humans prescribed an enormous amount of silly significance to fur color. Even though werewolves had been out for hundreds of years, there was something about a massive all-black wolf that affected people's psyche.

The frantic angry atmosphere of the club quieted. Not in the way an Alpha would bring stillness through dominance, and not in the way that Isaac could bring calm through compassion, but in the manner of an enforcer – posturing, animalistic, and harsh.

The crowed stilled, not out of respect, or love, or charisma, but out of fear.

Threat.

It made sense to Colin that it would be Judd who'd shift. He was the most practical choice because he was the most impressive wolf in their pack. Certainly, of the five of them there that night, he was the strongest and fastest shifter.

"Hey," someone grumbled, "I thought this was a fur-free club."

"Yeah, how rude," complained someone else.

But it was normal griping. The mob mentality had subsided.

"Everything all right here?" Tank's booming voice rang over the room, the one he never used because he just wasn't that kind of person.

"But that's Lexi Blanc!" protested someone.

"So what if it is?" Barked out Kevin, blood dripping down his face.

Tank pushed his way through the room from the front door. Looking impressively official in his Saucebox shirt. Suddenly Colin realized what a disservice Risa had done to them, putting them in the dumb stripper clothing. Bodyguarding included looking the part, and she had handicapped them with her stylistic choices. He glanced up at his mother on her balcony. Had she done it intentionally?

Tank turned to stand next to Kevin.

One of the regulars was having none of it. "Perhaps she just wants a nice drink, like anyone else. Wants a hot dude to keep her company."

Kevin snorted. "How'd you feel, if a lady you respected showed up to a club like this and some ugly nose-hair like you was all up in her craw?"

"What, Ginger Butch, you think you rank?"

Kevin laughed. "Hell no! Don't be gross. But I sure as shit look a whole lot better than you do, even with a broken nose. Fuck off and grow some style. That a beard on your face, or one of those air plants? What *do* you think you look like?"

Tank gave his pack mate a mild rebuke. "Be nice, Kev, them's paying customers."

"That's not a customer, that's a walking, talking succulent," objected Kevin.

Judd the wolf, apparently over his pack mate's banter, wormed his way under the velvet rope and trotted up the stairs. The poppy ear-bud was still draped over his head, making him look a little bit like a furry four-legged flamenco dancer.

"Uh, hey, wait a moment, Mr Wolf, sir!" The human bouncer obviously felt he was supposed to do something.

Colin explained, "He's with us."

"Glad he's with somebody. He going to stay that way? All furry?"

Colin shrugged and turned to his brother. "Where'd Tank go?"

"Back to the door. Someone has to." Kevin regarded Colin's new human bouncer friend suspiciously. "Who're you?"

"Oscar," said the bouncer. "You're Isaac's pack?"

"We're Alec's pack, but yeah, Isaac is one of us."

"Cool. Here." Oscar handed Kevin a durag to stopper up his still-gushing nose – with that much blood it had to be broken. Kevin would get hungry soon. Colin would have to keep an eye on his brother, shove some turkey jerky at him. Kevin always got peckish and waspish with accelerated healing.

"You got him back for that, I assume?" Colin gestured at his brother's nose.

"Of course," came the nasal response. "What you take me for?"

"Don't tilt your head back, that won't help," rebuked Colin. "Don't you ever listen to Bryan's medic tips?"

"I do when it's the fun stuff. Like the best way to knock someone out." Kevin pulled away the drenched rag and handed it back to Oscar.

The bouncer grimaced and let it fall to the floor.

"You should ask the bartender for a dishtowel," suggested Colin.

Kevin waved away his concern. "It'll stop soon. Meanwhile, I look like a total bruiser."

"Yes, dear, such a badass," responded Colin.

Kevin grinned at him. "Is it just me, or does this place kinda suck?"

Colin raised a brow. "Aw, are things too busy for you to flirt?"

Kevin grunted. "No one here to flirt with."

"Slept with them all, already, have you?"

Oscar watched this exchange with amusement. "You're the brothers, right?"

"Isaac talks too much," was Kevin's response.

The bouncer grinned. He had a broken side tooth – now *that* was badass. "Naw, dude. Tank told me."

"Tank?" said Kevin.

"Tank talks? Like, to humans?" added Colin.

The bouncer shrugged. "We're friendly."

"Tank has friends?" Kevin was definitely feeling waspish.

The bouncer rolled his eyes at them. "You two going up, now that all the excitement has died down?"

Colin looked up at the VIP balcony where Lexi Blanc was holding court in a big way. Apparently, the other VIPs were delighted to welcome her, including the missing Xavier. They were giving Lexi Blanc the royal treatment – champagne and raw foie gras with caviar on top in a cut-glass serving dish. She was standing at the railing looking down at the dance floor. Those below her had stopped tussling, mingling, or dancing and were, instead, looking up at her in awe. As if she were a fascist dictator. Only with selfies involved.

"Must we?" Kevin asked, showing some measure of pain for the first time since this all started. Or maybe it was just a broken nose and hunger pangs.

Colin gave him his best condescending look. "What, you don't want closure from mummy dearest?"

"I'll have closure when she's dead. Could we maybe just mildly eviscerate her, like in the good old days?"

"You mean when werewolves were *actually* monsters?"

"It seems like such a nice idea. I'm sure there's a temporary insanity clause in place for this kind of situation. Look, judge, she had to go, it was for the good of the planet!"

Oscar looked back and forth between them. "Aren't you supposed to be her bodyguards?"

"Well, yes, but just *look* at her."

Oscar looked. Clearly he didn't see what they saw. Didn't notice the way she tilted her head to show her white neck and tease the senses. The way she spilled her drink on the wait staff and never apologized. How she stroked Xavier's arm, even though his girlfriend was standing *right* there. How she put her hand out and snapped her fingers, expecting her manager to pass her a phone. How she gestured at Jojo to fix her hair, and then batted them all away petulantly when they tried.

"She's so beautiful," said the bouncer, in wonder.

Colin and Kevin groaned in unison.

"Wow, you really are brothers."

"I don't wanna," whined Kevin.

Colin patted his brother's shoulder. "There, there, you big baby." Since Judd was incommunicado at the moment, Colin added, "What would Judd have us do?"

Kevin looked at him, thoughtful. "Honestly? He'd want you up there, with him and better protected. He'd tell me to remain here and act first line of defense for the rest of the night."

"So we do that. And look, lucky you gets to stay away."

"I don't like you being sensible and I don't like you being around her alone."

And yet, Kevin had left him alone with their father, for years. Colin shook himself – that was bitterness talking. It really hadn't been Kevin's fault.

"I won't be alone, Judd and Isaac will be there with me."

"Judd is a wolf. What good can he do when her tongue starts wagging?"

"Don't worry about me, Kevin. Remember my greatest skill is to go unnoticed? With any luck, she won't even realize I'm there. Now, Oscar, do you think you could get the kitchen to bring my brother a burger, rare?"

"Sure thing."

Kevin grumbled.

"Eat the burger," Colin ordered.

"Fine." Truculent brother was truculent.

"Oscar, if he resists, just wave it in front of his face. Trust me, it's in both your interests that he eat something."

"You two are weird," was Oscar's only response.

With which Colin ducked under the rope and made his way upstairs.

He did, in fact, manage to go mainly unnoticed for most of the rest of the evening. He took up a watchful stance at the top of the stairs where he could see Kevin below and Isaac and Judd milling about the VIP lounge. He tried to pay very little attention to Lexi Blanc.

Surrounded by a dozen or so worshipful fans – important, moneyed, rich fans (not to mention the peons down below) – Lexi Blanc had not a barb to spare for her youngest. It seemed likely she'd forgotten Colin existed. Which was great.

Until, bored, Lexi started to make all kinds of fuss over Judd in wolf form. And then Colin was the one to incite contact.

"He's quite beautiful," she said, treating Judd like a pet. "Risa, get a photo of me with my leg over his back? We should have this one pose with me for the cover of my next album. Risa, make a note, that tour will be all about black. I can just see it now. Me and this gorgeous wolf, lying together on a bed of black satin with black tulips spread about us. So dramatic." She pointed at her manager. "Make another note, I should be seen on tour the entire time with a black wolf at my side – all interviews, photos, press tour, everything. Can you just *imagine* it? Perfection! I'm such a genius."

Colin felt so ill that he was moved to speak and he was rarely so moved. "Stop it, Mother!"

Lexi totally ignored him.

He was probably too timid about it. He sucked. Colin couldn't stand up for anyone, not even his own mate. Or the man he wanted for his mate. Colin's ears felt hot and he choked on frustrated tears and unspoken words.

Then there was a warm solid comforting presence next to him. Isaac's voice was mild but reproachful. "I don't think Judd will be available to tour with you, ma'am."

Lexi narrowed her eyes at him. "Next tour won't happen for at least a year. Who knows where he'll be at that time? Maybe he'll be with me. What color is *your* wolf? Two black wolves would be even *better* than one. You could both bodyguard me on the tour, and be in *all* the photos. Wouldn't you like that? Your *Instalamb* follower numbers would skyrocket. If you're very good, I might even make you my pack."

Isaac, whose wolf pelt was, in fact, not even slightly black, didn't bother responding.

"Mother!" Colin actually yelled. "Stop it!" But stopping Lexi Blanc from talking crap was like fist-fighting a sea urchin. She was all over sharp points and even if she had a squishy center under those barbs, it was undoubtedly salty and snot-like.

Colin did *not* like sea urchin.

Lexi rolled her eyes. Then someone handed her a drink and her attention was diverted.

Colin simmered. As if Lexi could lure Judd, much less *Isaac,* away to become her pack. *Ridiculous.*

Judd walked over and bumped against him, so tall his back was at Colin's waist. He gave a low whine of sympathy. As if, for some weird reason, he was worried about Colin, when he was the one who'd been insulted.

Colin reminded himself that his mother may be a werewolf Alpha, but all Alphas were not created equal. Colin knew, more surely than anything he had ever known before, that Alec was the stronger wolf. That he, Colin, was allied with the right pack and the right Alpha. That Judd, who was much older and wiser, would sense the same thing. That all Lexi's decisions, which had led to Colin becoming *who* he was now, had also led Colin to being *where* he was now. And that was good, because he was in the right place, with the right people, and with Judd. Judd would never abandon them, or him, to go running around with Lexi Fucking Blanc.

The massive sleek wolf clearly wasn't concerned with Lexi's comments or proprietary behavior. Possibly because as a wolf he didn't understand most of them. But more likely because he was unshaken in knowing where he belonged. Colin envied him that peace of mind.

Judd the wolf knew enough to understand his duty was to protect the strange female Alpha, but he also knew enough to circle and protect his pack mates– guard them, check in with them. He had sensed Colin's distress and come to him. Leaned against *him*. He wasn't going anywhere.

Colin lifted the poppy ear-bud off Judd's head and petted his soft ear.

The black wolf lolled out his tongue, then shoved his nose into Colin's groin.

"Seriously?" said Colin. Then he laughed. And everything suddenly seemed more absurd than anything else. Even his mother.

Especially his mother.

It was dawn by the time they got home, but Judd was still feeling wired. The house was silent, smelled undisturbed, most everyone else was in bed upstairs.

Only Bryan, in wolf form, ghosted up to them as they pulled into the driveway. It's possible Max was awake and gone for a run. Bryan usually took dawn patrol because of it. Max liked to run alone, gather his thoughts for the day. Bryan understood his mate's quirks and honored them by finding his own activities, which included early morning patrol.

Judd spoke carefully and clearly. "Trick will be up soon. He opens the café at seven. Can you escort him there?"

Bryan dipped his great shaggy head.

"You sure he understands?" Colin glanced between them.

Judd nodded. "If not, Max'll make sure Trick gets to work safely. After his run, he needs his caffeine fix. No one but Trick will do, apparently."

"Never get between Max and a crème caramel latte," agreed Isaac.

Colin yawned.

Judd swung a casual, not casual, arm around his shoulders. "Let's get you to bed, Gingersnap. You're not used to being out all night at these things."

"I did okay, though?" Colin nibbled his lower lip.

Judd wanted to physically stop him from worry, kiss away those teeth.

"I mean, I know I wasn't much use but it seemed to go all right, even with the dust-up at Saucebox."

"You did great," Judd praised.

Colin yawned again, jaw creaking.

Kevin laughed. "Come on, little brother, let's get you to bed."

"No need to be condescending. Some of us have daytime lives."

"Got class on Saturdays all of a sudden?" Kevin sneered.

"Shut up, buttwad," shot back Colin, inelegantly.

They proceeded up the pathway through the overgrown yard to the front door.

Judd held Colin back as the others went inside. "Come to my room?"

"Yeah? More lessons?" His mate looked so pathetically hopeful. Like he'd not expected it again. Like he deserved so little of Judd's attention.

"Unless you're too tired?" Judd was a gentleman. He gave Colin an easy out.

"Never!" Colin straightened noticeably. "What's in the syllabus?"

Judd crowded against him, permission given. He reached down to stroke him through those thin stripper pants. Such a big cock for such a slender man. Such a turn-on. It had taunted him all night.

"I was thinking blow jobs."

Colin's eyes went round. "Oh! You'll teach me how?"

"It would, without a shadow of a doubt, be my pleasure."

Colin smiled at him, cheeky now that he knew what to expect. "We shall have to find out if it's mine. But I have high hopes."

"I'm hoping they are low hopes." Judd let his gaze linger on Colin's crotch. It wasn't a very good joke, but his Gingersnap seemed to like it.

"Mmmm, definitely."

Colin went upstairs. Judd did a quick patrol of the house, from the unfinished basement, through the empty downstairs, and along the upstairs hall checking all the bedroom doors. His pack must be safe.

Finally, he took a quick shower. Switching to fur didn't make him more or less dirty, but for some reason he always felt grimy afterwards. It had been a long day and he wanted to put on a good performance for his Gingersnap. Make everything as easy and comfortable as possible.

Apparently, a little too comfortable.

Colin was dead asleep in Judd's bed when he finally got to his room.

Judd took a moment to appreciate Colin being there, vulnerable in Judd's space, surrounded by Judd's scent. He didn't mind waiting. Blow jobs first thing after waking were one of life's greatest joys. Plus, in daylight he could see all Colin's blushes. Judd was happy to wait. Judd had waited, one way or another, for over a century. He was nothing if not patient.

So he climbed into bed, pulled his mate close, listened to his soft regular breathing, and let himself be all over content.

When Judd woke up the next day it was, sadly, not to a blow job. He figured that would be too much for a first attempt. Still, he intended to negotiate open permission for the future. Whether giving or receiving, Judd liked to come awake sexed-up and happy.

But Colin *was* touching him, sweet smelling and sleep rumpled.

At some point they'd rolled so that Judd was on his back with Colin nested against him. Red head at the crook of shoulder and torso. A hand stroked down Judd's thigh.

Colin nuzzled, inhaled deep, pressed tight against Judd's side – cock hard and movements eager. Either he was turned on and still asleep, or awake but too sleepy to be cautious in his desire.

Judd adored it.

He curved the arm under Colin, cupped the back of that red head with one big hand. He bent to meet Colin's pretty mouth in a soft kiss.

No urgency to it, just acknowledgment and acceptance.

"Hello, Gingersnap."

"Judd." Colin's eyes stayed closed. His smile was small but unguarded.

"How do you feel about morning blow jobs, beautiful boy?"

"It's afternoon."

"How do you feel about afternoon blow jobs?"

"Resoundingly in favor. Just don't expect me to be great at it right away, okay?"

There it was, the expected caution rolling off his young lover like the funk of illness.

Judd was prepared for this. He'd put thought into it. More thought than he put into most things, frankly. "Would you like to start on me first, so that you know what to expect? Or would you like me to go down on you, so you can feel what it feels like? There's no wrong answer, Gingersnap."

Colin pressed his face into Judd's pec to dampen a forlorn sound. He obviously needed to do the right thing, but he didn't know what that was. Judd wanted to cry for him. Instead he ran a comforting hand down that smooth freckled back, feeling the bumps of Colin's spine.

Then he had a brilliant idea. Sixty-nine wasn't his favorite. He liked to be able to concentrate fully on what he was doing, or on what was being done to him, but in this instance it might be the perfect solution.

He threw the covers back.

Colin squeaked.

It was fall, but not *that* cold. Not in mid-afternoon. Not for werewolves. Colin was just being dramatic. He was also entirely naked. Which meant that last night, before he fell asleep, his mate had hoped for this. Fortunately, neither shock, nor confusion, nor shame dampened Colin's obvious eagerness.

He stared at Judd. "You're so gorgeous all over, every part of you. I look nothing like you, all pasty and freckled."

"You're the prettiest thing I have ever seen, I swear." Judd watched Colin's blush spread down over his neck and to his chest.

Judd scooted away and then flipped himself around. His head down near Colin's hard cock. It wasn't exactly comfortable, because Judd was so big. His feet were all up in pillows and headboard. He manhandled Colin downward, placing him in a better position, full on his side. Now both of them were comfortable.

The discrepancy in size meant Judd had to bend quite a bit. But he managed the right angle, as witnessed by a puff of breath on the tip of his own prick.

Colin let out a delighted little "Oh!" of pleasure.

Judd's academically minded lover needed knowledge more than anything. So Judd explained, "I think maybe you don't want me blowing you first, because you don't want all the focus on you. But you don't want to suck me first, because you don't know what you're doing."

"How'd you…?"

"You're my Gingersnap. 'Course I know where your head is at. So if we sixty-nine, it evens the odds. I do something to you.

You do the same thing to me. That way there's no confusion. I'll do to you exactly what I like, so you know, for certain, what turns my crank. And together we'll learn what turns yours. Sound good?"

"Perfect. Although I'm pretty sure your mouth on me will do it, in any capacity." Colin was obviously relieved. Poor baby, to be so terrified of the unknown all the time.

Judd continued his lecture. "What gets me hot might not work on you. So I'm gonna stop and check in regularly. Something I like, you might want softer or harder. You're gonna have to *talk* to me. Give me feedback. Okay?"

"Yes. And you'll do the same? I mean, I'll feel it, but that's not exactly the same as giving it, is it?"

Judd's answer was to nuzzle into the coarse hair at the junction of Colin's thigh and groin. He smelled best there, fresh and spiced and very much him. In the afternoon light, Judd could see that Colin's pubic hair was a darker red than the hair on his head.

Judd licked into the crease, eager for flavor.

Graceful, delicate hands were on his thigh. They gently pushed to get him to bend his top leg, exposing Judd to the same treatment. Colin rooted about, his tongue tasting Judd's skin.

Judd was old enough not to be self-conscious about any part of his body. Things flopped oddly in this position, but things flopped in general on a dude. His body was what it was. At various times, he'd worked it too hard and fed it too little, only to then indulge it too much. He'd changed it forever to werewolf at a later age than most. He had muscles, lots of them, and a slight softness to his stomach. His balls and cock were proportionate to the rest of him. He was proud of his skin, smooth and unblemished, and a beautiful dark brown color. His pubic hair was short and tight and a little patchy, sporting a few gray hairs, but no lover had ever complained of the texture. He liked how rough it was. Like him, it was coarse and crass and aggressive. His ass was too big by most standards – but when he found a man interested in fucking him, he'd vocally praised it as perfect to sink into. Judd had reason to be at peace with his body. He was also of an age not to give a shit.

Colin seemed to enjoy everything on offer.

Weirdly, that gave Judd a twinge of pride and relief. Guess he had been a little self-conscious, huh?

Judd focused on his Gingersnap. He smelled like Christmas in the old country – plum pudding, rich gravy, mulling spices. His limbs were slim and slender. His skin was very pale and so thin on his inner thighs that blue veins showed through. Judd traced them with his tongue. He found a small cluster of freckles on Colin's hip. Delighted, Judd kissed and licked and nibbled there. Colin twitched, tried not to giggle.

Judd moved on. He paid oral tribute to everything he encountered, except Colin's cock. Eager student, Colin did the same. Judd tried not to get lost in the fact that his broken, brilliant, perfect mate was letting him put his deadly mouth all over him.

Judd paused, checked in. "How we doing, Gingersnap?" There was gravel to his voice. He realized his own cock was heavy and his balls tight. All the teasing was turning him on as much as Colin. Not only because Colin was doing the same thing back to him, but also because the act of tasting his mate was painfully arousing.

Colin's beautiful cock in front of Judd was pointed straight out. It was a gorgeous pink color. The glans, pushed free of the foreskin, was even darker, glistening. It was almost the same color as Colin's pubic hair.

Judd glanced up to find Colin looking down at him. His green eyes were going orange. Judd had no doubt his own were yellow with arousal.

"We both need to keep our teeth under control." Colin's voice shaking.

"Absolutely. You good so far?"

"So good."

"You're a bit ticklish in places. No, don't get self-conscious. I like any reaction I get. But I'm thinking maybe you need a bit more teeth and roughness than me. So I'm going to try that. I'm a pain wimp myself, but not you, I think. So if you like what I do, then you relax into it. Let's not focus on me for a sec? It's okay to take a break and just enjoy. But, you say something if it's too intense?"

Colin nodded.

Judd focused on that cluster of freckles on Colin's hip. This time he bit – firm and hard.

Colin let out a cry of surprised need. He muffled his mouth against Judd's thigh, wet and panting. His pretty cock jerked and a tiny bead of pre-cum appeared. The smell of it – salty, spicy, and acrid – sent a spike of need from Judd's nose to his own cock. He groaned. This was why Judd loved blow jobs. It was so much fun to see, right there, what worked. Apparently, his Gingersnap liked a snap with his loving, a bit of pain.

Judd went a little rougher, testing Colin's limit. He knew it was pushing things, but he wanted to see if Colin would stop him.

Colin jerked and made an *eep* noise. "Too much!"

Good, he'd speak up for himself. Judd rewarded him with a soothing lick. Then moved to a different ticklish spot. He applied another bite, firm enough to leave a red mark, but no more.

Colin moaned. "Yes, that's… oh man, that's really good. I didn't know I'd like it, but it's like claiming or something. And it's not so ticklish. More, please."

Begging. His mate should never have to beg for anything, ever. Judd responded with tiny nibbles and bites all over Colin's stomach and thighs. His Gingersnap squirmed and whimpered, and arched and cried out in joy under his teeth. Judd wanted to eat him up.

He paused.

"Oh!" Colin was crestfallen. "I forgot to do my part."

"Look at my cock, Gingersnap."

"Trust me, I am."

"Does it look like I'm not enjoying this?"

"Oh yeah, I see. Could we maybe move on to that now?"

"Eager, are we?" Judd grinned at him.

"*We* certainly are. You're leaking like a faucet in disrepair, and my balls feel like they're going to explode. I'm young and impatient, remember?"

"Did you just compare my impressive manhood to a broken faucet?"

"If the dick fits…" Gingersnap was getting awful cheeky.

"Sucking cock makes you cocky."

"That's my point, I haven't *got* to suck yet." Definite whine to Colin's voice. They were getting near to begging again. Couldn't have that.

"Well, what are you waiting for?" Judd pushed his prick closer to that beautiful mouth. The one that had occupied his fantasies for too long.

Colin actually licked his lips. Judd thought he might blow just from that. This could get embarrassing. He was, indeed, leaking, yet Colin's mouth wasn't even on him yet.

Judd reached down with his free arm. He grabbed his own dick, smeared the head against Colin's perfect lips.

Colin licked them again. His eyes were entirely orange now. Which was unbelievably hot. Judd's cock leaked more. So Judd smeared Colin's lips again. His mate licked them again, moaning. They were spiraling.

"How do I taste?" Judd croaked out.

"Spicy and delicious," replied Colin, no embarrassment. "Like I always thought you'd taste."

Judd laughed. "My turn."

Instead of grabbing Colin's cock, Judd licked it from base to tip. He circled the shiny head with his tongue, dipped into the slit, hunted out Colin's flavor. Salty, creamy, bitter, spicy – delicious. He lost himself in it. Circling the head again and again.

Colin began doing the same to him. Wrapped that sinful mouth around him, coiled his tongue around the tip of Judd's aching dick.

Judd drew back, grasped the base of Colin's cock with one big hand. Then he went seriously to work – licking like a popsicle, swirling the head. He made his movements easy for a first-timer to imitate.

Colin was whimpering, getting lost either in what he was feeling, or in what he was doing, or both. He tried to thrust. Judd was too strong for him, even with only one hand. Colin couldn't move much. Which was a good thing – Judd couldn't deep throat. He had to stop Colin from thrusting too hard or he'd embarrass them both. Judd thought of saying something. Under similar circumstances, Colin could overpower a human lover. But Judd hated the idea that he was practice for someone else, and he loved Colin's getting lost because of him.

Colin did something wicked with his tongue. He was innovating. He was a goddamn genius after all.

Judd paused because he could feel his balls tingling. Too close.

Colin, after a moment, stopped and looked up. His eyes were bright orange and glazed.

"How are we doing, Gingersnap?"

"Oh my fucking god! So good. That's just amazing. The way you taste. How you feel on my tongue."

"You ready to try sucking?"

In answer, Colin grabbed Judd's prick firmly, and swallowed him down almost to the root.

Judd was by no means a small man, in any capacity. He'd had some killer blow jobs in his day – a few lovers had even managed to deep throat him. But never, in his wildest dreams, had he expected Colin to do it. Not on his first go.

"Holy cocktrumpeting cheeseballs!" Judd yelled, only just managing to stop himself from jack-knifing and coming at the same time.

Colin popped off, eyes twinkling. "You okay down there?"

"You glorious Gingersnap of heavenly goodness, how in seven hells do you know how to *do* that? You didn't even flinch, let alone gag!"

Colin looked, for the first time in their acquaintance, smug. "I'm inexperienced but not unpracticed." His voice was prim. "I got myself a very nice, well-sized dildo. I've been experimenting for years."

Judd reached down and squeezed his own cock hard to stop himself from shooting at that image. "Holy smokes, baby, I wanna see you do that for me sometime, okay?"

"Really?" Colin's head dipped. The blush was back.

"Oh yes."

"It's rainbow-striped."

"Of course it is."

"So, can I keep going? It's all right, what I'm doing?"

Judd let go of his own dick, under control again. He tilted Colin's chin with two fingers. Made him look down the length of both their bodies. Eyes meeting.

Colin was crimson-faced but his eyes were still orange. His expression was transcendent.

"Sweetheart, what you just did takes a lifetime of practice for most. I've had several lifetimes and I've never learned. I got an overactive gag reflex."

Colin grinned, clearly delighted. "You saying there's something sexual that I might teach you? That I might do better?"

Judd nodded, serious. "That's a real gift you got there."

"Gift of the gag?"

Judd let out a startled laugh. "Yeah, so get back to it."

"With pleasure."

CHAPTER THIRTEEN

YOU ARE MY MOONLIGHT

Judd tried to keep up with Colin suck for suck. Soon, however, he was worried about his canines. The sleep-mingled smell of mutual arousal overwhelmed his senses with spicy musk. Too much. He let himself rest his head on his hand. He floated on the feeling of Colin working him over. His Gingersnap gave a blow job with the unfettered joy of a man who has found something he not only enjoys but is also *really* good at.

Judd was never going to last long. Morning need, the boy of his dreams, and no gag reflex was a trifecta for losing control.

"Pull off now, Gingersnap. Finish me with your hand."

Colin shook his head, still sucking.

"You're sure? I blow big and hard." He wasn't bragging. Although, he didn't mind that it sounded like he was.

A nod this time.

Judd figured this was one way to find out how Colin felt about swallowing. So he threaded rough fingers through fine strawberry-blond hair, closed his eyes, and let go. He groaned out the shivery fire of climax, amazed at the unexpected additional jolt of pure joy. Connection, probably. This was what an orgasm felt like when he actually loved the person he fucked. Amazing.

Colin, as it turned out, was a champ. He couldn't quite swallow it all – Judd hadn't lied about his productivity. But his mate looked that much hotter with cum seeping out the side of his mouth – eyes still yellow, face full of pride.

"You're amazing," Judd praised, meaning it. He petted Colin's head, fine silky strands, sticking up from his previous grip.

Colin licked his lips, puffier than ever. His voice was dick-wrecked and croaking. "A natural cock-sucker?"

"Supernatural, even."

Colin sighed. "It was as good as I imagined. Better."

"We aren't done yet, Gingersnap."

Colin blushed as red as Judd had ever seen him. Lowered his eyelids. "I'm afraid we are for a bit. I kinda shot when you did. I couldn't help it, it was so hot."

Judd realized that Colin's dick in front of him was limp and spent. Judd's neck and upper chest were covered in jizz. He was a little disappointed. He'd wanted to drive Colin over the edge – see his face and taste his cum. But he was also beyond pleased that Colin had enjoyed blowing him so much that he'd followed Judd over the edge.

Judd dragged his fingers through the spend on his chest. Brought them to his lips. He could still taste.

Colin, watching, gasped. Eyes which had started to fade back to green, flashed orange.

"Sweet and delicious, like you. But also salty, and bitter, and spicy, like you are sometimes, when I'm lucky."

Colin rolled his eyes. "You're *terrible* at sweet talk."

"Talked you into my bed, didn't I?" Judd admired the small red marks he'd left on Colin's thighs and hips. They were fading, like memories of a journey left as footprints and blowing away. He *was* terrible at poetic courting. He stopped that line of thought immediately.

"And into a blow job."

"But you liked it." Judd wanted to be absolutely certain. He wanted Colin to come back to him, to keep up with the lessons.

Colin sighed. "Loved it. The weight on my tongue. I swear I could feel you throbbing."

"Bloody hell." Judd shifted. His spent cock gave a pulse of

renewed interest. "You, on the other hand, are really good at sweet talk."

"Hon, I don't mean to be condescending, but that was dirty talk. You got a serious problem if you're confusing the two."

Judd grinned. "Probably why I'm so bad at it. I like the *hon*, by the way."

"Honey bun."

"No, not that version."

Colin laughed. Then he sobered suddenly. Coming down off the endorphin high or, more likely, starting to question himself.

Judd was all too familiar with that worried look. He took a breath, prepared to battle his lover's feelings of inadequacy.

That wasn't where the conversation went, though.

"I don't know how aware you are as a wolf. I only remember things as if from a bad dream. But I'm a lot younger than you. Either way, I owe you an apology for the way my mother treated you last night. I'm not strong enough to stand up for you as I should have."

Judd flipped around so they could talk face to face. He'd only slightly followed the argument in the club. He didn't really process complex human interactions when a wolf. But he'd gotten the gist. Lexi Blanc had treated him like something to be used at her will. "I assure you, Gingersnap, I've had worse."

"Doesn't make it right."

Judd wondered if he'd ever before seen such earnest eyes. "No. But you stepped forward and tried. I know how hard that is for you."

"Shouldn't be. I should be bolder, stronger. I'm a werewolf, for fuck's sake!" Colin's anger was all for himself.

Judd stroked Colin's tense, freckled shoulder. "Yes, but is boldness in your nature? Was it ever?"

Colin looked sad. "Probably not. But I should like to know I can stand up for others, if not myself."

"You can. You did. And you stepped in with Trick and the selkie."

"But that was so hard. And I still wasn't strong enough. You had to come to my rescue."

Colin might as well have said that *he* wasn't good enough. Wasn't wolf enough. Wasn't powerful enough. Wasn't *enough*.

"But that's what brave is, sweetheart. Stepping forward, even when you know you can't win. People like me who do it all the time, that's because it's in our nature to be fierce. That's not bravery, that's duty."

"But the way she treated you!" Colin looked like he was going to be physically ill.

Judd pressed his lips together. He was exhausted by several lifetimes spent coping with not just bigotry, but others' guilt when they witnessed that bigotry. Even though the first came from a place of entitlement and the second from a place of affection, they were both burdens placed on him through no action of his own.

Judd tried to come up with a means of explaining. "You hate the way Kevin treats you, now, don't you?"

"What?"

"With kid gloves? Like he failed you? Like he's waiting for you to fracture, or to hate him? Like you didn't build up your backbone on your own while he was gone. Like you can't function without him."

Colin looked at Judd from under pale lashes. "Yeah."

Judd nodded. "So don't do it to me."

Colin's eyes went wide. He dipped his head.

"Pity, guilt, shame – they're toxic. To you and the person you coat them with. Admit it, hash it out, talk it over. You gotta tell your brother how you felt and why. So he can apologize and you can forgive him. It's what you both need. But mostly, it's so you can both let go of the past."

"And us? My mother?"

"Her words and actions aren't yours to own, Gingersnap. They never were. She didn't leave you because of something you did or said. She didn't cut me down because of anything I did. This isn't your issue to fix in any direction. You can't control the behavior of others. You aren't an Alpha, remember?"

"Far from it." Colin frowned at his hands. "But it's also my responsibility to stand up for those I love, isn't it?"

"Which you feel strongly because no one did that for you?"

"I suppose."

"I adore that you want to defend and protect me, but I'm still an enforcer. It still feels like you're weakening me by thinking I need help. Now, that's my issue. Those are my instincts. I gotta figure a way to reconcile with that, because part of affection is defense and loyalty." Judd didn't say love, although that's what he was talking about. He didn't say Colin was wrestling with the instincts of a mate, because that would be too much too soon. Although he hoped it was the truth.

He pressed on. "There's a huge part of me that wants nothing but to coddle and dote on you. Protect you from *everything*. Never let you see your mother again, least of all witness how she treats others. Not because it hurts me − like I said, I'm used to it, but because it hurts you."

"But you shouldn't *have* to be used to it."

"You gonna fight the world for me, Gingersnap?"

"I'd try." Colin's spine straightened.

"And you'd be hurt, and I won't have that. I can't."

Colin smiled, small and sad. "Impasse."

Judd realized suddenly what their conflict was. He was always one to act, to put the world into motion. Colin was the opposite, sitting back, hiding, trying to help through quiet sympathy. Colin did gentle, careful things. He cleaned the kitchen so Lovejoy would find it ready the next morning. He put sardines on the grocery list, so Marvin had a snack after work. He tidied the shoes in the cloakroom after everyone stripped for a run. He made certain the pack's computers and phones were updated and free of malware. He offered drinks to guests when they arrived and kept the dishes washed at potlucks. His actions were all understated. Which didn't mean they should be discounted or devalued, because they added good into the world in small doses.

Judd said the only thing he could think of that might get through. "I love the way you are and all the things you do for our pack. I know you do little things precisely because you don't want to be noticed, but you should know I notice you and them.

You don't think they're important but they are. Sure, they aren't grand gestures. Sure, you don't fight unless you've no other option. I know you think of yourself as useless. You try to avoid attention. So you do things that aren't bold but they *are* necessary. That makes you a *more* vital member of this pack, not a lesser one."

"Now you're making me blush."

"I love it when you blush."

Green, suspicious eyes were on him. "Oh! You do it on purpose, do you?"

"Maybe a little."

"That's terrible!"

"I always wanted to see how far down it goes. And now I know. It's adorable." Judd trailed fingertips from his mate's hot cheek down his slender throat to the top of his chest. He felt reverent, worshipful. There was a godless divinity to this moment.

"I'd rather be sexy than adorable," Colin grumbled.

"It's possible to be both, Gingersnap."

They'd moved past the heavy talk. For which Judd was grateful. He felt a bit of a coward about that.

Wrung dry of his defenses by fantastic sex and emotional conversation, Judd was also forced to admit something to himself. That *something* was love. Fixed and unmoving. He felt it – hard and fierce, tethering him to this boy. He wanted real, total, romantic love with this too young, too earnest, too perfect being in his arms.

He had no idea what to do about that.

Once again they met with Lexi Blanc at her rented house in Mill Valley – this time it was before a concert. Colin got everyone rigged up with communications and tested and ready to go without once acknowledging his mother. It was liberating.

She, of course, didn't notice him at all.

The pack wore the outfits that they'd worn the day before – washed, of course. Judd even had socks on.

Risa threw a fit when she learned they'd used an actual washing machine on their polo shirts. "Are you *animals*? Those are designer!"

Judd arched a brow at her.

Colin tried not to laugh. Kevin and Isaac didn't even try.

Jojo whisked Colin away for makeup. Colin enjoyed it, both the pampering and how he looked afterwards. He felt less insipid with his lashes and eyebrows darkened.

Judd said, "Don't even think about it," when Jojo gestured in his direction.

Colin instantly felt less good.

"I love it on you, Gingersnap. It's just not for me," Judd explained. Because he'd noticed Colin's discomfort. Of course he'd noticed.

Kevin regarded the exchange. "You can do me if you like."

Jojo waggled interested eyebrows at that. Kevin looked momentarily terrified, then submitted to the minimum of eye liner and mascara. Colin rather enjoyed that his brother's straightness was a deficit in the celebrity world.

"You look hot," Isaac reassured Kevin. "The ladies will love it."

Colin agreed. But then his brother always looked good. Somehow mascara made him seem more masculine, not less. Suddenly, Colin knew his own face to be far too pretty.

Judd's hand was at his back. "Stop it, Gingersnap."

From the house they piled into the stretch limo, which crawled its way (it really was a *most* impractical vehicle for the Bay Area) around Highway One and up the mountain to the amphitheater.

They arrived at around eight in the evening, but the stage was already up and running, lights being tested. There were a massive set and big curtains blocking off a back area. The stone seats were swarming with off-duty cops, who would form the bulk of the local security team.

Lexi immediately went backstage to put on more makeup.

Judd and Kevin stuck close to her. Colin activated the ear-buds and wandered around getting the lay of the land. He wanted to figure out the best location for monitoring both the tech and the pack's positions.

The amphitheater was pretty darn cool. Very Old World, like it belonged at Pompeii or something. It was a big half-circle carved into the mountainside with stone benches all around. The stage was at the bottom, with trees and then this amazing view of the hills behind. All around it were more trees and more mountains; it was just carved there in the middle of parklands. Colin climbed up to the nosebleed section. Below him the stage became a tiny thing far away. He couldn't imagine paying good money to see a loud concert with tons of other shifters and humans, only to be seated here. People were weird.

"Heya, red. You're looking spiffy." A scent of lush forest, honey chamomile, and predator assaulted Colin's nose – Hang Ten Viking.

He turned around with a smile. "Deputy Kettil, what are you doing here?"

"West Marin asked my department to help out. They don't have the manpower for something this big, and the money is great."

Colin was glad for the bear shifter's presence. He tapped his ear-bud. "We got us a friendly, boys."

Judd's voice: "Report?"

"Deputy Kettil is on stadium security."

"Tell him *hi*."

"Judd says hi."

"Who else of your lot is here?" asked the berserker, trying to not seem too interested.

"Kevin and Isaac. We're her ladyship's bodyguards."

"You brought Isaac? Seriously?"

Colin wrinkled his nose. "Pack reasons."

"Good for us to know, though. Omega in a crowd like this. Could be real lucky to have around, if something goes badly wrong."

"Our first responsibility is to our client, even Isaac's."

"I know, but it's still nice to know he's here."

Colin smiled. "I'll tell him you said so." He tapped his bud again. "Isaac? Deputy Kettil says hooray for you!"

Isaac chucked in his ear. "Well, I say hooray for him. Nice to have backup that big."

"Isaac says he's glad we have you for backup."

The deputy laughed. "Same deal applies, though. Our main focus is keeping the crowd under control."

Colin nodded. "That's fair."

"You look different." Deputy Kettil's shovel-sized hands swooped around Colin's face, not touching just indicating shape.

Colin blushed furiously. "I got makeup on."

The deputy nodded. "Huh. Looks nice. That what Trick does?"

"Yeah, most days. He looks really pretty, right?" Colin wasn't above a bit of teasing.

Deputy Kettil grunted an affirmative.

"They made me do this. But I'm not sure if I could, you know, keep it up…"

"Sure be a shame if you didn't."

Colin, feeling emboldened – someone who wasn't Judd liked the way he looked and had noticed. "Why Deputy, are you flirting with me?"

"What? No!" The berserker raised up both hands and backed away.

Colin felt warm and powerful and weirdly proud. All day yesterday he hadn't been certain about the look. He'd never worn makeup before, always wanted to, never had the guts. This time Jojo had done something to Colin's eyes, so they looked enormous, a burst of gold shiny stuff on his lids. Colin also had on some kind of gloss that made his already too puffy lips look wet and bee-stung. He thought it was too much, but maybe not?

A sudden presence was next to him and Colin turned. Judd was standing there, arms crossed, glowering at the bear shifter.

"Deputy."

"Mr Day." Deputy Kettil dipped his head. "I suddenly believe that I'm desperately needed elsewhere."

"I'm sure you are."

Colin turned to Judd. "That was weird."

"Was it?"

"I think he was flirting with me. I mean, maybe not intentionally, but still. And there was this lighting dude, too. Earlier. He kept staring at my mouth."

Judd muttered something.

"What?"

"Just come backstage with me. I know you don't want to be near your appalling mother, but I think you should stick close for the time being."

"You do?"

"Most definitely."

"Well, it seems the ear-buds are working, and they stretch all the way across the amphitheater so the pack should have full mobility without losing contact. I'm not sure I have anything else to do right now. Was there something you needed from me?"

"Yes, but it'll have to wait."

"You can't do it now?"

"I am many things, Gingersnap, including an exhibitionist, but you most certainly are *not*. And I don't think stripping you bare and sucking your cock in the middle of the Mount Tamalpais Amphitheater is exactly what you're looking for from our arrangement." Judd looked suddenly hopeful. "Is it? Because right now that's about all I want to do. That way every dude in this place will realize that you're *mine*."

Colin's mind shut down and he just sort of whimpered.

"Exactly," said Judd. "So instead, I'm going to kiss the stuffing out of you. Grope your amazing ass in those obscene pants. Turn us both on in a way that is bound to be embarrassing, and smudge all that ridiculously hot lip gloss. If that's okay with you."

Colin nodded, dumbly. *Definitely okay. All kinds of okay.*

Judd immediately had Colin in his arms, and suited his actions to his words, leaving Colin breathless, and Judd licking his lips and glaring down at him, impossibly smug. "Mmm, strawberry, very nice."

The lighting guy walked by. "Point made, big guy. Point made."

A ping came through on the com, Isaac's voice. "Uh, guys, there's something wrong backstage. It's the VIP pre-show meet and greet, and there's some dudes here smelling like, well, not roses, if you get my drift?"

Judd charged down the stone steps. Colin followed close on his heels.

Colin was going to be the death of him. But what a way to go. Of all the things Judd expected to happen that night, seeing the mate of his heart trotting about flirting with tech dudes wearing stripper pants, a cowboy shirt, and lip gloss was not one of them.

Colin smelled and looked bloody edible. Judd had a hard time keeping his hands to himself. It was worse than before. Somehow mutual blow jobs had given Judd's heart permission to *want*. His body always had, but the heart getting involved made it worse. Judd had to force himself to pay attention to his surroundings and not his lover, watching for threats to their client, and not threats to his burgeoning relationship. It was already a difficult task since, as far as he was concerned, they could have her.

When they'd arrived at the amphitheater, he was glad Colin focused elsewhere. Pert little ass wiggling about as he tested tech, adjusted cords, and consulted about sound distribution. Then Deputy Kettil made it perfectly clear that others probably thought Colin was edible too. So Judd had to go metaphorically pee on the kid. Because Judd was a stupid jealous wolf-man who'd never learned to share. And because it was Colin – scared, broken Colin – and men were pigs. Well, some men, some were wolves, and some were bears, but the point stood. Grrr.

Lexi Blanc had a special reception room set up to one side

backstage. It was all gold brocade and fine wallpaper. There she held court.

Apparently, a handful of VIPs paid thousands of dollars to arrive early and meet Blanc up close and personal. Shake her hand, take a photo, pluck her nose hair, or something equally thrilling. Since Judd wanted never to be in the same room as the woman for the rest of his life, he thought this a profound waste of money. Celebrity was weird. Humans with lots of dough were even weirder.

When he and Colin arrived at a run, Kevin and Isaac were squared off against a large round man and three bodyguards. The man didn't look familiar. Two of the bodyguards *did.* They all sure *smelled* familiar. Also, they were all wearing double-breasted pinstriped suits with no shirts underneath.

Judd said to Colin, "I know I just ran him off, but you should go get Deputy Kettil."

Colin's eyes looked even bigger than normal with whatever the makeup artist had done. "I'm on it." He scuttled off.

Judd joined his pack mates. "Fancy seeing you here." What had Colin called them? Oh yes. "Blubber Bozo One. Blubber Bozo Two." He nodded. He liked to be cordial before he beat someone into a pulp. "You gentlemen don't seem like country music fans."

The four selkie regarded him sullenly. They were much less posturing and aggro than they'd been in the café. Either because the extremely fat man with the extremely large mustache was their Alpha, or because Isaac was having a beneficial effect on them, or both.

"And you must be Blubber Bozo Three and the King of the Blubber Bozos?" Judd grinned at the other two selkie – showing all his teeth. "I see you've met Isaac."

"I have ticket." Blubber King showed his VIP pass. He had a strong accent, which Judd couldn't quite place. Greek perhaps?

"Yes, but your bodyguards do not." Kevin kept his expression bland and his arms loose and ready. "One pass per person. They can wait outside. If you like."

Judd glanced into the VIP room. Blanc was batting huge fake

eyelashes at an elderly couple drenched in fringe and jewelry. The ubiquitous Risa was the only one who'd noticed that the selkie had arrived. She was looking less icy and more surprised. These weren't the usual types to show up to a Lexi Blanc meet and greet. They seemed vested in a 1930s mafia don look, not country music. Big Bad Voodoo Blubbers. Judd supposed the selkie spent most of their time at sea, they probably didn't realize fashions had shifted.

He saw Risa press Blanc's bare shoulder and whisper something too quiet for even his supernatural hearing. The stylist gestured backstage.

Blanc nodded without looking at her.

Risa disappeared. She emerged a short while later with the heavy gold beaded jacket. Blanc put it on and continued with her line of sycophants.

The King of the Blubber Bozos was up next.

Apparently, he really was a fan. He left his guard as instructed and approached a known Alpha werewolf alone. He complimented Blanc in his heavy accent. He praised her singing, her looks, and her attire.

Blanc said something about the jacket being a special prequel to her costume that night. Wasn't he *lucky* to get to see it up close? He said yes, he was.

She called him, "My darling selkie daddy-kins." Batted those dumb lashes at him.

He gave her what looked like a real diamond tennis bracelet.

The audience ended.

The selkie exited, puffed and flushed. "It's like touching Venus!" His big brown eyes glittered. Then he glared at his guards. "She is innocent. She is pure. She is *glorious*."

"Oh fuck me," said Kevin.

"No one here porks your direction, brother dear." Colin trotted up, followed by Deputy Kettil.

The berserker had a frown on his face. He was focused on the King of the Blubber Bozos.

The selkie lumbered towards a corded-off seating area at the front of the stands, bodyguards in tow.

"Is that who I think it is?" Kettil's voice squeaked in shock.

Judd made an educated guess. "The head of the Pinniped Syndicate?"

"No. Not the *head*. That looks like Demetrius the Younger, his son."

The selkie made himself comfortable in the center of the VIP area. His blubber bozos settled faithfully around him.

"So, *Prince* of the Blubber Bozos?" suggested Kevin.

Kettil looked to the heavens and shook his head. "You wolves are exhausting. You know that?"

"Otters are worse." Isaac pointed out, mildly.

Deputy Kettil glared at him. "Stop it."

"Just saying." Isaac squinted to hide his amusement. It didn't work.

Kevin threw his hands up. "Man, dudes dating dudes is so much drama."

"Not dating," Kettil grumbled, under his breath.

Judd looked at Kevin. He crossed his arms and raised one eyebrow. "I know, right? You sure you don't suck dick, Kev? You're the biggest drama queen of us all."

"Fuck off, Judd."

They watched in silence as one of the blubber bozos produced a retro wicker picnic basket. It was packed with fermented fish wine, four whole lobsters, eight Dungeness crabs, two dozen oysters, in shell, a gallon bag of seaweed salad, and several containers of caviar.

The Prince of the Blubber Bozos ate his dinner. He was obviously prepared to enjoy the open air concert as much as his money allowed. Or his father's money.

Judd exchanged glances with the rest of his pack. "It's weird for a selkie mobster to have a crush on a country music singing Alpha werewolf, right?"

"Totally weird." Kevin nodded, fervently.

"Maybe he really is just here for the concert?" Colin sounded like he doubted his own words.

Isaac wrinkled his nose. "Anything is possible."

Judd focused on stratagem. "If he's here, though, I'm

thinking some other friends of ours will likely show up soon and..." He looked around. "There they are."

Up at the entrance of the amphitheater, on one side near the nose bleeders, stood Agents Faste and Lenis.

"How do they manage to look so much like feds?" Kevin wondered.

"It's the suits, no pinstripe," suggested Isaac.

"And they aren't double-breasted," added Judd.

"It's the stance," said Colin. "I wonder if they have lessons in how to stand in training camp. I mean, it's not quite like the cops. No offense, Deputy. But it's still all *we are here to watch you and we have the power to arrest you.* You know?"

"AKA we have sticks up our butts the size of baseball bats?" suggest Isaac.

"Whoa, kinky." Kevin snickered. "I thought you and Tank liked that kind of thing."

Isaac gave Kevin a level look. "You talk like you've given it a lot of thought. You keep writing gay checks that you never cash, Kev. There something you want to tell us?"

Kevin actually blushed. "Sorry, Isaac, none of my business."

"Mum-hum, thought so."

Colin was grinning as huge as could be. He clearly loved it when his big brother was taken down a peg.

Deputy Kettil's massive bearded head ping-ponged along with their banter. "Imma go. You know, see what they want."

"Good luck with that," said Judd. No love lost between him and the feds. He didn't like them sniffing round his pack's territory. That wasn't *ever* going to change.

"San Francisco used to be so nice and werewolf-free," lamented Kettil as he strode away. His long stride eating up the stone steps easily.

"You love us," yelled Isaac, after him.

"Likes otters better," muttered Colin, small smile on his face.

"Poor old sod," said Isaac, "we gotta be nice to him about that. I don't think he's ever had a crush on a dude before."

"Is that really any of our business?" wondered Kevin, waspishly.

"When has that stopped us before?" snapped Colin.

Judd said, before the two brothers could start bickering, "Isaac, I think you should be stationed right here at the front corner of the stage. You can watch the VIP access points, keep an eye on the performance, and monitor our blubbery friends there. Sound good?"

"Peachy." Isaac settled back, leaning against the side of the stage.

"Colin, how do you feel about the sound booth?"

Colin's looked up at Judd. "Indifferent. Why?"

"I like it as a base of ops for you." It was on the other side of the stage, slightly back. It was mostly shielded from audience view, but in good position to keep an eye on those things Isaac couldn't monitor, both backstage and high up towards the entrance.

Of course, Judd also wanted Colin there because he'd be protected from the crowd and safely away from any action. He decided to admit to that, so Colin didn't feel like he was being purposefully put to the side. "I'd feel better if you were away from our selkie friends."

"Bullshit." Kevin's grin was huge. "You want him away from the eyes and hands of all these shifters drooling over his ass."

Judd didn't deny it. He just glared at his fellow enforcer.

"Sound booth is fine." Colin went pink with what Judd hoped was pleasure.

"You did notice the sound guy is, in fact, a militant, tattooed Goth girl, right? She actually sneered at Mother during mic checks. I might be in love." Kevin gave Colin a smug look. "So of course Judd wants you there."

Judd snorted, but didn't deny he had an ulterior motive. He'd noticed Colin introducing himself to said Goth earlier. He'd also noticed that Colin seemed comfortable with her.

Colin confirmed this. "Paris. Yeah. She's nice. She hates country and is only here for the money. Totally your type, Kev. Way too good for you."

Kevin dipped his chin. "I know, right? Hot."

"Poor thing," said Isaac, shaking his head.

Judd wasn't sure if he meant Kevin or Paris, or possibly both.

Judd gave Colin a list of tasks to complete – cross checks and threat assessments, expected attendance numbers to weigh against security personal distribution. "Identify any holes, kid. Let Kettil know."

"Will do, old man," was his mate's cheeky response. Scuttling away before Judd could reply.

Judd watched Colin's gorgeous ass climb up onto the stage and trot over to the sound booth. Paris tucked him into a corner in a motherly manner and then continued her own work.

"Some brothers get all the luck," grumbled Kevin.

"True," replied Judd. "His ass is *much* nicer than yours."

"Dude!" respond Kevin.

CHAPTER FOURTEEN
SHE WORE GOLD SPANGLES

Judd found the concert, frankly, anti-climactic. Of course, it was bold and spectacular – a sensory overload. He admired its sheer brazenness. The opening band was decent – a local rockabilly sensation called the Squirrel Butt Kickers. They had too many flaming saxophones and an overabundance of beard glitter, but at least the tunes didn't grate on Judd's ears.

Judd caught Kevin bopping his head about while standing sentry outside of Blanc's dressing room.

"Seriously?" Judd gave him a look.

"They're not bad."

"Not good either."

"It's not like I'm actually dancing."

"Thank heaven for small mercies."

Isaac and Colin reported in every ten minutes or so. But nothing happened during the opening act.

Then Lexi Blanc took the stage in a blaze of swinging searchlights and a shower of glitter. She wore the amazing beaded gold jacket, a corset, a fringed scarf-skirt thing that barely covered her ass, and gold cowboy boots.

Judd would never admit that she had stage presence – but she had *serious* stage presence. She gyrated and wiggled all over the damn place, singing with all her heart. Not that she had much of a heart, but what little she had, she used up performing.

The crowd was wild for her.

There ain't nothing that I'd rather do,
  Than dance under moonlight, shiftin' for you!

She moved seamlessly from one hit to the next. No banter, no pause, no crowd work. She was there to give them a show. They were there to see her sing. She didn't even nod in the direction of the VIPs. If anything, she seemed to regard her roaring fans with an indifferent superiority mixed with mild contempt.

They lapped it up.

My baby gots paws,
  Ain't no stopping this wild sea-saw!
  When we get together, we don't howl,
  We goes yee-haw!

Judd: "Status, boys?"

Isaac: "No change with the blubber bozos. They're actually trying to dance. It's not pretty. I demand eyeball replacement surgery."

Kevin: "Dudes, I may never recover from this experience. That's my mother's ass out there. Like, her *whole* ass. I regret all life choices that have led me to this moment."

Colin: "Paris just gave me a La Coq soda. Have you had one of these? Guys, they're really tasty. I think mine is chicken liver-flavored."

You like it rough there, baby?
  You like my sweet, sweet lips?
  Just call me moon-mad lady!
  I'll shake my tail and hips!

. . .

Judd: "How much longer do we have?"

Isaac: "Blubber bozos still dancing. At least you don't have to see what I'm seeing."

Kevin (singing): "Sea people got, no reason, to dance?"

Judd: "Well, you didn't get your mother's voice."

Colin (small burp): "I take it back, this stuff is gross. Repeats on you."

Judd: "So sexy, baby."

Colin: "That's chicken liver-flavored sexy baby, to you."

Kevin: "What is happening right now? Are you two flirting via ear-bud? What alternate universe have I entered?"

Judd, Colin, and Isaac: "Shut up, Kevin."

Ain't no tail like a werewolf tail.
Ain't no sound like a howl at the moon.
Bet you're gonna feel my wail,
Bet you'll pull my tail hard soon.

Judd: "Is it over yet?"

Isaac: "I think it's just a costume change."

Judd: "Fuck me."

Colin: "Yes please."

Kevin: "Make it stop. Isaac, make it stop."

Isaac: "I have no control over the length of a country music concert, but I think it's only an encore. Shouldn't be too much longer."

Kevin: "I meant Judd and Colin. Make them stop flirting. Though the concert would be nice stopped too."

Colin: "Oh wait now... That *is* interesting. SBI is on the move. Approaching your position, Isaac."

Isaac: "I see them. SBI engaging with blubber bozos. So far, seems polite. Blubber Prince is annoyed. He wants to enjoy the concert, doesn't like the feds spoiling his fun."

Kevin: "Nothing could possibly further spoil anything this bad."

Judd: "Look sharp, boys, here she comes."

Kevin: "Oh my god, what is she wearing *now*? Jesus Christ on a Cutlet, is that even clothing?"

The crowd roared so loudly they drowned out even the direct communiqué of ear-buds.

The opening chords struck.

Colin: "She's doing *Fangs,* guys. Get ready. Isaac, you okay?"

Isaac: "Sure thing. SBI still engaged with the blubberers. Still playing nice."

Judd: "*Fangs*? What is *Fangs*? Oh dear god…"

The crowed roared again.

They said it would never work,
   When we walked paw in hand.
   They said you just can't play nice,
   Humans are weak. Werewolves are bad.

But I have your fangs at heart,
   I have your dreams in play,
   I've got your paws to start,
   I'll wag my tail all day.

Fangs, fangs, fangs,
   Fangs in the morning dew,
   Fangs on a moonlit night,
   Baby, I bleed for you.

. . .

Judd: "I. Am. Going. To. Stab. My. Own. Ears."

Kevin: "Is she stripping? Dude. I'm seriously gonna be sick."

Colin: "But this is mummy dearest's biggest hit. You saying it's not the *living end*?"

Kevin: "I hate you all right now. I hate my life."

Judd: "Well, I hate country music."

Isaac: "Man, if this work of genius doesn't convert you, nothing will. Did you hear she rhymed *hand* with *bad*?"

Judd: "Just, stop."

Colin: "Isaac, are you down a bozo?"

Isaac: "Nope, there he is. He was disposing of the shells. Had no idea one person could eat that many oysters."

Kevin: "What's she doing now?"

Judd: "It's that thing singers do when they bend down and slap the hands of the people in the front row."

Colin: "That can't possibly be hygienic."

Shifters don't love your prey,
Humans should fear the dark,
Skin and fur just don't mix,
Werewolves will break your heart.

Fangs, fangs, fangs,
Fangs in the morning dew,
Fangs on a moonlit night,
Baby, I bleed for you.

Isaac: "Prince of the Blubber Bozos is back up and dancing. Or at least jiggling a whole lot. Oh, he is *into* this!"

Kevin: "And she's stripping *more*. My eyes. My eyes!"

Isaac: "Aw, look, she's blowing him kisses."

Kevin: "And taking off her jacket."

Isaac: "And throwing it to our friend. Isn't that sweet? Aw, he's her number one fan. Look at his little mobster face. He's so happy."

Kevin: "Is he smelling it? I think he is. Gross."

Judd: "Eyes on the client, please, Kevin."

Isaac: "I didn't think selkies had a sense of smell."

Colin: "Why toss him her nice jacket? Will she expect it back or is it like a love token?"

Judd: "Well, if she's giving away a jacket like that, maybe you can keep those stripper pants."

Colin: "I'll keep mine if you keep yours."

Judd: "I'm sad I never got to rip them off you."

Colin: "Sooner me stripping than my mother."

Kevin: "Great, now I need to bleach my eyeballs and my ear holes later."

Judd: "And once more with feeling…"

Fangs, fangs, fangs,
  Fangs in the morning dew,
  Fangs on a moonlit night,
  Baby, I bleed for you.

Judd: "And we're done. Thank good glory shitgibbon for that."

The crowded hollered and shrieked, howled and roared, literally and figuratively.

Lexi Blanc took a long series of bows. She spun around so the fringe on her gold bra and undies flipped up. She reveled in their adulation. Alpha and celebrity, a potent mix.

Then she cast both arms out wide and shifted form. It took her an average length of time. It would have taken her longer had she not been Alpha. It was weird to see it done in the middle of a stage under strobe lighting. Generally, shifting was a somewhat private affair, like hot tubbing – for friends, pack mates, and lovers only. And best done in the dark, by necessity. Her clothing, such as it was, was designed to rip away like their pants. She was left standing in front of the roaring crowd on four legs in nothing but her own fur.

Which was probably a good thing, because a wolf would look bloody ridiculous in a gold lamé fringed bikini.

She threw her head back and howled.

The crowd went absolutely bug nuts. Half of those who could, also shifted form – mostly barghest and a few large cats. *That* caused a ruckus. Judd was glad his team wasn't responsible for crowd control. The ripped clothing, lost belongings, and public indecency citations alone. Poor Deputy Kettil.

Colin trailed behind the others as they went to collect Lexi from backstage. The SBI remained with the selkies and seemed inclined to stay there.

Apparently, the jacket was not for keepsies. Lexi threw the biggest prima donna fit about it not being back in her dressing room when she returned. Prince of the Blubber Bozos was prevented from leaving the amphitheater and directed backstage to return it to her, personally. He clutched at Lexi's hand and told her how wonderful she was.

His mother was gracious, but he saw Risa pass her a towel to wipe her hand the moment the selkie left.

Lexi's eyes were bright and feverish as they hustled her up the hill and into the waiting limo. They were driving down the highway before most of the concert goers had made it back to their cars. Those who had brought cars, of course. More than a few had run to the amphitheater in shifted form. Mount Tam was lovely hunting ground and unclaimed shifter territory.

Colin felt a little twitchy himself. He didn't usually experience the frantic energy of other shifters, the hum of quintessence, or the drive to hunt. But for some reason, tonight, even though it was nowhere near full moon, he wanted to run with his pack. Or was it just horniness? Maybe he really actually just wanted to fuck.

How novel.

He watched Judd from beneath lowered eyelashes.

Judd was still in full security mode. "Anything go missing tonight? Anyone make it backstage who wasn't supposed to?"

Lexi's manager shook her head. "You did good, and you did it while down two men from our normal security detail. We should have gone with werewolves this entire tour."

Lexi was still on a performer's high. Colin hadn't thought shifters got that way. "What a *fantastic* show. Didn't you love it? What a wonderful crowd. They adored me."

"You were great, Lexi. One of your best, darling," replied the manager.

Lexi glared.

"The best, definitely *the* best," she corrected herself.

Lexi's team then spent most of the rest of the drive telling her how amazing and talented she was. If Colin hadn't been relieved at how smoothly everything went, he would have been sick.

Finally they were back at the fancy house in Mill Valley that Judd said stank of eighties coke-fests and desperate tycoons with tiny, fast cars.

Judd and Kevin made sure Lexi and her people were safely inside the house. Isaac and Kevin swept the grounds while Colin and Judd did the same inside.

Their contract was up the moment the concert ended, but Judd was thorough and Heavy Lifting came by its stellar reputation honestly.

Lexi was taking a bubble bath when they left, so she didn't bother to wish them goodbye. Colin certainly wasn't cut up about it and Kevin had seen more of his mother than he ever wanted to. He was still complaining about it on the drive home.

They piled into the pack's pickup truck, Colin and Isaac in the back of the king cab, Kevin up front in the passenger seat, and Judd driving.

"Well?" said Judd, as they wended their way down the mountain towards Tam Junction.

"I hope you don't take this the wrong way, Judd, but if you

ever book us a country music gig again, I will eat your head," said Kevin.

"That selkie mobster is totally in love with her, and I wonder if that comes into play at all with all the stolen things," said Isaac.

"It'll never work," said Kevin. "Dad always said…"

"Surf and turf don't mix." Colin said it with him.

"Any other cogent observations, boys?" pushed Judd.

Colin couldn't stop himself from smiling. "I managed to keep the pants."

Judd turned just enough so Colin, who was sitting directly behind him, could see his smile. "So did I."

Colin gave a little cough gulp noise.

"Yeah, we all did. Shall we start stripping as another source of income?" Kevin sounded only party-joking. "I mean Heavy Lifting works either way. My stripper name is Big Guns MacCum."

"That's your porn name, dude." Isaac sneered at him.

"Yours is Oh My Gaga."

"Stop it now, Kevin."

"What's mine?" asked Colin.

"You're my little brother, you start stripping over my dead body. But Judd's is—"

"Don't bloody even, Kevin," said Judd.

Fortunately for Kevin, Judd's phone started ringing. Since he was driving, Kevin picked it up and looked at it. "Shit, it's the client."

Judd pulled over into the parking lot of a convenience store. "Give it here, MacCum. Hello?" Lexi's manager's voice on the other end asked if they had any additional contracts for tomorrow.

"No."

Would they be available to act as security again, starting around four in the afternoon? Apparently Lexi wanted to stay longer. Risa had told her about some shops she simply had to visit before they left the Bay Area. Same rate plus fifty percent for such short notice? Same team, please.

Judd didn't play along. "I'll have to ask my Alpha." Colin knew he didn't really have to, and this was a delaying tactic.

Would he be able to respond right away?

"Yes, I'll wake him when we get back. Should be twenty minutes or so."

Judd hung up.

They all looked at one another.

Colin said, "Well, shit, maybe she wants the pants back." Pause. "I wonder who has it."

"What?" said Judd.

"The stolen, uh fenced, uh whatever, money."

"Not our problem, that's on Lenis and Faste."

"Yeah, but I like the mystery."

They made it home, parked, and hauled themselves out of the truck, feeling more tired than nocturnal werewolves had a right to feel.

Judd's big warm hand steered Colin though the overgrown yard, into the pack house and up the stairs. It was both exciting and reassuring.

"You know what we should do?" Colin suddenly thought of something quite brilliant. Or at least his sleepy brain thought it might be brilliant. "We should show pictures of Lexi's team to Trick."

Judd pandered to Colin's exhausted whimsy. "Sure thing, Gingersnap. Soon as we wake up tomorrow, we'll do that."

"Cool. Because Risa and that jacket, you know. Suspicious."

"You gonna go out for a PI or something, baby?"

"Do you think I could?"

"Probably. You have the patience and you're smart enough, but I'd rather you stuck to computers. Safer."

"Ha, shows what you know. Computers is where the porn is. Nothing safe about that."

"Depends what kinda porn, I suppose. You gonna show me what you like?"

"Do I have to?"

"You could tell me instead."

Colin considered. "Now?"

"Nope, now you're gonna go take a shower, and then come to my room."

"Oh, yeah?"

"Imma ask Alec about us working again tomorrow, or tell him. I'm sure it will be fine, but best to involve the Alpha. I'll be right back."

True to his word, Judd was back before Colin finished his shower. Colin stumbled into Judd's room with a towel wrapped about his waist, the hot water having made him even more tired.

"We on for tomorrow again, then?"

"Looks like. I'm sorry, baby. I know you wanted to be done with her." Judd lounged on the bed, making a note in the contract.

Colin knew the pack needed the money, so he didn't mind. Feeling brave, he used the towel to dry his hair, standing naked before Judd. Judd really did seem to like the way Colin was shaped, didn't care about how slim he was. Didn't want someone shaped like himself. Which Colin supposed made sense – he didn't want someone shaped like himself, either.

Colin prodded at his feelings about his mother. It had been weird watching her perform. He'd seen footage online, of course. But being there, in person, was different. It made him realize something. They might look alike, but she was nothing at all like him. She was nothing to do with him. She was this other alien entity. The fact that she had once, a long time ago, given him birth, didn't really matter anymore. She had left him and gone away to make herself great. And why shouldn't she? Why shouldn't she want that? She was awesome at being a country music star and she was sublimely shitty at being a mother. She should do what she was good at, right?

He hung the towel on a hook behind the door, feeling shy and exposed. "She's impressive in her way, and she's good at it. Is it weird that I really don't care? I mean, not in the way Kevin cares."

"No, baby, I actually think that's healthy." Judd threw the contract aside. His eyes were hot on Colin, shifting towards yellow.

"She shouldn't really matter to me at all, should she?"

Judd looked proud, patted the bed next to him. "No, Ginger-snap, she really, *really* shouldn't."

"Cool." Colin climbed over Judd and under the covers, pretending that it was the most natural thing in the world, feeling almost like he belonged there. Because maybe it was and maybe he did.

"You look so good in my bed." How did Judd always know to say exactly what Colin needed to hear?

"It's better than mine."

"Yeah?" Such wistful hope in the fierce enforcer's voice.

"Bigger, softer, smells like you."

"Well, then, you use it whenever you want."

"You sure?"

"Yeah, baby. Now Imma go shower. You snuggle in. Go to sleep."

"But…?" Colin had seen those eyes go yellow and he was naked.

"Not saying I don't want you. But we're both exhausted. We can fuck when we wake up. Seems like it's kind of a thing with us now, doesn't it? And it sure is a great way to start the day."

Colin nodded, happy. Judd was right. It was a better plan. Plus if he were to have another lesson, he wanted to be wide awake and in good condition to appreciate it properly, pay very close attention. Right now his eyes felt weighted, his skin seemed stretched, and his bones ached.

He tried to stay awake long enough so he could drift off cuddled against Judd's fantastic body, but he was asleep before his lover got back from the shower.

Colin awoke feeling languorous, rested, and extremely horny. He was pressed up against Judd. At some point in the last few days, it seemed he had turned into a limpet.

He buried his nose in Judd's chest. His skin tingled at the prickles of short hair there. He thrilled at the scent of him, fresh and musky and spicy – rich and perfect.

Beneath his ear there was a small rumble as Judd too came awake. Big arms curled around him, lifted him up easily, so that Colin found himself entirely draped over Judd. The enforcer's touch was demanding, almost too rough as he stroked Colin's back, pressing him close and tight, as if Judd wanted to absorb him into his skin, share a shifted form. Colin loved it, of course. Gentle was too cautious. Gentle didn't show need or possession. Colin wanted Judd to want him down to his bones, amorphous though they might be. Maybe not bones then, maybe something even deeper, like wanting him at a cellular level.

Colin propped one bony elbow on Judd's sternum and rested his chin in his hand, so he could glare down into Judd's face from mere inches away.

"Want something, Gingersnap?"

"You said I'd get more lessons today."

"Did I, indeed?"

"I believe I was promised sex."

"Well, when you put it like that. I wouldn't want to break a promise."

"Yeah. It was as serious as a pinky swear."

"A penis swear?"

"How is that different from crossing swords?" Colin wanted to know.

"Ah, so, let the lessons begin. When you're linking cocks for an oath, you gotta stretch your junk kinda alongside mine and then under."

Colin squirmed about, tried to do as instructed, chuckling, but pleased that they were both very hard and interested, for all their ridiculous talk. Oh… re-*dick*-ulous. *Ha!*

He collapsed into giggles.

Judd lifted him back off, before rolling over to rummage in his bedside table.

"So penis swears are not this morning's lesson, then?"

Judd looked back at him over one shoulder, trying for coy, which looked ridiculous on a man of his bulk and fierceness. Also kinda adorable, but Colin definitely wasn't going to say that.

Judd waggled his ass a bit, while he leaned over and continued to hunt in the drawer. "Thought maybe, this morning, you'd like to fuck me."

Colin lost all his breath, all at once. Like he'd been punched hard in the gut. But not in a *bad* way because his own cock gave a painful throb at the idea.

"Seriously?"

"I am *always* serious about ass play, Gingersnap. You game?"

"Yes! Yes. I mean… yeah, great, let's do that." Colin winced. Could anyone possibly be less cool than him?

Judd didn't seem to mind, coming up, triumphant with whatever he'd been looking for. It proved to be a very large bottle of lube.

Colin was a little traumatized by the size of it.

Judd gave him a serious look. "Now, you remember this, young scholar."

"Teach me, oh wise one."

"There is only one hard and fast rule of butt sex."

"Hard and fast, got it."

"No… wait."

"Not hard and fast?"

"Definitely hard, but usually not fast. Nice and slow, okay?"

"Got it, hard and slow. That's the rule?"

Judd pretended annoyance at him. "Rule number one, go slow."

"Right. Hardness irrelevant. Got it."

"Stop it, kid."

"Sorry, *daddy*."

Judd flopped back on the mattress.

Colin was beyond pleased with himself. He was bantering. This was sexual banter, and somehow he'd just, kinda *won*. Except the butt sex wasn't happening, so maybe he'd lost?

"Please go on, oh great teacher of the gospel of lubrication."

Judd glowered at him. "That is not any better!"

Colin pretended to be a good student, sat up straight and raised one finger. "Rule one, go slow." He raised another finger. "Rule two?"

Judd handed him the massive bottle of lube. "You can never have too much lube."

"Judd."

"Yes, baby?"

"This is an awful lot of lube."

Judd rolled his eyes. "Well, you don't have to use *all* of it. But when in doubt, add more lube, okay? Every step of the way."

Colin swallowed, nervous. He was imagining steps covered in lube and how dangerous that would be. "Okay."

"Stop looking so scared. I'm a big, tough werewolf enforcer, remember? You can't actually damage me and you won't hurt me if…"

"I go slow and use lots of lube."

"By George, I think he's got it."

"Who invited George into the mix?" Colin was proud of himself for still being able to talk, even as he felt himself losing all capacity for complex thought.

"Are you always this snappy and perky right after waking up? 'Cause I have to say it's a major character flaw." Judd flipped himself over and crawled to his knees. He widened his stance, so that he'd be at the right level, Colin realized, for Colin to penetrate him.

"Oh, fuck me," said Colin, not at all eloquently.

"No, the opposite is the idea. Remember?"

If there was anything more sexy than this huge muscled man offering up his ass, Colin had never encountered it before and likely never would again. He couldn't help himself, he dropped the lube and just smoothed his hands over that perfect butt. Just worshiped it. Didn't care how slim and pale his stupid fingers looked, because Judd shivered under his touch. *Judd* shivered under *his* touch. Like it was something wonderful. Like Colin was wonderful. Like his hands were good, perfect, capable, glorious things.

Colin sank his fingers in, gripped hard. He remembered Judd had said he wanted that. It felt special and dynamic.

"What, you got your hands on my ass and you lose all your snark?" Judd's voice was a little gruffer than it had been.

"I just. Oh my fucking god, that's just… Gah!"

"Eloquent, Gingersnap. Now, what are our rules?"

"Slow. Lube. Got it." Colin fished about for the lube, having more success with finding it than finding words, as it turned out.

Judd would have to do the talking.

"Tell me exactly what to do," Colin begged.

And Judd did. Guiding him through the process of one finger, and then two, and then three. Of locating his prostate, and how to curve, and ways to tug on his balls, and all the things that made Judd squirm and whimper and cry out beneath him. Which made Colin feel so powerful. Powerful, for the first time in his whole life. Like he could do this and do it well.

This thing, this was what he was good at. And his own horrible white thin gay-as-fuck fluttery awful hands were turning Judd inside out – his hands on Judd were absolutely gorgeous.

Colin proved two things to Judd.

That it definitely was possible to use too much lube. Although neither of them minded. They'd just need to clean the sheets later.

Also that it was possible to go too slow. Because Judd was losing his mind, and Colin just wanted that feeling of power and pride to go on and on forever.

Finally, after losing his language for a while, not unlike Colin, Judd finally said. "Look, Gingersnap. Lube up that perfect prick of yours and stick it in me right bloody now, or I will not be answerable for the consequences."

Colin did as ordered. "Yes sir!"

"You are such a brat. How did I not know what a brat you were?"

"Apparently sticking my fingers up your ass brings out the brat in me."

"Apparently. Oh holy mother of god and French fries, yessss."

Which is apparently what Judd says when you're sticking your cock up his ass. *Good to know.*

Up until that exact moment, Colin had been more about the turn-on of what he could do, of how he could play on this man's hot buttons, on the power of someone so strong at his mercy. But the act of thrusting into Judd changed everything.

Suddenly, this silken hot vise was all around his cock, squeezing impossibly tight.

He was breathless with it. "Oh, wow. And I thought blow jobs were nice."

Judd's rumble of amusement came at that. "You like it?"

"Could I just, you know, stay here forever?"

"Gingersnap, if you don't move right-the-fuck-now, I will flip you over, and hold you down, and ride you so hard you'll see stars." Which didn't seem like much of a threat and was such an erotic image it almost made Colin come on the spot.

He squeaked and reached down to grip the base of his own cock. "Don't say stuff like that!"

"Oh, he likes that idea too, does he? Good to know. Now, remember my two rules?"

Colin groaned. Because as wonderful as it felt, he really needed to thrust. "Yeah, I remember. Slow. Lube."

"Good. So ignore them both now."

"Yeah?"

"I need you to move, baby. Hard and fast. Please."

Judd begging. Colin couldn't have that. He had to give him exactly what he wanted right now. Exactly what he needed. So he did it. Thrusting, hard and fast as he could.

Judd fell apart beneath him and around him, writhing and moaning, and crying out. The noises he made. God, those noises. The way he smelled, salt and eager, and all that beautiful smooth

skin, the most amazing ass in the world. And Colin got to fuck it
– fuck him. Hard and fast and free, just following where his hips
and his heartbeat led. Racing towards something perfect.

Until Colin himself was nothing but pulses of *need, joy,
need, joy*. Points of light and cum pushing out of him, trans-
forming into *love, mine, love, mate* and that was a death knell.
Terrifying. He was so glad Judd was a quivering mess beneath
him, eyes closed, face mashed into a pillow, because he
shouldn't see Colin right now. He shouldn't notice all the love
just pulsing out of Colin. Because the risk in that was way too
high. If Colin let himself give out love, when he returned to
reality he'd be empty. When he was back to being unnoticed, to
the place where Judd held him in easy distanced affection, Colin
would truly, finally, be nothing. Void and lost. He couldn't bear
that idea. He'd always known he was strong enough to be
ignored. But equally, now, he knew, that he wasn't strong
enough to *love* and be ignored.

Colin let himself fold over Judd, breathe him in. They were
both sweaty and gross but that made for enough salt and wet to
hide what tumbled down Colin's face. He was a dork to cry over
something so simple as sex. Something so easy for others.
Something he was apparently good at. He was a dork to love on
the basis of three encounters with a man who pitied him. Who
was just teaching him to be whole. A dork to think there could
be something more than that for someone like him.

Judd took his time recovering. Possibly because a goddamn
novice had just given him the best dicking-out of his very long
life. Possibly because he was weak and old and in love and
couldn't believe what had just happened. The smell of it. Of
them, though. That made it all so very *real*.

Colin's slim form, draped over him, was shaking. Either
from cold or exertion. Judd wanted to move – to turn and cuddle.
He was lying in a pool of his own cum. Colin's cock, shrinking
slowly, meant more was about to start leaking down his thighs.

Not that he didn't love that sensation, the remnants of being taken. But he should get up. He should do the waddle of shame down the hallway to the bathroom. Clean up. At the very least, find a t-shirt to wipe up the mess.

But he couldn't bloody move. He could barely blink.

What the hell just happened?

Colin rolled off him, flopped onto his back. Twisted his neck to look at Judd.

Judd turned his head. They were nose to nose.

Colin's eyes were fully green. He looked sad, scared, hopeful, and proud – all at the same time.

"Was that okay? Did I do okay? How was it?" His insecurity tumbled out.

Judd was reminded, again, that Colin was really bloody young.

Judd gave a broad grin. "Deep and thorough. Exactly how I like it."

Colin brightened. "Deep and thorough, huh? Like all good research?"

"No wonder you're great at schoolwork, Gingersnap. All is now clear."

Colin obviously didn't want to be serious. He wanted to play. "I like my sex like I like my research?"

"With proper citation?" Judd understood the need to be flippant.

"Mostly done in the library?

"Peer-reviewed?"

Colin giggled.

"Good lesson, huh?"

Colin's full lips twitched into a small smile. "The best. Bet I could ace an exam."

"Bet you could, baby."

"Will there be an essay?"

Judd chuckled. "Naw, it's multiple choice. In. Out. In. Out."

Colin snorted. "Ohmygod, you're such a dork. I thought I was the dork."

Judd pretended affront. "I can be dorkish."

"You're really bad at it."

Judd grumbled and levered himself up. "So... topping. Whatcha think?"

Colin clasped his hands together. "That was basically the best thing ever. Why would anyone want to do anything else?"

Judd laughed. "Don't get so cocky."

"But I did good, yeah?"

"Good enough that I'm feeling like the student is mastering the teacher. Maybe starting to want more." Judd tested to see how Colin might react. Tested possession and permanence... togetherness.

Colin took it the wrong way, of course. "You think I'm ready to leave the nest? Go on to try more things with other people?"

That was not *at all* what Judd meant to imply by *more*. But if Colin's big brain went that way, perhaps that was what *he* wanted? It was a stupid idea, anyway, the kid was way too young for anything more serious. This was meant to be just lessons – a dalliance. He shouldn't have pushed.

"Is that what you want?" Judd understood where Colin was coming from. They'd agreed this was temporary. It's only, Judd had thought it would be longer than three times together. He'd hoped to convince Colin for *more* with him. Even if that was selfish. Even if Colin should go out, sow his wild oats, or whatever young people sowed these days.

Honestly, Judd couldn't blame Colin for not being interested in a real relationship with him. Who would want some big, brash, possessive enforcer asshole around all the time?

"I..." Colin sounded crestfallen. "If you're ready to stop, I can be graceful about it. But I thought you said I was good at topping."

Judd's heart gave a great thump in his chest. Of course Colin would take it like that. Poor Gingersnap always assumed nobody wanted him. "The best I have ever had. No joke. I would *love* to do it again. And more. And other stuff. As long as you want. I was giving you an out."

Colin looked less scared and more determined. "Well, I am

young. Can't settle down too soon. I mean we agreed. Only lessons. Nothing long term or permanent. Right?"

Judd's felt shaky – wary and unsteady. "That is what we agreed, yeah."

"Okay, so maybe a few more times? Just to be on the safe side."

Shit, what the hell had just happened? How could he misstep so badly? Judd was confused and sex-addled, and hurt. What was going on in his Gingersnap's psyche that he always took everything so awry?

Still, it was better than either of them storming out. Although Colin looked like he wanted to.

Judd took a deep breath. Willed Colin to do the same. "Let's table this until we deal with your mother one last time, okay?"

"Alec agreed to have us bodyguard her today?"

"Yeah, at a huge up-charge. We're definitely earning enough for that extra bathroom. Good thing too. Can't have me waddling down hallways leaking your jizz down my legs."

"Why is that so hot?"

"Like a man who waddles, do you?" And just like that they were back on safe ground.

CHAPTER FIFTEEN
FOREVER AND EVER, WHIPPED CREAM

Colin felt so foolish. That he'd considered, even for a second, that Judd would want anything more than a dalliance with someone like him. This had been, all along, a favor Judd was doing for a friend. Stupid to forget that for even a moment.

Colin wasn't *that* stupid, though. He had noticed things that had given him hope. Like the way Judd always turned towards him in a room. The way the big man inhaled his scent, and relaxed when touching him. His obvious desire and eagerness in bed was reassuring too. Colin screwed his eyes shut in an effort to stop himself from thinking of these as anything more than casual affection.

He berated himself for feeling thrown away and used, when it had been his idea to take advantage of Judd's willingness to help in the first place. If anything, he had used Judd, not the other way around.

But how could he not want more? When Judd always saw him. Judd always listened. That very morning, after the relationship (such as it was) conversation had been tabled and the sex smells showered away, Judd had asked if Colin wanted to go with him. Where? To the café to talk to Trick. Why? Because last night, Colin had mentioned a mere notion that Trick should look at pictures of Lexi Blanc's team. Judd had taken him seriously. Judd thought Colin was smart and had something to give to the pack – had good ideas.

It took very little time for Colin to find and download images featuring Lexi and her entourage. Instalamb was particularly useful. Lexi was always so helpful with her hashtags: #mydaypeeps #mypethumans #humanpack and #foodislove featured prominently.

So while Judd was chatting with Kevin about preparations for escorting Lexi shopping later, Colin crept back upstairs and decided to try something brave.

He talked to Marvin.

Marvin did gay very well, and Colin thought while Judd was trying get him comfortable with one aspect of his identity, perhaps Marvin could help him with another.

It was Sunday, and with no active search and rescue cases, the merman was home, puttering about in the master bedroom. But his door was open, which was pack code for "come in and disturb me if you like."

Still, Colin knocked on the jamb to be sure it was okay.

"Marvin? Alec?"

"It's just me, Col. Alec's chatting with Bryan over at his place. You need something, babes?"

"It was you I was looking for, actually." Colin wandered into the room.

"Oh hooray! I love being wanted. How can I help?"

The master suite was one of the first things they'd remodeled after moving in. Because Alec was their Alpha and he worked so hard, and because, frankly Marvin liked things *just so*. If he was going to live on land, that land better restructure itself to his exacting, and sublimely spectacular, standards.

It was impressive. Marvin had a walk-in closet (for a man with a tail half the time, he was curiously obsessed with shoes). Marvin had a vanity with a very fuzzy pouf for sitting and all his fun creams and jewelry and makeup arranged just so (having scales just meant *more specialty product*). Marvin had big windows that looked out on the ocean. And the attached master bathroom boasted a truly huge slipper-shaped bathtub (so Marvin could salt the water and don tail if he wanted) and another window that looked back over the yard and open space up the hill. And Alec had his Marvin happy, which was really all that mattered to the Alpha in any given room – fancy master suite or not.

Marvin was at the vanity so Colin wandered over. Since that was what he wanted to ask about, anyway. "Whatcha doing, Alpha-mate?"

The merman looked up at him, smile sweet. "Planning the menu for next Saturday's barbecue. Friday is full moon, as I'm sure you're very well aware, so I know you boys will bring back a deer. I was thinking about trying a jerk sauce on it this time. Jerked venison? I could start a trend."

"You're planning a menu?"

"Yes, darling."

"Marvin, it's a potluck."

"There's no need to be pedantic about it."

Colin shook his head and moved cautiously to lean against the edge of the vanity.

He felt privileged to be there, in his Alpha's bedroom. The smell of comfort and care was all around him. The way it combined with Marvin's scent of salty sea breezes was delightful. It made him wonder if his dad's dumb saying about surf and turf was wrong. If maybe his dad had been wrong about a lot of things. And that made him brave enough to ask.

"Do you think you could…?" He lost all his bravery halfway through the sentence.

Marvin gave him the full force of blue-eyed attention. "I could what, sweetheart?"

The ocean was in his eyes, wide and welcoming.

"I thought maybe you could show me how to do my face? Just a bit?"

Marvin bounced up and launched himself at Colin, giving him a huge hug. He was all graceful wiry limbs and beachy smells and Colin loved it. Loved him. "Aw, babes, welcome to the magic place. Now, we start with primer, and then liner, and then *the sparkles*. Sit, sit."

Colin let himself be swept out to sea.

He returned downstairs about fifteen minutes later looking (as Marvin said) *fabulous*. Admittedly, he'd needed to hold Marvin back. "Maybe next time we have an event, you'll let me go all out?" the merman pressed hopefully. And because Colin felt so pretty, (and because he was Marvin, and Marvin was *so flipping cool)*, and because he was Alpha-mate and paying Colin attention and wanting to spend time with him (young, *geeky* Colin), Colin had replied, "Okay, maybe for the barbecue?" Rather injudiciously. He felt his stomach flip with nerves, and his throat close in fear. Because at the barbecue would be all their friends, seeing him trying to be beautiful for a man who really wanted him. Until Marvin had clapped his hands in an excess of joy at the very idea, and Colin had felt he would at least make somebody happy.

He looked in the mirror near the front door, waiting for Judd to join him, and studied what Marvin had done. It was subtle but his lids sparkled faint purple, causing the green of his eyes to pop. He thought he actually looked sexy. Maybe he held himself just a little bit taller because of it.

Judd noticed, of course. Judd walked right over to him, cupped his face, and stroked a thumb down his cheek. "You look really hot, Gingersnap."

And all Colin's worries were gone, just like that.

"Café?" Colin said, like it was his idea.

"You got the photos to show Trick?" Judd looked around as if expecting a stack of printed images.

Colin nodded. "On my phone."

"Oh, right, of course."

Colin was reminded again how old Judd really was. He'd been alive at the dawn of photography, how cool was that? Of course, he'd be slow to acclimatize to the digital age.

Trick was bouncing about happily behind his counter when they arrived. He displayed admirable cheer for a man under threat of imminent blubber bozoing. He was wearing a big yellow rose behind one ear and a pink peasant shirt with floaty sleeves and matching lipstick. Trick was not the type to let anything affect his fashion choices, even possible death. If anything, his attitude was: *If I die, I better be wearing the good stuff.*

As if sensing Colin's line of thought, Judd explained, "Dratsies really are ridiculous creatures."

"But so colorful." Colin looked up at Judd. "You like him."

"I like you. He's okay," replied Judd, without a second thought.

Colin tried not to be thrilled or read too much into it.

Max was on guard duty today. He was lounging in one of the comfy chairs at the back, looking arrogant and lazy and deadly, as was his wont. Colin had grown accustomed to the way the Magistar smelled – acrid coolant and hard cinnamon candy – pack mate and power. He didn't love it, but he didn't loathe it like he had before Max and Bryan mated.

The mage was eating something sticky and saccharine, and no doubt drinking the same. The man had a sweet tooth the size of an Alpha's canine – massive, and if applied frequently enough, liable to convert any normal man into an insane monster.

It amused Colin to note that Max, unlike the werewolves of the pack (or any decent bodyguard for that matter), hadn't bothered to sit at the front of the café near the door. He didn't need to. Max could do serious damage from a distance, even without his familiar. People thought the worst thing about Max was that the man could tear apart the fabric of reality. But that wasn't it. No, if bad guys came into his café, Max would simply stand up, saunter over and activate his true power – sublime, capital Q, Queeniest Cattiest Bitchiness. He might not actually be a werewolf bitch, but Max had a beastly tongue, and admirable skill at applying it. He was a weapon of mass discussion. Colin lived in fear and awe.

There was a small line at the counter, which they joined. Judd slung his arm around Colin's shoulders and tucked him hard against his side. Colin adored it, leaned into him, pretended they belonged together, and tried not to care how bony he was compared to Judd's big frame.

Trick twinkled up at them. "What can I get you boys? The usual, Colin darling?"

Colin nodded. *Why break with tradition?* "And Floyd's next as well."

Floyd gave him a salute of gratitude with his knitting needles.

Trick winked at Colin. "You look sexy as fuck, sweetie, love the war paint. You ever want to get together some time, share tips?"

Colin felt himself go red. "Thanks, but it's all Marvin."

"No baby, it's all you," shot back Trick.

Judd butted in to order a specialty protein shake. He practically growled at the dratsie, suddenly grumpy for some reason.

Trick rolled his eyes at the enforcer. "Big baby, I know he's yours. Which flavor you want?"

"Beef and cheese," grumbled Judd, looking part ashamed, part satisfied.

The regulars didn't order shakes, mostly because they were human, but also because the café's blender was louder than a turbine engine. However, Judd wasn't the type to limit his desire just because it inconvenienced others.

The blender whirled up. Floyd flinched and glared at them. Colin knew his face must be red. Amara, the writer who liked the front corner table, stood up ostentatiously, and flounced out the door.

"What I do?" Judd asked, looking around.

"No one gets the blended drinks here, Judd. Too noisy."

Trick banged the blender to loosen the contents.

"See," said Colin.

"Pathetic, the lot of you." Judd rolled his eyes at Floyd.

The knitting human flipped him the bird.

Judd laughed and took his drink from Trick, slurping it as loudly as possible.

Trick shook his head. "Go on with you. I'll bring yours over, Colin."

They joined Max at the back, although Judd was twitchy about it, too far from the door. He insisted on sitting facing the entrance, and didn't pull Colin into his lap. That hurt a bit, until Colin realized Judd wanted to be able to move quickly. So Colin sat as close as he dared to the enforcer, and let himself enjoy that their arms remained touching.

"Well, don't you two look cozy as shit," said Max, by way of greeting.

"Disapprove, do you?" Judd was instantly on the defensive.

"Only that it took you so long to get with the fucking."

Colin could feel himself blushing again. Fortunately, Max didn't notice. He was looking at Judd.

"Sorry for the delay. Did we inconvenience you with our lack of sex?" Judd shot back.

Max gave a vicious grin. "It's exhausting watching you two bob around each other. You should have been considering *our* finer feelings and screwed this one's little ginger brains out sooner."

"I object, my brains are not at all little," said Colin.

Max rolled his eyes. "Fair point."

"And if any brains were screwed out, they were mine," Judd added, taking a big gulp of his shake.

Max didn't even arch a brow. "Really? Well, I didn't know you had any left to screw out, old man."

"Oh, very nice." Judd slurped his drink again, then smacked his lips.

Max gave him a disgusted look. "Must you?"

"It's really good." Judd waggled the glass at him. "Wanna try?"

Max was horrified. "Smells liked congealed ass, no thank you."

"Like I said, really good."

Trick brought over Colin's foamy goodness at that juncture.

Colin whipped out his phone. "Trick, would you do me a favor and take a look at a few photos real quick? Let us know if any of these people look familiar to you?"

Trick, who really was a very good barista, checked the line

and said, "Let me finish with that last dude? Then I'll come back over."

Max sniffed. "Oh, so you had *purpose* in coming here, Judd, not related to slurping congealed ass? And... wait. Wait. What is that you're drinking, Colin?"

Colin looked at Max, scared of judgment. "Decaf latte with whipped cream on top?"

Max was instantly affronted. "Decaf. *Decaf!*" he sputtered, and then, "Did you say *whipped cream* on top? *Real* whipped cream?"

"Uh, yes," Colin practically whispered. He couldn't help it. Max was really intimidating.

Max threw his head back. "Patrick Inis, get your sexy ass over here!"

Trick came trotting back over. "I was coming. Line's just finished."

Max waved a hand at him. "Yes, yes, but Trick, darling, java king of my wounded heart..."

"Yes, Max, glorious prince of the sweetest shit I can pour?" Trick responded in kind.

"Why did you not tell me I could have *whipped cream* on top of a latte? Am I nothing to you? Do you not care for my soul? Do you ever even think of me with affection?"

Trick placed a hand to his chest. "Max, my own, my true one, my pudding cup – I had no idea. What kind of freak wants *whipped cream on a latte*? Except Colin of course. No offense, Colin."

Colin sipped his drink and glared at both of them. "That's *genius freak* to you two."

They both ignored him, caught up in the drama of it all.

"Trick. Pay very close attention now, beautiful boy."

Trick batted his eyelashes and cooed. "Yes, Maxi-poo?"

"Whipped cream on a latte. Whipped cream! Plus all that glorious foam. I mean *come on*, who *wouldn't* want that?"

"Most people, actually, darling. I mean, doesn't that strike you as overkill?"

"Trick, do listen closely."

"Yes, Max?"

"I get not one, not two, but *three* pumps of vanilla syrup in my coffee drinks. Do I seem like a man who can't handle overkill?"

"Five pumps when I add the cinnamon and hazelnut."

"Is that why the sticky bun one you make me is so nummy?"

"Yes, my prince."

"You, Trick, are a true genius godling of syrup squirt-i-tude. And yet now I learn that *you* have been holding out on me. You have *not been offering me whipped cream*. I am lost, forlorn, and abandoned. I am wasting away! You don't really love me at all, do you?"

"Max?"

"Yes, Trick?"

"Would you like me to go get you some whipped cream for your sacred libation?"

Max offered up his half-drunk syrupy latte and gave Trick very big eyes. "Oh, would you? How kind."

Judd shook his head at their antics. "You two are absurd. You know, Max, we actually need Trick's help with something important."

Max glared at the enforcer. "Are you saying whipped cream is not important, because if you are, we will have words, sir! Words!"

Trick returned with the latte, now piled obscenely high with whipped cream.

"You *do* love me." Max sipped it immediately. "Bliss. Now, carry on with your insignificant non-sugar-related business."

"Thank you for your kind permission," replied Colin.

Max blinked at him. "Aw, look at you, snookums! You're developing, like, baby teeth, or something. That's so cute and vicious."

Colin decided just to ignore Max, probably not possible, but worth a try. He showed Trick the photos.

"Do you recognize any of them?"

Trick bent over the screen. "No. I mean, not really. The short one looks kinda familiar."

"Like a friend of a friend?"

"No, like distant family. But it's hard to know for certain."

"How can you not recognize family?"

Trick drew himself up to his utterly inconsiderable height. "Us otter shifters aren't like you werewolves. We don't have pack the way you do. We don't bond with all the smells and the fur and the peeing and what have you. Besides, it's been a really long time since I saw anyone from my family. I *left* them, remember?"

Colin didn't want to cause his friend any pain. "Sorry, Trick, I didn't mean anything by it." Stupid Max, getting him all riled up.

"Oh, cutie, that's okay. I'm not like *hurt* about it or anything. They didn't reject me. Not exactly. I mean, I basically left them. But the short one does look vaguely familiar. What's her name?"

"Risa Ostrov."

"Well, there you have it then."

"We do? Have what? Is that a family name?"

"Not exactly."

Judd's voice rumbled out. "Trick."

"Sorry, evasiveness comes naturally to me. *Risa* doesn't mean anything, but *Ostrov* means *isle* in Russian, I think. Just like *Inis*. She might not be directly related, but she probably has dobhar-chú blood in her."

Judd shook his head. "She didn't smell like anything supernatural."

Trick looked at the photo again. "And she seems a bit big to be one of us. But we're like you lot, in that way."

"What do you mean?"

"Born and bitten. This woman might have been born to the dobhar-chú but never taken the bite, chosen against it, been a dud, or gone in as a human infiltrator. Hard to know."

"Would she keep family connections without a second skin?" Judd pressed.

Trick shrugged. "Might do. It's not like the family lets anyone ever really leave. I'll be checking my back for the rest of my life."

Colin looked at Judd. "SBI has been tracking goods moving over state lines, right?"

Judd grunted.

"What if it's Lexi Blanc that's moving them?"

"Your mother?"

"Or her team. Not a bad way to do it, right? She has, after all, been on tour all over the United States."

Judd stood then, tossed back the last of the cheese smoothie. "Great protein shake, Trick, but we gotta jet. Colin?"

"I'm done. See you later, Max."

"Can I have the last of your whipped cream?"

Colin grinned at the Magistar. "Whatcha got not enough for you?"

"Never enough, never surrender!"

Colin pushed his mug at Max, then trotted after Judd's retreating form.

Behind him he heard Trick sigh dramatically at Max, "They're gone so soon. Was it something I said?"

"Lack of whipped cream, I suspect."

"Oh, stop it, Max."

Judd hustled Colin back to the den to pick up Isaac and Kevin. Time for the last leg of the interminable bodyguarding contract. Only now Judd was excited, because the *hunt* was on.

He had hoped Blanc was the bad guy, but a werewolf couldn't have everything. He supposed country music superstar meets narcissistic jerk took most of her energy – no time for a life of crime.

"So, how are we going to get Risa Ostrov alone?" he asked, after he and Colin had explained their findings to the others.

They were driving to meet Blanc at yet another interview. Radio this time. Judd had forgotten radio still existed. Technological evolution was so weird – when he was born, cars barely existed.

After radio, she wanted to go shopping.

"Is it our responsibility?" wondered Colin. "I mean shouldn't we just tell the SBI what we know?"

"Should we, though?" wondered Kevin. "I mean, this is way more fun."

"What's more fun?" Isaac arched both brows.

Judd followed Kevin's reasoning. "Us knowing what's actually going on. The feds in ignorance."

Isaac tilted his head back and forth, considering. "Colin?"

Colin nodded. "Yeah, it's more fun."

Isaac shrugged. "Okay. But I'm telling Alec next time we see him."

"That's fair," agreed Kevin.

Judd let his lips twitch. That gave them most of the rest of the day. And a sense of truancy, don't tell big brother Alpha.

"So are we gonna catch us a thief?" wondered Colin.

Judd grinned at his mate, feeling fierce. "We absolutely are."

Colin clapped his hands. "Goodie. Will there be mayhem?"

"Maybe a little mayhem."

"And will there be blood and guts?" wondered Isaac.

"Probably some blood. Hopefully no guts."

"It's like it's your birthday, Judd. All your favorites, in one place." Colin really was cheeky once he got sexed-up.

Judd wondered if every time they fucked his baby would get snappy. Like Judd had snark-inducing jizz or something. He would like to encourage *all of this*. "Exactly. Lucky me. And it's all your doing, Gingersnap. Look at you, taking care after your man."

Colin went bright pink at the teasing – but also at the praise.

They hadn't talked about their morning misunderstanding, but it had pushed Judd to a decision. He was all in. He was too old for Colin, but he was also too old to care. Frankly, he was likely to be too old for any man who interested him at this point in time. Judd wasn't the oldest werewolf left in the world, but sometimes it felt like it.

Colin had been, without question, hurt at Judd suggesting *more*. Judd had meant *more* as in deepening their relationship.

Colin, it appeared, had thought he'd meant *more* as moving on to other people – done with lessons.

Judd's first instinct was to run away. Give Colin space to figure himself out, determine what he wanted. Hope what Colin wanted was Judd. Until Judd remembered that everyone who should love Colin had left him and run away, absented themselves. So that would be exactly the wrong move.

Then Judd realized that if Colin really was into him, he'd react exactly as he had – with pain and a sense of unworthiness. Colin always thought the worst of himself and his appeal. There was only one way to fix things with Colin. Judd might talk until he was blue in the face, but Gingersnap needed action. He needed to be shown that Judd wanted badly to take this beyond teaching and friendship. Fortunately, Judd was good at action. One might even say, it was his only skill in life.

So Judd was going to act like Colin belonged to him, with him. Judd was going to pretend that he belonged to Colin. Maybe then his mate would get it. Maybe then he'd decide that Judd was worth it – too old, too big, too fierce, and too *much,* though Judd might be. Perhaps Colin also might realize that they were perfect together. Judd just had to prove to him that the possibility was there.

Colin had them draped with ear-buds – small, yellow buttercups today. They were back in the stripper pants and fancy logo polo shirts again. Maybe if they got Risa behind bars, they'd get to keep the pants indefinitely.

Was that the best reason yet?

Probably.

The radio station visit was painless, although no one seemed to know Blanc was even scheduled to visit – including the radio station. This put Lexi Blanc in a very bad mood. But at least they didn't have to kill anyone.

Then Blanc insisted on visiting some fancy clothing boutiques. All eight of them had to go with her. Then they had to stand around, bored out of their minds, while she tried on the *entire* shop. Risa, Jojo, and the nameless manager told her how fabulous she looked. How that was *absolutely* her color, because everything was her color. And so forth.

Blanc ignored her bodyguards. Well, *mostly* ignored them. Except Kevin.

Today, apparently, Kevin existed in her universe. Not the other three, just Kevin. It was as if, after several days, she'd suddenly remembered she had a son. Only one son, mind you. She still ignored Colin.

Judd caught her, at one point, talking fast and hurriedly in Kevin's ear.

"Don't you think it would be fun? Mother and son, traipsing through Europe? Just think on it, darling – a European tour. I'd put you in charge. Who else would I have guard my back but my own child? You'd never have to take orders from *that other enforcer* ever again. It's beneath you, darling. Not to mention your silly weak Alpha."

Kevin looked pained and exhausted. He didn't bother to answer. He caught Judd's eye and shook his head.

Judd gave him their coded hand signal for *don't bother*.

Kevin responded with the British hand gesture for *fucking wanker*. One of Judd's favorites from the old country. He'd brought it with him to the New World. Ah, memories.

Blanc didn't follow the nuances of the exchange, but she understood they'd been discussing and dismissing her. She glared at Judd, true hatred in her eyes. Like most Alphas, she didn't like her will thwarted. Well, screw her, Judd intended to thwart to the best of his rank's abilities.

They kept a close eye on Risa. The stylist didn't behave any differently than she had previously. She helped Blanc into her various outfits. Apparently, even radio required *a look*. Then there was a different outfit for shopping.

Yeah, exactly. Blanc dressed up to go buy more things to dress up in. Bloody insane.

At the third boutique, Judd wandered around. Let Kevin do most of the guarding while his crazy Alpha mother bought half the store.

"I don't really like this, but I might as well buy it, because you never know." He overheard her say to Jojo at one point.

Colin drifted over to him. "Anything?"

"This is interminable."

"Agreed." Colin brushed Judd's hand, just the back of two of his fingers against Judd's wrist. Judd jolted at the delicious skin-to-skin contact. It was so subtle as to seem accidental, probably in case Judd rejected him or didn't notice. Judd struggled not to grab Colin's hand and tug him into an embrace – power and brute claiming, driven by his joyous shock. His Gingersnap had reached out, in public! Instead, he placed a hand to the small of Colin's back, steered him into a private corner – rewarding his tentative advance with equally subtle (if more proprietary) contact. Okay, maybe not *that* subtle. He caught Kevin rolling his eyes and grinning at him and suppressed the extremely childish urge to stick his tongue out at his fellow enforcer.

Forcefully casual, Judd pulled out a pretty, filmy, green blouse with a low, draped collar. He thought the color would exactly match Colin's eyes and the neckline would show off his slender throat.

Uh oh, he was getting poetic again.

"This would look nice on you," was what he said.

Colin looked between him and the shirt, wide-eyed and skeptical. "You think?"

What *had* he just said? Of course he thought that. "Yes."

"It's gorgeous." Colin fingered the soft fabric. "But super expensive."

Judd snorted at him. "You never spend money on yourself."

Colin took the blouse from him, looked at it wistfully. "I already cost the pack so much – my tuition, my textbooks. And I don't give back nearly enough in return."

That made Judd angry. But they were in the middle of a shop surrounded by the enemy so he only said. "You're ridiculous. It's one shirt, Gingersnap."

Colin nodded. "I'll remember the style and color for later. Next time Marvin drags me thrifting, maybe we can find something similar."

"Fine," replied Judd with ill grace. He really wanted to see the dumb shirt on Colin. He wanted to pet it, warm against Colin's skin. He wanted to peel it off him, slowly. Something good should come out of shopping with Lexi Bloody Blanc.

So, the moment his mate got distracted, Judd bought him the shirt. It was way overpriced for a thin scrap of fabric, but that's clothing for you. It was also delicate enough to tuck into Judd's back pocket, or it would have been if he hadn't been wearing goddamn stripper pants. With no pockets! Who makes pants without pockets? Risa, apparently. The woman definitely needed to be locked up.

He handed the shirt to Isaac, who smirked at him, and tucked it into his backpack. Because Isaac was sensible like that and brought a backpack full of snacks and other useful things when shopping with a female.

Smart dude, Isaac.

Finished shopping at long last, Blanc announced that she was peckish. Also, she really wanted to visit her darling son Kevin's new home town. Wasn't Sausalito supposed to be picturesque? Wasn't it just over there, near the water? Why not go honor it with a visit? Give the small town the thrill of a celebrity sighting.

To which Colin muttered under his breath that Sausalito was not the kind of place to recognize a country music star.

Blanc heard him, of course, and turned to Kevin for an explanation. "Oh? And why is that?"

"Mostly tourists, retirees, and rich old human hippies, Mother. Not your draw." Kevin explained.

"Oh, well yes, that doesn't sound like me at all. Imagine, anonymity, how novel. Shall we?" It was not a question.

They piled back into the stretch limo. Blanc chattered on about how excited she was to learn about Kevin's "little life in the Bay Area" and wasn't it all "so quaint and adorable?"

Judd up-tilted his chin at Kevin. With a sigh, his fellow enforcer kept Blanc's focus.

Judd relaxed back, Colin to one side of him, Isaac on the other. He lowered his voice so Risa and the other humans couldn't hear. If Blanc dragged herself away from her own voice long enough she might overhear them, but that seemed unlikely. Besides, he assumed she wasn't involved.

Kevin leaned forwards and angled himself. His big body shielding them from Blanc's view. He took all of her attention.

Judd lowered his voice to subhuman levels. "Let's get them to the Bean. See what happens with a confrontation."

"We're being followed, aren't we?"

Judd nodded. "Black SUV. Not the same car I peed on. I'm thinking it's blubber bozos. I'll text our two friends. Let them know our ETA and location. Isaac, you text Max we're incoming? Gingersnap, you text Alec?"

Colin nodded and pulled out his phone.

They all tapped quietly on screens for a while. Blanc and Kevin's nonsense talk echoed around them.

CHAPTER SIXTEEN

WOLVES IN WET PLACES

The direct result of their texting was that the café, when they arrived, was packed with pack. Colin entered the place tense as all get out and then instantly relaxed.

At a table at the front, furthest from the door, sat Alec and Marvin. It was a mark of the Alpha's confidence that he'd brought his mate along. Or it was just that Marvin was around, on Sunday, bored and nosy, and insisted on coming. He probably just wanted to check out the selkies, see if they really did wear suits without shirts. Colin was so pleased to see his Alpha that he had to stamp down on a desire to run over and hug Alec. Which was... what? He stopped to think about it. Nice. It was *nice*.

The SBI weren't there yet. It's possible they'd ignored Judd's text, the idiots.

Knitter Floyd was the only human still inside, because Floyd was part of the furniture. Plus, if there was about to be a rumble, Floyd wanted to see it. Frankly, Floyd would probably survive the vampire apocalypse by simply sitting, right the fuck there, knitting forever.

"Oh, this place is *so cute*!" cried Lexi. "Look at all its little windows. Is this how ordinary people behave on a Sunday? Are those people drinking *actual* coffee drinks? How precious."

Even without humans, Bean There, Froth That made to all appearances like a humming local café. Werewolves weren't exactly great actors, but Lexi Blanc wasn't exactly observant, either. Her three human followers, though, they got nervous. That prey animal thing engaged – a small section of their hind-brain kicked in, warning them of danger. They didn't do anything, though, too cowed by Lexi's will. Or too accustomed to ignoring their instincts because they'd been working for an Alpha werewolf for so long.

Trick was behind the counter, his usual bouncing chipper self. He was chattering at Max, who was ordering another mostly-syrup-with-a-caffeine-chaser and insisting on the largest mug with the difference made up by whipped cream. Trick was calling him a sugar junkie and criticizing his life choices.

Max said something about sticky bun lattes conferring upon the drinker the stamina and energy of a god. And so forth. Or was that, so *froth*?

Tank was tucked away in one corner, a quiet looming figure. Bryan and Lovejoy weren't around, but the odds in that café still tilted in the pack's favor. Even though Lexi had her entire entourage. After all, Lexi Blanc's support network was human. Their support network was badass mage.

Colin stood in line behind Isaac and glanced over at Alpha and Alpha-mate, letting himself revel in the comfort of their presence. Colin's nose told him that Marvin was drinking seaweed and fish sauce tea. The Alpha had mint. Because Alec was occasionally really bad at being a werewolf. What self-respecting wolf drinks *mint* tea? Still, both drinks were potent enough to permeate even a coffee shop with their scent.

Alec also seemed to be wearing Marvin's first drink. Colin hid a smug smile at his Alpha's tricky ways. The fishy smell totally disguised Alec's strong Alpha odor, not to mention Marvin's briny pong. Alec was also wearing a dirty lab coat and glasses. He looked like the young, skinny, geeky marine biolo-gist that he was, out on a date with an overdressed hottie who was talking a mile a minute and obviously way too good for him.

Colin turned back in line, looked up to find Isaac watching him with a small smile on his face.

Colin, feeling daring, bumped the Omega with one shoulder. "Why so smug?"

"It looks good on you."

"What does?"

"Pack. Happiness."

"Oh, stop it," said Colin, pleased and blushing.

As they neared the counter, Lexi became more high-pitched in her bubbling enthusiasm. "Oh look, Risa sweetie, how adorbs. They have beverages for shifters. One wouldn't think a place like this would be so... advanced. Bless their little hearts." Lexi took in the menu with the appearance of genuine delight.

Trick played his part to a T. Or tea. He spotted Lexi, put his hand to his throat in awe, and gushed, "Oh my gawd! Are you Lexi Blanc? *The* Lexi Blanc? Queen of Country Music?"

"Why yes, sugah! Yes, I am."

"I love your work. Just makes me want shake my hips and dance. When it doesn't make me cry, of course. Because you're sooooo talented."

"Well, aren't you just the sweetest little..." Lexi paused and sniffed. "...watery coffee boy creature feature, aren't you? Would you be so kind as to make me up one of those parmesan and clam juice carnivore special-teas?"

Trick would *not* be out-camped by an amateur. "Why, sure thing I will! For the great Lexi Blanc I'd do just about anything. I simply can't believe it's you! In my itty-bitty café. We are *so honored.* Would you sign this napkin, while I make your special extra-special just for you?" He slid a slightly soiled logo napkin over.

Lexi looked at it in disgust.

"I'll be sure to frame it for the wall," sang out Trick, manning the tea things with aplomb.

Colin swallowed a laugh.

Lexi's human entourage tittered with each other about their menu options. Clearly relieved to know that the threat their prey instincts were warning them about was nothing but the small barista. Silly humans. Apparently, it was of greater importance to decide if they could *afford the carbs* to split one of those *nice-looking chocolate orange scones*.

Trick assured them that the scone was low-fat and delicious, as he passed Lexi her tea.

"So," he turned bright eyes on Risa, "what can I get you, *deirfiúr*?" There was Irish in his mouth all of a sudden, lilting and sweet.

"What's it mean?" Colin hissed to Judd.

Judd shook his head. "Don't know."

Risa seemed to know, however. She tensed up, glared at Trick.

Trick tilted his head at her. "You didn't know you had family round these parts, did you?"

"Shit," said Risa. "They sent you to check up on me?"

Trick became one with his name. In that moment, Colin understood what he'd been before, what he was raised as – trickster in truth. Con artist probably, liar most certainly, and really good at all of it. It was a wonder his family ever let him go.

The dratsie didn't even bat an eye, played instantly on all Risa's fears. "You're late with the transfer, otter-kin. You didn't think we'd just let you fuck this up, did you?"

Lexi looked up from her drink. "Risa, pet? Why is the funny little coffee fishy man talking to you like that?"

"It's nothing, boss, old family friend, it seems."

Trick hummed, bright black eyes refocused on Lexi. "Old family, more like. You always keep duds in your retinue, Queen of Country?"

"Duds? I *beg* your pardon. Risa is the *best* stylist this side of the Mississippi."

Trick rolled his eyes so hard he had to rock his head as well. "Oh really? That jacket you're wearing any kind of indication? Because honey, trust me, it is way too much bling for coffee on a Sunday. Have you never heard of *dressing appropriately for the occasion*?"

Lexi gasped. Truly shocked that some two-bit small-town shifter would dare criticize her jacket. It was the really impressive metallic one from the performance the night before. Apparently, it represented her signature look for this tour and had to go everywhere with her.

She metaphorically clutched her pearls, which in a werewolf Alpha meant her canines dropped and her eyes started to shift. "Well I never! Who do you think you are?"

Colin bit his bottom lip to stop a laugh. Was his sainted mother about to have a fit of the vapors? *Excellent.*

He wondered if he should remind her that she was not, in fact, a Southern belle debutante but instead a forty-plus-year-old trailer trash from Boston. But it was too much fun to watch her pretend. Of all the people to take down his mother, Colin hadn't considered that it might be Trick. The little otter shifter was fierce as fuck. He'd practically left Lexi speechless, and that *never* happened.

Kevin sidled up next to Colin. "What, exactly, is going on?" His brother's voice was awed.

Colin shook his head in wonder. "I don't know. I mean, it looks like our mother is being humiliated by a tiny otter barista, but I can't believe it. I might totally love Trick."

"Hey," said Judd, mildly.

Risa, at this juncture, seemed to realize something was terribly amiss with her employer's plan to stop for coffee. The stylist cast desperate eyes around.

But she was human and, aside from Tank, no one in that café looked at all like a werewolf. And Tank was a quiet, still shadow, huge but utterly unthreatening. He had a hard hat resting on the table in front of him. Just some construction worker on break. (If you forgot it was Sunday.) Alec and Marvin were clearly a pair of college gay boys, couldn't possibly be werewolves. (Again, ignoring the lab coat on a Sunday.) And Max was too, well, Maxish, to be any kind of shifter. He'd taken up residence leaning against the counter to one side, looking bored. Because Max always looked bored.

Max never came off as a threatening super mage of doom. He was beautiful but all clumsy angles, seeming awkward and out of place *all of the time*. Right now, for example, he had whipped cream on his nose.

Finally, Risa's eyes came to rest on Floyd. "And what are you?" she asked, voice fierce.

Floyd gave her the most baleful look ever. "I'm Floyd. I knit. And that jacket is a fucking travesty."

Risa gasped.

Lexi looked wildly around for a moment, intentionally activating her werewolf senses for a change. "What the hell is going on? What is this place?" She took a deep inhale. But there were too many odors for even the best nose. All the smells of the beverages, including hers, the roasting coffee beans, her humans with those perfumes that she allowed them to wear standing close, as well as her own. Marvin's spilled drink. Alec's dumb mint tea.

Not to mention that her four hired bodyguards, still standing around her, were all werewolves. Everything smelled like werewolf.

Kevin said, "Nothing, Mother. This is just my local café. I told you, my life's not very exciting. This place is mostly human. You wanted to see how the little people lived. Here we are, the little people. What did you expect?"

Lexi glared at her son and pointed at Trick. "Little people are NOT ALLOWED TO CRITICIZE MY JACKET."

Colin could feel himself jerk in response. Had she just used VOICE command on them? Because of a *jacket*? What the *actual* fuck?

Kevin recovered first. "Mother! We weren't. There's no need to go that far."

Lexi waggled her finger at Trick. "He was!"

Trick didn't look particularly fazed. Apparently werewolf VOICE wasn't effective on otter shifters. Or he'd already allied himself so much with Alec, the Alpha's presence was protecting him. Or he was tricky enough to avoid the command by taking it literally. So he stopped criticizing the jacket and just criticized her.

"Whine, whine, whine, hot stuff. I wasn't disparaging that garish disco ball you're sporting – *on a Sunday* – as such. I was merely mentioning the fact that your out-of-touch stylist let you out of the house *in it* – on a *Sunday*. Bitch, puh-leez."

Lexi looked like she was actually contemplating shifting forms and jumping over the counter to maul Trick. She was truly incensed.

Trick was possibly too good at his role.

Out the corner of his eye, Colin could see Alec tense, ready to jump in if needed, but frankly Lexi and her people were too caught up in their web. The trap had been sprung. It's just that the San Andreas Pack didn't have any idea what to do with their prey now they'd caught it.

At that moment, a large black SUV pulled to a stop outside the café and disgorged eight very large men in pinstriped suits without shirts, all of them carrying equally large guns, plus one incensed Blubber Bozo Prince.

Selkie. What joy is ours.

Apparently the floppery had arrived.

Judd was actually relieved when the selkie showed up. Finally, something he could hit.

The level of critical discourse on the subject of inappropriate jackets was not one he felt able to handle. And yet, it *would* keep happening.

The moment the selkie entered the café, smell of brown butteriness carried alongside, the pack went into action. Tank moved to the counter, ready to protect Trick. Max straightened up and took a wide stance. He'd be their backup and remote fire-power. Alec stood, stepped forward, body shielding Marvin. Judd swung so that he was between Colin and the selkie. Isaac moved within grabbing distance of Risa. No one cared about Blanc and the rest of her crew.

"Who the hell are you lot?" barked out the country music queen in the coffee shop.

The Prince of the Blubber Bozos muscled through to the

front of his gang. "We meet again, goddess of my heart. Angel-voiced moonlight mistress."

"Fucking hell in a goddamn handbasket," said Max. He looked at Judd. "Seriously?"

Judd laughed at him. "Now you see what we've been putting up with for three days?"

"Dude." Max was blown away. "I don't know what to say."

"How novel," said Marvin, sipping his drink, still sitting at the corner table.

Trick was leaning on the counter, white-knuckled, scared eyes fixed on the big men in pinstriped suits with big guns and no shirts.

Blanc was looking confused. "Is this normal weekend activities for commoners in cafés?"

"No, lady love, you're special," replied her blubbery prince.

"Well, of course I'm special," shot back Blanc. "Tell me something I *don't* know."

The blubber prince approached her.

Blanc looked at Judd and Kevin. "Well?"

"Well what?"

"You're my bodyguards, defend me from him."

"He doesn't seem to want to hurt you," pointed out Judd. "And you allowed contact twice before."

"That was paid for! Kevin," she said, eyes narrowed, "protect your mother!"

"You don't seem to be in any danger," replied Kevin, not moving.

"Colin? Baby?" she turned to look at her younger son.

"Don't even start," said Colin from behind Judd.

Judd was pleased that his Gingersnap didn't budge from his side.

The Prince of the Blubber Bozos reached Lexi Blanc. He grabbed her hand, clutched it in both of his beefy ones. "You are even more beautiful in the daylight."

"Oh! Why thank ya, sugah." Blanc batted her lashes at him. "Is all this just for little old me?" She gestured to the invading selkie mob.

"My love for you is infinite," confessed the large man.

"Or at least worthy of… two, six, eight, mobsters? Are you mobsters? Please say you're mobsters. It's much more romantic if you are. The press might even make it front page news." She seemed to have decided to try to flirt her way out of the situation.

The selkie prince looked pleased. "The baddest of the bad mobsters, my pure one."

"How delightful. You aren't here to, erm, kidnap me or anything so *gauche*, are you? It's only, Kitty Cherry was kidnapped last month. So it's kinda been *done* recently, you know? I'd look like a copycat. Can't have that. Besides, much as I admire your persistence, my darling sweet cheeks, I can't survive under the waves with you. I'm still a land mammal, even in shifted form."

Prince Blubber Bozo nodded, jowly and sad. There might even have been real tears in his eyes. "The tragedy of our love, my precious gem, is in the impossibility of any future. So we are left to pine for each other, eternally."

Judd suppressed the instinct to gag.

Blanc looked nonplused. "Uh, yes, of course, sugah. Eternally, as you say."

Judd caught Kevin and Colin exchanging looks. "Surf and turf don't mix," the brothers mouthed at each other.

"Which is why, my love, I must ask you to forgive this transgression." Prince Blubber Bozo moved remarkably fast for such a big man. He lunged at Blanc, twisted her around, and then ripped the gold jacket off her curvy figure.

"What is with that jacket?" Judd asked the shocked room.

Lexi Blanc screamed in surprise and stumbled to one side. Recovering, she lurched after her coat, werewolf fast and Alpha strong, but it was too late. One of the other bozos had stepped forwards and put the muzzle of his gun to her temple. A shot that close to the head was too much, even for a werewolf.

"Uh uh uh, pretty lady," he said.

"But why?" Blanc cried.

"Fuck," said Risa.

"Duh da da dum. It's was the jacket all along!" Colin's voice was mocking. Like he was narrating a children's audio book.

Things moved quickly, then.

The selkies swung around, guns covering the pack. They either had done their research and knew all the San Andreas werewolves and what they looked like, or they were just that well trained. There was a military precision to their coordination; it spoke of structured colony arrangements and elite service. Navy Seals, perhaps?

Judd swore at himself. He'd miscalculated. He'd thought they were seal shifters – these were obviously sea lions. Well, shitgibbon.

Eight sea lions, plus their leader. While Judd had eight pack members, none of them with guns, and three in need of safe-guarding – Marvin, Trick, and Colin. Colin would hate to know he was numbered as one of the weaker elements. But Judd couldn't help how his brain strategized. Blanc and the humans were not predictable. He still wasn't sure whose side they were on.

The mobsters sensed wolf protective instincts in play. They knew what to do. Two guns pointed at Judd, but Colin was the real target. Two were directed at Alec, but only because he stood in front of Marvin. Same with Tank, who defended Trick.

Except everyone had forgotten about Isaac. Omega power worked in mysterious ways. It's not like their Omega wasn't standing *right there*, in line with them next to Risa. And yet they'd all mentally misplaced him. Even Judd.

Omega power. *Everyone* had forgotten, even the selkie. Which meant not a single gun was pointed at Isaac. Big mistake.

Isaac wasn't like Bryan, he hadn't the Beta's calming energy. And yet, for a breath, everything just seemed to pause. He'd been absent, and now he wasn't – a single pebble dropped into still waters. Judd grimaced. Poetry again? What had Colin done to him?

Isaac sent something out – a reverberation, a muffling – and that something intransigent subdued them all.

Blanc stopped screaming.

The guns didn't tilt down. The selkie seemed less affected, but even they were somehow less tense.

Blanc stared at Isaac, eyes full of avarice. "What *are* you?"

Isaac tilted up one corner of his mouth. "I am not the one you should be worried about."

Acrid ozone and sweet coolant came then. The prickling of hairs on everyone's skin. Quintessence shimmered about them, like air made of oil, responding to a pull. Judd didn't look at Max, he was too well trained for that. Instead he watched the Prince of the Blubber Bozos to see how he'd react. Out of the corner of his eye, Judd also monitored his Alpha. Alec was standing, quiet in the corner, trusting his pack to do what needed to be done. He was proud of them and their abilities and would only interfere if necessary.

Judd felt the joy of that sweep over him. To have an Alpha who loved and trusted them. Trusted *him* to handle this. To have Alec show up and not demand to lead an operation, but simply support it. It was a miracle.

Judd knew what Max was doing. He was showing his power. Without Bryan he couldn't safely control quintessence. Theoretically, he could hurl fireballs or convert energy into razor-sharp blades, but there was no way to know how much or where they'd go. Max without Bryan couldn't stop the selkie from shooting or strip them of their guns. With no familiar, Max was all power and pain and no focus or intent. But the selkies didn't know that. Blanc didn't know that.

Isaac dropped his hold over them then.

Max upped his draw on the quintessence. The smell got worse.

Blanc whirled and stared at their Magistar. "Who *the hell* are you?"

Gray nothingness shimmered around Max, undulating energy and matter mixed but not fully present, phasing in and out of existence.

"Oh," said Max, "I'm just one of those little people you said you wanted to get to know."

The selkie prince panicked. "Everyone just stop whatever the fuck you're doing or I will shoot you all. This is my jacket."

"Darling," said Marvin, still sitting and sipping, unfazed, "it's fabulous and all, but it will *so* not fit you properly."

They heard the sirens then. Police sirens.

Outside, a black car drew up, a familiar one, with a tire that smelled like Judd.

"SBI. Shit," said the Prince Blubber Bozo. "Everybody swim!" He gave Blanc a little bow. "Until we meet again, my one true love."

They ran out as a group, bypassing their own huge SUV. They bowled over Faste and Lenis. The two agents, leaving their car, were easily overwhelmed by nine enormous mobsters.

Neither of the SBI had time to shift. Apparently, even selkie could move fast when necessary. Although Lenis did pull her gun and shoot. If she hit any of them, it didn't slow them down.

"Kevin, Colin, stay here, grab Risa." Judd had enough wherewithal to bark out a few orders as he ran after the selkies. The rest of the pack joined him.

The pack was, in fact, much faster than any selkie, even a sea lion. However, the blubber bozos didn't have far to go. They crossed the street, ripping their suit jackets off as they went, leapt over the sidewalk, and dove down onto the sharp rubble shore-side.

Apparently they'd prepared for this, because spread out in some kind of order on the rocks were nine coarse brown fur coats.

The selkies belly-flopped onto their skins, and instantly nine huge sea lions were rolling into the ocean. They shed shredded suit-pants as they went. Selkie were handicapped by their reliance on an external shifting-skin, but they were much, *much* faster than shifters who didn't have skins. Five times the speed of even the fastest werewolf, selkie transformation was practically instantaneous. All their savage power was held trapped in one place. It was actually really impressive to see nine times over.

And that was it, barking and joyful, nine sea lions disappeared beneath the waves. One of them carried a beautiful gold jacket in his wide, whiskered mouth.

"Well, shit," said Agent Lenis, holstering her gun with a look of profound annoyance. She'd gotten off more than a few shots, as had some local deputies. But if any bullet stuck, it was only lodged in blubber now.

"It's okay," replied Judd, "we caught your thief for you."

"Marvin, no!" that was Alec's voice, desperate.

Judd's head whipped up. *Alpha?*

"STOP HIM!" Command, strong powerful, rolled over them. Judd moved, compelled to obey.

Marvin and Trick, running side by side, crossed the street.

The two water folk were lithe and quick and the werewolves confused. The voice COMMAND hadn't come fast enough, and it wasn't specific. Still, the San Andreas Pack lunged for the two smaller shifters.

It was too late. Marvin and Trick launched themselves off the sidewalk, diving in long arcs over the rubble into the water.

The pack leapt after them.

Tank and Isaac were in wolf form.

Judd fought his own instinct to shift as well. He was a better swimmer as a human.

They hit the sharp uneven rocks where moments earlier nine fur coats had been lying out in the afternoon fog.

Trick and Marvin were already vanished beneath the water. Trick resurfaced briefly, floating on his back, looked at them. He had jet black beady eyes, a cheerful face covered in thick brown fur, and serious whiskers. He waggled a webbed paw before rolling to dive. Barely a ripple marked his passing.

Judd wobbled over the rocks, prepared to swim after them. Isaac and Tank splashed into the ocean and began dog-paddling.

It was insane, of course – they were wolves. They couldn't outswim sea folk. But their Alpha had commanded them. And they would try their very best.

"STOP. COME BACK TO SHORE." A new command echoed out over the Bay, before getting muffled by mist.

They did as ordered. Judd turned, balanced precariously,

leaped up to the sidewalk using all his supernatural strength and agility.

Kevin and Colin had stayed behind as Judd instructed. Back in the café, they were out of COMMAND voice range. Alec stood on the sidewalk, leaning against Max. He looked terrified, but controlled. His mate was in danger. Judd knew how that felt. He glanced across the street at the open door, but it was too dark to see inside the café. The big front window reflected his own face back at him. Judd could only hope Colin was still okay.

"Sorry, guys, I overreacted," apologized Alec.

"It's fine," said Judd, the only one not in fur. "We get it. That's your mate out there."

"Yeah, it is."

Agent Lenis, Alpha werewolf herself, looked at Alec in mild awe. "Your VOICE is insanely strong, kid. I mean, I heard it before, but it's gotten stronger since we last visited."

Alec only rolled his eyes at her.

Judd gave her a small head tilt. "We're his pack."

"Yeah, but that extreme of a reaction? Two of you fucking *shifted* in response. That's a pretty big deal. Are you registered with DURPS as a class six Alpha?"

"Never tested. Too young. Last I checked, they wanted me to *settle into my role* for a decade or two. Their words, not mine." Alec didn't look away from the water.

Judd, who had experienced lots of packs, and not a few VOICE commands in his lifetime, knew Lenis was right. But he also knew that she didn't get it. It wasn't Alec's birth and bite that made him strong. "He has a true pack."

She turned brown eyes on him, measured, arrogant. "The implication being that I don't have a pack, so how could I understand?"

Judd shook his head at her. "We are, quite literally, his to command."

"Yes, as is the case with all packs. Are you saying it's different because you've a full complement: Beta, two enforcers, Omega? Is that what makes you so special and him so fucking strong?"

Judd snorted at her. Alphas, only ever seeing the power and the offensive play.

Agent Faste joined them. "We have a criminal to collect."

"Hardly does us any good without that jacket. It was the evidence we needed," Lenis grumbled at her partner. "Do *you* know why young Alpha pup here has so much VOICE control? Of course you don't know, you're a fucking bear shifter. Why is this my life?"

Agent Faste looked down on his partner. "Well, they love him. Right? I mean loyalty is one thing. But this is a pack that genuinely loves each other."

"You sappy motherfucker," said Lenis. She started back across the street.

Faste exchanged glances with Judd.

Judd raised his eyebrows at him.

"I'm right, aren't I?"

Judd clapped him on the shoulder. "'Course you are, big guy."

His Alpha was still distracted and worried, staring at the waves. Judd took enforcer initiative. "Come on, we've still got Blanc to deal with. And is that Deputy Kettil I see? You did bring us some serious backup, didn't you Faste? Thanks, dude."

"Things are always a mess with you guys."

"Yeah, but now you've got a fellow berserker to deal with, dontcha?"

"I do?"

Deputy Kettil, as if on cue, charged across the street at them. "Where the hell is Trick?"

Agent Faste looked adorably confused.

"Swimming with the fishes," said Judd.

Deputy Kettil actually growled. It looked like he too was going to shift and dive into the brink. Which would be a real bloody mess.

Judd smiled evilly and left poor Faste to deal with the man.

CHAPTER SEVENTEEN
STAND BY YOUR PACK

Colin returned his attention to the inside of the café. He was glad Alec hadn't projected VOICE in his direction. He hated VOICE. It took away all his will and made him feel pathetic, and he was already pathetic most of the time. Sure, he trusted Alec as his Alpha, but he didn't need a reminder of how weak that trust made him.

He too would have instinctively shifted form. He shuddered at the idea. The sun was only just setting. Shifting hurt a lot at the best of times, but a forced shift when the sun was still around? Gruesome. His bones ached just thinking about it.

Judd had resisted the pull somehow. Colin was impressed. Maybe it was an enforcer thing, or maybe it was an age thing, or maybe it was a Judd thing. Or maybe he just had the instincts to know he was better off staying human.

Their Alpha had calmed, or at least remembered that his power did not extend to the ocean. He had Max standing close, Isaac's white furry presence sitting on his other side, and Tank's massive wolf pacing back and forth behind them.

Alec didn't need Colin there too. He needed Marvin. But Marvin was chasing selkies and gold jackets beneath the waves. Honestly, what did Trick and Marvin think they could do? One merman and one river otter against nine selkie? Madness.

Colin was a little sad that he hadn't gotten to see Trick's otter shape. He bet he was super cute. Colin was also much less worried about the two water folk than the rest of his pack. Perhaps because he felt that, as the smallest and the weakest of the wolves, he had more in common with Trick and Marvin than with any of his other pack mates. Colin knew both Marvin and Trick were crafty and nimble. Water was their element. Those two were so much more powerful than they appeared, which made him wonder if he was too. Perhaps he could be like them some day.

Kevin had hold of Risa and, so far, Lexi seemed disinclined to object. Which was good – with Alec outside, if Lexi Blanc decided to exert Alpha power to save her stylist, there wasn't much either he or his brother could do about it.

She didn't seem to care.

In fact, she'd taken a seat at the big front table, with Jojo on one side, fussing with her hair, and her manager on the other side, taking photos.

"Perfect, Lexi. Just look at you, you're so *real*. You're so down to earth, so humble. So *relatable* in this setting! I love it. Gimme a little more of a pout. Show us the drink. And... sip! Oh yes, totally Instalamb-worthy." Suddenly the manager looked up. "You!"

Colin blinked. "Me?"

"Move, you're in the background of the shot."

So, yeah, Lexi didn't seem to be inclined to help her erstwhile employee.

Agent Lenis came marching in.

Alpha Lenis terrified Colin. She was strong, not so strong as Alec, certainly not over Alec's pack, but that didn't stop Colin from feeling the dominance pouring off her. She was also dangerous, unpredictable, and packless – hungry for something. She gave Colin the willies.

There were some local cops milling around outside the café as well. Agent Lenis paused in the doorway to yell at them for a bit – something about their inability to hold onto a *few fucking selkies* – before she marched in.

The only cop Colin recognized by sight was Deputy Kettil,

and he seemed more interested in the ocean, like Alec. Most likely because Trick was below the surface. Deputy Kettil probably thought that because Trick was a small otter shifter, he was weak.

That again.

But Trick had faced down Colin's mother. Trick had sassed Max over whipped cream. Trick wasn't remotely weak. Trick was just small, and cheerful, and fabulous. Trick was awesome. Could it really be that easy?

Agent Lenis ignored Colin, thank heavens. He didn't want to discover a modicum of backbone, only to have her chase it out of him.

She marched over to Kevin instead.

Kevin thrust Risa at her. "This is yours."

Agent Lenis looked to Lexi. "It's as we suspected?"

Risa gasped, clearly feeling betrayed.

Lexi Blanc stopped posing and glared back, but did not stand or approach the other werewolf Alpha. "Little pustule. Thought she could get one over on me, did she?"

Kevin said, "So you *were* working with the SBI? For how long?"

"Since Dallas. Didn't your little brat of a brother tell you he saw me with them? Colin, you weren't being *loyal* to me, were you? Stupid."

Colin winced at the unwarranted attack.

Kevin bridled. "Yeah, he fucking told us! Called a pack meeting and everything."

"Oh, brave little boy, runs crying to his pack."

Colin arched a brow. *Apparently, I can't win with her.*

Agent Lenis said, "Family drama again? Stop it. Did you collect the evidence we asked for, Ms Blanc?"

The country music queen shrugged. "Isn't evidence your responsibility?"

"Bullshit, now we really do need that jacket. Quarter of a million in real gold is sewn into the thing."

"No wonder it weighed so much," said Lexi, not seeming too

surprised. "Not that I minded, of course, Alpha strength and all. You know, I thought those were genuine Swoopski Crystals."

"Then the jacket would have been worth more than a quarter of a million," said Jojo, cheerfully.

Lexi laughed like this was a grand joke.

"This is a goddamn nightmare." Agent Lenis glared at Kevin, then Colin. "Why you felt the need to stick your collective noses into this business is beyond me."

Kevin huffed. "Did you miss the part where this is our mother? And you're in our territory? And we had a bodyguard contract in place?"

Judd came walking back into the café at that juncture.

Colin was beyond relieved to see him.

He was even more relieved when the big enforcer came straight over to him and squeezed his shoulder with one hand. "Okay in here?"

Colin let bitterness into his voice, "Apparently, the SBI doesn't have enough evidence."

Judd looked at Agent Lenis. "Do you actually know how to do your job?"

"Oh, that's rich. When you're running an interference op? Don't put this on me, Old One. You're still just a fucking enforcer, and your pack is nothing but local muscle. What the hell were you thinking, baiting a trap with *our* target, using *our* asset?"

Judd only crossed big arms over his massive chest. "Seriously? I texted you the moment we had Risa. You got the time and location. Not my fault a bloody colony of selkie mobsters moves faster than your governmental asses."

"What did you just say to me?" Alpha Lenis was still Alpha enough to bristle at that tone from a mere third-rank pack member.

Lexi decided to make her power known too, possibly because none of the attention was on her. "Oh, don't bicker, it's so unbecoming. You got your culprit, Agent. Isn't that sufficient? She's a greasy little thief and I'm well rid of her. I'm sure you can squeeze her tight enough to make her talk. Put her in one of my corsets. She's only human, after all."

"Mother!" said Kevin, shocked.

"Really, Mother," added Colin. "We don't talk about humans that way. As if they were disadvantaged."

"You forget, babies. I lived as a human long enough to give birth to you two brats. I know what it's like." Lexi gestured at her team. "They *are* disadvantaged, poor things." Turning once more to Agent Lenis, she added, "You should push her for all she's worth. Or are you another one of those pro-human Alphas? Save the food source, save the planet! That kind of thing."

"Mother! You can't *eat* humans." Kevin was shocked.

"Figure of speech, darling. Now, things seemed to be wrapping up here. And while this café of yours is quite precious, I think it's time we left, don't you?"

"We?" Judd looked down at Colin, as if he could explain anything his mother did or said. "I believe our contract has officially ended."

But all Lexi's attention was for her older son. "Kevin, baby, I thought we'd agreed. Europe, remember?"

Kevin only blinked at his mother.

She waved a perfectly manicured hand around. "Surely you don't want to stay *here*? You've now shown me the best that Sausalito has to offer. And I'm forced to ask, why on earth would you bother to stay? Quite apart from everything else, the place is positively crawling with selkies. Such a stench. How can you stand it?"

"Mother! That was basically your fault! Well, yours and Risa's," Kevin was moved to object.

Colin couldn't understand why his brother was bothering to argue.

"Really, darling, don't be preposterous. I've nothing to do with selkies. The fact that one of them has fixated on me is not my problem."

Colin looked at Agent Lenis. "The man in charge, Demetrius I think his name is, has a mad crush on our mother. He'll definitely want to see her again. You might use her as bait next time, if you like."

Colin caught Judd grinning at him, clearly pleased.

Agent Lenis looked intrigued. "Well, well, well, that is good information. Although selkie are always hard to pin a charge to, slippery buggers." She side-eyed Lexi. "Alpha Mangnall, I think you and I are going to have to have a little talk."

"Alpha *Blanc, please*," snapped back Lexi. "And we certainly don't need to *talk*. I did my part. Just as you asked."

Colin was confused about something, and Judd's supportive presence gave him enough courage to ask. "Why *did* you have Mother contact me first?"

Lexi answered him. *Oh, so she remembers me now, does she?* "Weakest link, darling. Agent Idiot over there was certain that the funny little barista was the one Risa was supposed to contact for the final handoff. They knew you frequented his café. Plus you saw the selkies first. I guess they thought you would be useful. Like I said, idiots."

Judd growled at her. Actually *growled*! At an Alpha.

Colin nudged him. "It's okay."

Agent Lenis sighed. "We never, for a moment, thought she'd attempt the handoff personally. Apparently, neither did the Pinniped Syndicate, given they also approached Trick."

Risa narrowed her eyes at all of them. But she wasn't stupid enough to admit to anything or try to defend herself.

There was a kind of excited shouting and hollering outside.

Kevin gave Colin the nod and Colin bolted for the door.

Outside, Alec was bent over, helping Marvin flop across the riprap and up onto the sidewalk. The merman could shift into his tail fast once in contact with salt water, but it usually took him a bit longer get his legs back. In the evening sun, he looked like some magical painting, his huge turquoise and teal tail sparkling, the skin of his torso tinged bluish white. It was a popular misconception that merfolk only changed their bottom half – they shifted entirely just like any other triple helix supernatural creature. It's just that their shifted top half still looked human, until you got them in the right light. Alec swooped up several of the discarded pinstriped jackets and used them to pat his mate dry. *Gah! They're so cute together.*

There was a loud chittering noise and Trick propelled himself out of the water onto the rocks as well. He was exactly as cute as Colin suspected he would be. Otters were, after all, adorable. He was big for an otter – so conservation of mass must be in play. There were some shifters, mostly those who traced their ancestry to Asia, who had more advanced density manipulation. Kitsune tended to be small as people, but even smaller as foxes – just very dense. Like mini, furry, fierce black holes. But Trick the otter was about the same size as Trick the person.

Max bent to help him. It was an awkward business getting an otter over shot rock. But once Trick was up on the sidewalk, he shifted back to human pretty smoothly. Apparently, dratsie had better shift capacity than either mermen or werewolves.

Deputy Kettil took off his shirt and handed it to Trick, who put it on without protest. It was like a baggy muumuu on him. Alec gave Marvin his lab coat.

Marvin gave Alec a waterlogged, heavy, gold metallic jacket.

"How on earth…?" The Alpha's eyes popped in surprise.

"How *under water*, babes." Marvin grinned wide at his mate. "We may be smallish, as shifters go, but we be fast."

"And fierce as fuck," added Trick, snapping his fingers for emphasis.

They all returned to the café.

Agent Lenis grabbed the jacket away from Alec. "Your merman rescued it?"

Marvin tossed wet hair at her. "Of course I did, it's totally my style! Wouldn't it look great with leather leggings? I mean, come on!"

Trick wandered behind the counter to find them clean dishrags to use for towels. "I helped, can I borrow it sometime?" He came back out, handed two rags to Marvin.

Marvin dabbed at his hair. "Absofuckinglutely."

"Gentlemen," Agent Faste cut in, "it's evidence in a case. Besides, we need to cut all the gold out of it."

"What?" said both sea folk together.

"Did you say *cut*?" squeaked Trick, big eyes tearing up.

"Oh, say it ain't so! Poor jacket," cried out Marvin.

They exchanged glances, then both went on their knees before the jacket and Agent Lenis.

"Their love was so brief and fleeting, they are going into mourning," explained Colin, for the benefit of the rest of the pack and law enforcement, who were all standing around, dumbfounded.

Colin turned to look at Trick. "But I thought you hated it. Weren't you fighting with my mother about how awful it was?"

"Oh no, never that. It's a wonderful jacket, just not for Sunday at the café, right? But on a Saturday night at a club? Come on!"

Marvin nodded gravely. "Oh, I entirely take your meaning. Shall we soliloquy?"

"Oh yes, I think we shall."

"Ode to the gold jacket we never wore." Marvin suggested the opening line.

"You were so beautiful and so pure." Trick was ready.

"We would have worn you with black or brown." Marvin kept a grave countenance.

"But not on Sundays, in downtown." Trick added, giving a head tilt to Marvin.

"You represent all outfits lost."

"Doomed to the ignominy of an evidence box," Trick finished with a flourish.

They stopped, bowed their heads.

Max started to clap.

After a moment, a few of the others joined in.

Colin said, "*Ignominy*, excellent word choice, Trick."

"Thank you, darling."

"Are you quite done?" Agent Lenis wanted to know. She had her arms crossed and was glaring at them. She turned to Alec. "Your pack is a goddamn nightmare."

Alec arched a brow. "But boasts damp poets extraordinaire, apparently. Poetry is too much for you to handle? No wonder you're SBI."

Agent Lenis just shook her head at him.

Max said, "Come along swim-team gold medalists. I'll buy you both pretty sparkly jackets that don't have a quarter of a million dollars worth of gold sewn into them."

"Good lord, is that all?" said Trick, standing up. "What a fuss."

"Yeah, we thought it was actually important," added Marvin. "You'll really take us shoppies, Max? You hate shopping."

Max looked morose. "True. I do hate it."

Alec shook his head at Marvin's theatrics. "It's Sunday, my heart, and you're both soaked. Why don't you let Max take you back to the pack house, have nice showers, and I'll take tomorrow off. Then we can go shopping on Haight Street together."

"Oh, me too?" Trick's voice was timid, hopeful.

"Of course, you too." Alec hustled his two dripping truants to the door.

Max trailed dutifully behind, wearing a pained expression.

"Wait!" cried Marvin turning to point an accusing finger at Colin.

"What?" said Colin, scared.

"You too!"

"Me too, what?"

"Shopping tomorrow, we gotta get you more fabulous. You know you want to."

Colin didn't have any classes on Mondays. "Uh, okay." He really *did* want to. He kept thinking about that unicorn shirt. And for some reason he really wanted a bright green hoodie. Like *apple* green. Very daring, since most of his wardrobe was gray.

"Perfect," pronounced Trick.

The mage took over from Alec and led the two water folk out of the café, presumably intending to walk them up the hill. Both of them were still mostly naked, but were so excited about plans for a city expedition they were entirely distracted from any possible embarrassment.

Colin looked at the others. "I didn't just agree to buy a sparkly gold jacket, did I?"

"Uh, agents?" that was Deputy Kettil's voice.

"Yes, deputy?" Agent Lenis turned to him, clearly annoyed.

"Shouldn't one of us take their statements?" He pointed after the two swimmers.

Agent Lenis arched a brow at the berserker. "Fine. Go after them, if you must."

With an expression of relief, Deputy Kettil turned to follow.

"Deputy, would you please remind Marvin there's extra smoked salmon in the fridge? They'll likely need protein after shifting and swimming so fast," said Colin.

"Sure thing, nugget." The berserker lumbered after the others.

Judd pointed at Floyd, still sitting to one side, knitting away. "You can close up the café, right Floyd?"

"What!" the old man looked truly affronted. "Just because Trick's loser boss is never here, no need to come down on my creaky old bones!"

"Can't be *that* hard," muttered Kevin.

"Trick may be a basket case, but when I said he was the best barista this side of the Bay, I was *not* lying. You think it's so easy to shut down a café, then you do it, big boy." Floyd was having none of their werewolf lip.

Kevin blinked down at the uppity human. "Seriously?"

Floyd waved a knitting needle. "Mop is over there."

Much to Judd's relief, Agent Lenis interrupted what could have been a very long argument between Kevin and Floyd by reading Risa her Panda Rights.

"Risa Ostrov, you are under arrest for money laundering. You are human, but Panda Rights are in effect as your crimes involve shifter protocols. You may request representation from an Alpha or equivalent rank, to whom you have allegiance. If you have no allegiance, an Alpha will be contacted on your behalf."

The two agents led Risa out of the café. The door closed behind them with a tinkle of bells.

"You won't stand Alpha for Risa, will you?" Kevin asked Blanc. Apparently he held out some weird hope that his mother was a decent person.

Blanc rolled her eyes at the very idea. "Sad really, she was an excellent stylist. Not sure how I can finish this tour without her. Not to mention my jacket. This couldn't have waited until *after* Seattle's performance?"

The pack looked at each other, trying to decide what to do about this woman.

The door tinkled. A group of human females bustled in. Most of them sported homemade scarves. Possibly knitted by Floyd.

Colin explained, "The Sunday Sunset Book Group meeting."

"You spend entirely too much time at this café, Gingersnap." Judd shook his head.

"Oh yeah, whatcha gonna do about it?"

"Make sure you spend entirely too much time in my bed, instead."

Colin grinned, wide and fearless. "Sounds fair."

The book group paused on the stoop, unsure as to what was going on.

"Is that Lexi Blanc?" one of them whispered to another, loud enough for every shifter in the café to hear.

"Oh wow! You think we could get her autograph?"

Judd pushed himself forward. "Don't even." He pointed behind them, back out the door.

"Uh?"

"We're closed," added Colin.

"Who *are* you people?"

"New management."

"What?"

Judd glared at them and advanced slowly. The book group backed down, and in a chattering shocked mass left the café.

Now it was just the pack plus Floyd, Blanc, Jojo, and the nameless manager.

Jojo and the manager were sitting and trying to look like this was all normal for them.

"Fucking shifters," said Floyd.

"Preach it, Grandpa Needles," replied Jojo.

Alec pointed at Jojo and then the manager. "You two as well, shoo."

The human pets protested. "But Lexi!"

Alec allowed his teeth to elongate and began a partial shift to third form. It was kind of horrific and a bit disgusting. Judd admired the ability greatly.

The two humans ran out after the book group. Even Floyd put down his knitting needles.

Alec tilted his now lupine monster head in Floyd's direction.

"No way, snapper," said Floyd. "Sausalito hasn't had this much excitement in fifty years. I ain't budging."

Alec morphed his head back to normal. "It's your funeral, weirdo."

"I'm the weirdo," shot back the old man. "You just had a wolf's head on a nerd's body. You're wearing plaid, for fuck's sake."

"Shut up, Floyd," said Judd.

"Well, boys," said Blanc, edging towards the door. "It's been real, but I must dash. I'm very busy and important, you know?"

"Wait just a moment, Mother. I have something to say to you." That was Colin.

Colin, who appeared to have decided to stand up for himself.

Judd felt a rush of pride and wanted to whoop.

Blanc whirled on her youngest child. "Listen, ankle biter. I wouldn't have looked you up if the SBI hadn't insisted. I'm sure you're a sweet summer child and all, but I really don't have reason to keep dead weight in my life. I'm sure you understand."

"No," said Colin, "that's not—"

Blanc didn't let him continue. "Sorry, sweetie. You were a painful obligation and an obvious disappointment before I left. It doesn't seem to me like you've made much of yourself since then."

"STOP." Alec's VOICE snapped over Blanc. Breaking over all of them.

Twice in one day.

Judd shivered under it.

Alec's normally calm, sweet face was red with anger. Their Alpha was listening to Blanc's words and not watching Colin's face. But Judd only saw his Gingersnap. Colin was hurt by what his mother said, but Colin had something powerful to impart, knowledge. Colin knew something that would undermine her.

Alec was strong, but Blanc was a fellow Alpha. She shook his VOICE off easily.

And now she needed to prove something to Alec. "I mean, sure you're smart, little Colin, but smart doesn't matter much in wolves or celebrity. And frankly, you aren't much more than smart, now are you, honeychild?"

"Mother. Enough." That was Kevin.

Blanc let out a long-suffering sigh. She looked around at the rest of the pack. "I mean, really? What good is he to you? Bless his little heart."

Alec got even redder. Kevin looked like he wanted to hit something. Probably his mother. Tank and Isaac looked like wolves. Because they were still in wolf form. Isaac cocked his head at Alec in query. Omega power wasn't as effective when they weren't in the same form, but Alec could order him to shift back and do his thing.

"It's okay, Isaac. I'm fine, Alpha. Please just let me do this." Colin returned his focus to his mother. "I *am* smart. Which is why I've been looking into your social media accounts."

"How intrusive. Stalker much?" Blanc pursed her lips.

"It's all public access. You know that, right?"

"Well, of course, sugah, that's the point." Blanc suddenly looked interested. "What did you *do*, puppy?"

"It's not what *I've* done, now is it? I found something very interesting with your Instalamb, now didn't I?"

Blanc's eyes widened, then narrowed.

"Alpha," said Colin looking at Alec, "do you think you could stop her, if you had to?"

Alec looked wicked pleased with himself, and with them, and with Colin. "Oh, I can stop her all right. What is she to me?"

Blanc bristled. "I'm an Alpha too, you little shit."

"Now, now, Mother," said Kevin. "Language."

Alec took off his glasses and set them carefully on the counter. "Yes, but you're an Alpha without a pack."

"Who needs a pack?" Blanc dismissed them all, sneering.

"You do," said Alec, and then he moved.

Alec was the fastest werewolf Judd had ever met – human or animal form. He was like a blur, like he shifted air. A second later he was standing behind Blanc, one hand covering her mouth, no possibility of VOICE, not that it would work on Alec. His other hand was around her throat. Squeezing.

Judd shuddered. Enforcers were deadly. He'd killed a time or two in the past. Okay, maybe more than a time or two. But mostly they fought out of instinct – quick, hard, fierce. Punching things was Judd's personal favorite. Tearing out a throat when he was in wolf form was pretty good too.

But what Alec was doing, coming in fast and mean and focused. That was *calculated*. Holding another Alpha close enough for their smells to mingle. That was gross. Alec's hands around her neck were just tight enough to remind her that even shifters needed to breathe.

"Be still," Alec hissed in her ear. He was about her height. "Listen to Colin. My Colin, not yours. You lost him. *Mine* now."

Then their Alpha nodded to Colin to continue.

Colin was beaming at him. "So I noticed Mother Dearest was using a weird hashtag."

Blank faces all around.

"You guys are such Luddites." Colin shook his head at them. "It's kind of like a keyword for tagging a photograph. Also works as a search term within the Instalamb ecosystem."

Judd didn't understand a single word his baby was saying, but Colin sure sounded confident.

"So occasionally in one of her many… many… photos, I'd catch these two super odd hashtags. One is clearly a jumbled code word, for searchability. The other is just a string of numbers. Neither of them means anything in Instalamb or to Blanc's followers. There's no point in hashtags like that, unless you're communicating to specific individuals. But since she uses a ton of tags already, no one really cares that there's this string of random numbers hidden among them."

Judd tried to gently press Colin along, because frankly none of them understood what the hell he was talking about. "What's it mean, baby?"

Colin's green eyes shone with victory. "One tag for searching, the other for GPS coordinates. She dropped these at different points all along her tour. Different locations."

Judd knew exactly what that meant. "Drop-off coordinates."

"You betcha."

"SBI could corroborate that those were all stolen goods being transferred." God, his baby was so smart and so hot.

"SBI could, indeed." Colin raised both eyebrows. "I also bet, if they looked into her finances, they'd find some seriously suspicious purchases and investments."

Judd nodded. "Money laundering."

"Yep."

Kevin laughed suddenly. "Colin, our mother is a criminal."

"I know, right? Finally, she does something for us to be proud of." Colin played along, pleased with himself.

Judd could feel the biggest grin split over his own face.

"You can't prove it was me," hissed Blanc. "My manager does most of the uploading to my accounts and such."

"Oh, dear me," said Alec. "Unfortunately, your manager seems to have departed. And who do we have left holding the phone and wearing the jacket?"

Colin was grinning. "Why, that would be you, Mother."

"Someone check Isaac's backpack for silver handcuffs, please," said Alec. "Very nicely done, Colin."

"Thanks, Alpha."

The backpack lay off in one corner, where Isaac had chucked it before running after the selkies.

"Of course Isaac has handcuffs in his backpack," said Kevin, rummaging about and extracting them.

Tank chuffed at him. Isaac just sat there, tail thumping, looking regal and pleased with his preparedness.

While Alec cuffed Lexi Blanc, Judd texted Agent Faste, to let him know that they might want to come back to Bean There, Froth That and collect Risa's accomplice. Or was Risa Blanc's accomplice? Or was Blanc just a pawn? Either way, it was fun to see her in cuffs. Even if Judd never got to hit her.

When they got back to the pack house, Marvin was in top form. They heard the music before they even got inside.

Fangs, fangs, fangs!
  Fangs in the—

"Oh hell no," said Judd, with feeling. He turned to Alec. "Alpha, make it stop."

They opened the front door.

Max was in the den sipping a glass of grape juice and egging Trick and Marvin on. They seemed to be having a lip sync battle meets slinky dance off. Lovejoy was in the kitchen making stew and humming along.

Lovejoy spotted them first. He was shaking his ass while he stirred the pot. He stopped, pointed the dripping spoon at them, and yelled over Blanc's caterwauling. "Where have you lot been? Leaving me alone to slave over your dinner with only these three characters for company. They come running in, smelling like salt, get sand all over our new carpet, and tell tall tales of gold jackets and selkie mobsters. I swear to god, you guys! I leave you alone for *one weekend*."

Alec raised his voice just enough to be heard. "Children, please turn that off. I believe this pack has had enough of Lexi Blanc."

Trick dove for his phone and unplugged it from the speakers.

"Boyfriend!" Marvin ran across the living room and threw himself at Alec, who plucked him easily out of the air. Marvin was wearing a silver fringed 1920s flapper dress. "You haven't sexed me up in days. You don't love me anymore."

Alec plopped his mate back down next to him. "We fucked this morning."

"Oh, yes, how could I forget?"

"I don't know. How could you?"

"You should remind me, babes."

"Now?"

"Now."

"Well, if I must suffer such hardship. I *was* just wondering what that dress would look like on our floor." Alec tossed Marvin over his shoulder into a fireman's carry. He spoke to the rest of the pack over Marvin's pert little butt.

"Everything okay now, boys? You lot are good? We caught the bad guys. Well, bad girls." He looked at Colin and Kevin. "You two aren't all torn up about your mother being a thief or anything, are you?"

"What?" came Marvin's upside-down voice. "What'd I miss?"

Trick clasped his hands. He looked back and forth between Colin and Kevin. "Oh, your mom is a criminal, too? Welcome to the family!"

"Thanks, Trick," said Colin, flopping into one of the big couches, opposite Max.

Judd sat next to him. Without hesitation, Colin snuggled up close, put a leg over his thighs. As if Judd belonged to him. It was awesome. Colin had initiated contact without a single flinch.

Isaac and Tank disappeared into the cloakroom. They reemerged in human form, wearing black waffle robes.

"What I want to know, Alpha," said Isaac, before Alec could proceed upstairs with his Marvin-shaped sack of potatoes, "is where I'm going to get another set of nice silver handcuffs. Those were my favorite, you know?"

Marvin squeaked. "There were handcuffs involved! Put me down, you big lug. I'm missing gossip!"

"But I thought you wanted sex." Alec's eyes twinkled.

"Sex can wait. This is important. Handcuffs were involved. Although I suppose that doesn't preclude sex."

Bryan came home at that juncture, looking tired from a long shift. He showed absolutely no surprise at seeing Tank and Isaac in robes, Marvin in a flapper dress draped over his Alpha's shoulder, Colin in Judd's lap, and Trick bouncing about on an improvised runway made of Mylar tape and sequined throw pillows.

"Hello, pack," said Bryan, a man of few words.

Max rose gracelessly and went to greet his mate.

Bryan cupped the mage's face, kissed his nose. "Everything all right?"

"Everything's perfect," said Max.

Judd lifted Colin completely into his arms. Colin fitted his head under Judd's chin. He leaned against him with a tiny sigh. Max was right. Everything was perfect.

Well, almost.

Then Alec said, "No more Lexi Blanc in this house, okay, boys? In person, in audio, or in chains."

Now it was perfect.

"Oh my god, will someone *please* tell me what happened with the handcuffs," yelled Marvin.

"Oh, I see," came Lovejoy's voice. "No one wants to know how my weekend at the food truck festival went? That's how it is, is it? Lovejoy, just come home, get to work in the kitchen, slave away making *everyone* dinner."

Tank moved to go help him.

Lovejoy waved him off.

"By all means," said Alec, putting down his mate, who was practically vibrating with curiosity, "tell us about *your* weekend, Lovejoy."

CHAPTER EIGHTEEN

YOU WILL ALWAYS BE MY MATE

It was a nice evening. Trick was fitting in with the pack – even his damp, grassy smell was changing a little. Still otter, but also ever-so-slightly *wolf*. After helping to retrieve the jacket, and hosting them in his café for several days, the dratsie seemed to feel it wasn't too much of an imposition to bunk down with them.

Judd was relieved. He didn't like the little otter sleeping in his car. Even if it was parked on their property.

"You can have Colin's room," said Judd. Pleased with himself for the idea.

"He can?" Colin looking up from his bowl of stew.

"Yep." Judd grinned at him. It was a grin that said: *Don't challenge me, kid.*

Marvin propped his chin on his hand, batted his eyelashes at them. "Oh my, but where, oh where, will Colin sleep?"

"In my room, of course." Judd tried to hide how proud that made him. Colin in his room for as long as Trick stayed. And with any luck, Trick was staying forever.

Colin raised his pretty head and stared at Judd with cool green suspicion.

Judd quieted under that gaze, tried to give him back yearning, and hope, and just… *Please.*

Please be with me. *Please* see the offer behind the demand.

Please see the wounded crippled old heart that Judd was laying down on that table before him. Like it was his kill as a courting gift. Like it was all he had to trade for this new shiny copper penny of a boy. Because it *was* all he had.

Colin chewed his stew, swallowed.

The pack held its collective breath.

"Okay," said Colin, and then, "Cool."

Judd felt the joy spear into him – pride and surety and confirmation. Colin was admitting to it, here, in front of all their pack, where promises were made and kept. This would work. Colin was his. And all those stupid obstacles of confidence, and age, and loneliness would shift to love, and sex, and affection, and just... belonging.

Judd had never had that. Over one hundred and fifty years on this planet, and Judd was finally getting the thing he'd always wanted – home. This slim red-headed man, with the cluster of freckles on his hip that only Judd knew about, and the blush that spread down his neck, and the eyes full of need, and the most beautiful hands in the whole world was going to come and sleep in Judd's bed. Was going to be with Judd.

Finally.

He looked up at his Gingersnap, shoveling in another bite of stew.

"Cool," replied Judd.

After stew, and gossip, and speculation, and laughter, the pack separated.

Colin showed Trick to his room. He selected an outfit for the next day's shopping jaunt and collected a few toiletries. They agreed to figure out the transfer of everything else later. Trick needed sleep – on Monday mornings the café opened at 6:30. Poor thing, he was having a rough week. Colin wondered if he could persuade him to just leave it closed for the day, come shopping instead.

They alternated using the bathroom, letting Trick go first.

With one more pack member in the mix, they really needed to get going with the remodel. Colin wondered if maybe they didn't need two additional bathrooms upstairs.

Finally, Colin and Judd were alone in Judd's big room. Colin searched for a place to put his little pile of clothing and his book and his water glass.

Judd swept a hand over the bedside table and dumped everything in an empty pillowcase – except the lube. "Put it here for now. Though I want you sleeping on the inside, please, easier to protect."

Colin shrugged – it's where he had been sleeping so far. He preferred it, because he had the window, and the walls, and the sensation of nesting. Colin was not the type to feel trapped. If anything, it was too much space and too much freedom that terrified him. Because that meant he could be left behind, again – forgotten about, again.

"I'll put in a shelf for you, next to the window, for your book and water and stuff."

Colin nodded.

"Oh, uh, here." Judd opened the top drawer of his dresser, which was empty.

"How long have you been planning to ask me to move in?" Colin teased, putting his clothes inside.

Judd actually looked embarrassed. "It's never had anything in it. The next one down is empty too. And half the closet." He opened the closet door. More than half of it was just bare hangers, dangling and sad. Hanging forlornly on its own at the end was a familiar-looking green blouse, soft and pretty, waiting for Colin. *He bought it for me.*

"I don't have that much clothing." Judd tugged on one ear, self-conscious.

Oh sure, that *was the reason.* A weird, joyful, scary suspicion wormed its way into Colin's heart. He didn't really dare believe it but…

As if at a loss for what to do while Colin processed, Judd stripped out of his shirt and, with a flourish, ripped off the stripper pants.

"Woohoo," said Colin, standing awkwardly near the bed.

Judd grinned and tossed the clothes into his laundry basket. Colin just stared at him. So big and powerful, dark skin stretched over bone and tendon, but mostly muscle. Those huge hands had felt so deliciously rough, stroking over Colin's body. They had made him feel safe and claimed. Those soft lips had worshiped Colin, those sharp teeth had demanded responses, that mouth had been coaxing and confident and – what? What had Judd been trying to tell him all along with his body, with his actions? Enforcers spoke in deeds, not words.

Colin frowned, trying hard to see the truth in Judd, and not just see what he, Colin, feared or wanted. "You were a loner when you first met Alec, right?"

"I was. I'd been looking for a very long time." Judd stood, naked, arms akimbo in the center of his room. Confident and lost at the same time.

Colin nodded. He'd sensed, when he met Judd, that the big man was looking for something or someone. Colin had hoped, for one red hot minute, that he was looking for Colin. But what could he offer someone like Judd? What was he to an enforcer? Barely a werewolf, no rank. Barely a man, even.

"Looking for the right pack?"

Judd shook his head slowly, focused hard on Colin. "A little, but mostly for the right person. For you."

"That is both sappy and ridiculous. No one is looking for me." Colin climbed onto the bed but not into it. He was still clothed, but he needed to be where Judd wanted him. He scooted over to the far side, snuggled down, smoothed the comforter in a nervous gesture.

"I'm an afterthought." Colin considered his pillow options – liked Judd's better, stole it. Hugged it in lieu of hugging Judd. "Like I'm a leftover from some restaurant meal that wasn't particularly good to start with. The doggy bag of werewolves."

Judd sighed, sat down on the edge of the bed. "And yet for all you say this of yourself, you're the only thing I saw from the moment we met. Do you remember that first time? Your old pack insisted you come on a hunt."

"I remember."

"You were just a pup, barely eighteen. This baby werewolf, so scared. Everyone ignored you, like you were an embarrassment. Like you weren't a hundred times better than every single one of them. Like only I could see how shiny and perfect you were. You were this green youngling, untried, unhappy, unwilling to be a wolf. I thought everything about you was wrong."

Colin flinched, focused hard on fluffing the pillow. He didn't want to hear this.

"And I thought you were the most breathtaking thing I'd ever met. Like hearing a beautiful piece of music for the first time. You smelled like fresh bread and mulled cider from my first real home. My first real pack. I thought, here is this precious, perfect man, and I want to put my brute hands all over him. I want to tell him dirty, crass things with my foul mouth. I wanted to see him wrung out and wrecked in my bed. Loose-limbed and well-loved, with eyes only for me and smiling only for me. You were all quiet, hesitant, and incandescent and I *ached* with want. I could barely look away. Still can't."

Colin's mouth dropped open. He couldn't fathom the implication of Judd's words... Of two empty drawers... Of a half-empty closet... Of that much longing.

Cautious and terrified, Colin opened himself up to rejection and asked with too much hope in his voice, "You joined this pack because of *me*?"

Judd gave another slow nod. "And moved across the country. And I'm a brash old wolf with too many seasons and too much loss, but I'm beginning to realize that makes me ready to take this chance."

"But I am so *not* perfect."

"Did I say that? No, it's true, you aren't perfect, no one is. But you're perfect for me. My mate, as I'm yours. I tried really hard to fight that because I'm too old for you, but I'm so tired of being alone."

"You know that I need you."

"No, Gingersnap, you got it backwards. I need you. How could you not realize that?"

"But you're the strong one!" Colin shook his head, confused. This was Judd – huge and capable, powerful and protective. The best enforcer, the most controlled fighter he'd ever met outside of an Alpha. And so very easy on the eyes.

"Is that all you see?" Judd sounded disappointed.

Colin couldn't stand that. He was tired of being a disappointment. So, feeling terribly brave, he said, "You make this thing between us seem so much more than just teaching. I mean, at dinner you basically insisted I move in with you. I'm confused." His hands fluttered as he spoke, his fingers desperate.

"Yeah, I know. Sorry. I'm too pushy. But hell, Gingersnap, you're so terribly young. I thought I'd be able to give you everything. Including the opportunity to not be with me. To go out into the world, be gay and fabulous. To learn all about yourself, learn your limits. I don't want to hold you back. But I'm too much *enforcer*. Too much wolf. I really just want to keep you close and tethered to me. My mate."

Colin loved that statement so much, his throat ached with it. "I *am* smart, though."

"Smarter than me, no doubt." Judd made a funny face. He was still sitting on the edge of the bed, not touching Colin – a whole galaxy away.

Colin inched towards him, let his hands do what they wanted – stroke Judd's broad, naked back, the divot of his spine, the curve of his shoulder blade. "Exactly."

He'd surprised Judd with that. The big man shivered – touch or word, hard to know which.

But Judd had just admitted that he wanted Colin to belong to him, which meant he wanted to belong to Colin. Which meant Colin had *rights*. For the first time in his life, he felt solid and sure and almost aggressive.

"So you should realize that I'm smart enough to know my own mind. Heart, too. I might not be old enough or wise enough to know much else, but I'm pretty self-aware." Colin kept petting, stroking, touching what was his. His too-pretty too-pale too-feminine hands on Judd's huge masculine body.

"Yeah, baby, I know that."

"So let's not go back to that *too young* thing. It makes us both unhappy."

Judd nodded, not seeming convinced. He turned, angled towards Colin so he might stroke over Judd's chest. Judd's eyes were bleeding yellow, hot and fierce. Colin felt the ache in his own gums, his canines tasting desire.

Judd looked down at Colin's fingers, tracing patterns over his skin. "God, I love your hands, Gingersnap." As if Colin's touch were a benediction.

Colin told himself to grow a fucking backbone. He owed Judd. Because otherwise the enforcer would keep doubting him and doubting them. There wasn't any other way to reassure Judd without giving him the whole truth. Every single part of it. "Do you know what I thought the first time I saw you?"

"No. You've never told me."

"I thought you were the most gorgeous and the most sad man I had ever seen."

"Sad, huh?"

"Sad." Colin reached for that memory, trying to explain. "And I thought you were meant to be my mate."

"What?"

"Listen to me, Judd. You started this thing between us, twisting me about, offering me lessons and shit. Pretending I'm too young to know who I am and what I want. And you forgot something really fucking simple."

"I did?" Ancient werewolf – big-eyed, startled. Enforcer – gruff, hopeful, looking for leadership. Looking for a reason to exist, for a purpose, for something to protect and take care of. Always, enforcers, they *cared* more than anyone else in the pack. People forgot that. People thought that enforcers fought because they were the strongest. That they were closest to their wolf. That they were warrior and guardian. And enforcers were all those things, but not because they were physically the most fit, but because they *cared* the most.

Judd's eyes were *still* the saddest thing Colin had ever seen. He hated that and he intended to fix it.

"What did I forget, Gingersnap?"

"You thought I was yours. You were wrong."

Judd jerked back, devastated.

"No, *listen* to me!" Colin hadn't realized how fierce he could be. How much iron was in him. How much enforcer. Judd's lessons had taught him more than just desire, they'd taught him a new way of caring. His hands, free from touching Judd, gesticulated wildly as he spoke. And for once, he didn't care, he didn't mind, because he needed them to help him explain.

"You're *mine*. And maybe, as I get older, as I learn all the things I can be, I'll develop that ego you all think I should have. I'll learn to be okay being noticed, and being loved, and being in a pack that supports me. *Then* I'll be yours. That's going to take time. Because I *am* young, and I can't give you everything until I have enough of myself to give. But that's not where you are. You've been waiting for me a really long time, Judd. And you're so much you. You've excess of yourself, and you really needed to give it, share it out. So you gave it to me. Probably in that very first moment. And I *am* really smart. I know what that means, and what a gift it is. And I'm going to fucking treasure it – treasure you. I will take such good care of you, Judd. Because I've never had anything that was mine before. And then today I woke up and I realized I got to have *you* and that's the best anyone could ever get, no matter how long I live. I will *never* forget that. Because I'm not an idiot. So just stop testing me already. Just be mine. Okay?"

Judd ripped his eyes away from Colin's beautiful, fluttering hands. Colin's face was flushed but determined. His eyes glittered orange, intent and earnest. He smelled of spiced memories.

Judd lunged across the bed, landed on top of him. He braced himself but only slightly. Judd was twice Colin's size, but Colin was a werewolf. He could take it.

Colin made an *oof* noise. He wrapped skinny arms tight about Judd's neck. He smiled against Judd's cheek. He ghosted warm breath over Judd's skin.

They clung, inhaling each other.

Trust, like warm fresh blood, burst over Judd's tongue. Nourishing and feral. Heated down his throat into his chest. The deadly responsibility of loving another person. Worse, letting them love him back. The reality of it bled into him. Judd would have to care for Colin's heart now, as well as protect Colin's body.

It was terrifying.

It was perfect.

Judd rolled them over, put Colin on top. That way he could unbutton and pull off his mate's silky shirt.

Colin laughed and told him not to rip it. It was currently the one of the few shirts he owned that he actually liked.

Then Judd got to do the thing he'd wanted to do for *days*. He ripped those stupid-tight, pinstriped, maddeningly hot stripper pants off Colin's lithe body. Just tore them away. The sound was very satisfying.

"All your pants should be Velcro." He hoisted naked Colin up to sit high on his chest. That way, Judd could bend his head and bury his face in Colin's groin, lick him where he smelled the most delicious.

Colin made gorgeous needy noises above him. Put those pretty hands on Judd's head, petted over his skull, down to his neck and shoulders.

Judd bit hard at the white perfection of Colin's thigh – left a mark, licked an apology over it.

Colin whined, arched liked a sapling in the wind, cock quivering.

Judd sucked him down. Showed him fierce power and encompassing love. Encouraged Colin to thrust into his mouth, to push possession into Judd, make him feel wanted and owned. Until Colin scooted away, panting. He slapped a hand, palm down, to Judd's chest.

"Roll over."

"Oh hell, yes." Judd did as instructed.

Colin prepped him with sure, confident fingers, beautiful graceful *perfect* fingers. One, then two, then three. Each time with a beckoning crook, the twist that Judd had taught him – the one that drove Judd into writhing madness and debilitating need. Come hither… cum.

Judd was close to tumbling over the edge. He would do that if that's what Colin wanted. He would come just from those beautiful hands inside him.

Then Colin stopped, pulled back, left him empty and yearning.

Judd whined.

Colin replaced his fingers with his cock.

And then, there was what he'd dreamed of, hoped for. Colin's hands grabbed Judd's ass. Strong lovely fingers dug in, held him hard, guided his hips, anchored him to sensation. Colin thrust that out-of-proportion cock deep into him. Pounding, taking, giving – spiking pleasure and invisible beauty into Judd, again and again.

Judd heard Colin's voice then, over the white noise of his own desire. Over the reverberations of his own moans, frankly a bit embarrassing – they were being awfully loud.

Colin was chanting as he fucked into him. "Mine, mate, my mate, mine."

And Judd believed him.

Friday's hunt was a long one – the nights were colder now and the deer more difficult to track. But they brought one down in the headlands and dragged it all the way home together. As a pack.

The smallest of the San Andreas werewolves, a beautiful creature with honey brown fur and rust markings, trotted grace-fully at the back, a little apart from the others. Until a huge black wolf with bright yellow eyes nipped at him playfully, nudged him forward, herded him back to the group. They ran together after that, tongues lolling.

The barbecue that followed was a big one. There weren't likely to be many more that year, so everyone turned up. Winter would soon make them prohibitively cold, if not wet. They didn't have to tell anyone the gathering was happening, either. Anyone who watched the moon knew the San Andreas Pack would be roasting venison on Saturday, and the cars started driving up and disgorging party-goers by around three that afternoon.

Max's old friend from DURPS, Gladiola, her boyfriend Chrysanthemum, and their leash of lovers were the first to arrive, bringing with them vast quantities of salads and even more gossip. Gladdy and Chrys were the kind of couple who gave up cell phones for *psychic resonance reasons,* got homing pigeons instead, and were then annoyed that everyone else didn't have homing pigeons. The pack hadn't seen them since Burning Sapien, and the little kitsune had *a lot* to say about the desert festival.

Trickle, Pepper, and some of their friends arrived next. The kelpie immediately went to find Max who was, for some strange reason no one understood but Trickle, her favorite human in the world besides Pepper. Pepper joined Lovejoy at the fire, discussing the finer points of jerk sauce, and whether they should break down the deer so the different cuts could roast at different temperatures, or leave it whole. Pepper had brought along her little sister, Saline, because Saline was in construction. Pepper thought Sal would be a good fit to remodel the pack house, and dared them with her eyes to say anything derogatory about her sister's diminutive size or busty appearance. Sal proved to be a militant female, with more tattoos than her sister, half her head shaved, and all of her determined and fierce. Colin, of course, liked her immediately, in that way that he always liked bold, strident people. He thought, from the way Kevin lurked near the fire and stared, that his brother very much liked Sal too. Which could get awkward if she started working on their house.

Marvin eventually absconded with Saline, demanding gossip

from the new human. Colin trailed behind because he was curious too and needed to get her drink preferences. As a result, they managed to learn nothing about Saline's skill as a general contractor and a great deal about her romantic life (recently single) and reasons for the last break-up (she wanted kids and he didn't) and her preferred beverage (hoppy IPAs). Still, Saline gave the impression of vicious efficiency and a fierce work ethic. She admitted to running her love life like she ran her crew, like a vindictive general. Colin shook his head. Kevin was doomed to fall totally in love with this woman.

"You saying you're the woman who brings all the balls to the yard?" asked Marvin, pleased with himself.

Sal wiggled her eyebrows. "Nothing but balls."

"Must be someone's fantasy." Colin arched a brow.

Trick popped up. "Did someone summon moi?"

"You're like a genie. Rub Trick's lamp and say *balls* three times, and he's sure to appear," Colin felt brave enough to say.

Everyone busted up laughing.

Over a week living with the pack and it was like Trick had been there all along. This was his first pack barbecue, but the little otter couldn't be happier. He was in his element (well, the one that wasn't water), flitting about, chattering excitedly, bouncing up and down, occasionally clapping his hands in an excess of delight. Trickle, the other river shifter, seemed to regard him with total exasperation. But with Trickle, annoyance was a good thing; it meant she liked you.

Because Trick was at the barbecue, and not at the café, Bean There, Froth That was closed for the day (it really didn't function without him), and several of the café regulars had wandered up the hill to visit the pack, or in search of caffeine. The place was lousy with humans because all the neighbors were there too. Marvin was smart about *human social mores* and the first thing he did when they moved in was invite neighbors to barbecues so he could impress upon them the fact that no, the new werewolf pack did not, in fact, wish to barbecue *them*.

Floyd had bagged a chair near the fire pit and was knitting away, complaining loudly about the lack of espresso. Gladdy's contingent, however, was from the East Bay, where the crafters grew strong and bold. Much to Floyd's apparent disgust and obvious delight, he was immediately joined by an angry tattooed crocheting vegan and a soft-spoken pink-haired wiccan sock-knitter. The needle-off commenced.

Some of Isaac's friends from Saucebox showed up, including the friendly bouncer, Oscar, with his girlfriend, Portia. Xavier and Lavish briefly graced them with their presence, specifically to thank Judd and Kevin for keeping things under control when Lexi Blanc visited their club.

A few of Isaac's shifter clients attended as well, awed and honored to have been invited to visit *the Omega in his own home*. Most of them could barely speak when introduced to Alec. After all, this was Isaac's Alpha, he must be very special. Deputy Kettil put in an appearance. He was in uniform and on duty. So mostly he came to eat some meat, stare longingly at Trick (who was flirting with anything on two legs, and a few things on four) before trundling off, huge shoulders hunched.

Only Mana wasn't in attendance, which meant everyone kept asking Lovejoy where she was. Which allowed Lovejoy to brag about the success of her latest cabaret, and the fact that she was taking meetings in LA at the moment, and might, in fact, be hosting the next great shifter reality show, *Hell's Bitchin' Undead Races* or something, and wouldn't *that* be amazing?

Colin wore the green shirt Judd had bought him – draped low at the front, showing off his slim neck. It was soft and elegant and he loved it. Marvin had persuaded him to pair it with a very tight pair of jeans, which made his ass look amazing, a fact that Judd made certain he knew, frequently. He also wore mascara and a little lip gloss, which Judd kept kissing off. Colin liked the whole effect, subtle and not too flashy, because flashy wasn't his thing and never would be, but getting admiring looks and sweet kisses was.

Of all people, his brother came up at one point, and threw an arm around Colin's shoulders. Colin relaxed into it immediately, not flinching at all.

"Hey, little brother."

"Hey, asshole."

"You look good."

"I know."

Kevin laughed. "Which is even better." Then Saline walked by and gave him a smile and he was lost.

Colin shook his head and went to make certain a newly arrived friend of a friend knew where to put their food offering, which cooler had beer, which cooler had the fruity drinks, and which cooler had the meaty fishy drinks (La Coq, of course).

He checked with Lovejoy and Pepper regularly, to ensure they didn't need anything from the kitchen. He was ready with the big platter when time came to carve the deer. Jerk venison was pronounced delicious by everyone but the vegans. Colin washed each pot luck bowl when it got empty and made sure its owner knew where to collect it later. He opened up dips and bags of chips. He ensured salads had serving tongs and that there were always plates and napkins ready.

Maybe, sometimes, Colin stopped organizing and chatted for a bit with Gladdy. Or laughed hysterically at Trick's antics. Or let Judd sneak him away and kiss him silly behind the outdoor shower. Maybe he got into an animated argument with Ms Trickle, a kelpie twice his size and fives times meaner, about the relative merits of government assistance to loners. But Colin knew Judd had his back, so he felt fine telling her that her ideas on internet security were antiquated, and frankly, concerning in a woman in charge of a government facility. And maybe he got so impassioned about it that he talked with his hands, white and fluttering about his face, like moths around a flame. And maybe, just maybe, he didn't notice. Or if he did notice, he didn't care how it looked because later that night he would get to put those hands all over Judd's body.

And maybe, once or twice, he stopped and thought about the whole situation in amazement.

He, Colin Mangnall, was wearing a floaty green blouse that his *boyfriend* had given him. He had on peach-flavored lip gloss. So what if his hands were gay as fuck, because *he* was gay as fuck. Maybe even a tiny bit fabulous. Throngs of people saw him like that and not a one of them minded, or flinched away, or ignored him. It was just endless roasted venison, and La Coq burps (the chicken liver flavor really was delicious), and laughter, and his pack.

His pack, who noticed him.

And he got to look up and catch Judd's eyes, bright with joy, searching him out in the crowd. Judd, attentive, heart's focus. Colin thought it was all a little bit wonderful, and he was awed by his own capacity for happiness.

So he let himself dwell – connected and significant and loved.

fin

AUTHOR'S NOTE

Thank you so much for picking up *The Enforcer Enigma*. Kettle and Trick are next up in *The Dratsie Dilemma*. If you would like more from the San Andreas Shifters, please say so in a review. I'm grateful for the time you take to do so.

Even more welcome are donations to your local LBGTQ centers (time, attention, money, whatever you can give). Mine is the San Francisco LGBT Center. Find them at sfcenter.org or @SFLGBTCenter on Twitter. Everyone needs a pack to come home to.

I have a silly gossipy newsletter called the Chirrup. I promise: no spam, no fowl. (Well, maybe a little wicker fowl and lots of giveaways and sneak peeks.) Find it and more at…

gailcarriger.com

ABOUT THE WRITERBEAST

New York Times bestselling author Gail Carriger (AKA G. L. Carriger) writes to cope with being raised in obscurity by an expatriate Brit and an incurable curmudgeon. She escaped small-town life and inadvertently acquired several degrees in higher learning, a fondness for cephalopods, and a chronic tea habit. She then traveled the historic cities of Europe, subsisting entirely on biscuits secreted in her handbag. She resides in the Colonies, surrounded by fantastic shoes, where she insists on tea imported from London.

facebook.com/gailcarrigerllc

twitter.com/gailcarriger

instagram.com/gailcarriger